ROAR

VOLUME 7
LEGENDARY

Edited by Mary E. Lowd

Bad Dog Books

2016

ROAR Volume 7
First publication 2016

Edited by Mary E. Lowd

Cover by Kadath
Copyright © 2016

Published by Bad Dog Books
www . baddogbooks . com

All stories copyright their respective authors.
PRINT ISBN: 978-1-61450-327-9
eBook ISBN: 978-1-61450-328-6

BAD DOG BOOKS

TABLE OF CONTENTS

For Fred Patten

Thank you for being a true legend of the furry fandom.

FOREWORD

Welcome to a LEGENDARY volume of ROAR! That's right, the theme
for the seventh volume is legend, and it will take you on a journey from
a fortune teller's bamboo hut to the end of the world in the coils of a dead
snake god, back in time to the Cretaceous and then up to the stars. You'll
meet tigers and cranes practicing Kung Fu, a singing frog, a gambling
pigeon, a rap-star bearded dragon, a rhinoceros who's friends with a goat,
and several creatures you've probably never seen before.

Last year when I edited ROAR 6, I actively searched for stories, seeking
out submissions both inside and outside of the fandom. This year, I waited
to see what stories would come, and I was amazed by what happened. In
spite of taking a more hands-off approach to gathering submissions, the
slush pile this year increased in both size and quality.

While I'm reading through the slush pile, I like to joke that I'm reading
ROAR: The Complete Unabridged Slush Pile Edition. Well, this year,
that was a pretty darn good book. It's hard to reject stories when so many
of them are really good. Of course, choices have to be made, and I believe
that you're holding an excellent tome of furry fiction in your hands—the
kind of book that you can sink into and lose yourself to the characters and
worlds.

The seventeen stories in this collection will take you on epic journeys and
then bring you home for small, meaningful moments. Because sometimes
legends loom large, but sometimes they turn out to just be stories.

Let the legends begin…

-Mary E. Lowd

We begin with a clash of dynasties, and a story that stretches across generations. Born from love and tragedy, this is the legend of tiger-crane style.

CROUCHING TIGER, STANDING CRANE

Kyla Chapek

The fortuneteller's bamboo hut was dimly lit by flickering candle-light. The air smelled sickly sweet from incense and opium smoke. Hesitantly the three young university students filed in through the doorway, which creaked closed behind them shutting out the cool night air. Though the outside of the hut looked dilapidated, the inside was neat and richly decorated with silk curtains and painted paper screens. A semi-transparent veil divided the one room shack, and the students could not see clearly beyond the veil. However, the outline of the fortuneteller was easily defined sitting on the other side of the curtain.

"Why have you come?" came a purring female voice from beyond the veil.

The voice made the students shudder. Whiskers twitched, feathers ruffled, scales quivered. The trio nearly lost their nerves. Then the boldest of them approached the veil. He was snake clan; his green scales looked black in the dim light. The son of the snake clan slithered forward and then removed his silk red hat with the end of his long tail. He bowed with respect before he hissed, "We have come for a story, Auntie Tigress."

The outline behind the veil chuckled. "There are many stories to tell, *Si Dai*. Do the three of you wish to hear what fortunes tomorrow brings you?"

"We wish to hear stories of the past," squawked one of the snake's companions. The son of the crane clan also wore a red silk hat, as well as a blue silk tunic with their University logo stitched over the left breast. He flapped his wings with urgency. "We wish to hear the story of the tiger-crane style. People say you're the only one that knows the truth."

This piqued the fortuneteller's interest. There were few that knew she could tell such a story. She parted the curtain slightly with the end of her pipe to take a better look at her visitors. A son of the fox, crane, and snake clans; all wearing the same uniforms. By their body language the three were friendly and familiar with each other. This pleasantly surprised the old mixed breed tigress. Any unnecessary cross clan interaction was highly frowned upon by the old dynasty. Back when she was a cub a snake could eat at a fox's restaurant, or buy fish from a crane, but it was abnormal for them to be in the same social circles and they were rarely educated together. The Manchu had upheld a strict separate but equal policy between the clans. Many things had changed since the revolution.

"Sit," commanded the fortuneteller, letting the curtain fall closed.

The three students got situated on cushions in front of the outline of the fortuneteller. "Did you bring the offerings?" she purred.

Three bowls were scooted underneath the curtain; one in front of each student. Each student filled their bowl with an item and scooted the bowl back under the curtain. The fortuneteller accepted the pouch of opium, gourd of wine, and sack of gold happily. Though she was less happy to recount the tale the trio sought. So many sad memories and restless ghosts to conjure up.

At least the opium and wine helped with that. The tigress packed her pipe with the contents from the pouch and took a drag from the long slender pipe. Her whole body relaxed and a pleasant shiver ran across her skin that made her striped and blotched fur stand on end. She then took a long pull from the wine gourd. The tigress had inherited both her father's skills and bad habits.

The trio started to become restless from the fortuneteller's extended silence. They had paid the proper offering, and they deserved a proper story. The tigress sighed, closed her eyes, and began to speak.

"To understand the story of the tiger-crane style you must go back years before its conception. The Manchurian government of the Qing dynasty had become corrupt beyond measure. At the same time the Shaolin style had become popular, gaining great respect and power within the martial arts world. The Manchu bastards feared this power. They also hated that the Shaolin allowed all clans, hunter, fisherman, and farmer class alike, to train side by side. The Manchu set out to destroy the many Shaolin temples throughout the country.

"One of the many pawns they used to destroy the Shaolin was one of the Five Elders, Pak Mei, who was one of the survivors of the original sack of the Southern Shaolin Temple. He was later captured, betrayed the Shaolin to save his closest comrades, and led the second imperial attack on the Shaolin temple, killing Jee Sin, another of the Five Elders, in the process. An act that set the fateful events in motion that led to the creation of the tiger-crane style. But our story begins with the first sack of the Shaolin temple and with two of Jee Sin's students who survived."

***

The sun shone red through the thick black smoke that rose from the Shaolin Temple. Hoong Hei Khoon, a young orange and black striped Bengal tiger, shook with rage inside as he ran alongside his master and comrades. Khoon's master, Jee Sin, another orange and black Bengal tiger signaled for the group of injured and tired Shaolin monks to stop and rest. He must have felt they had fled far enough for the moment. Khoon collapsed in a tired heap next to his best friend, Wu Wai Thien, another Bengal son of the tiger clan. They were lucky to be alive, many of their brothers laid dead back at the temple.

"What are we going to do, *Sifu?*" asked Thien, wincing as he struggled to his feet.

Jee Sin clutched his bloodied sword tightly and considered their options. Blood reddened the fur on his paws and brow. "We must scatter. Thien, you and half those of the tiger clan will come with me to Nine Lotus Mountain in Fujian. Pak Mei and the other Elders have fled there to take shelter. From there we will rebuild the temple farther south."

"Yes, *Sifu.*"

"Khoon!"

"Yes, *Sifu.*" Khoon was helped to his feet by Thien.

"Take the rest of the tigers and the other clans to the boats. Scatter to the four winds and do as we have discussed. Wherever the injustice of the Manchu exists so must be the Shaolin. We must sow the seeds of rebellion throughout the land if we ever wish to rid our country of this scum."

"It will be done, *Sifu.*" Khoon covered his right paw with his left and saluted his master. Jee Sin returned the salute and saluted the rest of his students.

As the tigers divided themselves, Khoon and Thien embraced in goodbye. They had been together since they were cubs and it seemed surreal parting under such circumstances. "Take care, *Si Heng*," said Khoon.

"Until we meet again, *Si Dai*," said Thien, and then the groups parted ways.

***

Khoon divided the monks by clan into the boats and sent them to the four winds like his master had commanded. Khoon's group of fellow Bengal tigers, clouded leopards, and snow leopards headed east. The fleet of Shaolin ships came to be known as the Red Boats. Day in and day out the monks continued to practice the ways of Shaolin on the decks of their boats under the guise of traveling performers. Wherever they went they used their skills of Shaolin to fight the injustice of the Manchu.

One day Khoon's boat sailed along the Yellow River and took anchor at a small river town to restock on supplies, earn some coin, and gather news. To keep up the guise of performers the boys made a big spectacle of exiting the boat. It caught the eye of travelers and locals that might be interested in watching the evening show.

The clouded leopards, with grey and blotched fur patterns, leapt from the starboard side of the ship before they were even properly docked. In tandem they landed on the dock on their front paws and somersaulted forward. As the boat was tied off, the snow leopards, their spotted fur smoky grey with white undertones, leapt into the air. They landed in the waiting arms of the clouded leopards who launched them back into the air. The snow leopards flipped through the air and landed on their hind paws with perfect grace and balance. A growing crowd of onlookers applauded.

Lastly, to get the attention of anyone who wasn't already looking, Khoon, along with the other Bengals, let out a ferocious roar and leapt from the boat and landed in the midst of the leopards. The leopards immediately closed in on the Bengals and the group began to mock fight, slowly moving the show off the docks and into the town square. The crowd, mostly made up of crane and otter clan, along with a few other fisherman clans, eagerly followed the show.

Reaching the town square, Khoon noticed a show already in progress. A small crowd encircled two cranes. An elder male crane struck out at a younger she-crane with a spear. The she-crane artfully twirled out of the spear's reach, the blade coming close enough to ruffle feathers.

Khoon guided his troop a respectful distance away and continued their performance. It wasn't long before the crowd gathered around the cranes were drawn away to watch the more ferocious looking style of the tiger clan Khoon's group displayed. When it was clear their audience was lost the elder crane shook his head sadly and began to pack up his spears. There would be other days. His niece took the snub of the crowd less gracefully.

The hotheaded Foong Chet Leong gathered up one of her uncle's spears and cast it into the midst of the dancing kittens. It stabbed in the ground at the feet of a particularly cocky looking snow leopard, right where she had been aiming. The look of surprise on his face made Leong snort with satisfaction. The crowd oohed at the challenge. The snow leopard Han's look of surprise turned into a mischievous smile. He walked forward to accept the challenge.

Han retracted his claws as he approached the she-crane. He didn't want to hurt the fragile creature, just use enough strength to put her in her place. Han made a big show of taking the tiger style stance, knees bent ready to spring, forepaws crossed in front of him left over right. In response Leong took on the strange looking crane style stance with her webbed feet pointing inward and her knees bent at an angle that would only be natural to the physique of a spindly legged crane.

With victory visualized within three moves Han sprung towards the crane, the crowd forming a new circle around the duel. Han lashed out with a fraction of his strength, aiming for the weak pressure points he had been taught since cubhood. To Han's surprise his strikes were gently brushed to the side by the crane's wings. Not exactly sure what had happened, Han lashed out again with a different combination. With the most subtle movements of her wings the crane brushed the trajectory of the leopard's strikes just off target. She then followed it up with a neck chop that surprised Han in its strength and forced him to stumble backwards.

Han's breath caught in his throat from the blow. The derisive sniff the crane gave him and the catcalls from the crowd made his fur bristle and anger burn in his gut. Han redoubled his attack, holding less back this time.

Khoon allowed the exchange to continue for a time. There was no real harm in it and to be honest Khoon was more than a bit transfixed by the she-crane. Her long slender body moved with such grace and control. Her strikes were executed with perfect accuracy and surprising power. The she-crane wasted no energy in her movements.

A warmth stirred in Khoon's middle that surprised him. In his youth tigresses had never strongly aroused his passions, allowing him to focus all his energies on Kung Fu and the way of the Shaolin. It was strange to him that this crane with such a foreign body from his own would stir such feelings within him.

As Khoon watched the duel he found himself entirely blocking out the world around him. His vision narrowed in on the she-crane's face: the sharp curve of her olive green beak, the patch of red bare skin on her crown, the downy pearly grey feathers around her eyes, throat, and neck; the rest of her feathers that were visible were snow white except for the secondary feathers at the tips of her wings, which were black. Khoon had never seen anything so beautiful.

Khoon was so transfixed by Leong's beauty it took him a few moments to realize the duel was getting out of hand. Han, who had begun the fight relaxed and controlled, was now letting his wounded pride get the better of him. Han lashed out with deadly force, his claws extended. Leong's defense remained flawless, but it only took one wrong move and Han could obliterate the crane's fragile body. The thought filled Khoon with such a sense of fear and dread he didn't even think before rushing in between the two.

Khoon blocked a powerful strike from Han, grasped his wrist, and used his own momentum to spin him into the crowd of onlookers. As Khoon was Han's *Si Heng*, his elder brother, Han should know to back down now that Khoon had interfered. Khoon did not get a chance to ensure this, however, as Leong struck out at the newcomer with surprising ferocity.

Removing Han from the fray had left Khoon open and Leong delivered a series of whipping blows to his ribs. Khoon winced and re-centered his focus. He had seen the crane style before, but there had been no practitioners of it at his temple, and he had little experience with the style. Despite this he was able to block another series of blows and pushed the crane back a few feet with an open palm to her chest. Khoon kept his claws retracted and purposefully missed the most vital points.

"Please, no more, I apologize for my friend..." Khoon tried to placate the crane. The last thing he wanted was to accidently hurt her.

She didn't listen. With a flurry of white and black feathers she attacked. Leong slipped her wings in-between Khoon's paws and batted them outwards to either side, at the same time she struck out with her beak and delivered a sharp blow to Khoon's forehead. Khoon stumbled backwards dizzy and half blind.

Khoon resisted his instincts to blindly lash out. He didn't want to hurt the she-crane by accident. Leong continued her attack with more pecks to the head with her beak and several whipping blows with her wings.

"Enough, Leong!" A spear stabbed into the dirt, separating Khoon and Leong.

"But, Uncle," huffed Leong.

The elder crane gave his niece a hard look. "Can you not see that he is not fighting back? You shame yourself if you continue."

Leong dipped her head in shame and abandoned her fighting stance. Leong's uncle walked over to Khoon and helped the tiger to his feet. "My apologies for my niece. She can get a bit overzealous."

Khoon gave the crane a respectful salute. "No apologies necessary. My man encouraged the escalation, it is I who should apologize. It would honor me if you and your niece would join us for dinner tonight on our boat."

Both Leong and her uncle seemed surprised by Khoon's invitation and then looked uncertain at Khoon and his men. Khoon supposed it was unsettling for two cranes to be invited over for dinner by a group of tiger clan. They might think they were meant to be the main course.

"My man, Han, who you have already met, makes an amazing tofu and sweet and sour stir fry," Khoon assured them, "and I would love to see more of your Kung Fu. Your crane style is truly formidable."

The cranes shared a look and then nodded.

***

When the cranes called to be let aboard, an excited shiver ran up Khoon's spine making his fur stand on end for a moment. He was pleasantly surprised the pair had decided to come. The moment Khoon and his men had returned to the ship he had sent them to work cleaning. He had also told Han to hold nothing back in preparing the meal tonight; he wanted everything to be perfect. Khoon had even changed into his best tunic suit. Black silk top with turn-down collar, four pockets with flaps, and pants.

Khoon was surprised with his sudden desire to impress the cranes. Specifically the she-crane, who he had learned was named Leong. As the cranes walked up the gangplank and Khoon went to meet them he idly wondered if Leong was engaged or not, and if her uncle was the relative to speak to on such matters.

The cranes had changed into fancier silk attire as well. Leong wore a pink tunic with white flower patterns, her spindly legs were bare. Her uncle wore a long black gown and a blue waistcoat with red stitching. Khoon greeted them with a salute and bow.

"Welcome to our home," Khoon said as he bowed.

The cranes returned the gesture. Then there was an awkward pause as crane eyes looked at cat eyes. Leong broke the silence, "You promised us food, Kitten. Where the hell is this great stir fry you've been babbling about?" Leong waltzed into the midst of the tiger clan monks and started making introductions as if she socialized with hunters all the time.

"Please forgive my niece, her manners are..." Leong's uncle trailed off.

"Think nothing of it," insisted Khoon. He was finding himself more drawn to Leong by the moment.

***

Within six months Khoon and Leong were set to be married. Leong's uncle sat down with Khoon the night before his wedding day.

"What did you want to talk to me about, Uncle?" asked Khoon. Khoon swayed a little when he sat down on the stool, he had already started celebrating with his brothers.

Uncle Crane refilled Khoon's cup with rice wine before filling his own glass. They sat in the common room below the decks of their ship. "To a happy marriage," Uncle toasted before downing half the contents of his glass. Khoon followed suit.

Uncle refilled their glasses. "Are you sure the two of you want to go through with this?" he asked, then took another long gulp of wine. "The Manchu do not look kindly on cross breed relationships, let alone cross clan. The two of you will be outcasts no matter where you go."

Khoon's jovial expression fell. His tail swished back and forth in solemn contemplation. "Leong and I have discussed this in length. We both understand the consequences of our relationship." Khoon let out a laugh. "It's not like I'm in good standing with the government as it is. As for Leong...you should know Leong will always go her own way."

Uncle rolled his black eyes and let out his own laugh. "That I know all too well. To a long and happy marriage." Uncle raised his glass for another toast.

***

A year after Khoon and Leong were married, Khoon received a message from his master, Jee Sin. It said that everything at the newly established southern temple was going well. The message also said that Wu Wai Thien was being sent to join up with Khoon, and that he would be waiting with his new wife in Xi'an. The monks changed course and headed that way.

They were many weeks out from Xi'an. Khoon stood at the rudder, gently guiding the vessel through the currents. Leong stood in the center of the main deck in her Kung Fu crane stance. Several of Khoon's brothers stood around Leong. They took turns trying to knock her off balance. Leong had been playing the game with the monks for months and they had yet to manage to knock her over. Khoon held the tiger style of Kung Fu above all others, but he was fascinated by the solidity of the crane style stance.

"Smoke," cried Han. The snow leopard was taking his shift at lookout.

The monks stopped their game and looked in the direction Han pointed. Khoon held a paw up to shield his eyes from the sun. Off in the distance several tendrils of black smoke rose towards the sky. They rose from the small river town they had planned on docking at that night. Khoon's face turned grim and his tail twitched. He did not have a good feeling about this.

***

The town was in complete ruin. Bamboo huts were burnt or burning to the ground; some looked to be simply trampled. The stench of death, smoke, and burnt flesh and feathers hung thick in the air. The only sign of life was a withered and bent otter clan crone who wandered through the ruins with eyes as dead as the corpses that littered the ground.

"What happened here?" growled Khoon. His claws strained as he stared up at the Manchu banner planted in the ground at the center of what used to be the town square.

21

"The governor wanted to take the baker's daughter as a concubine," coughed the old otter crone, who was being helped by Leong. "They weren't even the same clan. She would have been nothing more than a whore to him. The baker refused and the town stood behind him. This is what you get for standing against the Manchu." She laughed bitterly and kicked a charred piece of wood.

"Bastards! We'll get your revenge, Auntie," growled Han. The snow leopard clenched his paws so tight they shook.

Part of a house still standing collapsed off to Khoon's right. The noise made everyone jump. "Spread out and look for survivors," ordered Khoon. He wandered over to the house still partially standing.

The fallen wall revealed the corpse of a she-crane. Her lower half was crushed by debris. She cradled something in her wings close to her face. Khoon knelt for a closer look.

"Leong!" cried Khoon. He carefully picked up the brown and speckled egg.

"What is it?" She gasped when Khoon held up the egg. Leong cradled the egg in her wings and held it to her cheek.

"Is it…" Khoon couldn't finish his sentence.

"There's still life in it," said Leong with a sigh of relief, "but it needs to be nested."

"Take it back to the boat. We'll keep searching for survivors and bury the dead."

Leong nodded and hurried off to the boat. Khoon watched them for a moment with a flutter in his chest before turning and steeling himself for the sad work ahead.

***

Leong cooed her adopted son, Hoong Man Ting, to sleep, and then set him in his nest cradle. She wrapped a blanket woven of her own white feathers around the brown downy fluff that covered Ting's body.

"He hatched a bit small, but he's healthy and growing into a strong chick," said Leong. She spoke in answer to Wu Wai Thien's new wife Song's question.

The Southern tigress lounged back in a padded wooden chair. She draped a protective paw over her protruding belly. They were expecting a cub within a moon's turn. "It is gracious of you and Brother Khoon to take in the chick."

"It only seemed natural. All his family was killed, and Khoon and I cannot have our own." Leong looked longingly at Song's belly.

Nesting Ting had kicked Leong's maternal instincts into overdrive. Before Ting she had never pictured herself as a mother. She was feeling for the first time the true weight of the sacrifice she'd made to be with Khoon. At least it seemed Ting would fill some of the hole for both of them. Khoon was already acting the doting father to the young chick. Leong saw a new light in Khoon's eyes when he held Ting in his arms.

Song gave Leong a Cheshire grin, showing off her sharp teeth. The sight of the fangs sent an instinctive shiver up Leong's spine telling her to flee. She forced down the instinct that came naturally while around hunter clans.

"You know, Leong, I was very nervous about following Thien here," confessed Song. "I didn't know any details about any of you. I wasn't sure how you would react to me being of Southern breed and him of Bengal breed. It was a relief to see that you and Brother Khoon are of an open mind. My own family disowned me when they learned of the marriage." Song's whiskers drooped slightly making her grin look sad.

Leong was shocked. Cross breed relationships weren't common, but far more accepted than a match like Leong and Khoon. She draped a wing over Song's shoulder and gave it a squeeze. "The Shaolin is your family now. We are sisters you and I." Song's whiskers lifted and her grin turned sincere. "I'm surprised of such a conservative response from Southern tigers. I had heard they are more resistant to the Manchu ways in the south."

"My parents wouldn't have cared, but they have both passed on. My elder brother works as a government official and upholds their ways for the sake of his job. Sadly the Manchu influence is spreading and getting stronger. Despite the best efforts of the Shaolin. Just look at what happened to the Southern Temple and Jee Sin."

Leong looked at the door to the mess hall where Khoon, Thien, and the other brothers discussed the most recent turn of events. Her gut twisted with worry. When they had finally made it to Xi'an, Thien had awaited them with devastating news. The Shaolin Elder, Pak Mei, had defected to the Manchu and led an attack on the Southern Temple. Pak Mei, a white Bengal of the tiger clan, killed his fellow elder, Jee Sin, in a dual. Thien and Song barely made it out with their lives. Leong knew the men would take Pak Mei's betrayal personally and demand vengeance. She worried where such a path would lead.

As if on cue the door to the mess hall opened and in walked Khoon and Thien.

"Don't worry, *Si Heng*," assured Khoon. "We will get vengeance for *Sifu*."

"It will not be easy, *Si Dai*. Pak Mei's Kung Fu is the most formidable I have ever seen. We will have to train like never before if we have hope of beating him. Nothing will come of us rushing into a fight," said Thien. He came over and stood next to his wife.

Khoon nodded in agreement and some of the worry left Leong. Her husband had a wise elder brother. Something she was thankful for.

"So what now?" asked Leong.

The two Bengals shared a look and nodded. "We're going to abandon the Red Boats and scatter," said Khoon. "The Manchu have caught on to our guise. Thien knows someone that can get us papers. We will settle and lay low for a while in Qing Hai so we can re-group and increase our numbers."

***

"How did you and Thien meet?" asked Leong.

She leaned against the bamboo playpen and dangled her wing feathers above Song's son, Wu Ah Phiew. The orange and black striped tiger cub batted at his Auntie's wing with tiny paws. His sharp little claws just grazed the tips of her feathers. Little Ting stumbled over to investigate the game and pecked on Phiew's head when he wouldn't share. Phiew retracted his claws and batted his pen-mate back; Ting fell over harmlessly.

Leong smiled down at the children. It surprised her how gentle Phiew was with Ting. Despite being younger than Ting, Phiew was already larger and stronger. At first the mothers had meant to keep them apart when unsupervised, but soon Ting and Phiew would cry if separated for too long, and Phiew seemed to understand that he had to be careful with Ting.

"I lived in the village near the Southern Temple," said Song. She stood over the cooking stove preparing dinner. "I was drinking at the inn and Thien and a few of his brothers were there doing the same. My brother did not approve of me out drinking and sent one of his men to collect me. When I refused to leave he tried to force me. Thien came to my aid and beat down my brother's man. In return I struck him in the face and said I could fight my own battles." Song smiled at the memory. "Anyway, it was true love from then on."

Leong giggled at the story. Since they had settled on the small farm in southern Qing Hai she had come to enjoy her sister-in-law's company more and more. Leong liked her personality and respected her skills at Kung Fu. When their husbands worked in the fields, or were honing their skills for vengeance, the two females would often spar in between their day to day chores.

There was the sound of footsteps on the front porch and the front door opening. "The men are home early," noted Song. She wiped her paws on her apron and walked through the doorway towards the front of the house to greet her husband.

Leong was startled when Song's body was flung back through the doorway. The tigress hit the opposite wall and crumpled to the ground. Leong was at her sister-in-law's side immediately. Song was dazed, but unharmed. Leong helped her up.

Through the doorway walked four imperial officers of the tiger clan. A snow leopard, who was the leader judging by his head covering, backed by three Bengal tigers. The snow leopard gave the room an appraising look.

"Where are the criminals Hoong Hei Khoon and Wu Wai Thien? They are under arrest for conspiracy to incite rebellion against the empire. Give them up now and you and the little ones will be spared," growled the snow leopard.

"Get the children out of here. I'll hold them off until the men get here," whispered Song through clenched fangs.

"I'm not leaving you alone against them!" hissed Leong.

"Get Ting and Phiew safe. Promise me, no matter what, you'll look after Phiew!"

"Stop your whispering!" growled the snow leopard.

Orange tigress eyes held black crane eye for a moment that stretched an eternity. Many promises and goodbyes were made in a single second, and Leong bobbed her head slightly. That was all Song needed; her claws extended.

"Go!" Song snarled. She went down on all four paws for two paces and then lunged. The tigress tackled the snow leopard into the Bengals behind him. Two of them went down with the tackle along with the snow leopard in a snarling confusion of fur, claws, fangs, and blood. One Bengal managed to dodge Song's tackle.

As Song went after the soldiers Leong went straight for the crib, scooping up the double baby sling in the process and draping it over her neck. The Bengal that had managed to avoid the tackle jumped into her path.

"I don't think so, Birdie." He laughed when Leong took her fighting stance. He obviously didn't take the crane seriously.

The babies began to cry; Leong saw red. With a flap of her wings Leong lunged at the tiger that was twice her height and many more times her weight. She wasn't afraid, all that mattered was getting to the babies. The Bengal froze in surprise for a moment, but managed to get his paws up to defend just in time. Leong snaked her wings in-between the raised paws and batted them outwards. Then she struck with her beak several times, aiming for the eyes.

With a cry of pain the tiger sprawled backwards, nearly hitting the crib. Leong wasted no time in scooping up the children and nestling them in their double sling carrier. Ting was slung over her back in a feathery cocoon and Phiew over her front since he was so much heavier. She turned towards the back door, but it was blocked by her nemesis. The Bengal had deep cuts around his eyes, but he could still see.

The tiger took a swipe at Leong with his right paw. Leong blocked with her left wing, she gently brushed the tiger's paw aside at just the right angle that it missed her throat by inches. Then she rolled her wing over the tiger's forearm and gave him a whipping blow right to his snout. The tiger hissed and stumbled back. Leong was out the backdoor before he could recover.

Leong paused just outside and looked back at her sister-in-law. Song was squared off against the snow leopard backed by one of the Bengals. The other Bengal was motionless on the ground, a pool of red blood spreading out from under him. Song's mouth and paws were stained red and her right arm sagged.

"Go get reinforcements!" yelled the snow leopard. The Bengal ran for the front door.

Leong hated to leave Song behind, but she had to get help. Wishing her friend luck she turned and ran.

***

Khoon and Thien were too late. They entered through the back door and found Song on the ground in the middle of the room near the Bengal she had killed. The two Shaolin Bengals recognized the snow leopard that stood over her as Ko Chon Choong, Pak Mei's disciple.

"Noooo!" Thien let out a cry of anguish and fell to his wife's side.

"Choong, you bastard!" snarled Khoon. He went after the snow leopard.

As Khoon and Choong traded blows, none of them hitting their mark, Thien cradled Song's lifeless body in his arms. It took everything he had to not to fall to pieces. He longed to follow her to the afterlife. The thought of Phiew and vengeance were the only things that kept him together. At least Phiew was safe, hidden away with Leong in the fields.

Thien allowed himself one hacking sob and then laid Song on the ground gently. He put all his fury into his roar as he lunged into the fray between Khoon and Choong. Thien got three blows in at Choong's body, making the snow leopard wince. Choong blocked Thien's next attack and retaliated with a swing with his right paw followed by a spinning back kick; Thien was hard pressed to avoid both.

Khoon backed up Thien and attacked when there was an opening. Soon their attacks and defense fell into perfect harmony and they rained down blows onto Choong. Despite this, Choong was holding his own. He managed to block two out of three of the blows and landed at least one blow on the Bengals for every two he received. Khoon and Thein were relentless, however, and Choong began to tire.

Just when it seemed Choong was finished, a piercing whistle filled the air making Khoon and Thien fold back their ears. The sound of heavy footsteps came from the front of the house. Soldiers, all various breeds of the tiger clan wearing blue and red uniforms, flooded into the room. Khoon and Thien went on defense back to back as they were surrounded. They took down the first few that tried to close in on them, but they both knew it was only a matter of time before they were overwhelmed.

Thien looked down at the body of his wife. Then he glanced behind him at Khoon. He took in the soldiers and the window to his right that was the only unblocked escape.

"*Si Dai*, tell Phiew that his parents loved him. Raise him right, teach him the tiger style as we were taught," said Thien.

Before Khoon could respond Thien grabbed the back of Khoon's shirt, digging his claws into his pelt. Thien scooped Khoon up, spun him around for momentum, and then flung him through the window. Khoon was so caught off guard he only managed to let out a surprised cry of pain before he was flying through the air and then tumbling onto the ground outside.

Khoon tucked and rolled back up onto his hind paws. He spun around and looked through the broken window. The crowd of soldiers were closing in. Thien fought with the ferocity of the dying, but he was becoming overwhelmed. One soldier that carried a spear managed to stick Thien in the shoulder from behind. Thien let out a cry of pain and then disappeared from sight under a sea of blue and red uniforms.

Khoon wanted to run back into the house to aid his elder brother, but he would not belittle Thien's sacrifice. Feeling like his heart was being ripped from his chest, Khoon turned and ran before the soldiers could catch him.

***

A young Phiew laid on his belly and batted his new red ball back and forth between his paws. It was the day after his fifth birthday and the ball was his favorite present. The rhythmic motion of the ball along with the bright sun warming his back made him feel drowsy; he began to purr softly.

There was a flutter of wings, a shadow passed over him, and suddenly his ball was gone. "Hey!" cried Phiew. He jumped to his feet and looked to the sky.

"Ha, ha, can't get me," teased his elder brother, Ting. The young crane sat on top of the wall that encircled their house and yard. He held Phiew's ball between his webbed feet and dangled it just out of reach teasingly.

"Give it back," whined Phiew.

He jumped for the ball, but Ting pulled it out of reach. Phiew growled and clenched his paws. He thought it was so unfair that Ting could fly. Phiew was way bigger and stronger than his older brother, but that wasn't of much help if he couldn't reach him.

"It's mine now, Kitten." Ting laughed at the face Phiew made; he hated that nick name.

Phiew shook with anger and tried to climb up the stone wall, but he couldn't get a good hold. Ting laughed as he watched his younger brother struggle. He stopped laughing when a wet balled up shirt hit him directly in the face. There was a wet smack and Ting dropped the ball.

"Stop teasing your brother!" yelled Leong, who sat by the well doing laundry. "And bring me back that shirt."

"Thanks, Mother," giggled Phiew as he chased after his ball. Ting dropped to the ground and brought his mother back the shirt with his black feathered head hanging low.

"I was just playing," pouted Ting.

"Play nice," said Leong. She took back the shirt and gave him an affectionate pat on the head. "It is a *Si Heng's* duty to look after his *Si Dai.*"

"Yes, Mother," said Ting as he ran off after Phiew to play some more.

Phiew and Ting were in the middle of a game of catch when their father came out of the house. "Phiew, come. It's time for your training," said Khoon.

"Ha, ha, mine now," said Ting snatching the ball out of Phiew's paws.

"It's time for your training as well, Ting," said Leong, whisking the ball away from Ting. "Go stand!"

"Ohhh, but Mother…"

"I said stand!" yelled Leong in her no nonsense tone. She pointed with her wing.

Ting hung his head low and moped over to where Leong pointed. Then he took on the crane style fighting stance. Leong rolled her eyes and walked over to her son. She kicked Ting's skinny legs out from under him.

"Stand right!" she demanded. Ting picked himself off the ground and took the stance again, focusing on his form this time. Leong bobbed her head. "Better, stay like that until I am done with laundry."

Phiew snickered at his brother under his breath as he followed their father out the gate. Khoon and Phiew usually trained in the bamboo grove behind their house. "Father, why does Ting learn Kung Fu from mother and I learn it from you?" asked Phiew as they walked.

"Because Ting is born of the crane clan so your mother teaches him the crane style. You are born of the tiger clan so you learn the tiger style," explained Khoon.

"But why can't we learn both?" Phiew had always been curious about the style his brother got to learn. "Couldn't we combine them?"

"No!" said Khoon, harsher than he meant. Khoon was very much a purist when it came to his Kung Fu, if not in the rest of the aspects of his life. He continued in a softer tone. "The styles have been developed over hundreds of years to maximize the effectiveness of the body forms of the different clans. A crane couldn't use tiger style because they lack paws with strong digits and claws; conversely a tiger cannot use crane style because he lacks a beak and the stance would be completely unnatural."

His father sounded like he knew what he was talking about, but Phiew wasn't so sure. He had watched his brother practice before and thought that he could replicate some of the moves. When the pair of tigers came to their usual training area, Phiew pushed the thoughts to the back of his mind. He had to put all his focus in the lesson at hand if he didn't want to end up with too many bumps and bruises.

***

"Tiger style!" snarled a twelve year old Phiew. The orange and black striped Southern-Bengal mix lashed out at his crane clan brother. In his heated frenzy he didn't even remember to retract his claws.

Ting dodged, took to the air and landed behind Phiew. Ting gave his younger brother a rough shove in the back. "You'll never beat my crane style, loser," laughed Ting.

When Phiew got his balance he lashed out blindly behind him. Ting dodged, batted Phiew's paw down, and pecked him hard right between his eyes. Phiew stumbled back dazed; Ting hadn't held much back.

The fight had started over something foolish, but had quickly descended into the old argument of which style was better. Like many brothers Phiew and Ting were both best friends and rivals in most things. The fight continued on and became more out of control.

Phiew managed to get behind Ting and was going to take a swing at him, but his paw was caught by the much larger paw of their father. One look at their father's disapproving glare made them both brace themselves. In seconds they were both on their backsides in the dust with a few more lumps added to their heads.

"What in the name of Buddha are the two of you doing? You could have broken your brother's spine with that blow, Phiew!" growled Khoon.

"He said the tiger style was for losers," accused Phiew. He rubbed his head and glared at his brother.

"I called you a loser," corrected Ting, not wanting to upset his father more. "Not the tiger style."

Phiew opened his mouth, but Khoon spoke first. "Enough of this nonsense from the both of you." Khoon was well aware of the sometimes bitter rivalry between the two boys. He couldn't help but feel responsible for driving a wedge between the brothers by insisting on separate training. Khoon took a long breath to gather his patience. He sat down on the ground next to the boys and smiled to show he wasn't too angry.

"Phiew, when your father and I were your age we started training at the Shaolin temple." Phiew's ears perked up at mention of his birth father. He sat cross legged on the ground attentive to the coming story. Ting got comfortable next to him. "Though we learned the tiger style from your *Si Gung*, Jee Sin, we trained alongside brother Shaolin born of all the clans of the zodiac. At times we would test our skills against one another, but more often we would train to combine our skills into the ultimate attack and defense. Thien and I would often train with our brother, Feng, who was born of the snake clan. Where our style was weak his was strong, where his was lacking we were masters. We were unbeatable together."

"Where is Feng now?" asked Ting.

Khoon's voice caught in his thought for a moment. "He was killed along with Jee Sin when Pak Mei destroyed the Southern Temple." Khoon stared off in the distance for a moment and clenched his paws. Then he shook his head and smiled down at the boys. "Remember, boys, it is not the style that makes a fighter superior, it is the wielder of that style. Neither of you could ever hope to defeat me, or your mother for that matter. The only hope you have is to learn to fight in unison." With that Khoon left the boys to contemplate his words.

***

A seventeen year old Ting hid himself in the shadows on the rooftop of their family home. He wore a conical bamboo hat and a white and blue tunic. Phiew concealed himself just inside the shed wearing a red and black tunic and pants. He crouched low, his muscles were tense and ready to spring. They were in position and ready to attack.

Within minutes their father wandered outside. When he was halfway across the courtyard the boys attacked in unison, Ting from above and Phiew from the ground. Khoon was ready and met them head on. Even fighting in unison within five moves Ting was flung into the air and got tangled up in the laundry lines, and Phiew was sent sprawling into a rack of practice weapons.

Khoon barely broke stride and continued his casual stroll across the courtyard and out the front gate. "The two of you are improving," was all he said as he passed his downed sons.

Ting and Phiew picked themselves up and brushed themselves off. They heard their mother's harsh voice from inside the house inquiring on the commotion. The teenagers looked around at the mess of wooden weapons and laundry scattered across the courtyard.

"Walk to town?" asked Ting.

"More like run," said Phiew. The brothers ran out the front gate already feeling the switch their mother would have prepared for them later.

The brothers raced for a long time, neither willing to slow their pace or give up first. When they finally stopped they were tired and panting heavily.

"I almost landed a strike," said Phiew.

"You wish, *Si Dai.*" Ting lightly stepped on his brother's tail. "Remember, most of the time we shouldn't attack at the same time. I attack while you defend and vice-versa. We need to get our timing better."

Phiew rolled his eyes and swished his tail out of Ting's reach.

"Please! No!" shouted a panicked feminine voice from up the road.

Ting and Phiew rushed towards the voice. They rounded a bend in the road and came upon a mixed group of two rhinos, two Gibbon monkeys, and three raccoon dogs; all males. The group, with knives and cudgels, surrounded a lone clouded leopardess. A still form laid motionless at the she-leopard's feet. The young leopardess was trying to hold her attackers at bay with a walking staff.

No words were needed, the brothers went into action immediately. They instinctively went for the rhinos first. With a flap of his wings Ting took to the air and went for one rhino's eyes, being sure to avoid his sharp horn. Phiew went for the other rhino's legs. He used the strong straight swipes of the tiger style. Extending his claws he aimed for the weak points at the joints. Within moments the rhinos were on the run, abandoning their comrades.

The Gibbons recovered from their initial surprise and attacked the unwelcome newcomers. Phiew and Ting dodged the initial attack of wildly swung knives. Then the monkeys took to the trees. Ting flew after them and Phiew leapt into the branches to follow. The crane faced off against one of the monkeys on a thick branch. Ting immediately attacked, but the monkey swung around the branch, holding on by his tail, and came back up behind Ting. The brown furred and black faced monkey raised his knife to stab Ting in the back.

Phiew pounced on the monkey with a feral growl. The two fell to the ground and when Phiew stood, the monkey's body was crumbled and lifeless. "No one hurts my *Si Heng,*" Phiew hissed, shaking with adrenaline. He felt sick to his stomach when he stared down at the Gibbon's corpse.

Phiew took a deep breath and turned to the remaining raccoon dogs. Ting came up behind to back him up.

"Thanks for the save, *Si Dai*," said Ting.

"Anytime, *Si Heng*." Phiew's whiskers and tail twitched with pride.

The brothers readied themselves to take on the brown and grey striped raccoon dogs. Before they could attack, the leopardess came up from behind the raccoon dogs and struck with her staff. They were sent running with bruised and bleeding skulls.

Once her attackers had fled the leopardess fell to the side of what looked like an elderly clouded leopardess. She broke into hopeless tears and hugged the body close. Phiew and Ting rushed to the girl's side to comfort her.

***

Khoon stood just inside the doorway of their small home. His sons didn't know he watched them play in the courtyard. What had been an errand to fetch water for the baths had turned into a water fight at the well; that had somehow turned into a balancing act on top of a spear lain across the dowel that drew up the bucket. Ting was nineteen years in a moon's turn; Khoon wondered if his sons were ever going to grow up.

The balance the boys displayed was impressive. Phiew had it a bit harder of the two boys being heavier, but the tiger was holding his own. That is until Mingmei, the clouded leopardess they had taken in a few years back, walked by and giggled. Phiew became completely distracted by Mingmei and wobbled off balance.

He fell into the well and Ting had to flap his wings to keep from doing the same. Ting laughed and Mingmei rushed over to help Phiew. The tiger's ears were bent back with hurt pride and he refused the paw Mingmei offered. It had not escaped Khoon's notice that Phiew and Mingmei had been sneaking off together quite frequently.

Khoon shook his head. *I hope I did right by you, Thien.* Khoon thought of his old friend often. Though they had not shared a drop of blood, Thien and Khoon had been the dearest of brothers. Khoon had found a safe place and had raised the boys in peaceful seclusion. They were grown now, though, and he had spent years honing his Kung Fu; it was time to keep the promise they had made so many years ago. Their *Si Fu*, Jee Sin, had to be avenged. Phiew's parents had to be avenged.

With a twitch of his whiskers Khoon came to a final decision. He would spend one last day with his family. Tonight he would have a final bout with the boys. He would even let them each land a blow. Then he would set out before the sunrise. If the fates were kind he would be back with his family in time to celebrate Ting's birthday.

"Not yet," came Leong's musical voice from behind Khoon. He turned to face his wife; she always seemed to know what he was thinking. "You're not ready yet. I saw what Pak Mei's disciple, Choong, was able to do; your tiger style wouldn't be a match against his master."

"Thanks for the vote of confidence, Wife," Khoon said with mix of bitterness and sarcasm in his tone. This was an old argument.

"Let me teach you some of my crane style. Even mastering some of it would give you the edge you need to defeat Pak Mei. I'm sure of it."

"No!" snapped Khoon.

Leong's black eyes were watery. Khoon breathed out his frustrations and walked over to his wife. He wrapped his arms around her delicate body and held her close, stroking her soft feathers. How could he blame her for being scared? She was only trying to help, but she knew his reasons.

Jee Sin had taught him pure tiger style. Khoon would avenge his *Sifu* using that style. He would leave it to the younger generations to evolve the styles. Khoon glanced out the doorway at the young ones. All three of them were laughing at some joke.

"What should I tell the boys?" asked Leong, her voice muffled by Khoon's shirt.

Khoon squeezed Leong a little tighter. *Such a strong creature in such a fragile body*, he thought. "Tell them I went on Shaolin business to meet Han. By the time they figure out differently, it will be too late for them to stop me."

Leong let out one sniffle, but refused to shed a tear. "They'll never forgive you if you don't come back," she warned.

Khoon laughed and released Leong from his embrace. "Come, Wife, let us enjoy the day."

***

Within a week Ting and Phiew had figured out where their father had really gone. They were furious that their father had left them without saying goodbye, but they were wise enough not to take it out on their mother. Leong was over the edge with worry and was barely keeping it together. She never let the boys see, but she cried every night and prayed that her husband would return to her.

When Ting's birthday came and went and there was still no sign of Khoon everyone began to fear the worst, but no one gave voice to their worry. Phiew was home alone practicing his tiger style when a lone figure came into view walking up the road. The traveler was clearly tiger clan. Hope bubbled in his chest and Phiew ran out to meet the traveler.

The hope sunk like a stone when Phiew recognized the traveler; his pace slowed to a walk. "Uncle Han," said Phiew when he came close. The middle aged snow leopard limped along with a staff and his right arm was in a sling.

Han stopped in front of Phiew. The snow leopard shook his head sadly. "I'm sorry, Phiew, I helped him fight his way into the temple, but he had to go up against Pak Mei's top students before he could face the master. He was already worn out and injured by the time he faced Pak Mei."

Phiew couldn't grasp what Han was saying. A ringing started in his ears that blocked out Han's voice and his face felt hot. Dead? Hoong Hei Khoon couldn't be dead? His father was the strongest tiger he had ever known. Someone, somewhere, had to have made a horrible mistake.

The ringing subsided and Phiew was able to hear Han's voice. Han was shaking Phiew gently and asking if he was all right.

"I'm fine," said Phiew, perfectly calm.

He turned and strode into the house. He knew exactly what he had to do. It didn't take long to gather all he needed. Han was still limping towards the house when Phiew emerged with a sack slung over his shoulder.

"Where are you going?" asked Han. "Your father wouldn't want this."

"My father is dead!" yelled Phiew. He continued just above a whisper. "Both of them are dead." He was silent for a moment in order to keep from crying. "Tell them where I've gone. Give them my love."

Phiew headed off down the road at a fast run. He couldn't risk Ting or Mingmei catching up to him and trying to stop him. If he gave it all he had, he would beat Ting to Pak Mei's temple even if Ting flew to catch him. He would get vengeance once and for all, for his birth parents, his *Sifu*, and his *Si Gung*.

***

Ting and Mingmei were surprised to find the injured snow leopard on their front porch when they arrived home from town. Ting knew the meaning of seeing Uncle Han without his father.

"Where's Phiew?" was the first thing out of his beak.

Han shook his head. "I couldn't stop him. He's heading for Pak Mei's temple."

Ting's head drooped. His *Si Dai* was so reckless sometimes. This time it might get him killed. Mingmei let out a dread filled gasp and her paw instinctively went to her belly. The movement did not escape Ting's notice. Mingmei gave him a pleading look.

"Does Phiew know?" asked Ting.

Mingmei shook her head. "I wasn't sure until recently. He was so worried about your father I didn't want to burden him more over what could be nothing. I can't lose him, Ting."

Ting put a comforting wing on Mingmei's shoulder and placed the other across the paw over her belly. He had already come to think of Mingmei as his little sister. Now she would truly be his sister-in-law and he would soon be an uncle. He had to stop Phiew. His *Si Dai* didn't stand a chance against Pak Mei. His child would not be raised never knowing their true father like they had.

"I'll fly as fast as I can for the temple. I may beat him if the weather is favorable." Ting went in the house and retrieved a sack of food and his conical bamboo hat.

"The rains are coming," said Han, struggling to stand. "They'll slow you more than they will Phiew. I'll sail down the river, I may beat you there if the weather is extreme."

"I'm going with you, Han," said Mingmei.

By the look on her face he knew better than to argue. "We need to leave before Leong gets back. She would lock us all down and go after Phiew herself. Leave her a note before you leave." Mingmei nodded and Ting took to the air.

***

Phiew ran on all four paws night and day towards his destination. He stopped only to eat, drink, and catch a few hours of sleep when he was absolutely exhausted. Ting flew just as hard to catch his brother. Flying was faster, but it wore Ting out and he had to stop and rest more often than Phiew. When the rain Han had predicted hit, Ting was hard pressed to keep flying, but he pushed through the foul weather.

Phiew made it to the temple first. He rested for a few hours in the woods and then sprinted up the steep stone steps leading to the front gates without much of a plan. The young tiger was scared if he stopped to think about what he was doing for too long he might back down from fear.

The temple's defenses were weakened from the recent attack from his father. Phiew met little resistance and easily fought his way into the inner sanctum of the temple. For the first time Phiew laid eyes on the white Bengal tiger known as Pak Mei. The legendary Shaolin Elder turned traitor sat in a decorative chair atop a dais on the opposite side of the room. He wore white and blue robes and a long chain of prayer beads around his neck.

Phiew's face felt hot and the ringing started in his ears again. His claws extended and he pointed his paw at Pak Mei. "You!" he growled.

Pak Mei shook his head and his blue eyes looked sad. Dozens of Pak Mei's disciples flooded the room between Phiew and his father's killer. Phiew crouched to spring at the closest obstacle; he would tear apart anything in his path.

"Hold!" cried Pak Mei, holding up his paw. His disciples relaxed and backed down. "I will face him."

A snow leopard standing to the right of Pak Mei's chair bristled. "He is not worthy of your efforts, *Sifu*. Let me handle this. I will make short work of the intruder."

Pak Mei shook his head. "I said I will handle this, Choong. There has been too much death of late. I would have this finished quickly." The white tiger stood and walked off the dais. His students parted to form a path for them both to meet in the center of the room.

As Phiew walked to meet Pak Mei he gave the snow leopard who had spoken a careful look. He knew his parents had been killed by a disciple of Pak Mei's, he thought his name was Choong. Once he was done with the master he would take care of the student.

Phiew refocused on Pak Mei. They squared off five feet apart in the center of the room. Phiew's muscles tensed and without a word he struck out. Using strong straight swipes he precisely aimed each clawed digit at Pak Mei's weak points. Phiew's strikes were on target, but never hit home. Pak Mei moved faster than Phiew had ever imagined possible. With each strike Pak Mei would move just centimeters out of reach.

The white Bengal's strikes were just as fast as his defense. When Pak Mei decided to attack he moved in and landed three strikes to Phiew's body before he could even blink. Pak Mei withdrew and Phiew fell to one knee, clenching his fangs against the pain.

"This is your one and only chance, boy." Pak Mei looked down at Phiew. "You have no chance against me. Leave now and I'll spare your life."

Phiew saw red and lunged at Pak Mei with a feral growl. In his fury Phiew abandoned his disciplined style and took powerful but telegraphed side swipes at Pak Mei. The white Bengal slapped aside one of Phiew's strikes; this left Phiew's side open to attack. Pak Mei delivered a series of blows to the young tiger's side, aiming for his vitals. Phiew cried out, doubled over, and coughed up blood.

Realization of his situation finally dawned on Phiew and he felt like a complete idiot. How did he ever believe he would succeed where his father had failed? There was no way he could beat Pak Mei. Phiew felt desperate and cornered.

Phiew thought of Mingmei and how she always said that there was no shame in running from a fight you couldn't win. Picturing Mingmei, Phiew gathered his strength and jumped to his feet. Instead of attacking Pak Mei he turned and ran for the exit. He leapt over a row of Pak Mei's armed disciples and made it outside.

At the top of the stone steps that led down through the gates, Phiew stumbled. Phiew's injuries were greater than he imagined and he could not keep himself from falling down the steps. Each strike of flesh against stone a reminder of his failures and inadequacies.

Pak Mei calmly strode out of his temple and watched the tiger's body roll down the last few steps. There was an icy stab to his heart as he wondered how he had wronged the boy; he probably belonged to Hoong Hei Khoon somehow. Fate had forced the old tiger to make impossible decisions. He struggled with the results of those decisions every day.

He knew he should kill the boy. Leaving him alive would only be sparing a future threat. Yet he hesitated. There had been so much death lately. That had never been what he had wanted.

Choong approached his master and put a gentle paw on his shoulder. "We must end this."

The Manchu still held several members of Pak Mei's original temple captive, along with their families, to insure his allegiance. He was charged with the eradication of any and all potential threats to the Manchu reign. This boy had great potential to become a Kung Fu master one day, and his pure hatred for Pak Mei was evident.

"Finish him," ordered Pak Mei with a heavy heart. *What wasted talent*, he thought.

Pak Mei's white fur bristled and he let out a roar of frustration. For a more physical outlet he kicked over a large iron sconce sitting at the top of the steps. Burning coals went everywhere and the sconce made loud gong sounds as it rolled down the steps after Phiew.

Phiew lay dazed at the base of the steps and was unable to move out of the way of the red hot iron sconce. It rolled over his right front and hind paws. Phiew heard the crunch of bone and smelled the stench of burning fur. He let out a cry of agony. Through blurry tears Phiew could see Pak Mei's disciples closing in on him. He wondered if he would meet his birth parents in the afterlife.

A familiar shadow crossed over Phiew's vision. A white feathery blur fell into the midst of Pak Mei's disciples. Phiew blinked his eyes to clear his vision and recognized his *Si Heng's* hat. In a flurry of feathers Ting used forward wiping motions with his wings to deflect the blows of his nearest opponents, and then used the same motion to eye gouge one opponent and throat jab the other.

Ting bobbed his long slender neck out of the path of a spear one disciple wielded. The crane blocked another thrust of the spear upwards with his forewings crossed in front of him. He kept contact with the shaft of the spear and followed the shaft forward towards its wielder. Ting struck out with his beak and gouged at the clouded leopard's eyes. The leopard dropped the spear and covered his eyes with his paws, letting out a cry of pain.

"What are you doing here?" cried Phiew. His pain fogged mind was still trying to process the situation.

"Saving your ass," grunted Ting as he bobbed out of the way of a Bengal's large fist. "It's a *Si Heng's* duty to protect his *Si Dai* after all. Now get the hell out of here. I'll hold them."

"I'm not leaving you," growled Phiew. Not that he would be of any help. He couldn't even stand.

After downing another clouded leopard, Ting gave Phiew a frustrated look. Then he smiled at something behind Phiew. "Get him out of here!" yelled Ting.

Furry paws gently grabbed Phiew and dragged him away from the fight. In a panic Phiew began to fight, but he relaxed when he recognized Mingmei and Han. "I won't leave him!"

"Sorry about this, kid." Han hit Phiew over the head with his walking staff. Phiew's body went limp and the leopards dragged the tiger to a horse waiting with his cart. Mingmei loaded Phiew into the cart and Han slipped a bag of silver in the horse's saddle bag. The horse broke into a trot with a satisfied whinny.

Phiew began to regain conciseness as they rode out of sight. His blurred vision cleared in time for him to see a large white tiger holding a limp crane form high above his head before bringing the crane down hard across his knee. Phiew slipped back into unconsciousness.

***

Phiew was shocked out of his drunken stupor by a stream of icy water poured over his face. He clumsily scrambled to his feet, extended his claws, and looked around for the threat. What he found was his mother standing in the doorway of the shed holding a bucket between her wings and death in her eyes.

"Wake up, you useless drunk," Leong practically growled like a tigress.

Phiew rolled his eyes and sank to the floor. The shed smelled of wine and vomit. He wondered how he had ended up in the tool shed; last night was mostly a blur. The tiger cradled his mangled right forepaw in his lap and picked up an abandoned wine jar that sat forgotten amongst rusting farm tools. Phiew gave the jar a hopeful shake and was disappointed to find it empty. He brightened, however, when he noticed his opium pipe on the ground at his side that still had a few drags left in it.

Leong kicked the pipe away with her webbed foot before Phiew could grab it. Phiew let out a long sigh. "Just leave me alone, Mother, please."

Leong shook her head and wondered if both her sons were truly dead. With a sniff of disgust she stalked out of the shed. "Maybe you can talk some sense into him," she said to Mingmei, who stood just outside.

Mingmei rubbed her swollen belly with her paws. It wouldn't be long before the baby was here. She needed to find a way to snap Phiew out of this depression. He blamed himself for Ting's death and destroyed himself for his failure to defeat Pak Mei. Mingmei took a deep fortifying breath before entering the shed.

She looked down at her broken love wallowing on the ground. "Why don't you come outside, my love? Train some of your Kung Fu today. Your paws are healed now…"

"My paws will never be healed!" snapped Phiew. Though they no longer pained him greatly his paws were permanently mangled and lacked any real strength. He limped when he walked and could barely hold chopsticks. "My tiger style is a joke with these. They are as weak as…as…"

"As wings!" snapped Mingmei, getting angry now. "Seems to me you're making up excuses. Your brother handled Pak Mei and his men with his spindly little wings far better than you did with your oh so powerful paws. Stop feeling sorry for yourself, Phiew, and start acting like the tiger I fell in love with." Mingmei ran out of the shed before Phiew could see her crying.

Phiew was shocked silent, not so much by Mingmei's rebuke, but by her comparison of his damaged paws with wings. Something dawned in his mind. He sat on the ground of the shed for a long time mulling over the long conversations he had once had with Ting comparing their styles of Kung Fu. He envisioned the exercises Ting and their mother had done out in the courtyard all his life. Though he had never tried them, he knew the basic crane forms nearly as well as his tiger forms.

When Leong and Mingmei left to go buy food in town, Phiew finally emerged from the shed. He was shamed by his state and limped over to the well. Splashing his face with cold water, he washed the smell of wine and sick out of his fur. He then stood in the center of the courtyard and tried to mimic Ting's fighting stance.

In tiger style you stayed on your toes, ready to spring at any moment. Ting had told him that with crane style you stayed flat footed and pivoted on your heels. Though it felt unnatural at first, Phiew found the movement more accommodating to his weak paw. Phiew struck out his left paw with a tiger style swipe and then did a forward wiping motion with his right paw, pads down, imagining his mangled fingers jabbing into an opponent's eyes.

Ting's voice whispered in the back of Phiew's mind, *Crane style is all about staying relaxed and loose. If you're tense, your opponent can control your energy. If you stay relaxed you can feel where their energy is and deflect it or loop right around it.* The tiger envisioned the loose whip-like blows Ting would deliver in quick succession when they had sparred. If Phiew used his energy correctly he could generate a great deal of power with the motion, even with his mangled paw.

Phiew was beginning to incorporate crane style defensive movements in unison with tiger style attacks when he heard his mother's voice from behind him. "Your stance is all wrong. Roll your hips under to straighten

41

your spine. Have your weight on the inside of your feet." Phiew made the adjustments and looked over his shoulder at his mother standing just inside the gate.

Leong bobbed her head. "Better."

"Teach me crane style?" asked Phiew simply.

Leong considered her son for a long minute. "Only if you promise not to face Pak Mei again until I say you are ready."

Phiew hesitated wondering if this was some ploy of his mother's to keep him forever out of harm's way. He recognized the look in her eyes, however. She wanted vengeance as much as him.

"Very well," agreed Phiew.

Leong bobbed her head again and passed her packages off to Mingmei who stood beside her. "Let's get started." Mingmei went into the house to prepare dinner while Leong drilled the basics of crane style into her tiger clan son.

***

With his forearms Phiew batted the two wooden rods that stuck out from the post behind the leather dummy that swung to and fro. He then palmed the chest of the dummy in quick succession. The tiger paused at the end of the sequence to check his form. His whiskers twitched with satisfaction; he was right on target.

Hissssss. Phiew smiled at the sound. Pride bubbled in his chest as the sand poured through the tear in the back of the dummy and his leather foe deflated.

"Yay! You did it, Daddy," cried a small tigress.

The mixed breed tigress, with a unique striped and blotched fur pattern, pounced on the shell of the dummy and ripped the remains to shreds with her sharp claws. Ng Mui practically purred as she tried to mimic her father's fighting style.

Phiew smiled down at his daughter and was filled with fatherly pride. Her technique wasn't half bad considering he had yet to give her any formal lessons. Perhaps she was getting old enough to begin her training.

After shredding the dummy, Mui's little ears perked up and she scanned the yard. "That's the last one, Daddy."

Phiew's ears perked up as well. He turned and scanned his large practice yard. Forty nine other posts stood bare save a few shreds of rope that once held leather dummies.

"So it is," he said, hiding the satisfaction he felt. "Why don't you go tell Grandma."

Mui turned and scampered into the house. "Grandma! Grandma! Daddy finally did it. Grandma!"

Mui soon returned with Leong and Mingmei close behind. Leong crossed her wings in front of her and studied Phiew's handy work. She finally bobbed her head, giving it her stamp of approval.

"Honestly, you did it faster than I expected," she said. "I thought wearing out fifty dummies without using your claws would take you at least another year, but you have been dedicated, my son."

"Four years was enough for me." Phiew cringed at the memory of the grueling hours he had spent training over the years. He knew he was ready. The only question was, did his mother think the same?

Phiew looked to Leong for confirmation. Orange tiger eyes held black crane eyes for a moment that stretched an eternity. Leong saw Phiew's birthmother in those eyes. Her heart broke all over again for all the loved ones she had lost. She prayed to Buddha and all the ancestors that Phiew would not join those she mourned.

"You are ready, my son. There is nothing more for me to teach you. I will send word to the others. They will help you in what is to come."

Mui cheered happily, not understanding what her father's success meant for them all. The adults stood stoic and grim faced.

***

Phiew walked down the gangplank of Uncle Han's boat to join the others on the shore. Han had said it was one of the last remaining original Red Boats, and the very boat that his adoptive parents had been married on and traveled on together with his birth parents. Leong had been in a fog of nostalgia the entire trip to Pak Mei's temple. She followed just behind Phiew onto the shore. They were a mile up river from Pak Mei's temple.

"Are you sure you want to do this, Mother?" asked Phiew. He had spent much of the journey trying to dissuade her from coming.

"This is as much my fight as it is yours. I made a promise a long time ago, and I intend on keeping it. Pak Mei is all yours. I'm just here to get you to him in one piece." Leong used her tone Phiew knew couldn't be argued with.

With a sigh of resignation Phiew looked at the Shaolin brothers who had answered his call. Along with Uncle Han, there were two sons of the snake clan dressed in red and blue silk capes, an elderly raccoon dog wearing a conical hat and a long chain of prayer beads, a massive rhino, and a white rabbit with pure red eyes dressed in black robes. They were all survivors, or students of survivors, of the sacks on the Shaolin temples. Phiew was not the only one who had been preparing for this day for many years.

Phiew saluted his allies. "Thank you for coming, brothers. You all know the plan. Today is our day for justice."

"May Buddha bless us," said the raccoon dog. His bamboo conical hat reminded Phiew of Ting.

"May Buddha bless us," echoed the others.

Taking a deep breath Phiew flexed his mangled paws. He had done special exercises to rebuild their strength for years. Phiew only ran and walked with a slight limp now. His crane style made up for the strength they still lacked.

"Let's go," he said before breaking into a run and falling down on all four paws after a few strides.

The others fell into formation behind Phiew and they ran towards Pak Mei's temple. Leong took to the air and scouted out the landscape ahead of them to ensure sentries or a trap didn't await them. They met no resistance until the front gate.

As planned, the rhino went first. Along with his massive horn as weaponry he also wore several golden rings on his forearms that protected from claws and blades and transformed his massive arms into even more formidable clubs. The rhino charged up the steep stone steps and rammed down the gate. He was followed closely by his comrades.

Pak Mei's disciples were caught off guard, but they responded quickly. Those practicing in the expansive courtyard went into defense mode and the alarm was raised. The rhino charged deep into the courtyard, batting any resistance aside with his massive horn and his ring clad arms. At the other side of the courtyard he finally came to a stop. Many disciples surrounded him armed with swords and spears. The rhino took the low and wide parallel stance of his style. When the disciples converged he swung his arms in circular motions that deflected all the weapons and busted open the skull of any disciple that got too close.

The other Shaolin followed in the wake of the rhino's carnage. Those of Pak Mei's disciples that weren't surrounding the rhino were hard pressed against the attack of his comrades. The snakes slithered in an incomprehensible pattern before jumping into the air and throwing themselves at a squad of Bengal tigers, spitting venom as they went. They took as many tigers to the ground as they could. Snake style were experts at grappling, with their chokes and joint locks.

Armed with a matching pair of hooked swords, the rabbit turned into a white and black blur, cutting down anything in his path. The raccoon dog relieved a clouded leopard of his staff weapon with a straight powerful jab to the chest. Before continuing on he took a long pull from a dried gourd that hung from his belt. Then with a look of perfect serenity on his face and an artful twirl of the staff, he charged with the ferocity of a mad man.

Phiew spearheaded the attack towards the inner sanctum of the temple flanked by Han and Leong. Though more disciples poured into the courtyard, the group slowly fought their way inside. They tried to stay as a tight group and not get separated until the last possible moment. When they breached the doors to the main hall Pak Mei's remaining disciples retreated to surround the dais on the opposite side of the room.

Five of Pak Mei's top students stepped forward. "This insolence will not be forgiven, boy," said Pak Mei from his seat. "I will not be as lenient as I was last time. Kill them all!" The top students came forward, three Bengal tigers, a clouded leopard, and a snow leopard.

The Shaolin squared off. Both the snakes went after one of the Bengals, their attack perfectly coordinated. The rhino took on one of the other Bengals and the raccoon dog took the third. Han pounced on the other snow leopard and the rabbit took the clouded leopard. The remaining disciples split off to back up the top five. They threw in cheap shots here and there, careful not to get into the top's way.

Phiew leapt over them all and charged the dais. Pak Mei's first disciple, Choong, leapt into his path. The snow leopard held a spear in his paws, "To get to my master you will have to go through me."

"Fine by me," growled Phiew.

A blur of feathers came from above and landed in-between Phiew and Choong. "He's mine," said Leong. Taking her stance she faced off against Choong. "Stay focused on your goal." Leong bobbed her head towards Pak Mei, who was finally standing from his chair.

Phiew nodded and redirected his attention. Pak Mei stretched casually and sauntered down the steps of the dais. Phiew took a deep breath; the moment had finally come.

"You know, I remember them all. Your *Sifu*, Khoon, your birth father, your brother, even your *Si Gung*, Jee Sin. They were all fools." Pak Mei shook his head sadly. "They didn't know how to evolve with the times. They couldn't see that going up against the Manchu was a losing battle. Seems you are such a fool as well, boy."

Phiew saw red at the corners of his vision, but with a calming breath he kept his emotions in check. "My name is Wu Ah Phiew! Enough talk, it's time for you to die, Pak Mei."

Pak Mei's whiskers twitched with amusement. "We will see, boy."

Phiew charged with a snarl. They traded a few blows, but none of them hit their mark. The two tigers parted. Phiew adjusted his stance, shook out his paws, and cracked his neck. Pak Mei looked surprised and reevaluated Phiew with his blue eyes.

"What style is that?" asked Pak Mei, adjusting his stance and getting serious.

It was Phiew's whiskers that twitched with amusement this time. "It's my style," he snarled and struck out again.

The tigers traded several more blows. Phiew used his crane style techniques to block Pak Mei's attacks while simultaneously striking with his powerful tiger style punches. Pak Mei was as fast as he remembered, but Phiew kept contact with him so when Pak Mei dodged, Phiew could feel where his energy was going and where he could strike next. Phiew both gave and received several blows that landed.

When they finally parted Phiew had a swollen eye and bruised ribs. Blood dribbled from Pak Mei's mouth and stained his white fur. They stared at each other for a moment. Pak Mei felt a twinge of doubt that he might not win this fight. He hadn't felt that way since he had faced his Shaolin brother, Jee Sin, so long ago.

Phiew went in for a final attack. Pak Mei brought up his paws for defense. Phiew feigned a strike to his groin, but then his paws swam upwards and in-between Pak Mei's paws. With a grunt Phiew batted Pak Mei's paws outward to either side and then struck with his mangled paw right between Pak Mei's eyes, picturing his paw as the beak of a crane.

The blow reverberated through Pak Mei's skull, making him stumble backwards and lower his guard. Phiew lashed out with a series of palm strikes to Pak Mei's chest aiming for all the main pressure points. Pak Mei wore a look of pure shock and let out a little cough. Blood blossomed from his mouth and his lifeless body fell to the ground.

There was a ringing in Phiew's ears as he watched Pak Mei's body fall in slow motion. For a moment he didn't comprehend that he had actually done it; vengeance was his. When the body hit the ground the ringing died to nothing and Phiew comprehended the rest of the world around him.

With the death of their master the few remaining disciples fled. One of the snakes had fallen and was cradled by the other. The rabbit had also fallen, pierced by several different spears. The raccoon dog drank from his gourd and muttered prayers over the dead.

"You did well, my son," said Leong. She sat near the body of Choong, who had his own spear jammed in his chest. "Come, help your mother up and let's go home."

Phiew smiled and went to his mother. He pictured Mingmei and Mui. Wings fluttered in his chest at the thought of seeing them again. He could never thank Ting enough for his sacrifice.

"Yes, let's go home, but first, burn this place to the ground," said Phiew.

The rhino nodded and with a powerful kick he knocked down a burning sconce. Red coals went everywhere and set alight a set of tapestries. Phiew led the Shaolin outside and they fled to the last Red Boat before the smoke could draw any unwanted attention.

***

"...and that is how Wu Ah Phiew defeated the great Pak Mei, by combining tiger and crane style and creating his own style." The fortuneteller had put quite a dent in her gourd of wine and opium stash by the time she finished her story.

"So that's how the Shaolin defeated the Manchu," hissed the snaked in awe.

The fortuneteller started. She had been so engrossed in her own tale she had forgotten about her audience. "No!" she snapped. "It was merely the beginning of the end of the Manchu. The Shaolin had to fight for years to overthrow them. Phiew's family never knew true peace until those scum were eradicated." The mixed breed tigress took a long pull from her wine gourd thinking of all the spilled blood she had seen. "Even now the current Ming regime is not so much better. They have ended segregation but are just as corrupt in their own ways."

Was all the sacrifice worth it? she asked herself, not for the first time.

"Tell us about how the Shaolin defeated the Manchu?" asked one of the students. The tigress thought it was the fox but wasn't sure; her mind was a little garbled by the wine and opium. Something seemed off about the fox to the tigress, but she chalked it up to the inebriants.

"That is another story and would require another offering on another night." The fortuneteller grew tired of conjuring ghosts, she wished to be alone. "Leave now."

There was a bustle of whispers on the other side of the veil. "We're not leaving," squawked the crane.

The fortuneteller grew annoyed and ripped the curtain aside with a snarl. The three university students cowered backwards in fear and supplication. "What he means is we won't leave until we learn your name," added the snake quickly. He and the crane practically hid behind the fox, the only one who managed to somewhat stand their ground.

"You're her, aren't you?" asked the fox. "Your Phiew's daughter, Ng Mui."

The tigress straightened at her true name. She hadn't heard that name in a long time. "That is the name I was given," she admitted.

Ng Mui prepared for an attack. She had been the target of many assassins over the years seeking vengeance against her and her family. To her surprise the students fell and bowed low, their faces pressed to the ground.

"Please take us as your students, *Sifu*," begged the fox. The crane and snake sent up their own pleas.

Surprised, Ng Mui lowered her guard. "Why do you wish me to train you?" she asked, still suspicious.

"I wish to learn the ultimate crane form, the tiger crane style," said the crane.

"I've been told you are the only one living who knows the Shaolin snake style. I wish to learn," hissed the snake.

"I wish to learn to fight," said the fox. "I fear you are the only one who might be willing to teach me."

Ng Mui was confused for a moment and then realized what was off about the fox. The fox was a female and her motives became clear. Under the Ming, females were discouraged from training martial arts and were barred from most schools.

The tigress sighed deeply. Would she just be training them to die one day? She had buried too many students.

"What is your name, *Si Mui*," she asked the fox.

The fox stood and looked the tigress in the eyes. Ng Mui recognized a great determination in those eyes. "My name is Yim Wing Chun, *Sifu*," she said, saluting the tigress.

Ng Mui evaluated the three for several moments. She turned her back on them with a huff. "Come back tomorrow. Bring more wine and be ready to train."

Why does Frog sing? And what would he do if anything ever happened to his voice?

THE FROG WHO SWALLOWED THE MOON

Renee Carter Hall

In the earliest days, Frog had a beautiful voice. All through the long summer twilights, he sang sweetly among the reeds while fireflies blinked lazily and the earth settled itself into evening. Around that first pond, the other creatures always gathered to listen.

"Such a lovely voice," Salamander said.

"Just marvelous," Turtle added.

"So sweet and clear," Mallard said with a sigh. "How *do* you do it?"

Frog always looked embarrassed and gave the only answer he could think of, which was also the truth. "I don't know. I just love singing."

One night, having sung a particularly long tune about how beautiful the moon was and how sweet the summer breeze and how wonderful it was simply to be alive, Frog drew a bucket of water from the pond to soothe his dry throat. The full moon shone like a silver coin on the surface of the water, and Frog gulped the whole bucketful down.

The night went black around him, like a candle blown out.

Frog swallowed hard, hiccuped, burped, and swallowed again. It felt like a stone had settled in his belly. "Oh, dear," he said—and every time he opened his mouth, moonlight burst out. "Oh, *dear*."

Everyone had gone home after Frog's last song, and being all alone made things even scarier. Keeping his mouth slightly open so he could

51

see the way, Frog hopped to Salamander's home among the damp stones and dead leaves at the edge of the pond.

Salamander listened to Frog's story, shielding his eyes with one hand against the flashes of light that came with every word.

"What does it feel like?" Salamander asked.

"Sort of cold and fizzy," Frog said miserably. "What should I do?"

"We'll go see Turtle. He's older than any of us. He'll know what to do."

When they reached Turtle's mossy log, they had to knock on his shell several times before he emerged, blinking sleepily, to ask what was the matter.

"Frog's swallowed the moon," Salamander said.

"Dreams and nonsense. Go back to sleep."

"But it's true." Salamander nudged Frog, and Frog opened his mouth. Blue-white light flooded the log.

Turtle squinted at them. "Hm. Thought it was a little darker than usual tonight. What'd you ever do such a silly thing for, anyway?"

"I didn't mean to. It just happened."

Turtle sighed a deep, slow, heavy sigh, as if this sort of thing had happened a dozen times before and he was heartily sick of dealing with it. "Well, there's only one creature in this pond who can help you, and it isn't me. You'll have to go see the Sister of the Moon."

"Who's she?" Salamander asked.

"She lives in the center-of-the-center of the pond. You'll have to take the moonpath to get there."

"But there's no—" Frog's moonlight blinded them all again when he spoke, so he tried to move his mouth as little as possible. "There's no path out there. I've been all over the pond since I was a tadpole. And the only thing in the center is some mud and marsh-reeds."

"Didn't take the moonpath, though, did you?"

"No, but—"

"Then it wasn't the center-of-the-center, was it?"

Frog looked at Salamander. Salamander shrugged.

"I guess not," Frog said.

"Of course it wasn't. Only full moonlight shows the path, and then you have to be looking for it. So go on with you and look." With that, Turtle pulled back into his shell, muttering about lost sleep and unexpected company and how you could certainly bring a bit of fish or at least a nice worm or two if you were going to wake someone up in the middle of the night for such a silly problem as swallowing the moon.

Salamander followed Frog back to the edge of the pond. The water lay dark and still, and stars shone on the surface like white speckles on a black egg. Frog opened his mouth, and the beam of moonlight speared the blackness, skipping over the surface of the water. Then a soft glow appeared, and another, and another, each following the last, until a path of pale stones shone in the moonlight, leading out into the water.

"The moonpath," Frog whispered.

"Do you want me to go with you?" Salamander was whispering too, and he sounded like he hoped the answer was no.

Frog swallowed. The moon in his belly felt colder and heavier. "I guess I'd better go alone."

From the edge of the pond, the stones looked hardly large enough to hop onto, but they were dry and just rough enough to keep Frog's webbed feet from slipping. He glanced back at Salamander, who waved and tried to smile. Frog was about to smile back when he saw that the stones behind him had already disappeared. He swallowed again, faced forward, and went on.

It didn't seem to be the pond he'd known as a tadpole. In the stark light of his moonbeam, the pale stones led him across an expanse of water larger than he'd ever seen before. Soon there were no more marsh-reeds or cattails at the edges of his sight. There was only darkness and the moonpath, and when Frog dared to look up, even the stars had disappeared. He didn't look up again after that, keeping his light and his eyes focused on the stones just ahead.

In time, although Frog could not have said how long, there was a glimmer of silver light ahead. At first he wasn't sure if his eyes were playing tricks on him, but as he got closer to it, the light became a shape, then a structure, and at last he saw a little temple of pale stone, barely more than a roof over thin columns. The stone was veined with silver, and this was the light he'd seen. It glowed brighter as he approached.

The temple lay on a small island, just big enough to give Frog something to scramble onto as the last stone sank from underneath his feet. He rested beneath the roof, watching the veins pulse and glow like ripples on water. He had no reason to, but he felt safe.

There was no sign of anyone else, though. Where was the Sister of the Moon? And more importantly, *what* was she? He had no idea what sort of creature to look for. Whatever she was, he hoped she didn't eat frogs. He hummed a little to himself as he waited, bits of the song he'd last sung. The silver light pulsed in time with the rhythm, and he cocked his head and watched it. Light moved along the veins, drawing his gaze toward the center of the roof, where a silver bell hung. The light played over its surface until the bell seemed made of white light instead of metal.

Frog reached up and tapped it.

A clear, brilliant note sounded. It became part of the stone, part of the light, part of Frog himself. Its perfect tone ached within him, and he knew that anything beautiful he heard from now on would be compared to it.

Beyond the temple, the dark water stirred. A white shape moved beneath it, turning in slow arcs. It rose closer to the surface, and finally Frog saw a white fish, bigger than any he'd ever seen, far bigger than he was, with scales that glittered white and silver. Her fins trailed out behind, translucent and delicate as frost. Silent as fog on the water she came closer, until Frog could see every scale, every ridge of her fins, and the flat, sharp disc of her eye.

"Sister of the Moon," Frog whispered.

(((*So I have been. So I am. So I shall be.*)))

Her voice sent ripples through his mind. It didn't hurt, but it felt strange, almost ticklish. (((*You carry my sister.*)))

"It was an accident."

(((*It must have taken great power to pull her from the sky.*)))

"Not really," Frog mumbled. "I just sort of swallowed it. Her. By accident," he repeated, wanting to make that part of it clear, at least.

(((*Ah.*))) Her fins rippled as she turned slowly in the water, eyeing him. (((*Moon and water are tricksters. So they have been, so they shall be. Better than you, master Frog, have been snared.*)))

He felt a little better after that. She was odd, but at least she didn't seem angry with him. In fact, she almost seemed a little amused, though it was hard to read a fish's expression. So he told her what had happened, and then she *did* laugh, in a mist of bubbles.

(((*I could have chosen a far worse guardian for my sister's light. Will you carry her always, so that I call you brother, or shall we return her?*)))

"I'd much rather put her back, ma'am. Er—your majesty?"

She waved his concern away with a slow fan of her tail. (((*There is a price, of course.*)))

Frog nodded. He knew enough strange old tales to know that much.

(((Pondflesh can only bear so much of my sister's power. I can call her from your body, but your voice, I am afraid, will not be as it was.)))

Frog stared at her. "Will I still be able to sing?"

(((After a fashion, yes. But your voice will be a rough echo of what it is now. You have had the sweet; this will be bitter. You have had the light; this will be shadow.)))

Frog thought of the warm summer nights, his friends gathered around to listen. He thought of the joy of hitting each note, of adding something beautiful to the stillness around him, until his voice seemed like an extension of the night itself. Then he looked up into the dark sky, and thought of it staying dark.

"It really isn't much of a choice, is it," he said quietly.

(((There are always choices. There are not always pleasant ones.)))

The sympathy in her voice gave him courage. "All right." He stood up as straight as a frog could. "What do I do?"

(((Only sing, and that will be my gift to you.)))

He remembered the song he'd sung earlier that evening—if it was still the same night, which he was no longer sure of. A song about the beauty of the moon, and the wonder of being alive. The opening notes floated into his memory, and he sang.

It was the same song, but bigger, richer, sweeter. It was the moon and everything it looked upon. There was the same joy, the same beauty, but there was an edge of sorrow, a rim of shadow like the moon held just as it began to wane from full. It was his same voice, but the way he might have sounded after singing all his life, deeper, purer. There was no effort, no thought, only song pouring out in utter perfection. Somewhere he began to weep, and yet he sang on, in a song that became all his longings and strivings and dreams given voice. And then he felt it ebb, felt the light slipping away from him, drawn out of his body. Part of him wanted to clutch at it, pull it back. The rest of him merely watched it go.

The last note died away. Frog took a ragged breath and looked up. The sky was scattered with stars, and among them the moon hung full. He swallowed. The heaviness was gone, and his throat was sore. He felt cold, and empty, and tired.

The first word he tried to say came out so rough it was barely a sound.

(((Gently.)))

"I'll... never sing again, will I. Not like before."

(((No.)))

Sudden anger closed his throat. "Why did you call that a gift? Why give me that, to remember, when I can never—"

Her sadness washed over him. (((*What is the memory of joy but a gift?*)))

Frog gave a shuddering sigh and blinked away hot tears. "Well. At least it's all right again." He looked up at the moon again, trying to feel satisfied, trying to feel pleased. "I guess I'd better get home, before they start worrying."

The Sister of the Moon stirred her fins. (((*Farewell, then, brother Frog. May you find a voice again, and remember joy.*))) Then she dropped deeper into the water, her faint light moving away, and in the ripples of her wake, the stones rose up one by one to lead him home.

***

No one saw Frog around the pond the next day. Salamander took him licorice tea with honey for his throat. Frog said he was fine, though he knew he didn't sound fine, but he didn't tell Salamander what had happened, and Salamander didn't ask. That was why they were friends, and Frog was grateful. Besides, everyone had seen the moon come back to the sky, and that was all that mattered—or so Frog told himself.

As evening came on, Frog huddled in the corner of his reed house. If this were any other night, he thought, he would have been out by the water, greeting his friends, thinking of what songs he might sing. Instead, he felt like going as far away as he could from the pond and never coming back.

He wondered if they were still out there, Turtle and Mallard and Salamander and all the others, waiting for him.

Reeds rustled. "It's me," Salamander said. "How's your throat?"

"Better."

They sat in silence for a moment.

"Are they out there?" Frog asked finally.

"They'd like to see you. They've been worried."

"I don't know."

Salamander nodded. "I'll tell them you're all right."

"Maybe tomorrow night," Frog said.

Salamander nodded again. "Because—I mean—you're more than just your voice, you know." He hesitated, then slipped through the reeds.

Late that night, when everyone else was asleep, Frog sat by the black water, gazing at the moon.

After a fashion, he thought, remembering the Sister's words.

No one would hear.

He had to try sometime.

He drew a breath and opened his mouth. It sounded more like a belch than a note.

He went home.

"Why bother?" he told Salamander several nights later. "It's not even singing, really, anymore."

"But you love it."

Frog sipped his licorice tea. "I used to. Not now."

It was a lie, of course, and they both knew it, but neither pointed it out. That was why they were friends.

Frog told the others it hurt too much to sing now. That wasn't a lie, though it was a pain that no amount of licorice or honey could ever ease.

And yet, he *did* miss it. Not just the summer twilights and the expectant hush of the audience and the praise that came after. He missed the feeling of it, the way a song rose in him and demanded to be sung. But every time he tried, all he could remember was the brilliance of that moon-song, the Sister's cursed gift, that perfection he could never even strive for anymore. And so night passed into night, and except for the crickets, the nights were silent.

"If I could forget how it was before," Frog told Salamander, "maybe I could be happy."

Salamander sipped his tea. "Maybe you could forget just for a little while. You know. *Pretend* to forget."

"Mm," Frog said.

In the end, it was the full moon, again, that was Frog's undoing. One warm, clear, windless night, the beauty of it all tugged at him, and a new song welled up, and without thinking he gave it voice. The sound still disappointed him, but he was getting used to it, and this time he tried singing higher and lower, drawing the notes out, then clipping them short. It wasn't anything like the voice he'd had before—and it still hurt that it never would be—but maybe... Maybe...

So he pretended to forget, for a little while. He set aside the perfect beauty of a silver bell and a white moon and listened instead to the mud and the reeds of Frog, to what it was and to what it might be.

The sound of his new voice didn't surprise him anymore. But the happiness—the crazy, rough-edged, imperfect happiness—did.

He thought of new songs and practiced them far from the pond, where no one else could hear. At last, when he felt at least half ready, he told Salamander, and Salamander told the others, and once again the creatures of the pond gathered to listen. He sang quick and low, earthy and bold, a song about the strangeness of the moonpath and a sky dark of stars. It was rough, but there was life in it. There was joy in it.

When the last note died away, heart pounding, he waited.

The silence hung like cold fog. He watched one look to the other. No one seemed to know what to say.

"That's very… innovative," Turtle managed. "Quite clever of you."

"I've never heard anything like it," Mallard said brightly.

One by one they drifted away, their polite comments hitting him like raindrops. Some rolled off. Some soaked in. Salamander was the last to remain.

"Give them time," he said softly. "They'll learn to love it."

Frog swallowed. "Maybe sometimes I am just a voice."

"Maybe," Salamander said. "But not to everyone."

And that was why they were friends.

***

In these later days, Frog has a beautiful voice. No crowds gather at that first pond now, to praise his songs' sweetness and clamor for more. But there are some who still count his voice as rare and precious as before—perhaps even more so—and so he sings for them. He sings for the beauty of the world and the joy of being alive. He sings for himself, for the memories of joy and for the joy that dwells in the singing of a single, present note. And over it all the moon hangs bright and full, its light gleaming on the mirrored pond like the sound of a silver bell, its echoes rippling on and on, into the summer night.

Captain Electron is a legend, but Rob Cantor is an aging Dalmatian, trying to figure out if yesterday's legend is even relevant today.

The Torch

Chris "Sparf" Williams

Rob's hackles rose as he stared down the escalator at the wide hallway outside of the main ballroom that served as the autograph area. The multitude of people in a relatively small space produced a wide array of scents that was difficult for his canine nose to process. That said nothing of the occasional attendee who lacked some fundamental hygiene. No matter how many times he made these appearances he always had to fight down his instinctive desire to flee. The Dalmatian desperately wanted a drink. He adjusted his tan sport coat to distract him from those thoughts.

The fidgeting of the short, pudgy, young corgi standing next to him on the escalator as they descended snapped him out of thoughts of an early morning drink. He tried really hard not to drink while "on the job," and besides, the stuff was so strong that one drink was about all he could stand.

Rob leaned a little more heavily on the escalator railing for support than he used to. His lower back hurt him nearly constantly, and he'd lost some of the upper range of his hearing. The corgi was probably a third of Rob's age, if that, and nearly two feet shorter. Rob chuckled to himself; the handlers at these things kept getting younger. The corgi stared determinedly forward, risking little sidelong glances when he thought the older dog wasn't looking.

"So, you're my handler for the whole convention?" Rob asked. "What's your name?"

"I'm Jake. And yes, I'm with you for the whole convention. They wanted to assign staff on a rotating basis, but I told them that it was a good idea to keep a single staff member with a guest through the entire con, that way they get to know the person they're working with."

Rob reached behind him and rubbed futilely at the dull ache in his lower back.

"Sounds like a plan, Jake," he said, reaching out to shake the young corgi's paw. The corgi took his timidly but excitedly, giving it a firm shake.

"I hope you don't mind ending up a little bored. My table isn't so much a big draw these days."

"Are you kidding, Mr. Cantor? You're Captain Electron! Your show was awesome! I still pull out my old VHS tapes and watch the reruns I taped as a pup! I used to tell my little cousin about your adventures as bedtime stories! He liked them better than any old fairy tale."

The corgi was practically vibrating.

Rob chuckled and shook his head. "I was Captain Electron. Now I'm just this guy, you know? By the way, you can call me Rob if you want."

Rob pulled up his chair at the table and began placing neat stacks of publicity photos in even rows while he waited for Jake to stop panting madly. Rob glanced in both directions, taking in the lay of the land in the signing hall. His table was located in the corner of the end farthest from the escalators. Not the most ideal location, but the fans would make their way back to him.

***

"Mommy, Captain Electron's here, let's go! Let's go!"

The little Dalmatian's shouting caused Rob's ears to perk up. He sat up straighter in his chair and looked over the table at the pup, readying his biggest kid-friendly smile. The boy was just tall enough to see the copies of Rob's reproduction photos over the top of the table.

"Well, hello there!"

The pup paused, cocking his head.

"Who're you?"

"I'm Captain Electron! See?" Rob held up a photo of himself in the old costume, grinning and looking every bit the consummate superhero.

"You're not Captain Electron! You're too old!" the little boy barked. To their credit his parents, dressed the way parents who don't go to conventions dress when they go to conventions, reacted quickly. The mother shushed the child and led him away to the line to see the "real" Captain Electron. The father shuffled awkwardly, offering Rob a shrug and a forced smile.

"I'm sorry—"

Rob raised a hand. "No worries, son. It happens sometimes."

"I am going to get him started on your series soon, but I really wanted to see the new movie and I didn't have a pup sitter and—"

"Like I said, it's fine. Stop by later."

The father gave another quick nod and a smile, rushing to catch up with his wife. They wouldn't be back, Rob knew that. They were here to rush through, get John Pierce's autograph, and get out.

The former Captain Electron glanced down at the convention guidebook that had been left for him. Front and center on the cover was John Pierce as Captain Electron, with an old pulp-style cover design surrounding him and praising his virtue. Along the bottom, in what Rob always thought of as the "But wait! There's More!" area, a small, humble typeface announced that "Also featuring the legendary Rob Cantor, the original Captain Electron!"

Legendary? That was a nice flourish but probably untrue. His show might be legendarily campy, perhaps, but he himself? He'd really just done regional theatre since the show aired. His agent hadn't been able to get him seen for other parts. Sometimes, it was because of Captain Electron, sometimes just the bad luck that comes with a life spent as an actor. Being told 'no' became second nature to the Dalmatian long ago.

He cast his eyes down the exhibition hall, noticing a handful of other minor actors setting up at their tables. Most of them were younger than he was at this point. Maybe he'd been at this too long. The spotlight wasn't his anymore.

The line for Pierce's autograph was huge, and despite winding through a long series of velvet ropes and out through some glass doors to a below-ground concrete courtyard and then back inside, it still managed to block several tables.

In the line were dozens of parents of various species with their children, including the young Dalmatian. Rob felt a pang in his heart. Pierce had better take damn good care of those young fans.

He stretched out and leaned back in his chair to loosen the tension he hadn't realized was building.

Kids used to love him. They'd turn up with their store-bought or homemade costumes, their autograph books, and their Captain Electron comics, and smile so brightly when their hero—sent out in character by the studio—spoke to them. That had faded with the ending of the show, though, until he only got a few kids at the appearances any more.

The kids dropped off to a trickle, and then to nothing at his last few costumed appearances, but Rob did his duty, just as Captain Electron would have, and kept showing up. Occasionally he was rewarded by a particularly enthusiastic fan. Once he'd even given away Captain Electron's prop badge. Rob had not been particularly fond of the choice to deputize the hero as a de facto police officer, but the studio had said they wanted no confusion for children about vigilante justice.

"Mr. Cantor, it's an absolute pleasure to meet you finally. Can I shake your paw?"

Rob snapped out of his thoughts and looked up to see a tiger, roughly half of the Dalmatian's age, grinning at him from across the table, paw extended. He wore the robes of some kind of space wizard that Rob didn't recognize. Probably something pretty new.

He shook the tiger's paw, and listened politely for a few minutes as the fellow, who spoke at a rate usually reserved for the legalese at the end of car advertisements, gushed over him.

"Well, you know what I mean, Mr. Cantor, I mean it's like, yeah, Pierce is all flashy, and he's got a super cool version of the car and all but I just love how simple and fun your show was."

"Well, thanks. I'm glad—"

"You're the real Captain Electron as far as I'm concerned. I just want you to know that."

Rob smiled and gestured towards the stacks of photos. "Could I interest you in any of these?"

"I can't, right now, but I'm thinking about coming to the photo session later so you can count on me!"

As the tiger scurried off to other pursuits, Rob turned his attention to his itinerary.

"So, what are my official signing times?"

"Well, uh," Jake paused, gnawing on his lip for the briefest instant. "We don't have any set times for you."

Rob's head jerked towards the corgi. "What do you mean? I always have at least one official time slot."

"Well the, uh, the con staff decided—this is totally off the record, by the way, sir—that they only had the budget to arrange the free signing deal with one guest. On the bright side, you can keep your own hours at your table." The corgi's ears were pinned flat against his skull.

Rob's spotted tail swished violently. "Which guest has scheduled times?"

"I...uh..."

"Just answer the question, kid."

"It's Mr. Pierce, sir."

Rob blinked. He'd been at giant conventions, tiny conventions, and everything in between. There had never been a one that hadn't arranged a time for him to sign. There was room for both Captain Electrons. He'd have agreed to concessions if he'd had to. This put him on the same level as some of the character actors and bit part players at the other tables in the signing hall. Not that they weren't talented, but they'd played Professor Moriarty once on a show that wasn't about Sherlock Holmes, or they'd been aliens or side characters or henchmen. They hadn't been the main character!

What did a big-shot like Pierce need with a tiny convention like this one? Rob had seen some glory hounds in his day. The guy who played Doom Bringer had been, as the British would say, an arrogant prat. He'd traded on a pawful of major theatrical roles for decades, until finally no one remembered them. He persisted even after that, and drove everyone on the Captain Electron set nuts.

Rob sighed, pushing away the uncomfortable thoughts. "Okay, so no official signing times. What events am I slated for?"

Jake wiped sweat from the tan and white fur of his forehead. "Well, there's the photo-op session this afternoon. You'll join Mr. Pierce for the joint photos at 2:30." Rob clenched his fists at that. Jake took no notice and continued. "Then from 3 until 3:30 are the solo pics with just you and the fans."

Rob sighed and offered Jake a wan smile. "Okay, terrific."

It really wasn't terrific. He'd turned down a decent one-night engagement in his local theatre's concert version of Coyote of La Mancha to be here. The fame from his years as Captain Electron had opened a few career doors for him (even if it had shut others). He owed the character and his fans this much.

"And then there's the Q&A session, of course."

"Of course." Even the character actors with the smallest, tangential careers usually got a Q&A for fans of their particular series.

"Oh, and there's a second Q&A tomorrow afternoon, but that's optional. Mr. Pierce's people wanted to offer you an invitation to share the stage with him for a big Captain Electron Q&A. That's if you're interested, of course."

Rob blinked. That was new. Probably they anticipated a lot of questions about the 'reboot' of Captain Electron, and figured there would be a lot of older fans who wanted to ask him what he thought. At least it would be a different set of questions than "Did you really kiss Ethel in the episode 'The Bank Robber's Daughter?'" or "What was it like on the set?" or the personal bane of the Dalmatian's existence: "How did you remember all those lines?"

Still, though, did he really want to put himself out there for a literal side-by-side comparison with Pierce?

"Anything else?"

The corgi's ear flicked uncomfortably.

"No, I think that's it. I brought this," he said, pulling out a thick vinyl banker's bag. "I'm also your cashier, that way you don't have to do anything but sign."

Rob sat and waited for autograph seekers and fans to make their way to his table. Over the span of about three hours, he was visited by exactly ten people. All of them were old enough to have watched him as Captain Electron in the show's first run. He smiled and talked with them, answering a few brief questions, and advised some people to bring their questions to his Q&A session. And, of course, he signed autographs.

That second Q&A weighed on the Dalmatian's mind. Should he do it? He really stood to gain nothing from it except helping promote the studio's new golden boy, but on the other hand, he had originated the role on screen. Though they were fewer and fewer with each passing event, he still had fans who looked up to him as some kind of mythic figure. He'd had cartoons making fun of his campy old series, and himself, for years, to the point that he and his version of Captain Electron might be more myth than mortal. If he went and did the Q&A, he could—what? What could he really do? He could legitimize the reboot, certainly. Maybe he could get some brownie points with the studio, maybe snag a cameo or a few lines in the sequel film which everybody and their brother knew was coming the way Hollywood handled franchises these days. It might, too, give him some final dignity in handing the role off formally.

No. The studio had made the decision to cut him out of involvement, and it wasn't like he was difficult to find for Pierce to get in touch. He was out there on all those social media things, and unlike John Pierce or Paul Vanzant, he didn't have an intern or manager handling his postings. The Q&A wasn't until tomorrow. He'd decide later. Maybe.

Thirty minutes after the last fan had dropped by Rob's table, John Pierce's line was still snaked outside and all through the hall. Jake fidgeted in his chair, holding onto the light cash bag. Rob couldn't see the new Captain Electron for the crowd. He found himself wishing that he'd looked up more information on the new movie, and maybe gotten some background on Pierce.

"I warned you it might be boring, Jake. I'm sorry it seems to be a ghost town."

"Oh, no! It's fine! I'm not bored! I'm sure more people will come by after the photo shoot and your talk."

"Sure. I'm…sure they will. Hey, I'm going to take off for a while, grab a drink and maybe a sandwich. Would you mind watching the table while I'm gone?"

"Sure, no problem. That's what I'm here for. If you want I could just go grab you something."

"No, thanks. I just need to think for a bit. I'll be back."

Rob shoved his chair back, slipped past some convention goers dressed up as rolling mechanized plumbers, and hopped on the escalator. There was a bar attached to the hotel's overpriced, and exceedingly pretentious, restaurant. He'd earned a drink, at least. Hopefully the bar had some decently aged single malt scotch. That might take the edge off of the growing sense that he really didn't belong at this convention.

From near the top of the escalator, he could see that a circle had formed around an open floor space at Pierce's table, and Rob, with his irritatingly less-than-decent vision, barely made out the rough outline of a Dalmatian kneeling down in the familiar red and blue.

Actors rarely came out in character any more, even the ones from the famous sci-fi shows and movies, so the fact that Pierce did struck Rob as a throwback to his own days in the costume. Curious indeed.

The lobby floor was packed with a few dealers that the convention hadn't been able to squeeze into the clearly overcrowded dealer's room, selling or displaying models of spaceships and custom painted holiday ornaments. Rob sidestepped them, trying to squeeze his way through the mass of various species in their outlandish costumes or their pop-culture mashup tee shirts to get to the bar. He got a few polite nods from some of the fans who had dropped by his table, though mercifully they all seemed to be polite enough not to interrupt a Dalmatian on a quest for scotch.

The bar teemed with convention attendees, as well as the occasional normal who'd wandered into town for a business conference, or some stop along a longer road trip, and who were all confused or amused or just plain bewildered by what they saw. The Dalmatian stifled a grin. No matter how long he came to these, the reactions from the normals always made him think of leaves being caught up in a hurricane.

A seat opened up at the bar, which Rob claimed. The bartender was swift and ruthlessly efficient in taking his order of a seventeen year old scotch, neat. As the Dalmatian sipped on the liquified peat bog, his mood darkened. He'd hoped it would be improved by getting some distance from his replacement's infinite autograph line, but instead it grew from grey skies to a rumbling storm cloud.

He hadn't asked much of the studio. He'd offered, in good faith, to consult on the new film and they'd ignored him. Well, to be more precise, they'd glad-handed him.

We'd be happy to talk about you consulting on the new movie! Of course! Don't call us though, we'll call you when we need you.

Two-faced studio executives had always been a way of life in Hollywood. That wasn't about to change. But it was different and somehow worse, when they took the only thing you were ever really known for and didn't even offer you a cameo appearance. Even the guy who stole Spider-Folf from his partner got a cameo in the movie.

He sipped his scotch again. No use crying over spilled milk. If truth be told, the studio had never had much support for either Captain Electron or Rob Cantor. After the show was canceled, they made such a halfhearted and half-assed attempt to get it picked up that Rob wondered whose daughter he'd accidentally jilted, or whose bratty nephew he'd snubbed.

The signing appearances had gotten smaller and smaller, going from big convention center venues and television interviews down to grand openings of furniture stores and costumed appearances in front of the cereal aisle at the chain supermarket. Those were usually the worst. People rushing past with a cart full of groceries, wondering why they were having to veer around this extra impediment.

Rob sipped at the scotch again, then downed the remainder of the glass.

He'd tried to stay positive in those days, hoping that if he just kept making the character look good that popular support would convince the networks to change their minds, and at least one of them would bid on returning the show to the airwaves. And those fans who turned up were always kind and genuinely seemed pleased to meet the great Captain Electron, especially the kids. He'd carried on for so long for their sake.

***

His scotch gone, the Dalmatian laid a twenty on the bar and slunk off in the direction of the escalators. Like it or not, bitter or not, he had a job to do and he didn't want to disappoint anyone who actually did turn up looking for a signature. The corgi, Jake, looked positively relieved as Rob reappeared and lowered himself back into the chair.

The ache in his lower back returned with a vengeance the moment he sat down, and he was forced to lean over on his knees, staring down at the ancient yellow and brown carpet. The pain lessened enough to sit up, and he passed a few minutes glancing around at the crowds and at the outdated, gaudy wood paneling of the hotel hallway, and his undisturbed stacks of photos, and his empty autograph line. Suddenly he felt his insides knotting up a little, and wondered if maybe he'd eaten something that disagreed with him. He stared mournfully down the concourse at where the throngs of people were dispersing from "Captain Electron's" table.

Rob closed his eyes briefly, to rest them. This was no good. He could sit and mope all he wanted and formulate all the reasons why the world was unfair and how dare that young whippersnapper steal his glory, but it wouldn't help. It wasn't John Pierce's fault that he was popular and that Rob was a mere afterthought. Hollywood didn't have a decent original idea in its collective brain; reboots and remakes were the norm. As he rubbed his eyes, a voice spoke from across the table. Blue eyes snapped open, and he sat up, like a clockwork toy freshly wound.

"Um, excuse me, sir. I'd like this picture, and if you could sign it 'to Jake'?"

He'd all but forgotten the pudgy little corgi who had now stepped around the table. He was holding out a twenty-dollar bill. Ten for the photo (he'd chosen one of Rob's favorites; his fight with Doom Bringer in the prime time special they'd done at the height of the series), and ten for the autograph. He stuffed the bill into the banker's bag and grinned sheepishly. Rob smiled and signed the photo, before giving it back.

"Thanks! Sorry for not waiting, but I figured you might get busy after your Q&A."

"No problem, Jake. Hey, I'll be right back, ok?"

"Sure thing, sir. Just remember that you've got fifteen minutes before you have to be on stage!"

Only fifteen minutes? Time had flown by already. He'd have to be quick. Rob strode through the crowds leaving John Pierce's table. Hopefully he could catch the actor before he was rushed elsewhere. At least to say hello and introduce himself properly.

Unfortunately, by the time he reached the table, Pierce was gone. A pair of security staffers and a convention handler tidied up the table. Rob slumped. He'd waited too long. He'd really wanted to bite the bullet and get the first meeting over with on his own terms.

The handler packed up Pierce's photos, placing them into one stack and leaving only the top one visible. On that one, Captain Electron was lit from above amid eerie, dark shadows, the outline of the costume's colors and the Dalmatian's own fur creating an ominous effect. Captain Electron is coming, it seemed to shout, and he isn't happy.

It fit with everything he'd heard in recent years: that the comic producer had taken the character, Rob's character really, in a dark, approaching anti-hero direction, which was pretty spectacular in Rob's mind for a character still named Captain Electron.

Having failed to catch Pierce, he trudged back to his table, feeling somehow abandoned by the universe. His rational mind fought that feeling back. He knew better. But his head knowing and his heart feeling were often irreconcilable. It didn't matter. He had to be on stage. That would perk him up. Hopefully.

***

"So, yes, I did actually kiss her in that episode, but neither of us enjoyed it very much, and afterward we each spent a week recovering from whatever plague we'd contracted."

The crowd, filling approximately the first third of the theater space, rumbled with laughter. The stage lights kept Rob from focusing on any one member of the audience aside from whichever person was lit at the house microphone, but they all seemed to be his older fans, most of whom had already dropped by the table, he figured.

"Are there more questions? I've got time for a few more, I think!"

The Dalmatian was all smiles and energy. Being on stage or on camera always brought it out in him. He'd probably pay for it with a mood crash later, but right now, it was important to keep the performance going. A heavy set badger waddled up to the mic and asked the question he'd been dreading.

"Hi, Mr. Cantor. Huge fan ever since I was a kid. I was wondering, um, well…did the studio consult you on the new Captain Electron film?"

Rob forced a big, energetic smile, though he could tell from the way it felt on his muzzle that it would've looked terrible on video.

"No. There were some discussions that I'm not at liberty to discuss, but in the end they decided that it would be best to go their own route."

The badger sunk, looking as if he'd lost a bet. "Um, well, a follow-up if I may?"

Rob glanced behind him. There was nobody waiting in line.

"Sure, go ahead."

"What do you think of the direction they're going? Your Captain Electron was a good guy through and through. I believe you were even legally allowed to hunt down criminals. What do you think of what they're doing, making him dark and brooding and, well, meaner?"

Rob took a sip of water from the provided glass.

Tread lightly

"This is a different Captain Electron, for a different time and a different fan base. By drawing on the more recent comics, I think the studio is doing what they think the fans want."

It was a good answer, and he felt some of the butterflies in his stomach dissipate with it. Diplomatic, unlikely to get him sued or have him show up on TMZ.

"Not all of us," the badger mumbled, then wandered back to his seat in the darkened theater.

Me either, friend. Me either.

Mercifully a few more creatures lined up at the mic to keep rob from having to dwell on either the implications of the question or of his own response.

Rob answered a handful more questions, including the dreaded, "How do you remember all those lines," before time was up and Jake appeared in the wings to take him back to his table. The flashy M.C. Fox enjoined the audience to give the legendary—there was that word again—Rob Cantor a big round of applause, and while the roar of it didn't shake the huge theater the way a packed audience would, the sound of it made the Dalmatian grin just the same.

He gave a wave and strode confidently off stage, pausing in the wings to lean against a chair and catch his breath.

"So, we've got the photo shoot next, Mr. Cantor," Jake said, leaning down to look Rob in the face, probably to make sure the old dog wasn't about to keel over.

"Right, right… let's go. I'm feeling good and limber after that little bit of exercise. Maybe I can even hold up a prop or two this time!"

He patted the corgi on the shoulder, and the two made their way out the stage door.

***

Rob's grey-tinged ears perked up to better hear what was going on inside as he and Jake approached the photo room. The line was out the door. Creatures of every species and walk of life were there waiting to get their photo taken with the star. The mix was incredible, with everyone from Dalmatians to swift foxes to a couple of weasels and a sloth waiting their turn to step into the hotel suite which housed the photographer's equipment. Rob noted that the carpet here was plush and a rich crimson which contrasted with the beige, ribbed wallpaper. This area had either been added on after that god-awful convention space or it had been remodeled.

Of course, he didn't have to wait in the line. He was a few minutes early, but Jake ushered him through the crowd to the farther door, into the sleeping quarters attached to the suite. There were some murmurs of recognition among the crowd, and Rob felt some of his tension melting away. They remembered. At least some of them did anyway.

"Okay, they're on the last few single-shoot ticket holders for Capt—er, for Mr. Pierce. Then you'll go in and the people who bought the picture with both of you together will get taken. And then it's your individual photos."

"Right," Rob said distractedly. He was staring at the immaculately made, undisturbed bed, and at the electric blue bundle of fabric resting on it.

"We didn't figure you'd want to try to dress up in the full costume, so we got—"

"You got the mask and cape, huh?" The Dalmatian reached down and felt the material. It was a perfect replica of his old one, even down to the soft satin texture and its slight metallic reflectivity.

"You don't have to wear it if you don't want, sir, I—we just thought—"

"It's okay, Jake. I'll wear it. It's nice. You know, you guys do a pretty good job here. Lots of small conventions would have just had somebody cut a mask out of cheap blue felt and made a cape out of a towel." Rob forced a smile. The corgi was going out of his way to make him feel at least somewhat wanted, and that was golden.

An older vixen with a touch of grey in the dark fur of her ears, much like Rob's, stuck her head into the room. "We're ready for you now, Mr. Cantor."

Rob nodded and pulled the mask up against his face, tying it in the back automatically with a muscle memory that had not dulled over the years. Then he pulled the cape over the shoulders of his sport coat. He caught a glimpse of himself in the mirror and stifled a chuckle in spite of himself. He looked like some sort of modern day Coyote of La Mancha, a businessman gone mad and determined to live in a fantasy world.

The vixen—whose name was Dawn, Rob gleaned from her name tag—held the door for him from outside with one arm. He stepped into the room, squinting to adjust his eyes to the brightness of the space, enhanced to retina-scorching levels by the photographer's studio lights. The photographer had set up one of those grey backgrounds with the light area in the center and lit it with two big umbrella things and a couple of smaller lights from underneath. There was a huge set of French doors with gauze curtains letting the light stream in from the outside as well, and a few members of staff were manning some tables nearby where incoming subjects could place their bags and costume props and such to be picked up when the photo was done.

By the photographer's backdrop, standing slightly taller than Rob—even before age had taken its few inches—and in full red and blue Captain Electron costume, was John Pierce, flanked by his manager, a chubby pine marten who seemed to be glued to his smartphone, a very chipper young cacomistle with a very large and expensive looking camera dangling off his neck, and a female retriever making notes in an old fashioned leather date book.

Rob had to admit that the costume flattered the other Dalmatian. He was lean, muscular, and the costume showed off a superhero's physique. Rob had never been in that good of a shape. The popularity of the show at the time meant that he'd had a steady paycheck for the first time—and one of the only times, in his life as an actor—and he'd indulged himself a bit too liberally. After the first season aired, he remembered, they'd had to squeeze him into a girdle for a couple of public appearances, and from then on his contract contained an exercise clause.

The costume was a fairly faithful re-interpretation. The red was darker, a deeper and somehow more serious crimson, and the blue looked brighter by contrast. The texture of the fabric suggested something more like woven Kevlar. Even the gun had been given a less retro-futuristic look.

"Rob Cantor!" the other Dalmatian called excitedly, waving in his direction. Rob didn't move, caught off guard. "It is absolutely amazing to see you. Come on, come over here!"

Rob made his way over to the photographer's backdrop and shook Pierce's waiting outstretched paw. He'd expected a typical autographs-and-sunglasses movie star, not a warm and enthusiastic young male. As he approached the backdrop, Rob caught a whiff of something that smelled like paint. That probably answered the question of how long ago this room had been remodeled.

"Listen, before they let in the next group, could we, you know, get a picture of just the two of us, in the Justice Spots pose?"

Rob furrowed his brow but couldn't keep from smiling a little with nostalgia. The pose was stupid comic book mubfubbery, but it always looked great on camera somehow.

"Yeah, sure, why not."

"Great, over here! This tape mark! We good, Mr. Photographer?"

The cacomistle gave a thumbs up, and Pierce's manager meandered absently out of the frame, eyes still glued to his phone.

"Okay, ready?"

Rob nodded. He hadn't done this in a very long time. Right paw in a fist, against his left shoulder, bent at the waist, left arm straight at a 45 degree angle, paws slightly more than shoulder width apart, head up. Pierce took the same pose with his arms reversed, though with considerably less popping of joints and lower back pain.

"On the count of three, look defiant and say 'Justice'. Ready? One, two, three!" The two 'heroes' complied, and the lights flashed brightly. "And one more, one, two, three."

Again they repeated 'Justice' and again the lights flashed.

"Hey, Mr. Cantor, thanks so much. I'll get this signed before the con is over."

If your endless fans don't slow you down.

As Rob looked his young counterpart over he caught something wrong in the Dalmatian's left eye. It took Rob a moment to realize that it was an ice-blue contact lens slipping down and revealing a brown iris underneath. Masking heterochromia probably. Not a bad job.

The crowd for the double photo was older, though still younger than Rob had expected them to be. And there were quite a few of them. Males in their thirties who had grown up on reruns of his show. Most of them were canids but occasionally an otter or feline would pass through. Rob settled into his old habits, offering a warm smile and a paw on the shoulder for each photo.

"And that's it for the doubles," Dawn the vixen said from the doorway. "They're lined up now for your solo shoots, Mr. Cantor."

"Can't imagine this will take long," he muttered to himself.

"All right, I've got to go change. Are you going to be at the Q&A. I think it's tomorrow afternoon. Eh, Jean? Tomorrow afternoon, right?"

The retriever flipped the page of her organizer, "Yes, Mr. Pierce."

"Great! Think you'll make it?"

"I don't know if I'll be able to. These things take a lot out of me." He could tell just by the feel in his joints that he was going to be sore later, but really, he just wasn't sure he wanted to see a huge crowd cheering on this young new hero.

Pierce's ears pinned momentarily, and a faint whine reached Rob's ears. "It would mean the world to me if you'd come, but I understand if you can't.

And then he was gone, and Rob was left in the suite with Dawn the vixen, the cacomistle photographer whose name he didn't catch, and the four or five older folks who came in to get their photos with him.

***

After a quiet lunch the next day in the hotel's little overpriced cafeteria, Rob debated just going back to his room and taking a nap. It was nearly 4:00 in the afternoon, and if he was going to constantly feel old, he might as well act the part.

He thought about the Q&A offer with John Pierce, turning over the younger male's eagerness in his mind. He'd seemed genuine in his enthusiasm, but still. Would it be a good idea? Probably not.

He tossed the last few bites of his soggy, prepackaged turkey club into the trash on the way back out into the main autograph hall.

Jake trotted up in a tizzy, panting heavily and trying desperately to catch his breath.

"Oh, Mr. Cantor. Rob. Sir. Uh… yes… Um…"

Rob tilted his head, perking one floppy Dalmatian ear—his best one. "What's going on, Jake?"

"There's a Labrador at your table waiting for an autograph. He seems to be in a big hurry. I told him you'd be back soon but—"

"Ok, well, let's get over there."

The corgi turned on his heel and wove his way through the crowd of convention patrons, creating a tiny bubble of empty space in his wake which Rob fell into.

His table was at the other end and was obscured by the crowd admiring a spaceship model crewed by puppets on display outside the video viewing room. Rob never got that British stuff anyway.

When the pair had made their way close enough to Rob's table, there was no one standing near it, just a sign informing fans that Rob Cantor would return to his table soon.

"Oh gosh, sir, I'm so sorry! I told him to stay here and I'd be back quickly, but I guess he couldn't wait."

Rob gave a halfhearted nod and flopped back down behind his table, removing the "back soon" sign. He hoped the fan would come back. He'd hate to have caused the poor guy to miss his chance to say hello and get an autograph. Still, biological needs were biological needs. Lunch had to happen at some point. Now that it had, the Dalmatian felt a bit sleepy and so pulled out a well-worn paperback copy of The Adventures of the Scarlet Pimpernel to keep himself awake and focused.

He'd just read another delightful humiliation of M. Chauvelin by the crafty fox when he glanced up at the increased foot traffic and noted that the line for John Pierce was queuing up through the stanchions once more. Rob checked his watch, holding it closer to his nose so he could better read the hands through the scuffed crystal. He'd been reading for nearly two hours now!

Rob stood up once more, stretching and feeling the glorious popping of his joints.

"Back in a second."

Jake said something in reply, but Rob didn't catch what the corgi had said. He focused on the big time signing table beyond the sea of creatures lined up. He should probably let Pierce know that he wasn't going to join him on stage, just so he was warned ahead of time.

Trying to make his way around the crowd took some doing. Security let him through because of his badge's "guest" designation at least, but there were just so many people!

Finally, more out of desperation than cunning, he made his way out of the crowd and over to the outside wall, past which the fans who had received their autographs were walking on their way out. Rob sidled along it until he was finally able to see Pierce at the table being handed photos each in turn and personalizing each signature for each fan—probably with a pre-set group of phrases to pick from as Rob had learned to do.

He was dressed in the costume, that modern, stylish costume, just as he had been for the photo session. Rob noted that his energy level was just as high with the fans in line as it had been upon meeting him for the photo. He was all smiles and chatter, looking his fans in the face and chatting with them about where they'd come from, or what they did for a living. The convention staff and his personal aides managed, but only just, to keep the looks of annoyance off their faces.

Rob smiled and started to sidle back along the wall, but stopped short when the next fan reached the table in front of Pierce. It was a little pup, couldn't have been more than five or six years old, staring down at his paws and holding out his picture for Captain Electron to sign without even looking up.

"What do you have for me, there, little scout?"

Little scout? Rob blinked. He'd always called his young fans that, both because it fit and because it was what the fan club members were called. There hadn't been a fan club in decades though, at least not for children.

Rob watched as the little fox shuffled uncomfortably, looking everywhere but directly at Captain Electron. The fans in line fidgeted and checked their phones, while the attendant staff behind Pierce's table began to look at each other as the seconds stretched on. Pierce finally rose from behind the table and crossed around it to kneel down in front of the kit.

"Would you like me to sign your picture?"

The child sighed and nodded, holding it out and looking up for just a moment into the smiling face of the dashing Dalmatian.

"And what's your name, little scout?"

It took a gentle nudging from the boy's mother before he'd speak again. "Kevin."

"Well, Kevin," Pierce said, placing the photo on the corner of his table and uncapping his marker, "I'll sign this for you and—"

"Mommy says you're not real."

Pierce paused and looked to the mother, a nicely dressed vixen in her late twenties or so. She clamped both paws over her muzzle, her ears pinned and tail down, embarrassment evident.

A great writer once said, "These are the times that try creatures' souls," and this was one of those situations. Rob had been there. He kept his ears pricked and pointed sharply to pick up every bit of the ensuing conversation.

"Well, remember, little scout, Captain Electron has many enemies. Sometimes it's safest to pretend I'm not real, but you know what?"

The child perked up, daring to look, finally, at the superhero. "What?"

"I'm real as you are. You can even shake my paw if you want. So what do you say?" He extended his paw

"I knew it! I knew Mommy was wrong!" the kit yelped, bouncing up and down excitedly and looking at his mother with bright, shining eyes. The mother, for her part, looked relieved and mouthed a quiet "thank you" when the boy's back was turned and he was vigorously shaking his hero's paw.

Old memories tugged at Rob's heartstrings. The exchange felt so familiar. He knew every beat of the drama before it played out, and Pierce had played it perfectly. The line was moving again, he'd delighted a young child and soothed the embarrassed mother. He knew all the tricks already, and maybe, just maybe, better than Rob ever had.

With the crowd moving again, Rob took his cue to slip away, past the serpentine queue and the tables of occasionally engaged, occasionally bored, character actors, until he reached his own, with Jake sitting dutifully behind it.

"Jake? What time was that Q&A?"

***

Backstage once more, Rob felt the butterflies swarming in his stomach, not so much butterflies as angry bees now. This wasn't part of the plan. He should be having a glass of scotch in the bar right now, running through his travel checklist and preparing to get out the next day and return home, then deciding what to do about any future conventions.

Before seeing Pierce with the fox kit, that decision had been so clear. He'd gracefully retire from the convention circuit and focus his theatrical efforts on teaching or stage performance.

Now things were muddy. Hearing those words, seeing that interaction, tugged at the Dalmatian's heartstrings. He'd been that hero once, and Pierce was that hero now, in every sense of the word. Clearly there were still people who remembered Rob's Captain Electron and yet were still excited about the new.

The green room was abuzz with con staff, Pierce's personal staff, and security monitoring the door. Once again, his convention badge did its job, and he was ushered in past the overweight but muscular wolf security guard. Pierce was seated in front of a broad mirror surrounded by lights. Rob squinted to get a look, but the lights hurt his eyes, and he had to look away.

"Forty-five minutes, Mr. Pierce," said a badger, clothed in the black of a stage manager and wearing a microphone and earpiece.

"Thank you, forty-five!"

At his acknowledgement, the badger scurried off to her other duties.

Rob stood to one side of the door to stay out of the way of the bustling activity. He tried again to look over at Pierce, but the makeup lights were really something and left glowing green and red spots in the Dalmatian's vision.

"Mr. Cantor's here, Mr. Pierce."

The bright lights were shut off, and Pierce stood and faced Rob, who tried without success to blink away the spots in his vision.

"You made it! That's fantastic!"

"I saw you with the kid, earlier," Rob said, rubbing at his eyes. "You were really something."

Pierce stepped closer, a softer smile now sitting on his muzzle, one of warmth and not the glee of a fan. The lights must have really done a number on Rob's eyes because the other dog appeared to have all black fur on his muzzle and around his eyes. Rob's nose twitched. There was that paint smell again…

He stared long and hard at the grinning superhero, blinking as the glowing afterimage began to fade. The dog that stood before him bore the black fur and brown eyes of another breed entirely. The paint Rob had smelled, and smelled now, made more sense.

"You're not a Dalmatian?" Rob blinked.

"Nope! Labrador!" Pierce wagged his spotted tail. "But I can sure pass for one, huh?"

Rob gritted his teeth, fighting the sudden urge to tell this upstart mongrel off once and for all. Seriously? Changing your breed for the sake of a role? Sure, it wasn't like a fox trying to play a wolf. They were both still dogs, but just because it wasn't species prejudice, that didn't make it right.

The look on Rob's face must have been more apparent than he'd thought. Pierce took a step back, ears pinned. The room fell silent, all of the attendant staff staring at the scene unfolding.

"I know, it's pretty unusual, but the studio and everybody was cool about it—"

"Oh, I'll bet they were!" Rob snarled. "The Studio was cool with everything because The Studio only sees one thing: dollar signs. They don't see years of a person's life and hard work. They don't have any respect for the craft itself unless it makes them money. So what if you're not really a Dalmatian? As far as they're concerned, there aren't any Dalmatian actors out there waiting for a shot, so let's just get some other breed to fill in!"

Pierce looked wounded but stood his ground, backing up no farther. The security guard at the door had stepped inside, eyeing the situation tensely. The Labrador waved her off, though she stayed planted a few feet away, just to be certain.

"Who ever gave you the notion that this was a good idea?" Rob glared, the afterimage having faded completely from his vision now. The half-painted Labrador looked for all the world as if he were fighting back tears.

"You did," he answered softly.

Rob opened his muzzle to shoot off something else but was halted when Pierce lifted something off the side of his belt and held it out to Rob in offering.

Rob, now feeling a vibe of chill confusion swirling amid his white-hot rage, took the object without thinking, and stared at it. When he did, all of his rage melted away.

In his paw sat a five-pointed star made of shiny silver metal. The emblem at the center was Captain Electron's logo.

"Where did you get this?"

"You gave it to me, Mr. Cantor. You gave it to me when I was just a little pup, during an appearance at a big supermarket."

Rob looked up into the other dog's brown eyes. It had been thirty years. He'd seen lots of fans, but that time…that time he remembered very well.

"It was you?"

***

"Well, hello there, little scout," Rob had said, in his deep, booming "superhero" voice. "What can I do for you today?"

The little boy immediately looked down and fidgeted. His black ears could not decide whether they should be pinned back or perked up excitedly.

"What's your name," Captain Electron said, trying once again. It wasn't that he was in a hurry. Not at all. There was no pressure here. Most of the people passing by took no notice of him or his signing table. His manager was outside smoking and probably having a nip of brandy from the flask that he didn't want Rob to know he carried. He just knew, from experience, that he couldn't depend on the child to say something on his own. That either overeager parents would interfere or he would simply run off from sheer shyness.

"Um…" The boy turned his head to look behind him.

Rob looked up, following the boy's gaze until he saw a well dressed Labrador couple, quietly urging the boy on from a distance. Rob admired that. They wanted the boy to take the step on his own. The pup looked back in Rob's direction, still not making eye contact.

"I'm not s'posed to tell. It's my secret indemnity."

The masked Dalmatian's muzzle broke into a grin. Of course! Secret identity, or 'indemnity' as the case may be, was critical to any superhero, and the boy was completely dressed up, mask and all. He was playing an excellent game of pretend. Rob couldn't not play along. This was his favorite part, when the young ones really got into the swing of things.

"You're certainly to be commended," Captain Electron said. He dropped his volume conspiratorially as he leaned in closer and cocked a floppy black ear. "But if you can't trust Captain Electron, then who can you trust?"

The little boy looked up then, his eyes meeting Rob's, ears coming forward, tail wagging furiously. He was smiling now, and his brown eyes were full of wonder. "Okay," he said, excitedly. Then forcing himself back to proper superhero composure, leaned in and whispered, "It's Jonny. You gotta promise not to tell."

"My word as a member of the Justice Spots," Captain Electron whispered in return, winking.

"I have...um... a very important question to ask you, Mr. Captain Electron, sir."

Rob leaned across the table on folded arms. "Well, better ask, lad. I'm all ears."

"When are you gonna come back...um...on TV? They put on some stupid thing with a really creepy puppet at the time you used to be on."

Rob felt his heart sink beneath the costume's embroidered chest logo. This question was the worst.

"Well, you see... I've had to start doing more low-profile crime solving."

"Oh! Like a secret mission?"

"Yes, something like that." He hated that the boy was completely unfazed by the lie and took it as gospel truth. But he couldn't ruin the kids' fantasy by telling them the reality of the situation. CBS had decided to cancel the series.

"Will you ever come back on? It's boring without you."

Rob looked up, hoping to see the boy's parents coming to take him away, but they hadn't moved. The father's arm was wrapped around the mother's shoulder, whose paw was placed gently on his, admiring the imagination of their little pup.

"I can't say for sure, maybe one day."

"When I grow up, do you think I could join the Justice Spots...?"

This was safer territory for Rob.

"Well, normally, members of the Justice Spots are only Dalmatians. It takes someone of special character to be admitted otherwise. Do you think you have what it takes?"

The boy's tail lashed excitedly back and forth.

"I do, I do, I really, really do!'

Solemnly, Captain Electron came around the table and knelt before the child. He slipped his paw to his belt and lifted the heavy costume badge from its place. The shiny prop had been made by the same company that made a number of actual police badges. He didn't like wearing it, but the studio was insistent that a vigilante superhero like Captain Electron actually be shown as a duly deputized law enforcement officer, just so that kids weren't given mixed signals about lawbreaking.

The badge was splendidly detailed with Captain Electron's atom logo as the cloisonné design at its center and five rounded points extending outward like a marshal's badge from one of the spaghetti westerns. It sparkled in the fluorescent light of the supermarket.

"Then by the authority vested in me by the Justice Spots, I hereby induct you as an honorary junior member," he pronounced as he knelt, placing the badge into the pup's outstretched paws. "And maybe, when you're old enough, you can be a superhero too, just like me."

The kid practically vibrated with excitement, his eyes as wide as saucers staring at the badge in his paws. Impulsively, he wrapped both arms around his hero and hugged him tightly.

"I hope you come back on TV soon so I can watch you with my dad. He's a big fan too."

The little Labrador pup named Jonny turned and scampered off back to his parents. Rob couldn't hear what he was saying, but he was jumping up and down and showing the badge to both parents who grinned and laughed. They soon left, waving at Captain Electron for making their child's day.

***

Rob shook his head in disbelief. "It was you. I can't believe you held onto this." All the burning anger and humiliation he'd felt moments ago drained away, replaced now by a sense of shame at his outburst and a desire to reach out and hug the young actor.

"Are you kidding? I was obsessed with Captain Electron. He was always my favorite! You're the reason I got into acting in the first place. I mean, once I found out that your show wasn't actually real, that is."

Rob had been told that, occasionally, by some young creature at a signing table. He'd hear how he'd inspired them to chase their dreams, and even when they found out they couldn't be a real superhero, they wanted to be other people. It was a nice sentiment, but hearing it like this made Rob's old heart do some joyous backflips.

The staff and others in the room finally breathed a sigh of relief and returned to their bustling. The security guard stepped outside, holding the door as someone else came inside amid the flurry of activity.

"When I found out they were finally going to be rebooting Captain Electron, well, I hired a stylist and a makeup artist," he said, indicating the pair of foxes who had been dutifully grooming him before Rob had walked in. "And we worked out how to turn me into a Dalmatian. I'm just sorry that you didn't have time to be in the movie! I had a great scene for you all picked out!"

Rob's ears perked forward. "What are you talking about?"

"I asked the studio if we could have you in to play my father, but they told me you weren't interested."

Rob's face burned, his smile faltering. "That's really interesting. Nobody ever told me."

Pierce yelped. "What? I can't believe that!" He yanked out his cellphone and began dialing.

"Honestly, it's fine," Rob said.

"No, it's not fine. If they want me back for the next film, I don't care what contract I'm under, they'll put in the dad scenes! They're so important! Without them… You know what? They'll get an angry phone call on Monday."

"I still can't believe you stuck with being a fan all these years," Rob said, willing his voice not to break.

"Hey, listen. Meeting you meant everything to me when I was eight. You gave me permission to chase my dreams."

He reached out, lifted up the badge from Rob's paw, and held it up, grinning sheepishly. "They, uh, wouldn't let me wear it in the movie, y'know? I tried."

"So, now you're me. That's pretty impressive, kid," Rob said.

"Nah, I'm not you. I'm me. You're you. And we're both Captain Electron. But you're the legend, here."

That funny, loaded word again.

"So, are you still going to do the Q&A with me? I mean, I totally get it if you don't want to now," Pierce said, looking down at the carpet.

The indecision fluttered in Rob's stomach.

"I'll do it. You kept that dream of yours alive because of something I did. I think it's only fair that I keep doing this, for the fans, because of you." He nodded, tail wagging. The butterflies disappeared from inside, replaced by a warm glow.

"That means the world to me, Mr. Cantor."

"Call me Rob. I think you've earned it."

"Okay, then. Rob. So, uh, Have you watched the movie?"

Rob shook his head and laughed. "Avoided everything about it. It all pissed me off so much at the time that I couldn't see straight."

"Tell you what, I'll have my manager drop off a Blu-Ray in my suite, and we can watch it together. You can give me pointers. They

green-lit two sequels already, and there are talks for a new TV series."
The Labrador's tail wagged.

"You've got a deal. But you supply the popcorn and the brandy, and I get to make fun of you as much as I want."

"Deal. Now, I gotta finish getting ready. I plan on talking about nothing but how much your show inspired me and colored my performance, and then I'm going to demand that everybody come and get your autograph."

The Dalmatian grinned. "Okay, but remember, I'm old. You're going to aggravate my arthritis by making me sign so much."

"Bah, occupational hazard when you're Captain Electron."

"When we're Captain Electron," Rob corrected. As Pierce returned to his makeup chair, the Dalmatian heard a strange, high-pitched noise from behind him.

He turned around to look for the source and nearly bumped straight into Jake, who was standing immobile, paws clasped firmly over his muzzle. He practically vibrated with excitement and made little whining noises to accompany his furious wiggling.

"Hey, Jake, calm down. You'd think you just saw a superhero or something."

Sometimes chasing a legend—even a small, silly one— can help you figure out where you're going. Or at least, where you are.

A ROCK AMONG MILLIONS

Skunkbomb

I woke up to a text from my best friend saying, "Hiking. You and me. DO IT." After sending out resumes all summer and getting no reply, I figured I could be an outdoor cat for an afternoon. Maybe some fresh air would clear my head or, at the very least, distract me from my unemployment.

"Dude, this park is awesome," Leif said as he pulled into the parking lot of Oak Lake Park. His tail thumped against his seat as he pointed to the gathering of trees at the base of a rocky cliff. A river curved its way to an oval lake. "And we're going to the top."

I shielded my eyes from the sun's glare. "I thought we were just going to take a lap around the lake or something."

The collie shook his head. "We have to go to the top, Alec. There's this rock up there—"

"There are rocks all over this park."

"No, but for real, there's this rock," Leif said, holding his paws out wide. "Huge rock. Legend says that whoever touches it gets good fortune." He grabbed my arms and leaned in closer to me. He spoke to me in a whisper full of Taco Bell-y dog breath. "And we're gonna touch it."

I fought to keep my claws from poking out. Leif's my best friend, but his canine enthusiasm was a little overbearing. "Rocks don't have magic powers."

"Come on, where's your sense of adventure, mister investigative reporter tabby?"

Leif had dubbed me that ever since I picked Journalism before I started my freshman year. I don't want to be the guy writing articles about a new grocery store opening. I want to write about the unfair wages and hours the grocery stores give their employees.

"Can you at least get a little psyched for me?" Leif said as we climbed out of the car. "I've got a week of freedom before I start that insurance job. By the way, how'd that interview go for you on Friday?"

"I woke up to an email saying the position was actually an internship," I said. It was getting harder not to extend my claws. "They still offered me a spot, but I've done internships all through college. I should at least have the experience for an entry-level position, right?"

Leif's ears flattened. "Shit, sorry bro. Something will pop up at some point. Hey, maybe once you touch the rock, you'll get that dream job."

"Let's just walk, okay?" I said. I looked up at the sign with arrows pointing toward all the different paths. "Which one of these leads up?"

***

Once we entered the woodsy part of the trail, the shade provided enough protection to keep Leif from panting too much.

"Try not to mark any of the trees," I said.

"That was one time!" Leif whined.

"Twice."

"Whatever!"

Rocks jutted out of the ground, so we had to step across them. Well, Leif did. I had more of a graceful bounce. Leif found a group of rocks overlooking the lake, and he lay back against one like a lawn chair.

"Dude," Leif said, placing his paws behind his head. "Take my picture!" As he shifted his tail into the sunnier part of the rock, he said, "Tag your sister in this. Show her what she's missing."

I wrinkled my nose. "Never happening."

"She still playing college soccer?"

I nodded. "Apparently some scout for the Olympic team watched their practice last week."

"And your brother?" Leif asked. "Is he still boring?"

"Kinda," I said. "But he's doing accounting for some big business."

"Whatever it was, it gave him a sweet company car," Leif said, grasping the air in front of him like a steering wheel. "I saw those pics online."

I glanced at a shaggy caterpillar inching across the stone next to me. "It's not a company car. He bought that." It was as if my brother had been handed the job as he walked off the stage with his diploma. Actually, it was like half of his graduating class was already wearing business suits under their graduation gowns. Had I missed some sort of requirement in college? I took all the right classes, but here I was walking to a park in the middle of a Wednesday afternoon.

"This rock is actually super uncomfortable," Leif said, his smile faltering. "Mind if we speed things up?"

I took out my phone and snapped a couple of quick shots of him. "Okay, now give me 'paint me like one of your French girls.'"

Leif slipped a finger between his belt and shorts. "Don't take this the wrong way, but can you take the pic again, but with me naked?"

I lowered my phone. "What the hell kind of way am I suppose to take a question like that?"

"You take it as 'yes, Leif. I'd love to help you score a date with an outdoors-y artistic nude pic,'" Leif said. "You sure you don't want to send it to your sister?"

"She has a boyfriend," I told him as I slipped my phone into my pocket. "She's had one for two years now. Also, if you take your pants off, you'll get bug bites on your ass."

Leif thankfully took his paw away from his half-loosened belt and stood up. "Somebody sounds bitter. You get laid yet?"

"I'm focused on job searching," I grumbled.

"Haven't you been offered, like, three jobs since the summer started?"

"The right job."

Leif scratched his ear. "If someone shows up offering you a job, it's the right job. Look at my insurance job. I wasn't looking to work in insurance, but then I got the offer. Seriously though, do I look like the kind of guy who would sell insurance?"

I shrugged. "You're friendly and you're a smooth talker. You could do it. Plus, 'tail insurance' sounds just innuendo-y enough for your liking."

"It's totally real, man," Leif said. "You try walking around without a tail and see how many times you fall flat on your ass." As if to make a point, he stood on one leg at the tip of another rock. "Lots of pop stars and athletes get it. Who knows, maybe I'll do the insurance plan on some dog's tail and he'll get me a part in his next movie."

"Looks like you've got it all figured out," I said, my paws shoved into my pockets. I fell behind him so Leif wouldn't see me scowl, but he slowed to match my pace.

"Yeah, but I have to wear a suit," Leif said, wrinkling his muzzle. "Don't get me wrong, going classy like James Bond every now and then is cool, but the whole week?" He shoved a hanging tree branch out of the way. "And I have to work Saturdays, dude. Saturdays! Okay, only, like, every other Saturday, but still! Who starts the weekend by thinking, 'Hey, let's buy an insurance policy'?"

I curled my tail closer around my legs, the fur standing on end. "We've been walking for an hour. How much longer?"

"I'll check the map," Leif said as he pulled out his phone.

I looked over his shoulder. "Which path is this?"

"The Sunset Path," Leif said.

The Sunset Path arced loosely until making a tight circle around the lake and back to the visitor center. "This isn't anywhere near the top of the park!"

"Oh shit!" Leif said, a hint of a laugh in his voice. "I thought this was called "Sunset Path" because people looked out at the sunset at the top, not at the lake. My bad!"

I glimpsed at the sinking sun. "Whatever. Let's just head back."

"No way!" Leif said, shoving his phone into his pocket. "We have to get to the top!"

"But the park closes at dark," I said, already making my way back.

"Hold on!" Leif said, grabbing my arm. He scanned the surroundings, sniffing the air like he could smell a shortcut. "The rock's not that far from here. It'll be a half hour tops to get there and that long to go back down." He loosened his grip. "Come on. What's another hour for an adventure? We can find this rock."

I folded my arms and turned back to him. "It's just a stupid rock. What's so important about it?

"You're in a bad place, Alec," Leif said. "You get rejected enough and you'll be all 'why bother?' Well, even if this rock isn't magical or whatever, I'm not leaving until we've both touched it. Once we've touched that rock, we've succeeded. If we keep going, we haven't failed."

I pinched the bridge of my nose. His tail wagged. It was like Leif was waiting for a treat. "Fine."

***

The overhanging trees blocked out the last bits of light the moon provided, and a cricket chorus played on. My thighs ached. The next pebble I stepped on, I was going to chuck it as far as I could. "You're sure we're almost there?"

After a few seconds, Leif said, "Pretty sure." He panted, a bit of saliva dripping off the tip of his tongue.

I pulled out my phone. "If you won't check the map, I will."

"Come on, have some faith in my navigation skills."

"Well excuse me for wanting to know where I'm going," I said. "Blind faith doesn't always cut it. The least you could do to help is pull up your flashlight app."

"Checking the map earlier drained my battery," Leif said. "My bad."

"Okay, seriously," I said as I stopped. "Leif, it's dark, and we can barely see where we're going."

"But you're a cat," Leif said. "Don't you have night vision or something?"

"That's not the point," I hissed. "Let's—"

"Dude."

"What?"

"Between those two trees," Leif said. He wasn't smiling, but the swishing of his tail spoke for him. "What's that look like?"

I squinted. There was certainly something with a thing sticking out of it. Still, it was more than what I'd seen during our search. Leif jabbed my shoulder, and we raced over to the something. When we got there, I held up my phone and turned the flashlight app on.

A rectangular sign pointing downward diagonally read, "Visitor Center: 1.5 miles."

"I swore it was here," Leif said, looking around.

"I'm leaving," I said, turning around.

"It has to be nearby," Leif said. "I bet we find it in five minutes. No, less than five minutes. Then we can head back down."

"No, here's what's going to happen," I said, my claws sliding out. "I'm going back down, I'm getting in my car, and whether or not you're with me, I'm leaving."

"Alec, don't be like that."

He put his paw on me, but I swatted it away. "Look, this was fun at first, but I'm not sticking around to get another bug bite so you can touch a rock because it's somehow more special than the million other rocks here!"

"It brings good fortune," Leif growled.

"Why the hell do you need good fortune?" I said. "Your family's loaded, you coasted your way through high school, still managed to get into a good college, and you're starting a job soon."

Leif shoved his face close to mine. "What, you think once you've got money and a job that everything's going to be fine?"

I wrinkled my nose at his dog breath. "That does seem like the winning combination."

"It's not that simple!" Leif barked, grabbing the front of my shirt.

"Well excuse me," I scoffed, putting my paws up. "You make it look easy. Now let go!" It was supposed to be a push, but it surprised me how much strength I put into it. The front of my shirt tore and Leif staggered back.

Then he wasn't there.

"L—Leif?" I called. I stepped forward and almost tumbled over the edge of the path. I slipped into a crouch, staring into the black beneath me. "Leif!" Only crickets answered. I grabbed my phone to pull up the flashlight app. As I pulled the phone out of my pocket, it slipped from my hand and was swallowed by a darkness my sight couldn't penetrate. I dug my fingers into the dirt and opened my mouth, but my throat was too tight. Even my voice was gone. I wondered what it'd be like covering a story like this and what the headline in tomorrow's paper would read. "Local Resident Kills Friend in Petty Argument Over Rock." I could see myself in handcuffs being led to an awaiting patrol car and the reporters swarming me, asking me why I did it. I wouldn't give them a sensational story, just the truth. I killed my best friend because I was an idiot who was scared of my future or lack of one.

"Asshole!"

"Leif?" I said, my voice high and thick. His voice was loud and blessedly close. I slipped over the edge of the path, hanging by my paws, and let go. I fell into a crouch about a yard down. Leif lay on his back on an earthy jut of land hanging from the path.

I hopped down and knelt by his side. "I'm so sorry! I didn't mean it, I swear! I'm going to pick you up and carry you back down. I might drop you, but that's because I don't have any muscles."

"Shut up," Leif said, his chest heaving. "Just the wind ... knocked out of me." I reached out, but he shook his head. "Just give me ... a few minutes ... to catch my breath."

It's awkward standing over someone, so I lay down next to him. If a park ranger found us, it'd look like we were chilling and I didn't just almost murder my best friend. On this spit of land, the trees didn't reach out far enough to block out the sky. A spattering of stars freckled the night sky.

"My bad," I said.

"You could have killed me," Leif said dully.

"I was freaked out."

"I wasn't going to punch you or anything."

I sighed. "No, it wasn't you." I rested my paws on my chest. "I've applied to that journalism job more times than I can count, but it's like they don't notice me. I'm like a rock."

"You're not a rock," Leif said, rolling onto his side. "Your head's just as hard as one sometimes."

I snorted. "Thanks, but I feel like one."

"Compared to your siblings?" Leif added.

I rolled over to face him. "A master accountant and an Olympian to be. I can't compete."

"There's something you need to know to get through life," Leif said. "When it comes to other people, especially your siblings, don't compare them to you or whatever. Just do you and be awesome at it."

I smirked. "I'll try to squeeze that in between all the panicking."

"Hell, I'm still panicking," Leif said. "I was going into my last semester and I realized I had no clue what was after college. I was, like, 'now what?' I threw my resume at everyone so someone could rescue me and give me that step."

"Well, it worked out," I said, rolling onto my back.

"I don't even know how I got this insurance job," Leif said, scratching his ear. "I think they were at a job fair, but I don't remember giving them my resume. Then I got a phone call, which turned into an interview, which turned into a second interview, which turned into a job offer. I didn't even think. All I knew was that someone gave me my next step and I took it.

"I was happy at first because I wasn't panicking," Leif added. "But then the closer I got to my start date, the more I realized when someone asks me what I do for a living, I'd have to tell them I sell insurance. What cub grows up wanting to sell insurance?"

"And touching a rock would have fixed that?" I asked.

"Well, it wouldn't have hurt."

I shrugged. "Fair enough. Did you talk with your parents about the insurance job?"

"A little bit," Leif said. "I'll just do this until I find my calling or I hate the hell out of it. I mean, we're in our early twenties. That makes me feel super old, but compared to my parents, I'm still a cub. We've got time to figure this out, right?"

"Don't look at me. This is your motivational speech." I traced the crescent moon with my finger. "The whole getting-my-shit-together thing still seems far away."

"Yeah," said Leif. "But until then, we can panic together." He sighed. "Shit, it's dark."

I sat up and grabbed my phone from the ground. There weren't any new scratches on the screen. "I've still got my cell phone light."

Leif shook his head. "I almost died once tonight. Let's not go deeper in the woods and find some chainsaw-wielding hermit. You know what'd make this night better? Pizza."

I stuck my paw out and pulled Leif up. "Sounds good, if you're buying."

"You almost killed me tonight. If that doesn't earn me a free meal, I don't know what does."

I clicked my flashlight app. "You're going to hold that over me for life, aren't you?" Leif laughed and I found myself laughing too. I gave him a little head butt because it was dark and we were alive.

As we walked down the rocky path to the visitor center, I was tempted to race up that mountain or drive anywhere. Maybe it was the lack of light pollution or my eyes adjusting to the dark, but my path seemed brighter tonight.

Epol is a skilled gambler, but how much would he risk to become a legendary one?

THE PIGEON WHO WISHED FOR GOLDEN FEATHERS

Corgi W.

"I'll wager," said the pigeon, a smile coming to the edge of his beak, "that the next roll will be... a one on the black, a four on the white, and... six on the red."

The lion snorted, in the same fed-up way that he had done all night. "It doesn't matter," he spat, "I've lost already. What little you've left me with will barely cover my trip home. Just roll, so I can be done with this loathsome kingdom."

In avian society, gambling was a sacred affair. Games of chance were divine mediums, through which the gods declared their will. As some read signs in tea stains, and others looked for guidance in the stars, birds turned to gambling, whenever they wished for divination.

They would bet on anything, if given the situation. Putting one's possessions at the gods' mercy was said to be one of the highest virtues. A fortune rivalling an emperor's could be found in the drawing of a card, the rolling of a ball, the flipping of a coin, or the casting of a die. It was in this eternal pursuit of ever changing wealth that Epol found himself betting against a lion, under the dim light of a tavern, looking out over the ocean.

Epol chuckled, passing the dice from his left to right claw, throwing them into the air and balancing them on the tip of his beak. "You oughtn't visit us birds," he began, rolling them into the space between his eyes, blinking rapidly, then pouring them onto his shoulders, "if you struggle with losing. I've rolled well, but that's only because the gods wished it. Clearly they think it better for you to return home, and with the way you've handled our game, I cannot say I fault them."

The lion grumbled, his mighty jowls drooping. In his state, no trick would amuse him. Epol had seen all the faces that opponents made when they lost. The lion, he decided, was a sore-sport, but dignified enough to not fly into a rage. He might have even known that Epol was cheating, but damned if he could work out how. When the time came to pay, he would hand over what he owed, perhaps holding onto a few insignificant coins, in a gesture that would let him say to himself, 'I really pulled one over on him', as Epol cleared his pockets. His mood could not have been improved by the discomfort of sitting on a perch, trying his best to treat it as a stool. In an avian tavern there was nothing to eat but bread and seed.

"I'm curious," said the pigeon, finishing up his trick by juggling the multi-coloured dice. "Why come to us birds? I've been all around this country, seeing swans, hawks, falcons, and crows, but never anything wingless. I can't imagine you're passing through, else you'd have never sat down to play me. What business might a lion have in lands such as these?"

The feline gave a toothy smile. "Information is valuable," he said. "Something we can put a price on. So how's about I wager it? In exchange for a chance to win back what you've taken."

"Come now," laughed Epol, placing the dice on the table in a stack. "I only said I was curious. Whatever it is that you know can't be worth an entire night's winnings. I'll wager your information against buying you another drink. That's fair, right? Feathers such as these aren't won in such silly bets." At the mention of his feathers, the pigeon spread his wings, pointing to the few pieces of gold that shone from within. "One day I'll have them all set like this; solid gold, you see." He tapped his claw against the metal. "Very fashionable, for those with the money. The only other bird that I know to have entirely golden wings is our emperor, and I hear that some of his are just unusually shiny brass."

"Ah," the lion exclaimed, "then my quest would be very worth your knowing. I came here to make my fortune. If you wish for riches, you'd be foolish not to take my offer."

Epol thought for a moment, then leaned over the table, spreading his wings to make himself seem larger. "Half," he said, meeting the lion's gaze. "If you win, I'll waive half of what you owe."

"All," the lion insisted, slamming his fist between them.

Epol's form shrunk, his wings wrapping around himself as he leaned backwards on his perch. Across the room, he spotted an anxious pair of eyes. He gave a nod to the dove, bringing his hand to his beak. For as long as Epol's master had watched him, he had warned the pigeon against any unnecessary bets. The dove would have told him to take the money; for him, it was as simple as that. If the pigeon refused the bet, he would bring a smile to the white bird's elderly beak.

Yet something in Epol would not allow for that. He knew he could win by controlling the faces that the dice would show, a technique known as rhythm rolling, a highly illegal skill. Sat before him was his chance to prove himself in the art. There was a sharp difference between practising by himself, and having a fixed pair of eyes watching the subtle movements of his wrist.

In order to be a gambler whom the world would truly remember, he would have to take silly bets such as this, of which the tales would tell. When they remembered it all, they would recount the time that Epol had put a small fortune up against a useless tidbit.

"I'll do it," he said, picking up the dice. "I'll wager it all, but you're going to be honest with me."

The dove looked away in shame, as the lion jumped from his perch. "Something simple," said Epol, "a truly godly game; whomever rolls highest on two dice wins, best of three. No strategy or tactics, no skill or ability, a game of pure divination."

The lion grunted his agreement, taking the dice and subjecting them to a close inspection. Epol doubted the feline knew what he was looking for. With the eyesight of birds, and the stakes that they played for, weighting dice was an art in and of itself. Still though, it was common enough for people to inspect them, not with the hope of catching any foulness, but as a way to warn against it. By taking those cubes and giving them so much time, the lion was warning Epol that he did not trust him to play fairly.

"I want you to go first," the lion demanded, handing the white and black dice over.

"I like the red," replied the pigeon, stretching out his hand. There was no significance to the red die, it was the same as all the others:

unweighted, made of a light metal, with perfectly rounded golden inlays. What mattered more was that the lion thought it was important.

By placing emphasis on the dice, which were not the source of his cheating, Epol could fool the lion into thinking that they were. His opponent would fixate on the dice, not watching the way they were rolled, utterly convinced that the dice were somehow 'off'. The worst he could do would be to give the dice another inspection, looking as closely as he could, but unable to prove the pigeon was dirty.

And so, Epol waited for the red to be handed over, placing the white aside.

Reluctantly, the lion yielded to the request.

Taking the die in hand, the grey bird considered his roll. Going first was a disadvantage. If he were to roll nothing but fives and sixes, the lion's suspicion would only rise, but to pick a number too low would give the lion a reasonable chance to beat it. Ideally, Epol would win the first round by a very slim margin, lose the second, then give all he had for the third. To lose on the first round would mean that he would need to roll unusually high for the second and third, giving results that would be hard to put down to chance.

Considering it all, he threw the metal cubes to the table, spinning them in such a way so as to give himself a four and a five. Nine was a good score; not high enough to seem odd, but not low enough to leave the lion much of an opportunity for victory.

"Your turn," said Epol, pushing the red and black cubes over.

The lion eagerly made his roll, finding only a six and a two.

"Close," said Epol, smiling, as he took his dice back, tossing out the black and picking up the white. It was important for the second score to be low, but not so low that it looked to be diversionary. The pigeon could bring forth two ones, but that would be far too obvious. A score of five or six could be beaten quite easily, without requiring extraordinary results. The dice rolled; the upwards faces showed a two and a three.

The lion took his turn, landing another six with and a two. "Hurrah," cried the lion, leaping backwards from his perch.

Seeing the lion cheer, before he had even won, filled Epol with a desire to absolutely crush him. He wished to throw two sixes, then laugh, as the lion's odds sunk in. There was an immense satisfaction in watching one allow themselves to become invested, praying that the gods would favour them, whilst they never had a chance. Epol liked to imagine that was how the gods felt when they meddled in the affairs of mortals.

On the other side of the tavern, the dove cast an irritated glance. The lion had already known that something was wrong with the game. For Epol to win in the extravagant way that he wished, he would have to once again pull against the lion's whiskers, revealing the pre-determined nature of the rolls. The dove's mood was already sour, scornful that the bet had ever been made.

Switching the black and white dice once more, Epol doubted what to do. For the sake of the dove, and to keep the lion from fighting, he ought to be sensible with his results. A four and a six would be valid, unlikely to be beaten, mundane enough to seem fair. But the temptation of two sixes rattled about in Epol's mind. Clacking the metal pieces together, he felt his wrist fall dull, unable to make the precise movements needed to keep the dice tumbling in the ways that he wished. In an attempt to feel which side was where, the pigeon loosened his grip. And, mistakenly, he gave the dice enough room to spill out. The two cubes clattered onto the table, falling apart. The red landed on a one. The black landed on a two.

A roaring laughter sounded from the lion. "Three," he said, pointing to the table. "I don't even need to take my final turn. If you wish, for your own sake, I'll accept your defeat right now."

A long sigh left Epol's beak. "You might as well go. The game's not over until you've rolled."

Snatching up the dice, the lion let out another hearty roar. "If you wish to drag this out," he announced, smashing the dice together between his paw.

He threw the dice. The pair bounced across the wood of the table, knocking against Epol's mug, jumping back towards the lion. They landed unceremoniously in the center of the table.

To the shock of both players, the red and black die both displayed a one.

"Twooo!" screamed Epol, spreading his fluffy wings, as he snatched up his drink.

For several seconds, the lion's jaw hung open. A sudden disbelief surrounded the game. Of all the combinations of numbers, for whatever reason, this had seemed the least likely. In truth, the probability of the result was the same as any other; two sixes, a five and a four, a three and a two, etcetera, they were all equally as likely to come up. But there was a strangeness to the scenario into which the dice had been thrown. It was moments like this that revealed why birds put such faith in the idea that these games were decided by the gods.

A low rumble came from the lion, his teeth grinding against one another. Compared to a lion, a pigeon's body was nothing. With a single swipe, the feline could break Epol's neck. The pigeon's hand crept into his satchel, fingering a slightly larger pair of metal dice, using his wing to cover what he was doing.

Surrounding the rhythm were a great many secrets, one of which was this: 'Satellite dice', as the dove had named them. With the exception of the 'one', each face had an inlay of silver ball-bearings, designed to explode in different directions, when thrown correctly. It was a dangerous weapon, used by advanced practitioners of the rhythm, for making an escape, if they were ever caught. *"You've got to be certain with 'em,"* the dove had warned. *"If you ever need to use 'em, the 'ones' have got to land facing you. Any other side and you'll end up hurting yourself. It's a weapon meant for use with the rhythm, but only for those with the skill."*

Seeing the lion's form hang over him, Epol readied himself to throw, searching for the nearest exit. If any of the tavern's innocent patrons were hit, he would have to be ready to flee.

The lion took another glance at the dice, then took them between his paws. He threw them against the floor, shouting in a tongue that Epol did not understand. Seeming as if he had calmed himself, the lion returned to his perch, and drowned his muzzle in drink.

"Sooooo," began Epol, leaning over the table. "What's your business here?"

The lion snorted, his eyes seeming to shrink. With an angry motion he reached into his pocket, shuffled about his hand, and produced a folded piece of paper. Flicking it over, he raised himself up. "The money's upstairs, in my lodgings," he grumbled, forcing his way from the table.

He returned several moments later to toss a bag at Epol.

***

Alone, Epol unfolded the paper and waved over the dove.

"What's it say?" he asked, twisting his head about.

A pronounced tut sounded from his white feathered friend. "You've not been practising your letters lately, have you?"

"It doesn't matter. I've got you for these things, now come on, what's it say?"

An unsure look overcame the dove as he read. He glanced at Epol, then back to the sheet of paper. The pigeon knew the look well. When Olanthun read something that he did not want Epol to know, his wings drooped slightly, and his eyes began to dart about. There were a set of feathers that existed just beside his beak which rustled up whenever he was uncomfortable.

And upon reading those words, his feathers were more scrunched together than Epol had ever thought possible. At times like this, the pigeon really wished he could read.

"So, what's it saying?" pressed Epol. "I can always find somebody else; you know I'm not above that. Remember in Yerno, when I pretended to be blind because you wouldn't tell me that somebody had written swears on the side of the tavern? I've no qualms against asking somebody here to read it for me." If Epol was being honest, he found the thought terrifying. People who could read always irritated him. Upon admitting his illiteracy, he felt they were looking down their beaks at him.

Olanthun groaned, then held the paper flat on the table. "Put your hand on it," he said, "stretch out a finger and place it on that letter, there. Now, what sound does it make?"

"Not now. There's people about."

The dove's claw was steadfast.

"'A,'" said the pigeon. He hated whenever the dove would do this. Olanthun would seize upon any opportunity to try to teach him to read, and, every time, the pigeon would make the sounds in the most dismissive voice he could muster. The dove would halt them at any passing sign, refusing to continue the journey until Epol had read what was written. Whenever letters were present, the dove treated it as a study session for the pigeon.

"And that one?" he asked, moving his claw along.

"'T', and that one next to it, that says 't', too. And there, look, another 'a.'"

"Right, and with the two 't's' together, it's only a single sound. Now carry on with the rest."

"'E,' 'n,' 't,' 'i,' 'o,' 'n.' Atten-t-i-o-n.' That word says 'Attention,'" Epol triumphantly declared.

For the best part of an hour, the pair continued in that fashion: Olanthun telling Epol where to look, the pigeon making the sounds and waiting for approval. By the end, the content mattered less than the form. What mattered most to Epol was that he was reading what was written. It was only when he encountered the last full-stop that he took the time to consider what he had said.

"Attention," he began. "You have been invited to take place in a tournament of the gods. By your love of gambling, and faith in the gods' will, you have been offered a place at the table. On the first day of summer, present this letter to the priests of the temple of Fading Winter. Upon the fated day, the gods' shall decide who is worthy of their temple's fortune, through the medium of dice.

"That's a months' time" exclaimed Epol. "The fortune of a temple… We won't ever need to travel about again. We have to go."

Olanthun merely grunted. "We'll discuss this outside," he said, preparing to leave.

***

For the better part of their lives, Epol and Olanthun had wandered. On the first Monday of each month, they would pick up whatever they could carry, spread their wings, and move to the next town. Constant travel was essential for their income. Inevitably, if they stayed for too long, somebody would wise-on to their ways of dice rolling, and to be found cheating in any of the gods' games was a crime worthy of death.

They camped not far from the village of Herar, hidden away within a small clearing, far enough from the village so as not to be heard, but close enough to get an idea of what was happening. If Epol could have had his way, they would have found comfortable rooms at an inn. Beside their tents, they built a fire.

"You can't go," was the first thing Olanthun said, rubbing a stick between his claws, creating sparks, then a small fire. "You're not skilled enough in rhythm rolling, you'd be caught. There's a reason we keep to small towns. In cities and temples, they train to spot the rhythm. The art must constantly change, if it's to have any chance of eluding the eyes of the priests. I've not spoken with any other practitioners in years; I've no clue of what's what with the technique."

For the dove, the conservation was over. Olanthun did not decide upon much, but the little that he did, he would do.

"Hold up," said Epol, "I can always go myself. A temple's money; we wouldn't ever need to travel again. We could settle up and live in the winter house all-year-round, with good seed, servants, whatever we wanted."

"But you wouldn't," said the dove. "You'd get bored and wander again. If either of us wanted to be rich, we could have earned our fortunes already. It's not much to hit three places in a week. If we didn't tarry about like we do, we'd be earning in a month what we do in a year. Aint' that simple though. Rhythm's not meant for it. You're not meant for it. Nobody who wants to be rich ever is. They can earn all they like, own all the stuff in the world, but, sooner or later, something else grabs their attention, and they think they need more. 'Sides, you go, they'll catch you rhythm rolling and cut your head off. I didn't teach it to you just so you could get yourself killed."

"You didn't teach it to me for anything worthwhile. What's the point of the rhythm if you won't ever use it for anything that matters?"

The dove said nothing. He reached into his tent and took out a golden feather-comb. Epol had never learned where he had gotten it, but it was the only thing of value that the dove kept in his possession. Stretching his wing around his front, he took his feathers between his claws, gently brushing each one until he was contented.

"Well?" said Epol. "Why teach me anything that you don't want me to use?"

"No respect for the history…" the dove whispered, keeping his eyes fixed upon his grooming. "It was never meant for this…"

"Don't give me that!" The pigeon pressed. "Tell me how the rhythm's meant to be used."

"The way we've been using it," said the dove, his attention still upon his feathers. "It's meant to be a trick you teach the kids with the poorest lots in life. You teach it 'em so they can earn a bit for themselves, not needing to join a gang, or sell their feathers for arrows. It weren't ever about being rich. You were meant to learn your letters, find a craft, earn an honest lot."

"And that's what you did?"

"Nope."

"So it's fine for you to live on the rhythm?"

"Yep."

"How's that work?" Epol yelled.

"I've the patience, and I don't want to be rich. True masters in the rhythm understand its ways. It's more than just your hands that do the rolling. You've got to feel it through your body: push the wind through your wings, keep your mind in the right place, feel the subtle movements in your waist and use them with your hands. It's about knowing when to lose, to make it all seem fair, watching your opponent's soul and knowing how to respond. The rhythm, not that you would care, was an art devised by the priests, using the bags of dice they carry about as weapons. Those with a conscience turned it into what it is today, teaching it to the poor. I respect the tradition, I follow the rules, and though I'm not a master, I can feel its purpose. If you want to survive on the rhythm, that's what you'll have to learn. I've told you this before, but you never listen. Unless it's what you're looking to hear, your ears close up to it.

"You're young, impatient, you want to enjoy your life. To you, it's just rolling dice for money, and that's all it will ever be. Put this nonsense aside. The temple's fortune ain't for you to take. Now, get your book, read aloud for me. You've not been keeping with it, and it showed tonight."

Reluctantly, Epol did as he was asked. With the dove leaning over his shoulders, he began to read aloud. "O-n-c-e," he began, as he always did.

It would take him several minutes to finish a single page of the book. The letters were large, with innocent pictures beneath. Though he lacked much reference, Epol could tell that it was written for a child. Other books, he had heard, were a great deal more interesting, and less embarrassing to read. He hated every moment of it. The only thing that got him by was the thought that, once he had a decent grasp of it, there would be no more looking down on him. Reading was something special, which everyone else could hold above him.

At the end of each line, he stopped to look at the dove. "Well done," he would say, whenever Epol had gotten it right. Even when he had not, a small smile still appeared at the edge of Olanthun's beak. It was a distinctive smile, which evoked something strange in the pigeon. He never saw that smile during any of his dice games, regardless of his winnings. If he returned with the gold of all the kings and emperors that had ever walked the world, he doubted it would bring forth half the glee that the dove displayed when he heard Epol reading. "I can't believe anybody would take this up for fun," said the pigeon, turning over to the end of the book. Despite the dove's teaching, he never felt himself improving. Reading was for the clever birds; the hawks and the eagles. It was not something for pigeons.

The night had slipped by without him knowing; the crescent moon hung high. In Herar, there was quiet. Not far from where the two birds camped, the ocean lazily lapped up against the shore, as it too fell into an uneasy sleep. Without much need for talk, the pigeon and the dove put out the fire, crawled into their tents, and drifted off to slumber.

***

At the break of the next morning, when the air was chilly and light, Epol crawled from his tent. In his claw, he grasped the lion's letter, in the same way that an elderly miser might hold his final coin, telling himself 'at least I still have this'. The ocean was almost silent. No lights could be seen in Herar.

The grass in the clearing was wet, though the mud remained hard beneath Epol's feet. Taking a deep breath in, he pushed his chest forward. Olanthun was still sleeping, as usual. The dove, in a sign which Epol took to be the start of his old age, generally lay in his tent until midday, when he would wake and act as if it were still a reasonable time for breakfast.

If my name's ever to be said in the taverns, I'll have to earn it alone, thought the pigeon, reaching into his belongings. Taking the previous night's winnings, he began to divide the coins. *I'm sorry, but you've taught me all you can. I'll never be good at reading, writing, fishing, baking, or anything you've ever thought I should learn. I'll go to this tournament, win my fortune, then gamble it again. Through the rhythm, my story will be known.*

With the money unevenly split, Epol placed the slightly larger bag beside his friend. He put on his old leather cap, whose style had been forgotten since long before he was born. Taking a small stick, he began to write in the dirt. For two hours, he struggled with what to scrawl, often having to stop and think about which letter came next. *Goodbye Olanthun. Thank you,* was all that he could manage, checking it several times to ensure he had spelled it correctly.

Pulling his goggles over his face, he allowed himself a final glance towards the dove's tent. Feeling his eyes become wet, he spread his wings wide. Bounding forward, he took off into the sky.

***

On his first day, Epol had flown into the coastal town of Ter. In the white stone houses, an unusual number of ravens dwelt. When he had asked how to get to the temple of Fading Winter, he had been pointed to a shop selling maps. From the little he understood, the temple was built beside the city of Inar, which was three days flight from Ter. By the end of the week, Epol had begun to check over his shoulder for the dove. After a brief bout of gambling in Ter, the pigeon took off once more.

***

On his way to Inar, the pigeon passed by several more towns, where he made a series of small wagers. He bought his bedding and meals in the taverns, taking the time to find himself a new set of clothing. Hats with golden trim, he had heard, were very popular amongst the larger birds, with chains hanging from the sides, and ornate decoration upon the brow. The tailor whom he spoke with insisted that one had to be 'more than simply presentable,' when attending a tournament of the gods. With the coins he had left, Epol bought another golden feather. As time drew on, he found himself less worried that he would encounter the dove, the fear replaced by an odd sense of hope. With each white bird that he spotted, a part of Epol prayed, briefly, that he was looking at Olanthun. He never was, of course. "It's for the best," he would say, feeling less convinced each time.

With two weeks until the first day of summer, Epol flew into Inar. Years had gone by since he had last been so close to a city. The buildings managed a uniformity in their difference, painted in pastel shades of blue, pink, red, and yellow, never allowing two walls of the same colour to touch. In cities built by birds, roads tended to be few. The new was built atop the ancient, stretching upwards like an artificial mountain, thousands of doors and windows dotted throughout. Lying not far from the city was the temple of Fading Winter, an open-aired stadium with an altar in the center.

The pigeon flew towards the top, and purchased a room from which he could see the temple.

On the terrace beside him, Epol spotted a hawk.

"Are you also here to know the will of the gods?" he asked, turning his attention to the pigeon.

"I'm here for the tournament, if that's what you're wondering" replied Epol.

The hawk gave a nod. "I thought as much. Don't be surprised; I see it all the time. This morning I woke and saw a drop of water sliding down my window. I asked the gods if I would meet any of the tournament's participants today; if it went left then I would, if it went right then I would not. The droplet landed leftwards, and I have been watching ever since. And now you have found lodging in the room next to mine. In such a world, how can anybody doubt that events are set in motion by the gods?"

"Are you also here for the tournament?" was all that Epol could think to ask.

"Yes, though not as a competitor. I have been sent as an adjudicator, to guard the sanctity of the divinations," said the hawk, with pride in his words. "My kind have a reputation for the keenness of our eyes. There must be those who guard tournaments such as these. Though I would never think you capable of it," he forced out a laugh, "some would bring foulness into the god's revelations. The dice that I keep shall be the ones used in the games. Each roll shall be judged under the clarity of my vision. When the gods give out their fortune, it attracts an undesirable amount of wickedness from those seeking to steal it. Usually, invitations are only sent to those who are deemed to be worthy, yet they often return with different owners. I have been on a constant vigil, watching for those who would enter into the gods' divine games."

A weakness came over Epol. His hands felt as if they were dragging down his arms. His wings were useless, unable to lift him from the ground, even if he wished it. The hawk seemed deadly serious about his duties. Looking at them now—the bulging, glassy, beads, burning orange, with a perfectly rounded blackness in their center—it was as if there was nothing that the hawk could not see. If Epol so much as tapped his toe, the hawk would notice. For a moment, he thought to throw away his invitation. He doubted that even Olanthun would use the rhythm roll near the hawk.

Thinking back to his friend, Epol wondered what the dove would do. Not realising that he had frozen, beak slightly parted, the pigeon thought desperately on what his friend would say.

'Be careful' was the first thing that came to mind, quickly replaced by the words, 'fly away, whilst you've still got the chance'. But despite his desperation, Epol could hear nothing of what the dove might say. Olanthun was clever; he never would have gotten himself into this.

"W—what happens if you catch any…"

"Cheating?" the hawk interrupted. "I always catch somebody try it, nothing escapes me. So long as you are an honest pilgrim, such things need not trouble you. Show yourself at the tournament, trust that the gods know what is best. Win or lose, it is what the gods have decided. I am simply thrilled to be a witness. If you wish to earn the gods' favour, you must pray, and make sacrifice on the pyres."

Epol nodded, took a step backwards, then disappeared into his room. From his bed, he tried to spot the terrace. Leaning around the wall, he saw the hawk, eyes still fixed upon him.

***

For the remainder of his time, Epol locked himself in his room. He had no money left for travel and could barely afford food. On his table, he had been tinkering with his satellite dice. Since his encounter with the hawk, he had taken the time to disarm and practice with them. On average, he could make the 'one' face him four fifths of the time. The satellite dice were slightly larger than standard, made considerably heavier by the weight of the mechanisms inside. He had picked them up and rolled them across his table, then the floor, using his other dice to record his successes and failures. The tournament was the following morning, and he still did not feel comfortable in their use.

He put the dice aside and picked up his final coins. Heading into the lower rungs of the city, he decided to eat well that evening. After an expensive meal, he flew back to his room, penniless, and uneasily settled down atop his pillow.

Unable to sleep, he spied movement near his window. Between the wooden frame, it seemed, if only for a moment, that two orange eyes hung against the darkness. As quickly as they had come, the eyes disappeared.

***

As the sun rose upon the first day of summer, Epol armed his dice. Opening a pocket, he carefully lowered them inside. The sky was filled with spectators, all heading to the temple. The hawk was not on his terrace when Epol stepped outside.

Atop the temple's walls, birds stood with bows. Flying to the entrance, Epol showed his invitation. Two priests set upon him and guided him towards the altar. Olanthun had once said something funny concerning priests, bows, and temples, but Epol struggled to recall what it was. Standing before the crowds, he would have given almost anything to hear that joke again. At the table, three of the ten competitors awaited: another pigeon, a crow, and an owl next to whom Epol was seated.

To Epol's horror, three hawks circled. Between them, the pigeon could not decide with which he had previously spoken. Each bore a thick leather helm decorated with silver. Epol's breath caught in his throat. Beneath the table, his hands instinctively made the motions of the rhythm.

He wished it were a month ago, when he was still camping with Olanthun. He wished it were two months ago, when they had first flown into Herar. He wished it were six months ago, when he could remember eating bread, perched on a broken wall, speaking with his friend. He wished it were several years ago, when he had first watched the dice pass between the dove's claws. He wished it were still the night in which he had fainted in front of Olanthun, feeling himself lifted into the air, placed atop a soft bed in a room that smelled of chai. He could hear the roar of the crowds, sense the eyes of the hawks. Beside him, the owl gently hooted. Yet never before had Epol felt so helplessly lonesome. They would catch him if he tried to use the rhythm. If he lost, he would be back to living on the streets. His golden feathers had never felt so cold. He peeked up into the crowds and looked about the temple. Thousands had gathered to watch.

And amongst them, Epol saw something wonderful.

White feathered, an old hat covering his eyes, wings held close together, a dove, immaculately clean, was watching. He gave a quick nod the moment that Epol spotted him. There were so many things that Epol wished to say; 'sorry' being first among them.

As the other competitors flew in, the pigeon could not stop his eyes from wandering back to the shining speck of white. When the head priest started talking, Epol could barely hear it.

"The rules," he declared, "are as follows. Each player shall be given fifty dice. At the start of each round, they shall choose how many they wish to roll. The dice that are chosen shall be returned to the temple, once the round has finished. Whomever has the lowest score at the end of each round is defeated. To decide who is to go last, two dice shall be rolled by each player, at the start of every round. The highest scoring player shall be the last to decide how many dice he wishes to roll. Is that clear?"

Those around the table nodded. From the sides of the temple, the priests bought forth silver bowls, filled with dice. Once each player had declared that they had fifty, the game had officially begun.

***

On his first round, Epol was lucky, being sat beside the owl who won the first roll. By the time it came to the pigeon, each player had decided upon an average of two dice. Following the average, Epol picked out two. As the players rolled, they did so individually, the priests looking down and calling the results to the spectators. Servants stood behind each participant, holding boards which declared how many dice they had remaining.

By the third round, Epol had forty three dice in his bowl. He prepared to roll again, when the hawks swooped down and took hold of the owl that sat beside him.

Grabbing the owl's hand, they held the dice to the sky.

"These are weighted," one declared.

"Definitely," the other replied.

As quickly as he had flown in, the owl was taken away, struggling and protesting as he went. The owl must have been fast, Epol thought, for even he had not seen the switch. Nervously, he picked his own dice up once more and spilled them out onto the table, earning himself a decent score, to which the crowds cheered.

***

The day continued in that manner until only three competitors remained: a crow, a raven, and Epol. The pigeon had no need to resort to the rhythm; his position had remained strong throughout. In a profound sort of way, a magnificent thought occurred to him. "I might actually win," he started thinking to himself. "Without rhythm rolling, without any form of cheating, I may actually have a chance."

During the fifth and sixth rounds, the crow placed the highest bets, leaving himself with only ten dice remaining. The raven fared better with fifteen in his bowl. Epol felt comfortable, sitting with seventeen. On the roll to decide who would declare their dice last, the crow scored the highest.

"Ten," said the raven, placing the dice on the table.

"Eleven," said Epol.

It seemed certain that the crow would lose. In the next round, the most Epol would have to face would be the raven, with five dice to his six. What he hoped for, though, was that the crow would attempt to make it to the end. He had ten dice; he would stand a reasonable chance if he used six or seven of them. But if he did, Epol would only need to roll against three or four in the final.

The crow's eyes sharpened. "Four," he declared, to the surprised gasps of the stadium. When the priest called out the number, even his face seemed to ask, '*have I heard that correctly?*' "Four," the crow repeated, counting them out. "The gods favour me," he said, turning to his competitors. "With four dice, I can roll up to twenty-four. That's enough to beat ten, or eleven. I'll show you the love that the gods have for me."

Epol attempted to multiply four by six with his fingers. *He's desperate,* he told himself, though he could not deny the passion with which his opponent had declared his intentions.

When the crowds silenced, the raven picked up his dice, cupped them in his hands, and shook them about. The dice crashed to the table. The eyes of those who could see scanned for any sixes. In the stands, if only for a moment, Epol thought that he saw Olanthun leaning forward.

Laid out on the table, the highest scoring die showed a four. The rest were ones, with the very occasional two. In total, the raven scored nineteen. A silence gripped the temple, followed by the chattering of the crowd, as if there was a collective agreement that the time had come to talk. A smile emerged at the very edge of the crow's beak.

Epol rolled next, receiving a score of forty-three. He was into the finals with six dice in his possession.

The crow was the last to roll, picking up his dice. Casually, he shook the wooden cubes, released them, and let them pour onto the table. Two fives, a six, and a four. The raven had a score of twenty. A wild cheering engulfed the temple as the priest called out the number. "I saw no foulness," cried the hawks, "he truly is blessed by the gods."

Even if the sharp eyes of the hawks had missed it, Epol caught what had happened. The subtle movements of the body, followed by an almost imperceptible twitching of the wings. Epol had seen a rhythm roll. In the first moment, he wanted to call to the hawks, and declare what he had witnessed. *But they'll want to know how I saw it,* he thought, *and then they might become suspicious of me. Besides, if they haven't seen it, they won't believe that I have. There's nothing for it, he's going to rhythm roll again, and so must I.*

"We are left with our final competitors" the priest called, silencing the temple. "For the final round, the players shall roll simultaneously."

Epol wished that he knew what that last word meant. By the way that the others looked at him, he supposed that he ought to be doing something. Reaching for the dice, he noticed a positive response. Copying the crow, Epol cupped the cubes. It was six against six, a fair match, for those unacquainted with the rhythm.

Slowly, Epol began to make the motions. An energy rose from his hips, travelling to his chest, falling down along his arms, his hands, and then, into the dice.

The eyes of the hawks were watching, but Epol no longer cared. He could get his rhythm past them. In that moment, there was nothing but him and the dice. All noise ceased, replaced by a blubbering murmur. For all that Epol knew, he could have been shaking the dice into the evening. Looking across the table, he saw the same within the crow.

Through grey and black feathers, the eyes of the two birds met.

'*Are you ready?*' the crow seemed to ask.

Epol gave a nod.

The hawks had not stopped him, his hands were ready to open. Hopefully, he would get a score above fifty; a high number, but within the realm of probability. The pigeon's claws would have opened, if it were not for the speck of white amongst the crowds.

The dove was shaking his head.

Across the table, Epol heard the falling of wooden cubes, yet none of them were rolling. The crow had placed his dice in front of him. Something cold wrapped around Epol's arm. A moment later, his wings began to sting. The three hawks had grabbed him.

"That's a rhythm roll," cried the one who held his arm.

Feebly, Epol's dice crashed onto the table. A whisper found its way into his ear.

"Come peacefully," they said.

The pigeon had never been in a real fight before. Against larger birds, his species could barely put up a scrap. Grabbing the dice from the table, Epol aimed for the hawk's eyes, hoping that his skill with the rhythm would ensure his accuracy. The predatory birds let out a series of screeches. From the brief glance that Epol thought to take, he saw that the hawk's heads had begun to bleed. Not all of the eyes had been hit, but the moment of confusion had loosed the hawk's talons enough for Epol to break free.

Several arrows flew at him; some found their way inside his wings. Guards had already massed by the door that he had been hoping to escape through. Reaching into his pocket, Epol pulled out his satellite dice. The hawks were right behind him. If he stopped, fumbled for even a moment, their talons would set on him again.

As he ran towards the guards, Epol began to flex his wrists. The metal dice seemed impossibly heavy now. With his final rhythm roll, Epol launched them forward.

Everything went dark after that.

***

"It was a good effort, 'specially towards the end," said Olanthun, between the iron bars. "But what did I tell you about rolling satellite dice?"

"To always place the 'one' in the flattest part of your claw," replied Epol, laying back down on his bed.

"Right. I admire the attempt, but that's not something you can be certain of whilst running."

There were thick bandages covering most of Epol's wings and legs. The golden feathers were gone, probably turned into jewellery.

From what the pigeon had heard, of the three satellite dice, only one had landed as it should have. On the others, the five and six had faced him, knocking him off his feet, allowing the hawks to catch up.

The sun was setting on the fifth day of Epol's imprisonment. Though it had taken the entire time, Olanthun had finally been let through. The pigeon was to be tried the following day.

When Epol asked how his sentence was to be carried out, the dove looked down at his feet. "They'll tell you tomorrow," he said, trying to avoid the topic.

"I'm sorry," said Epol, gazing up at the stone. There was nothing more that could be done.

"Don't feel bad about the loss," said Olanthun. "I saw the crow using the rhythm. More skill than I could ever dream of having, never seen anything like it."

Captivity had not been how Epol had imagined it. He had thought that it would be louder. He had thought he would peck against the bars, dig into the stone until his claws were whittled down to stumps, or shout that he was innocent until the guards came to silence him.

The pigeon had done nothing of the sort. Everything presented itself with a hitherto unknown veridicality. The tiny holes in the stone seemed so much larger, the dove's words came slower, weightier, filling the pigeon's head with magic. It was like being on anaesthetic: seeing that his body was broken but being unable to feel it. Time passed slower; yet tomorrow would arrive too soon. His wounds ached, but he had almost lost the care needed to acknowledge it.

The dove accepted the apology, and for a moment, Epol was contented. Until Olanthun was dragged away, the two birds spoke—not of anything that mattered, not to anybody else, but of things that they had done. When the sun finally set, Epol began to weep.

***

A clanging woke him at the break of the following morning. The guards who came to take him reassured him that it would be over by the end of the day, probably sometime before lunch.

Lunch had never been so appetising. The pigeon wondered what the men who carried him would eat: grainy bread, probably, porridge, if they were hungry. Grainy bread and porridge seemed the food that emperors ate.

With his legs in the state that they were, Epol had to be dragged along the chambers, the backs of his feet scraping along the stone. Movement hurt, stinging the places where the ball-bearings had torn through. The pigeon's mind began to wander, his eyesight blurring, the noises around him becoming a series of thuds within his skull. In a brief moment of lucidity, Epol spotted a hawk, his face bandaged, casting a scowl his way. The hawk approached one of the guards, though the words were far beyond the pigeon. His captors nodded and turned, pulling him backwards. A darkness overcame him, the pain in his wings and legs temporarily vanishing, as his mind swam about in the aether.

When his senses returned, Epol found himself in a small, perfectly square room. The same bandaged hawk sat across from him, facing him from behind a wooden desk. A series of leather straps bound Epol to a chair, keeping his wings firmly pressed against his back. It was tight and dug into his injuries, but of all the things to experience, Epol counted himself lucky to endure even that. The hawk placed a piece of parchment on the table, rotated it, then pushed it towards Epol. Looking down, the pigeon tried to recall the dove's teachings. He made a conscious effort to avoid the hawk's gaze, as he stared down at the first letter, imagining the sound it made.

"T," he whispered, followed by, "h."

"Pardon?" said the hawk.

Epol froze. "I… I'm sorry… I'm not very good with my letters. Could you…" he swallowed, disgusted that he had to ask the question. "Read it for me?"

A biting snicker came from across the room. "You must read it. This is a legally binding document which you must sign yourself. The signature must come from one who has fully understood the conditions and agrees with what is stated. The use of an intermediate in such affairs is strictly prohibited; I could make you sign any number of things, otherwise."

Epol gulped. The letters had turned to squiggles; black ink against parchment, the intention behind which was vague. Whenever Olanthun had asked him to read, he had told him to be slow, look at the words, then break them down into their letters. As he started on the first word, the pigeon could almost feel the dove leaning over him, whispering the sounds. The words were smaller than they had been in any of the books, but, upon closer inspection, no matter how fancifully they were scribbled, they were the same. There was a strange familiarity to them.

"I," he continued, "'s.' 'Th'-'is.' 'This,'" he said.

"By obligation, you may take as long as you require," said the hawk, sounding bored and rapping his claw against the desk. "If you cannot do it, feel free to say so, and we can carry on as planned, putting this silly development aside. Personally, after what you've put me through, I was hoping for the chance to take your head myself."

Epol wondered for a moment as to why the hawk had spoken. If he could read one word, then he could surely understand the rest. His eyes withdrew from his first cut into the document, his vision gliding over the entirety. The word "this" was unrecognisable amongst the solid block of letters. With a quick count, the pigeon found that there were one hundred and fifty lines of text.

"And the back," the hawk said, to Epol's despair. A part of him was tempted to simply write his name along the dotted line. *They're going to kill me anyway, what's the worst they can do?* he thought, picking up the quill and turning the document over. Olanthun had told him of several things worse than death. Flipping the paper back, Epol stretched out his claw, and placed it on the first letter next to the word "this."

***

It took the best part of three days for Epol to make it to the end. The hawk had come and gone, his frustration increasing with each visit. The pigeon had survived on half a cup of water and the crumbs of stale bread, requiring a guard to accompany him whenever he needed to relieve himself. Sleep was difficult when bound so tightly to an uncomfortable wooden chair, and, from what Epol could guess, he had only rested for two to three hours at a time. There were no windows, only a candle, which was replaced periodically.

By the end, Epol had shed several tears. In brief, the letter stated the following:

This is the confession of Olanthun of Ypther, for the crime of cheating in a tournament of the gods. Not only have I committed such a crime, but I have forced another to do it on my behalf. Epol of Ihass, who was previously thought to be acting of his own volition (Epol had needed to ask the meaning of that word), *was, in fact, nothing more than my unwilling servant.*

Through repeated threats, I forced the young man to enter and taught him the rudimentary skills needed for rhythm rolling. His deeds were borne from fear, as opposed to any greed or malice. In recent days, I have come to regret my actions. I take full responsibility for Epol's supposed crime.

In exchange for his release, I offer to place myself at the mercy of the gods. In addition, I am willing to share my knowledge of rhythm rolling with the priesthood, if it will ensure Epol's safety.

Beneath what Olanthun had written, Epol noticed another way of writing; a more organised arrangement of letters, with identical spacing between them.

I, Epol of Ihass, declare the statements of this document to be the truth, they said, followed by the dotted line.

"Can I see him?" asked Epol, upon the hawk's final visit.

"No," the hawk replied.

"Even if I sign?"

"Even if you sign. If you refuse to place your signature, in the eyes of the law, you shall remain the guilty party. Sign, and you shall be released immediately."

Epol sat in silence. For as long as he could remember, Olanthun had been there for him. Without the dove, he would have been nothing: a beggar, at best, though he likely would have starved. If the dove had walked away, the pigeon would have understood. It had been his choice to enter the tournament. His own misguided stupidity had led him here.

Yet, despite that, the dove was still willing to save him. Before Epol was a final opportunity to live—to learn to read, to write, to make something better of himself. Through a mixture of weariness, hunger, and pain, he allowed himself to break out into tears.

Taking the quill, he placed it on the paper, beginning with the *E*, not removing it until he brought it up for the *l*.

He wished he could have been braver, sitting in the chair, arms folded, refusing to allow his mentor and friend to take his place. He wished he could have done that.

The hawk snatched the papers, and called for Epol to be untied.

***

Later that afternoon, Epol was taken from the cells. Before he was allowed to leave, the guards demanded he wait. A small wooden box was brought to him, carried by the hawk, who practically threw it onto the floor. "All the prisoner's belongings. As a token reward for his knowledge of the rhythm, he was allowed to pass this along. Even *that* is too much, in my mind." The hawk growled, a noise which Epol had not imagined any avian was capable of.

"I'm sorry," said the pigeon, meekly, as the hawk stormed away. Of all the things to regret, throwing the dice at the hawks suddenly ranked amongst them.

Inside of the box was a set of ten quills, made from white feathers, perfectly groomed. A note was written in the base.

Keep at least two. Sell the rest. If you ever wanted to know why I spent so long combing my feathers… I had plans for ten more. Your inheritance once I had passed. Pulling them hurt. Do something worthwhile with your life. Carry on reading. Learn a skill. Get a job. Marry. Do not waste what you have been given.

Night had fallen when Epol finished reading the note. Taking the box under his wing, he limped his way from the prison. Looking back, he wondered if any of the lights were Olanthun. "I won't waste it," he yelled, hoping that the dove would hear. "I won't ever forget you," he whispered, taking another look at the quills.

***

White quills sold for a good price; better, if they had been well-kept. True to the letter, Epol kept two, using a portion of the money to buy them a finer box. When his legs could once again carry him, the pigeon left the city of Inar. Those whom he passed recognised him from the tournament and cast strange glances, some filled with wonder, others carrying contempt.

The pigeon settled after that. His wrists, having practised with the rhythm, adapted well to other tasks. Unbeknownst to him, he had an affinity for weaving. When travelling with Olanthun, he had been shown how to fix his clothes. Finding a craftsman who would take him as an apprentice was his priority during the year that followed the tournament. He settled in a small village, where he quickly became known for being an expert judge in any game involving dice. In his spare time, not caring for what others thought, he found a place in the local school.

Though it took until he was middle-aged, Epol finally learned to read and write. In celebration, on the day he left his schooling, he opened the box which held Olanthun's quills, and began to write. For the rest of his life, he wrote the dove's story, admitting to himself that he could not prevent embellishments of certain details. When he visited Olanthun's home, he sought out a game of dice. His eyes had dulled to the ways of rhythm rolling, but upon seeing it, the elderly pigeon's memories returned. Ypther had several practitioners skilled in the rhythm roll, to whom Epol handed Olanthun's story.

The dove's legend spread amongst the circles of the rhythm, held up as the ideal practitioner. When Epol left Ypther, he felt he had finally done the dove justice. He kept fond memories of him, placed the quills atop his mantle, and remembered why he lived whenever he glanced at them. Neither money nor fame could tempt him whilst he kept those feathers close.

This story was inspired by Dwale.

UNBALANCED SCALES

Bill Kieffer

F rosty Pine felt something warm and wet between his toes. He looked down and was appalled to see the crazy Fox girl who Bling-Bling had brought to the after-party gently sniffing at his feet.

She caught him looking at her and, totally misreading his pose, began to suckle the gray-white padding of his large claw-like feet. A Mammal, she made the common mistake of concentrating on his face... not taking into account his physical expression. She could not see his disgust.

"Bling-Bling!" he bellowed. Then switching to the street version of the Xeno-Vox, "Get this sloppy tongue bitch off me, you hear?"

Her ginger tufted ears zeroed in on him, and she looked up a little amused and a little confused. Frosty pulled his pillow over his head just as the lavender-headed Anole swooped into the bedroom. His dewlap blossomed into an amused grin as he plucked the naked Fox off Frosty. She gave a token protest, used to being manhandled to a certain extent, and Bling-Bling laughed, "You leave Dr. Ice alone, you hear now?"

Now the protesting began in earnest. Frosty had repeatedly explained over and over to the girl (was her name Ginger something?), that he wasn't Dr. Ice... he was just a fancy roadie, a high paid stage guy that just happened to also be a thin Bearded Dragon with the same coloring. He cursed BB for teasing the girl. His right foot shot up in the air trying to kick the drying saliva free.

Disgusted and unsuccessful, Frosty slowly climbed out of bed. He checked the sheets for damage. None, unless you counted the Fox hairs all over the bed. He shuddered with a full body grimace. Shedding every hour of every day, how the hell did Mammals get to be the dominant species?

Frosty staggered towards the showers. It was noon. He would have to have gotten up in the next hour or two, anyway.

In the bathroom, he locked the door. Not for any modesty; he'd hadn't even bothered to wrap the sheet around himself since his privates fit easily inside of him. Once, one of the groupies had tried to steal one of his Tzitzis for a souvenir. While he couldn't consider himself a proper Chromatic any longer, it would be devastating to lose any of his little badges. Using only his right hand, he unclasped his birth Tzitzit, a little two inch bit of green braided strings with a black triangle symbol in the middle, from one of the "beard" scales below his neck. He laid it on a hand towel on a sink as he recalled the name image of his mother. A misty forest, cool but welcoming. He felt her love as if she were in the room now. His father's name image came to him as a static charcoal drawing of a spartan evergreen. A lone pine empty of depth. A hermit's dwarf tree.

The other Tzitzis came off in the proper order, Frosty extending thoughts and images as he did so. He thanked god for his life and thanked Mosaic for giving them all a path. Paths, actually, but Mosaic had codified many observations and granted a uniformity across the many different Breeds and Species of Sentience. The Anthro and the Xeno, the Warm and the Cold, the educated and the uneducated, the rich and the poor. These observations cut across all these lines, so that in every thing one did, one could glorify god the creator or at least testify to his greatness.

Except, perhaps, with Rap Music.

Frosty checked himself. By taking off his badges (including the six stupid gold ones Kudzu insisted that he wear and really meant nothing), he had unburdened himself of the past. He got his knees on the bathmat and then bowed in the direction of Homeland. "Creator, the one and the many, hear my humble submission and plea that I should be guided by your hands. That the words of the Prophets should occupy my thoughts." He could not bring himself to wish his band and family the Creator's blessings.

"Forgive my weakness," he added, lamely.

Dr. Ice yelled into the bathroom, "Come on, Frosty, there other people out here, yo?"

Frosty ignored the singer and took the shower. Also keeping to tradition (except for strict conservation of water… they were a long way from the desserts of Homeland, after all!) he cleaned himself. He might have missed some fox hairs in his pocket, but his exterior was furless now, at least. He toweled off the way he'd seen other, non Chromatic Repts do. The traditional way just took too long, especially when one was soaking wet and not just damp. And it felt good.

He also spread moisturizer and sanitizer on his skin. Dry Rept skin could carry bacteria if one wasn't careful. While Kudzu insisted that the Plague Stories were merely Warm Propaganda, Frosty had seen the science. Plus, anything to prevent ashy scales. If he had a vanity, it would be the perfect green of his outer arms and legs. Most of the rest of him was snow white, tinting a mint green around his fingers, toes, and his orifices. Like Dr. Ice, he was a rare "sport" Bearded Dragon. Unlike the performer, Frosty thought vanity was a flaw.

His ablutions completed and the Tzitzis returned to his chest, Frosty stood, hating that he felt forced to praise God, hidden from the others. He was the only half decent Chromatic in the *The Large Scale Event*. He no longer felt the comfort in his lone dedication that he once might have.

Dr. Ice was gone, probably to use one of the suite's other bathrooms. Other musicians were beginning to wake up now. Large Scale Records had given their artists a choice for this tour. Each group could get their own room or all the performers could share a huge high class suite at each stop. The talent decided to go with the huge suite. It quickly became a party suite around the clock.

Frosty felt himself being sucked in little by little. That thing last night with the Fox. He thought they'd just snuggled, her warmth seeping into his limbs so sweetly during the night. It bothered him that he might sin so easily and not even wake up fully for it.

They'd be here for three more days. Then another opening of another show at the next city on the list.

Frosty stepped over a few sleeping bodies, naked but not exposed. He didn't bother lifting his tail. Mimic, the beat box Turtle with the disfigured plates, snored from beneath a pile of Rept ladies of various species. Soon, they would need to gather up their crap and begin their walk of shame. He let them all sleep for now.

This was their first tour as a label outside of New Netherlands, and Kudzu had made it very clear that he was in charge of the tour. Kudzu had the tour and production experience to make it work.

It was nice to meet people outside of the Green Band, but they were all so demanding and he never knew what they expected of him. He had hated leaving New Amsterdam, but his parents wanted him to keep an eye on Kudzu, his older and bigger brother.

Kudzu, you see, was insane; a steam roller in the shape of a Bearded Dragon. He was the most dynamic Rept that Frosty had ever seen. It was frustrating. What made it worse was that no matter what bad choices Kudzu made, everything worked out for him.

Everything.

He could hear Kudzu in the suite's dining room holding court as Saint George. As the coffee was poured, Frosty eavesdropped a little. Reporter. Typical Kudzu. Kudzu liked to see his name in print, even if it was just his stage name. He only heard two voices. Frosty sighed and poured a glass of ice water for Kudzu, who would talk until his voice was hoarse.

"No, it's not that I don't think that Reptiles are a superior race," Kudzu said provocatively to an Avi reporter who held out a cigarette pack sized recorder. "But we've been conquered by sheer numbers and we always will. And the more we allow ourselves to be a part of soul crushing religions, sects, and political parties, the worse it gets as a whole for the Cold Blooded."

Frosty did not see the PR person around. That was worrisome.

He meant to just discreetly leave the glass at Kudzu's side, but the huge green and brown Rept jumped up, his gold chains rattling. His gold plated ivory sun glasses were on his face, despite being indoors. They countered the mirrored coated sunglasses that sat atop the bill of his baseball cap. Kudzu's whimsy. His gold coated Tzitzis shimmered like a gaudy rash on his right shoulder. The man had no respect.

Kudzu was huge. He'd grown like the weed he'd chosen as a name, smothering and crushing all other life about him. If he stood up straight, he'd be nine feet tall. Having him bend over you so his head floated at eye level was somehow worse.

Then Kudzu smiled and his lower set of teeth were gold capped. His sharp upper teeth had been etched with the words 'ST. GEORGE' and then inlaid with gold. Frosty disguised his reaction by grabbing his brother's spare set of glasses, as if the glare from his brother's smile had been too much. He pushed the snoutbridge shut with a very non-emotive Dr. Ice hand gesture as Kudzu introduced him to Dave Sterling from

Force magazine. The colorless claw from the feathered arm felt like a Rept's but lighter, and disturbingly warm.

Unlike Kudzu, Dr. Ice moved to a purpose only. Once he sat, he stayed still, moving only to sip his coffee. From behind the glasses, Frosty studied the Avi reporter. Sterling was a Duck, or so the Rept thought from his bill and his exposed web feet. He wore a blue grand boubou, embroidered with gaudy golden ankhs. With this draping garment, he didn't need pants, but then most Avi did without these days anyway. As he sat back down, Sterling casually adjusted the back of the brocade blouse so his tail feathers would stay pointed in the right direction.

Kudos to him for letting them grow out, Frosty thought. *Shame he's not letting them out, but then nobody wants to see those silly short things curling all different ways.*

Before the reporter could ask the elusive Dr. Ice a question, Kudzu began his own manifesto again. Frosty maintained Dr. Ice's bored and cool persona, throughout the rambling diatribe. As Saint George, headliner of the Knights of Saint George, Kudzu spewed out a lot of verbal crap to see what would stick to the wall. Journalists got to pick and choose what sentences to use. If anything came back to bite Saint George in the tail, his brother would rightly claim the sentence was taken out of context.

The context, of course, being pure nonsense.

Frosty, as Dr. Ice, watched the Avi to see if he was onto his brother's game. Most of the best reporters were. They laughed at anyone who took Saint George seriously. He did have a growing fan base, and he was poised to be the first rap superstar from the East Coast in years. Interviews with the bedazzled Bearded Dragon sold issues.

Frosty allowed himself a small smile that the Avi might or might not notice. Everyone knew how to read Mammal expressions. One grew up watching them on television. Every blink, twitch, facial muscle tug, pretty much meant the same thing across every Mammal breed.

Avi and Repts were more subtle than that. Repts had hand gestures, head bobbing, blink series, color changes, and tail slapping. Some species even had dewlaps that expanded and colored, like Bling Bling. Avi had crests, eye shapes, head motions, and a few facial muscles that they could shape into a smile behind their beaks if they practiced.

Unlike the Avi where every bird-like gesture meant the same thing, each Rept breed had their own tells.

"The West Coast rappers," Kudzu said, grabbing Frosty's attention again, "they are all against us. And by us I mean myself and my Knights, Dr. Ice here, and the entire Large Scale Records talent stable. There's this basic philosophic attitude that they are unbending on, that only true rap can come out of places like Compton. But what they are forgetting is that hip hop began in the Bronx, that Grandmaster Coldblood brought it to The Harlem Opry, that Rept:DOA brought it to television. Poor money management is what done in the East Coast hip-hop labels. The scene didn't collapse; it didn't go away. Just the labels went bust. The East Coast Nightclubs are bigger than ever. That's why PumpDaddy, Street Dog, and I founded Large Scale with Dick Dagwood, a rap fan with all the musical talent of a cash register."

"They call him Ka-ching," Frosty interjected. Dagwood had been producing since his college days on Loon Beach Island. He had plenty of talent which included a nose for finding fresh talent, and he knew how to manage the money. They really owed their continued success to him, perhaps more so than their own talent. He was a good man, for a Bear.

Kudzu laughed at this outright lie with a hardy laugh. Sterling took this as his opening to ask Dr. Ice a question, "What's your view on the West Coast/East Coast feud?"

"I din't tink mush ov it you'know," Frosty mumbled, "But them depth threats... feh, they coward anyhoo. We got nuthin' to worry 'bout."

Kudzu made a dismissive gesture so obvious even a Mole couldn't miss it.

Sterling dove at the bait. "What death threats have you been getting?"

"No death threats," Kudzu said. "Just big talk from little men. Don't mean a thang." This was, of course, exactly the thing to say. "Any divisiveness among Repts serves no one but the Warm Blooded Power Structure. It is of the utmost importance that we remember that."

The interview continued on in a similar vein until Kudzu decided it was over. The Duck looked a little frustrated as they shook hands. Once he closed the door, Kudzu turned to Frosty and said, "You know, I think Dad has a dress like that."

Frosty made himself chuckle. "It's called a boubou. And it looks better on Father."

He wished he had the kind of relationship with his father where he could just simply call him and say, *I saw something that reminded me of you today.* He had no idea why all of his father's loving attention had gone to Kudzu.

***

"What happened with Jarvis Pettifogger?" Frosty folded his arms across his chest. "You promised you wouldn't give interviews if he wasn't here."

"I fired him," Kudzu spoke with disarming frankness. "He insisted that we downplay the East Coast/West Coast Feud."

Frosty's head bobbled with annoyance and his tail slapped the ground trice. "But that's exactly what you did!"

Kudzu smiled his ivory and gold smile. "Did I?" he asked, heading back for the kitchen where breakfast for the posse was finally getting under way. "Did I really?" Then he laughed and glanced back. "Go put some clothes on, my brother."

Grumbling, Frosty did as he was told.

***

Frosty found himself in the stairwell of the hotel. A cell phone in hand and a guilty shadow hovering behind him. He didn't recognize whose phone it was, but it was probably one of the rentals LSR got for them. Luckily, he knew his parents' number by heart. It rang and then his mother's sweet voice. Her "greeting" seemed a little strained.

"Mom, it's Frosty. Is everything OK?" Then belatedly, he responded, in kind, "All things come from the creator."

Her voice warmed up, "Oh, everything is fine. We've just been getting the strangest calls. Your father says we might have to get an unlisted number. *Your brother said he'd pay for it. Imagine that.* Him volunteering for the extra expense and all that."

Frugality. The Green Band wasn't known for spending more than they had to. Just another reason this Saint George business must be eating his father alive. The excess of Kudzu's rise to stardom flew against everything their father ever taught them.

"What type of calls?"

"Oh, the press," his mother relented as if he'd kinked her tail. "They asked how we felt about someone declaring war on Singe. I really had no idea who they were talking about. It's your brother. He got a new name, again. Again! You can tell him he can make his own Tzitzis this time. I saw what he did to the others. Such a waste."

Lamely, he said, "Chromatics change their names all the time, Mother."

"No," she said sharply. "No, we express our name-image differently. As we grow older and wiser, we reinterpret ourselves. Furthermore, your brother has made it quite clear he no longer follows Mosaic as prophet and guide by taking the name of a mass murderer. And this attempt to create a Gold band... pure mockery. Your father can barely roll out his sajada at the mosque without hearing disgruntled murmuring."

Frosty looked at the cell phone in disbelief.

"I didn't know Chromatics could be rude during worship," he said honestly. He rather liked the idea. It made his people seem human.

"Well, mostly it is the young men. The new ones. Your father ignores them."

Frosty took the plunge there. "Is father there? I saw something that reminded me of him today. A boubou. This one was blue, not green, but the embroidery was identical."

Suddenly, the line went dead and a strange dial tone came out of the cell phone.

Dr. Ice was in the stairwell then and took a judgmental stance. They were almost mirror images of each other, except for their obvious attitudes. Frosty could see the singer was mad at him, but he didn't know why. He felt sure he should know. Dr. Ice held out his hand for the phone, and then suddenly Frosty remembered whose phone this was.

Sheepishly, he let Dr. Ice have the phone.

***

Shedding Skin Studio was an unimpressive concrete block. Paint peeled off the building in foot long swatches, almost as if to match its name.

To this, Kudzu had dragged a million dollars worth of equipment and talent. This time, it was not just Frosty that cast doubtful looks. The big Rept smiled and cajoled and got the crew and talent moving.

Kudzu began cursing at the front door. It took only a few moments for everyone to realize the giant Bearded Dragon was stymied by an old fashioned set of "man doors."

And that he was stuck.

Before there could be too much ribbing, a young Gecko with an absurd penciled-on mustache appeared. He expertly extracted the large Rept. He introduced himself as Felix Climber. Climber explained the building's history, first as a Speakeasy and then as a recording studio. The narrow doorway controlled traffic and helped bar entry.

The Gecko pointed out two small black and white signs. The bigger sign said, 'Warm Entry,' and the smaller one below that said, 'Cold Entrance,' with an arrow pointing to the right.

"Follow me," the Gecko said, turning to the right. He kept up a steady patter worthy of a professional tour guide down a well worn path around the building to a barn door. Above the door were several signs in different styles declaring this the 'Reptile Entrance.' "As these signs came down in the 50s, my grandfather made it a point to nail them up here. Each one, a little victory for Rept Rights."

Inside, the walls were floor to ceiling knotted pine paneling. Black and white pictures of various obscure Rept performers were mounted in an oddly low line across the walls. On the tables were various pieces of equipment. "This looks a museum," Frosty said, still dubious.

"Yes, actually, we are legally listed as a museum. It keeps the doors open," Climber said, "but we are still a fully functional studio."

If fully functional counted as 8-track analog recording deck, then Climber was absolutely correct. Climber got to working out the details right away. A baby grand took up much of studio one, and the equipment was sensitive enough to pick up a strange echo on the test, which pleased and annoyed the sound techs. Rearranging the mikes and baffles seemed to do the trick.

Jonny Heartland arrived, looking gray and dusty. He wore black shorts and a white, heated hoodie, although it was a warm summer day. Both were well broken in, almost too worn for wearing. Frosty gave Kudzu a dubious look, and for the first time, Kudzu gave him an equally dubious double blink back.

With the sound close enough for Jazz, Kudzu began the introductions and the assignments. Everyone supposedly already knew who'd be singing what and had had time to listen to the original versions of their songs. They all knew there'd be no time for retakes.

The old one was pleasant and modest. He was almost overwhelmed by the attention. His teeth were like Indian corn, some white, some brown, but most of them yellow. Only the white ones seemed sharp; the 'Gator either had dentures, or he still had teeth growing in.

Heartland was especially interested in meeting Mimic. The Box Turtle was almost as famous as Saint George, and his fame was certainly longer lasting. It turned out that Heartland had been in the same protest mob when the cops let loose the water cannons, disfiguring Mimic.

The Turtle awkwardly avoided talking about his martyrdom and seemed to embarrass the 'Gator a bit.

"Well, the reason I brought it up is, I've been watching your career, young man… and it seems to me you started as something of a novelty act. But you transcended that. The sounds you make with your body… well, son, they remind me of my friend Lefty Terrapin. He went off to 'the Last Great War' and came back with two legs and an arm missing."

"Land mine?" Mimic asked dutifully.

"No, he got tangled up in some barb wire. Ripped himself up something good, did Lefty, and of course, everything's infected by the time they get him to a M.A.S.H. Unit. Fool surgeon, overworked, cut off the arm and legs, thinking they'd grow back."

Several of the Repts flinched, including Mimic. Few Repts could grow a portion of their tail back. It was a common Warm misconception. Almost every Rept family had a sad story involving that myth.

Mimic's plastron deformities had made him what he was today. The Turtle, at least, had been able to remake himself, if not reshape himself.

"Now, we promised Lefty a place in the ensemble if he made it back alive… so we made him this." The alligator took out a tie box. It's a little weird, but I thought you might be able to use it in your act."

Mimic pulled out some vealgut strings strung between two odd pieces of wood and metal. He raised an eyebrow at the Alligator. "Lefty was a bass player. If you clip this on the bottom of your… um, vent there… " Mimic just looked dumbly at Heartland, so the old 'Gator just clipped it onto Mimic himself with a clinical mechanical air. "And this part here…" The top piece was obviously a compact headstock with tuning pegs and clipped to the plastron, pushing the Turtle's head back. Mimic took this with remarkable good humor tinged with a little embarrassment.

"Mr. Climber," the old Jazz artist called out, "Do you have a two inch pickup I could borrow?"

Climber scurried away as Frosty and Kudzu exchanged looks. Heartland hadn't signed anything yet; all the agreements were just verbal. Over one hundred hours of studio time would be wasted if the 'Gator didn't sign.

"Now…" The 'Gator looked at Mimic as if the Turtle had just come back into the room. "Now, do you know how to play a bass?"

"Ummm, no," Mimic said trying to tilt his head to a comfortable position.

"No worries, Lefty hadn't a clue either but he learned. At least, you won't need your tongue for the cord changes." He clapped Mimic on the back as Climber handed him a small piece of wood roughly shaped like a toddler's brass knuckles. "Yes, this should do."

The 'Gator stuck the wood between the strings and the Turtle's hard stomach. He tuned it 90 degrees, and the strings hummed a bit as they slid into notches. Mimic made a little noise himself.

"Now, I'd tune you myself, but my arms are too short to go around you."

"Dr. Ice can play bass." Kudzu volunteered and Frosty rolled his eyes. They were burning valuable studio time and Heartland had already made it clear he would not, could not travel out of state. Before he could say anything, Dr. Ice stepped forward and put his arms around Mimic from behind.

***

Dr. Ice tuned the gimmick on Mimic's chest, quick and easy. Mimic stood stiffly, trouper that he was, with his arms out straight and his fingers twitching with embarrassment.

Then Dr. Ice just held him for a moment from behind. He ran his hands up the Turtle's plastron from below the vent, then up and around the holes and protrusions that marked his orange-brown front. There were some giggles as Mimic looked victimized. He moved his head awkwardly, and Dr. Ice blew on his neck. The living beatbox stiffened, eyes wide, at the unexpected sensation. "I'm going to play you now," Dr. Ice said in a velvet whisper and the Turtle's eyes went wider still.

He didn't exactly look terrified.

Kudzu counted down, 3-2-1… Dr. Ice led the way, playing "From Brooklyn to The Bayou" as he remembered it. Mimic surrendered to Dr. Ice, straightening and relaxing as the Bearded Dragon directed.

Mimic squirmed within the green and white embrace. He pressed a hand below his vent as the sensation came close to overwhelming him. Then, finally, he could stand it no more. He looked up at the ceiling and opened his beak. Instead of a scream, he released a series of shrill wheezing sounds and then the screech of a turn-table scratch.

As Dr. Ice continued to pluck at him, producing sensations and music directly into his brain, Mimic sung out a living percussion beat of harmony.

Heartland had pushed the stool away from the piano and spread his legs in a catcher's stance almost two feet from the keyboard. His body bent forward in an arc until the chin of his toothy mouth rested on the baby grand. His arms were too short to play it any other way. Then he froze with a Gator's stone, hard, unblinking stillness.

Dr. Ice looked cool and steady while Mimic trembled with excitement. Dr. Ice reached forward and slapped his palms on the Turtles chest like he was playing bongo drums. Mimic sucked in a breath before spitting out bongo noises.

Then Jonny Heartland threw in the piano, wild and kinetic, in synch with Dr. Ice and Mimic but with a slight counterpoint that suggested this piece was not at all tamed. From the tip of his thick serrated tail to the end of his flat snout, the Alligator was in motion, swaying in time to the music.

Jaws dropped on the other side of the glass.

The 'Gator was not done with his surprises yet. When he opened his mouth to sing, it wasn't the smooth, longing, velvet voice of his younger days. A strong, steady, but harsh voice of bitterness escaped his body, turning the love song sour. He didn't sing in Aenglish, but in the noble, slang-free Xeno-Vox of his youth. Click Clack, they'd called it in the Age of Jazz.

And when the song called for Brooklyn, he sang out Harlem, instead.

The song ended at 3 minutes and 14 seconds. Mimic kept saying, "Oh my stars, oh my stars," and he had to cover his crotch to keep from embarrassing himself. Dr. Ice patted the Turtle's head. Together, they then helped Heartland outside to cool off.

***

"Got it on the one take," Frosty said when he was done listening to the playback.

Kudzu nodded, a big shiny smile on his face. "Good thing, too. We couldn't get Mimic to do that again."

"That old man is just about ready to go again." Frosty could barely believe it. "You did good with this plan of yours, Singe."

"Oh, you heard about that, did you?"

Frosty nodded. "Mom let it slip."

"I'm going to spell it with a dollar sign instead of an 'S.'"

Frosty rolled his eyes. "Of course, you are." He raised a bowl of cold chai in a salute. "Here's to $inge."

His brother raised his mineral water and clinked their bowls. "Here's to Dr. Ice, for getting this thang going on a high note."

Frosty hesitated for a moment and then shrugged. It wasn't like he expected much personal recognition but then Dr. Ice had really knocked it out of the park.

The cold chai felt surprisingly good on his rough throat.

The next recording was with Lady Pink. It was a duet, *One House/ Two Rules,* his first single. They both crooned it, but as father and daughter instead of husband and wife. Heartland's velvet was still there, just a little thinner. A little sadder. In the end, even Lady Pink sounded sad and brokenhearted to be declaring her independence.

Once again, the vocals were completed on the first take. The second take was for the piano only. Listening to the playback on his head set, Heartland rolled out the notes smoothly and professionally. He hit the keys without looking at them, his body arched again so his short arms could reach all of the ivory without trouble.

The next five sets continued as wonderfully as the first two.

Mimic eventually came out of the water closet and did his assigned set with Heartland. It was a gimmick comedy piece that the 'Gator had done with the USO Orchestra near the end of the Last Great War.

The last session was the hardest. Bling Bling just hadn't picked up on all the excitement that the old Jazz musician had created. In fact, he seemed a little surly and resentful about the whole thing.

After a dozen takes, Frosty pulled him out of the recording booth and into Climber's office. "What gives?"

"Boo, this is taking all day. It was supposed to be just two hours here. A little vanity project just to get the old guy to sign over his catalog."

"Do you not hear how good he is? This isn't about your little legal CYT any more. This old man is going to net us legit awards and press."

"Everyone lifts tracks, Boo."

"Not half a album's worth." Kudzu poked the Anole in his chest. "Get back out there and sing Cold Charlene like your life depended on it."

"Does it have to be Cold Charlene? It's going to sound a lot like the first track on the album."

Kudzu rolled his eyes. "Well, big surprise there."

Frosty thumped his tail thoughtfully. "Can you play an instrument? Besides the tambourine and rainstick?"

The lavender head shook out a negative.

"OK, well, then be a good sport today and we'll figure it out tomorrow."

By then, Heartland had figured out that BB's heart wasn't in it. He played Cold Charlene as a half slow blues song. Suddenly, BB's apathetic, robotic droning turned sorrowful, regretful, pathetic, and guilty without the Anole tumbling onto the fact that this might be the best song of the day.

Frosty turned to Kudzu. There was the obscene golden smile again. Another miracle turn around. Everyone stood the second the red light was off. The small building exploded with applause.

Exhausted and spent, Heartland declined to grab dinner with them. He signed the contracts and Kudzu gave him a much bigger check than he had expected. The 'Gator looked ancient now and he barely had the energy to put the check in his wallet. Humbled and embarrassed, Jonny Heartland asked for a ride. He'd missed the last bus home.

***

"That could be us one day," Frosty said to all of them on the way to the club Lady Pink had recommended.

Kudzu smiled again. "Not me, I plan to die young and leave a pretty corpse."

Frosty chuckled. "We should probably knock you off soon, then, before you get any uglier."

Everyone laughed, except the driver and BB. He sat there sullen and annoyed. Finally, he appealed to Kudzu. "Big guy, we aren't really going to use that last song, are we? I know you feel sorry for the old river log, but… it just doesn't fit the rest of the songs we did."

Kudzu stared back at young rapper. He wished he could see his brother's coloring just then. With only the passing streetlights, the depth of Kudzu's mood was hidden from him. The Anole went to say more, but Kudzu cut him off. "Let's wait and see what we got at the big mixing table when we get back to New Amsterdam." His voice reminded them all that he was the boss.

At the club, they entered with a lot of bravado and splash, calling more attention to themselves. The packed scene bellowed, "Saint George!" Drinks were held high in salute. The house DJ played Kudzu's most controversial song, *The Cold War*. The patrons were all Repts. They danced with their tails in the air. Their arms pumping in time with the beat.

Frosty was still too much a Chromatic to be comfortable in a scene like this, but he mixed a little. He was more interested in the scene than making the scene. Frosty allowed himself to fade into the background almost instantly.

He watched Kudzu smiling, showing off his gilded smile and chest to a throng of female Repts gathered about him several feet thick. What were these whores to him? Or more importantly, what were these women to their families?

He watched Mimic for awhile. The Box Turtle had limited himself to merely two women, as he often did. He'd had fame most of his life. He caught Frosty watching him and his eyes went deep. He looked exposed, like a deer recognizing a hunter for what he was. Almost shy.

Frosty gave him a smile and raised his mineral water to him. Mimic smiled back.

Frosty caught sight of Bling Bling. The Anole's mood seemed to have improved. He'd narrowed in on Dr. Ice and together they sneaked out a side door, casually.

***

Frosty Pine awoke as warm hands and a wet tongue fondled his right foot. Incredulous, the slim Bearded Dragon sat up. Sweet Ginger gave him another suggestive look from between his own claws. He shook her off, careful not to poke her eyes out. "Bling-Bling!" he bellowed as he wiped the saliva off his feet. BB did not swoop in immediately, so he bellowed again. Another Anole, the sea green Knight Moves, showed up with one of tour security. By this time, the fox was kissing and fondling his crest. "Bounce this Bitch," he ordered the guard.

The guard scooped her up much the way Bling Bling had yesterday morning. She laughed like a mad woman and waved good bye. *At least, she was enjoying the ride.*

Frosty turned to Knight, "Bling Bling has got to stop bringing these crazy whores in here."

The singer shrugged. "Actually, we thought she was with you. Besides, BB didn't make it back last night."

Frosty stopped cleaning himself and looked at the bed sheet, surprised at the amount of hairs on it. On the whole bed, actually. He felt incredibly uneasy, as if there was something he should know or do.

Realizing that the back-up singer was waiting for a response, and uncertain of the question, Frosty gave a halfhearted, "Hmph."

That gold-digging Fox with the foot fixation must have slipped me something. Deep in thought, he almost didn't hear Knight say that he'd tried calling Bling-Bling's cell phone.

"That damned fool is just pissed that he's not getting his own way with his first release," Frosty said dismissively. "He'll be back with an agent by lunch, you'll see."

The Anole went to say more but seemed suddenly indecisive, so Frosty saved him the trouble by staggering off to take a shower.

He was not, they knew, a morning person.

He went through his morning ablutions in the locked privacy of the bathroom, taking the now familiar shortcuts and trying not to think about his hang-over. He didn't drink. *But people do have blackouts when they drink,* he thought as he re-attached his little badges. *Sometimes.*

A terrible guilt swept up through him and his tail began thumping on the floor so hard it hurt. "No," he whispered. "This is just free-floating anxiety. Not guilt. Not guilt."

When he looked in the mirror, he noticed that his Tzitzis were all out of order. He barely remembered putting them on. "OK," he told the mirror. "Now, I feel a little guilty." He took them all off and put them back on in the proper order.

"I'm losing myself," he told his reflection. "This isn't my life. I'm not supposed to be here."

"You got that right," a voice from beyond the door growled. "Other people need to take a dump, you know."

Dr. Ice. Frosty closed his eyes and gathered himself.

***

Frosty sat with Kudzu at the breakfast table, close to 2pm. They were eating beetle filled crepes. Everything tasted off. "So, where'd you go last night?" Kudzu asked with a full mouth. "You missed a great photo op."

"I don't like photo ops," Frosty said sourly. The coffee tasted tinny. His mood wasn't improving. "What happened?"

"I 'accidentally' ran into EnFamous Raptor and his West Coast posse last night. Threats were made in front of a wall of paparazzi. It was glorious." Kudzu's head bobbed in a silent and satisfied chuckle. "The cops showed up, all of them Warm and fuzzy, and the crowd just went wild. They literally chased the cops away. The club owner took care of them, convinced him we were being dramatic and that no one had gotten hurt. They went away."

"Just as you planned," Frosty half accused.

"I could not have planned it better," Kudzu agreed and denied at the same time. "How did you not notice this?"

Frosty did not want to admit anything. Had it been date rape? He didn't feel victimized. In fact, he felt vaguely guilty. "I was getting quite drunk."

Kudzu did a double-take and then smiled. Not a Saint George golden smile, but the more subtle Rept smile; open mouthed slightly, no teeth showing, and a loosening of his facial muscles around his eyes. Much as Mimic had smiled at him last night. "Frosty..." Then his brother stopped, and forgot whatever he was going to say. He seemed to look deep into Frosty's soul and then glanced about to make sure they were alone. "I know this tour's been hard on you, and I really do want you to loosen up and have fun. But I still want you to be yourself. We don't need another me."

Another me.

"I just worry. I don't want you to end up like Heartland. You just live on the edge and burn through cash. We've seen so many record labels fail... and I worry." It was an awfully lame lie, but at the same time, it felt like something that needed to be said.

"I've done a lot of growing up since becoming St. George. I've learned a lot about business hands-on when we were getting Large Scale off the ground. I've got investments. I even have a will. It all goes to you. That's why I wanted you along."

Frosty nodded, willing his tail not to slap down. Their parents had wanted him to go with Kudzu. Obviously, his big brother hadn't vetoed the idea, but that was a long way from wanting him along.

"You just can't get by on simply singing, anymore." Kudzu said wisely.

Frosty nodded his white head knowingly. He should be relieved that Kudzu had another serious side to him. Yet, the thought that his brother had been showing him only one of his sides—until now—bothered him.

"Speaking about Heartland, I spoke with Pumpdaddy and Dagwood last night. You know how we were going to just do a one off label with his stuff so we can justify BB's lifting it?" Kudzu paused to let Frosty nod painfully. "We're going to make it a prestige, reprint label. Rescue the old music and make a buck or two. Do some serious music." Kudzu gave another natural smile, not showing off his grill.

Frosty smiled back, although it was a little forced. "Did you tell BB, yet?"

Kudzu's pose hid all expression. "Not that he has any say in the matter, but no. I haven't seen him this morning."

"Knight said he didn't come back last night."

Kudzu waved a dismissive green hand. It looked oddly naked without his gold rings. "He vanished when the cops showed up. Knowing him, he probably had more weed on him than our lawyers would have liked. And who knows what else."

Frosty sipped at his coffee and the tinniness hadn't gone away. "Ugh, can you pass me the sugar?" He asked, reaching out to his brother for it.

Kudzu froze in the act of passing the sugar bowl, startled. He stared at Frosty's hand and then glared at Frosty's face. Confused, Frosty looked at his hand, half expecting to find it blood-splattered and covered in gore.

Instead, it was a nice clean hand with a white palm, tinting green on the edges and finger tips. It was his hand, each claw tip scrubbed and filed to safe round tips. Nothing monstrous at all about his hand, reaching out for the sugar bowl.

Then he realized that this was his left hand, and he snatched it back, ashamed. He hissed, trying not to curse, confounding his sins. His right hand pressed the offending hand against his own chest, careful not to let either hand touch his badges. Frosty looked at his brother, horrified, trying to form an apology.

Kudzu burst out laughing. He pushed the sugar bowl across the table, using a fork to get it right next to Frosty's coffee cup. "I'm telling Daddy!" he mocked and then, in their father's voice, "I don't blame you, son. I blame those people you've been hanging out with."

**

New Herp Community Theatre was one of those landmark buildings that, in order to survive the late Twentieth Century, had to be converted into something else. In this case, the old Herp Community Schools building. Most of the building had become a community center while the elementary wing had become a museum of Xenostudies, Rept History.

The high school and lower level auditoriums had been combined to create one decent sized venue, but it was also the smallest venue on the tour. There was no room for official merchandise in the lobby; part of the orchestra pit had to be dedicated to the sound boards. Gaffers made a track event of taping down wires. The DJs, each with their own machines and layouts, had to organize a tight ballet of switch-outs with the roustabouts for each of their acts.

Bling Bling was still among the missing.

Taking the day to rehearse a full show had been a good decision in the cramped space. Frosty was in his glory organizing things and making practical decisions with the roadies. Everything began to take shape.

The merchandising was moved to the cafeteria where the reception would be held for the local VIPs and the press. A white backdrop with the Large Scale Event logo and each group's logo checkering was hung, so everyone with a backstage pass or prestige could have their photo taken and posted to LifeBook and Stumbler. Frosty ignored the occasional looks of irritation. It was just better to get things out of the way.

After Dr. Ice's sound check, a rough hand grabbed his and pulled him into the shadows. He'd have yelled at anyone else but Mimic. The rude words died in his throat as his eyes moved to the craters in the Turtle's chest.

"I've been looking for you," The beat box said softly in the Xeno-Vox, adding a small layer of privacy to their talk. He didn't let go of Frosty's hand.

"You've seen me," Frosty said, staring at the hand. Watching Mimic's thumb stroke the back of his right hand softly. His evergreen skin against Mimic's brown, black, and orange scales. "You seen me lots of times." He kept it all Aenglish.

"Not since the recording session," Mimic said keeping it quiet, but with an intensity. "Not... alone."

Confused, he looked up into Mimic's eyes. They were big and wide, full of some unknown need. Frosty was vaguely aware that it had something to do with Mimic grasping his hand the way he was. "I... I don't know what you want me to say."

Mimic licked his beak and swallowed hard. His eyes crinkled into what passed for a hopeful smile. "You don't have to say anything..." Mimic then reached out with both hands and wrapped his dark, stubby fingers around Frosty's already captured hand and pulled gently. "I know you're shy, off stage."

The session with Heartland, Mimic, and Dr. Ice flashed into his mind with lightning brightness. The Turtle squirming against the other green and white Rept. Dr. Ice blowing on Mimic's neck, strumming the steel strings tied to the plate covering the Turtle's loins. The rapture they shared as they made wonderful music together.

Frosty leapt back and pulled his hands out from the coarse grubby hands. "You're confused, Mimic. I'm not… I'm not interested in you like that."

"But," Mimic started towards him, an arm outstretched.

Frosty slapped the hand away. "I'm not! I'm not! I'm not!" His heart pounded in his chest and he tried to control his voice. He took a deep breathe and looked the Turtle straight in the eyes. "Don't be gay, ok? Just don't! You got played like an instrument. That's it, nothing more. OK, Mimic?"

Frosty was dizzy with his breath gong in and out so fast. He watched something break in Mimic's eyes. The Turtle's eyes seemed to get shiny and then blink rapidly. "My name… is Michael."

"Whatever, Michael. Don't go gay on me."

Mimic began hissing softly. His body shook with spasms as he turned around and tried to walk away with some dignity. He didn't look back as Dr. Ice stepped up next to Frosty.

Frosty was confused. He should know what those sounds Mimic was making meant, but—as before—his mind could not and would not make the leap. Dr. Ice patted him on the back and took off the dark glasses.

"Thanks for taking one for the team, Frosty," the rapper said, placing a white and green arm over Frosty's back. He shuddered, strangely unnerved.

"I don't understand what's happening," Frosty complained, his dizziness increasing.

"Well, we have to save your reputation. Mimic's going to tell someone you're gay, sooner or later." Dr. Ice pulled him forward. "So, we need to establish your bona fides. Get it, Boner fides?"

Frosty tried to shake the performer loose. "Not really, no."

"Good, you keep playing the good boy. You're good at that." Dr. Ice laughed at some private joke as they entered the part of the school still set aside as classrooms. Mannequin Rept children sat at desks in various stages of attention. Different classrooms represented different decades. "I'm going to introduce you to someone who'll make you feel better."

Then, suddenly, the Vixen was there with them. She didn't seem so gross and slutty then. He felt his loins stirring, He tried to back away. Dr. Ice pushed him forward. "I know what you're thinking. You'll like this. You always do. And, yes, we are using her. But she's just a Fox. Not even the Aesopists think much of Foxes. Look at her… she wants to be used. Just say her name and she's yours."

Frosty stepped forward, a roaring in his ears. "Sweet Ginger Hunt," he whispered, not even knowing that he knew her full name. Her warm body embraced him and he felt himself unfolding into that blessed, loving warmth.

***

Frosty woke groggily to the ringing of his cell phone. Cold floor. Warm legs wrapped around his tail. He was trapped beneath a furry weight. *Oh, the Fox girl...* much more pleasant to be waking up first. They were in a dark room, with street light pouring in. Giant creepy dolls looking away from them politely. He felt rested, for a change, not at all cranky. It took forever to move, however, and when the ringing stopped, he slid back down on the cold floor to sleep.

A moment later, the ringing started again. "Hello?"

"Frosty Pine? This is Sgt. Wilkins."

"Yes? Hello." Frosty tried to sound sober and alert. "I'm sorry, Officer. Was I speeding?" Frosty started laughing. "I'm sorry, you just woke me up."

"Mr. Pine, I'm sorry to inform you but there's been a shooting. Your brother's been shot."

"Blessed creation! Is he all right?" Frosty felt himself sobering up a little.

"He's in serious condition, but his type's hard to kill. He's at Herp Community Hospital in the ICU. You should be here."

"Yes... officer, I'm in no shape to drive and my phone's about to die."

"Give me your location and I'll send you a cab."

The dummies blurred and the street lights threw rainbows at him in the dark. He felt the icy path of death before him. He remembered the drugs. "Maybe... you should send an ambulance; I'm not feeling well... at all."

"Mr. Pine?"

"I'm in the creepy classroom at the Community Center having a little private party..." And then he fell back asleep. In a moment, Sweet Ginger pulled them together and wrapped him in her furry limbs. The police found them a half hour later.

***

Frosty had a few bad moments… before they pumped his stomach, the hospital put him through what they called "procedures," throwbacks to a time of the segregated schools, intended to sanitize Rept skin of any diseases they might unknowingly carry. He woke up twice to burning skin and eyes and once to something stinging and cold poking into his cloaca. He did not remember this much, except in nightmares over the next few days.

He slept for almost a whole day before he was awake enough to talk to the police. They were polite, having gotten most of the story from Sweet Ginger.

There weren't there for him, but for Kudzu aka Saint George, soon to be also known as $inge. They were Warm cops, who didn't understand at first that he and Kudzu were brothers. They thought they were separate species, which was somewhat understandable. Kudzu might as well be, as he was at the extreme size range of Bearded Dragons while Pine was slim with a very flat crest—what most Mammals would describe as "normal" sized.

After he assured them that he hadn't tried to kill himself—that he'd only taken, he thought, enough to help him relax—they laid out the facts of Kudzu's shooting as they knew it.

***

Frosty did not have to explain what had happened to his parents when they arrived. Before his stomach pumping was even over, Dick Dagwood had gone over to his parents' house and briefed them. Showman that he was, the Black Bear had them give a quick press conference asking for prayers for both of their sons. Their father only said that, "Mosaic would tell us that forgiveness is the second most visible proof of God, second only to Love. It is often as hard to find as Love, but it is less fleeting," before asking everyone to join them in prayer.

Dagwood got them on his private jet right after that. One of the roadies had picked them up at the airport in a tail friendly van. They rushed in to see Frosty once the police left.

They gasped, for he knew he looked terrible. His skin was so irritated that it almost felt warm. In an hour or so, it would start shedding, and he wished he had slept long enough to be spared that. He hadn't shed his skin since his teens.

His mother wailed from the doorway and then tried to cover her mouth, as if to take it back. His father, unreadable other than exhausted, just looked on over the shoulder of his saffron colored wife. His full body evergreen coloring matched Frosty's limbs. Both of his parents were dressed in heavy somber green layers and a bit too much for the summer heat. Typical Chromatics, he thought, willing to repeatedly dress and undress rather than get heated suits.

Still, he felt some comfort in their normalness. He felt more comfort in seeing Repts of his size and shape, other than Dr. Ice. He felt glad of their attention.

"Hello," he said, not feeling up to the traditional greeting. He felt uncomfortable, stuck on his back, every ridge on his back being pushed the wrong way. He was stuck like this until a nurse came to take the probes and stuff out of his more delicate orifices.

He didn't realize how tired he was until his mother hugged him. He was dizzy from the effort of hugging her back. He gave her a soft peck. She straightened up and dabbed at her eyes with a green moist cloth. *A misty forest, cool but welcoming.* He could smell the forest scent on her.

His eyes went to his father, standing as upright as any Bearded Dragon could. *A hermit's dwarf pine, drawn in simple, yet bold strokes on rice paper.* As if with great effort, his father reached out and placed his right hand on Frosty's right knee. The older Pine turned away, as if momentarily shy.

His father turned back to face his son. "Both my sons injured the same day severely... you have *both* frightened us completely out of our lives," Father said softly. "Please, promise that you will not do it again."

To Frosty, it was more than he expected, less than he had hoped for. "Once," he said in charcoal flavored words. He paused to savor the iron even as he had to cough to clear his breath. "Once was enough." Then, Frosty was rather surprised to feel himself falling back into the numbing darkness. The last thing he heard was the voice of another visitor. Dr. Ice, maybe? Dagwood? He wasn't sure, but he was grateful for the rescue all the same.

***

It was a whole day before Frosty was able to drag his tail out of the hospital bed. Getting that tail into a wheelchair proved demeaning and impractical. He forced the nurse to let him put on some street clothes, if only because Dr. Ice threatened to sue. There were already threats because his clothing and his Tzitzis had vanished somewhere between the emergency room and his room, not to mention the scorched Earth routine with his skin.

They found him a pair of baggy pants that he couldn't pull past his tail, a belt that was able to pull over his tail, and a large hockey shirt with the hospital's logo on it. He hated it, so maybe he'd start a fashion trend.

After getting his own discharge papers, Frosty made his way to his brother's room. The elevators were car-sized boxes with plenty of tail room. Dr. Ice met him there. "Shouldn't you be on tour, Dr. Ice?"

"People expect me to be here," Dr. Ice answered from behind his mirrored sunglasses. "Besides, I think you need me."

Frosty nodded gratefully, his eyes closing in gratitude. He stepped over to give the performer a hug, but stumbled and missed, nearly falling against the wall over the button. "Whoa, easy there, Scal'eee. Those drugs messed up your coordination. That's how come the po'lee know that you didn't shoot your brother…"

The doors opened and Frosty gingerly stepped in, clutching the handrail. He kicked his own tail into the car when the doors began to close. His coordination was definitely off. "They think BB did it."

"I imagine so," Dr. Ice said, staring at Frosty's reflection. "He did start out as a roadie; he was the go-fer on every tour. We all asked him for everything from drugs to bitches; he got the connections. Opportunity. Saint George was going to delay, if not cancel, his record deal. Motive."

"But he didn't do it," Frosty complained softly.

Dr. Ice shrugged in green jogging suit-covered shoulders. "If they ever find him, they can ask him."

Frosty was unsettled by the response, but then the doors opened. They had to get out before others could get in.

Frosty was checking room numbers and almost missed seeing his father entering the stairwell, heading upstairs.

"Guess, it's almost that time," Dr. Ice said derisively, echoing Frosty's private thoughts. Afternoon prayers.

A small part of him wanted to join his father. It'd been awhile since he'd prayed outside. Longer since he prayed with his father. Plus, sunlight was good for a healing Rept, better than the UV lights they used here. Before he could decide, however, Dr. Ice barged into Kudzu's room. Knowing his mother might mistake the rapper for him, as so many did, Frosty leapt forward.

His mother looked up from her prayers and started. "My, what an entrance you make." She made no move to cover her skin. Dr. Ice wore all greens, so to her mind, he must be family, too, or at least in the same Green Band. She simply continued to ritualistically re-attach the Tzitzis to her chest. Frosty doubted Dr. Ice was anything like a Chromatic.

When she was finished, he helped her up and rolled up her prayer mat for her. She was a traditional Chromatic woman of the Green Band. Deferential to the men of her family, protective of her children, and very, very emotive. Growing up, he sometimes had been so embarrassed by her. Still, he never doubted her love for an instant. She'd never flashed dark colors at him or said a cruel word to him. He did not escape her sharp tongue, but time had often proven her right.

His father had been the opposite in most ways. Frosty used to think it was because his father had been born into the Black Band. They were known to be insular and liked to be seen as mysterious. That proved to be true, in its way, but spending time with young Black friends, Frosty had learned that around family alone, they laughed more, smiled more, and opened their hearths and pantry to any Black Banded brother in need of food or shelter.

Frosty never saw that in his father.

Except with his brother, Kudzu, named after his surges of wild growth spurts. Wild Kudzu. Giant Kudzu. Unstoppable Kudzu. His father ran himself ragged keeping up with the little monster. Pure puny Frosty, only "normal" sized, got pushed aside too often.

He got his mother, and Kudzu got their father. That wouldn't have been bad, except his mother loved Kudzu, too. In a different way, but she did. She told him that his father loved him, too, in a different way. He tried to believe her.

Frosty cast a glance at his brother. The large man was on his right side, back to the door. His tail was supported by another gurney, strapped to keep it from moving off. It was large and thick enough to pull him out of bed, should it fall. A quick tug on the gurney proved that it, in turn, was braced to the bed in such a way that it couldn't be turned over.

Thought of everything, did the hospital.

He crossed over to the front of the bed, to face his brother. Kudzu's eyes were closed. His face was smoother than he expected. Not dry and flaking from the abrasive and corrosive cleansing the hospital had imposed on Frosty and countless other Repts. "He got around the procedures?" he asked, aloud, his voice flat, his outrage gagged in his throat.

"Don't be angry, Frosty," their mother said, seeing through him. "You were an overdose," she said, choked up to admit this aloud. "They didn't know where you'd been and what you'd done... what hellhole you'd crawled out of... And the creature that was all over you... unhealthy little whore... I'd have scrubbed you with boric acid myself, if you'd come into my home."

"I'm sorry, mother," he said meekly. "I just wanted to relax... We've been so busy."

"I warned you both your lifestyles would catch up with you," she said, her fury mostly spent but her duty not yet complete. "I never imagined, the Creator would cast your fates upon you both the same night."

Kudzu opened his eyes. Dull with pain pills, his eyes still wide with shock and fear. His lips moved, pleading... but Frosty could not make sense of the words.

***

Frosty found his father on the roof, rolling up his sajada.

Uninvited, Dr. Ice mumbled, "Ah, good timing." The roof was empty but for the three of them on a helipad that doubled as an open air worship center. The Xristios Bible, the Fables of Aesop, the Wisdom of Mosiac, and the books of a dozen smaller religions were stocked in an alcove, behind glass doors to keep them dry. Frosty flinched when he heard Dr. Ice spitting on them.

Well, you couldn't say he was a hypocrite.

Frosty didn't want to excuse or explain the rap artist. He was just glad he had a friend to back him, to help him confront his father's neglect.

His father had worn shades of green again. He glanced at his skinnier son and his older, evergreen face split into a wide, open mouth smile. "You look like a teenager again," he said warmly.

The tone threw Frosty off. Then he realized how goofy he must look. He peeled about three inches of dead, papery skin off his face and let it go in the breeze. "It burns worse now than it ever did. I can't believe they still do this to Repts."

"They forget we are people," his father said, turning back to the cityscape to the west. "We defy what the Warm Bloods know of life. Their words for us mean 'alien' and 'death'. From Cat to Dog to Rhino to Mouse, they all have almost the same silhouettes. From Anoles to Phrynosoma, we all not only look different but express emotions differently."

"You forgot the birds," Frosty said, almost teasingly. With Dr. Ice within hearing range, Frosty made sure he put a little edge into his voice.

"Avi," Frosty's father chided. "Actually, science is coming around to our way of thinking. The Avians all evolved from the great dinosaurs." He turned to face his two-tone son, ignoring Dr. Ice. Maybe he had heard the other Rept spitting after all. "There was a time we could talk about science and nature for hours."

Frosty was floored. "I think you misremember. We only talked like that when Kudzu was in camp."

His father's expressions withdrew. Part of Frosty was satisfied to have hurt him in some small way.

"Hush," Dr. Ice whispered in his ear. He squeezed his shoulder, and Frosty felt braced by the green and white hand on his green and white shoulder. "Let him do all the work this time."

Frosty felt Dr. Ice's steel slip into his body. It, somehow, changed the shape of the silence between him and his father, sharpening the edges. The silence had a weight it never had before. To his wonder, his father seemed to feel it, too. A swirl of gray unease dappled the older Rept's cheeks.

His father looked at him sideways, thinking, as he leaned a little on the railing. The old man's eyes were level with Frosty's. A sigh escaped the green Dragon and he turned to face Frosty more directly. It was a relaxed pose, but merely a pose.

"Did my records help you, any?" His father asked. Then, to Frosty's confused expression, he explained, "Heartland's recordings?"

Frosty was confused and did not understand what his father was talking about. Dr. Ice once again stepped in. "Oh, yes, very inspirational. We got to meet him and got some great music out of that. One of our singers is even doing a tribute album."

Frosty was mildly surprised. He'd been aware of his father's love of Heartland. It was one of the reasons he had exposed Bling Bling to it. No, wait, Frosty chided himself for getting confused. So, even as his father beat around the bush, speaking with Dr. Ice, Frosty forced himself to get this over with.

He might never be so alone with his father again.

"None of that is important," Frosty huffed after Dr. Ice had explained his session with the old 'Gator. "I want to ask you why you like Kudzu more than me!" He poked his father in his chest. "Why don't you love me as much?"

"I love you, Frosty," His father's pose expressed humble surprise. "You're so very much like me.... and so like my brothers... I thought you understood."

"Oh, spare me," Frosty snapped. "I already heard this story. That Kudzu needed you more. I might have bought it as a child, but it's been so long." Frosty felt his chest tighten as his tail slapped so hard and fast, he felt scales popping off against the concrete. He imagined his whole face and crest were turning black as rage consumed him. "He made a mockery of our religion and you let him! You let him!"

"I let him?" His father seemed actually shocked. "You went along to keep an eye on him. You weren't supposed to follow him into blasphemy!"

The accusation slapped at Frosty so hard, he reeled. His ears rang and he felt that he was at the bottom of a well. Because there was truth in it; he had slipped and failed, but it was so hard to live a life of devotion amidst the glamour and hedonism. His mother had reached out for him repeatedly but not his father. His father could have saved him, instead... he'd sent records.

No, wait.... Frosty tried to grab onto a fleeting thought. Dr. Ice had brought the records to Bling Bling. He saw it now. The Anole's wedge shaped lavender head sliding up and down slowly in pleasure. The ivory thumb scraping his finger claws with the old scratchy jazz. Dr. Ice was pleased, also, but for different reasons. Why?

At the end of the tunnel, he could hear the rapper speaking urgently, steadily, almost maliciously. Frosty clawed his way back to the real world. He found it impossible to work at the mystery of the jazz records and force his will into his own body and make it behave at the same time. Oh, Mosaic do not ever let me try drugs again, he begged.

The Prophet remained silent, but Frosty could hear his father arguing back with someone. The young Rept realized that Dr. Ice had been sticking up for him. He was grateful but more appalled that they hadn't noticed how he'd almost passed out.

He cut off his father's words with an aggravated scream, not stopping his head bobbing and tail slapping. Frosty was not usually so dramatic, but he felt like he was drowning in sensations suddenly. "Stop it. Stop it! Shut up! Shut up!" He screamed at his father, his friend, and his wild emotions. "Just be quiet!"

He batted away Dr. Ice and flailed about with his claws as they too betrayed him. His breath came fast and Frosty grabbed at it, forcing it to slow steadily. In a moment, he reduced it to a series of slow, soft hisses.

"Frost... please don't cry," his father said.

"I'm not crying," he growled defensively. Frosty took a deep breath, aware that he'd just had a tantrum that had left him dizzy and feeling almost unreal.

"Just tell me. We're all grown up now. I can't tell you why I need to know. I just... do. I just do." Frosty cut off another hiss before it could escape. "Please... it's driving me crazy. I have to know."

His father nodded yes, but turned away, looking at the cityscape. Something Frosty said had frightened him.

"You never met your grandmother, my mother that is," the older Dragon began after a moment, his voice soft but otherwise expressionless.

"She died before I was hatched," Frosty said, if only to keep the conversation going. A trickle of excitement ran up his spine at the thought that this was hurting his father. The truth was finally going to come out.

"No," his father said, after a moment of hard silence. "That was a lie. She died when you were three or four, locked away in an asylum. She killed my clutch. Every one of them."

Frosty didn't have to do the math to know that wasn't exactly true. "Wasn't Uncle Night from your clutch?"

A short nod, or a head bobbing flinch, answered him. "Silent Night... that was another lie. He killed himself. He became unwell, haunted. He refused to become..." He sighed and made an effort to swallow. "He stayed in the Black Band when I became Green. Everyone knew about our mother there. He felt safer there than I did... until, at the very end, he no longer felt safe anywhere... and he tried to teach himself to fly on wings of madness."

Frosty was stunned and he turned to look out at the city. For a long time, he could process only the thought that his parents had lied about these things. That his mother's sharp tongue had never betrayed these secrets was impossible to accept. "Does Mother know?"

His father's head bobbed and flinched again. "That insanity runs in our family? Yes, she knows."

For a moment, Frosty was impressed at his mother's willpower but then the simple factual horror of his father's admission struck him with hurricane force.

Insanity runs in our family.

The railing steadied Frosty as he tried to figure out why the idea of insanity should bother him so instantly, so deeply. It wasn't as if he thought he was crazy.

"She killed my father, too." His father gave an open mouthed sigh, as if he had just let go of a heavy box he'd been carrying for a long time. "No, not your grandfather, Blaka. He raised us as if we were his own. We both had nightmares growing up, but we'd forgotten… He helped us pick out our names, loved us. I can't imagine a better father, but we still had nightmares."

Frosty gripped the railing, trembling, wondering if he'd pushed himself too hard. He forced his head to stop bobbing; Frosty refused to give his father the satisfaction. "I don't see what that has to do with me."

"The reason I spent so much time and attention on Kudzu…" The man's thick green tail slapped the concrete. His father's tail kept twitching as if it wanted to hit the floor a few more times. Mustard colored eyes darted towards his son looking for help. "Do you remember what happened when you were about three years old?"

Over the ringing in his ears, Frosty shook his head no. His straightforward father had picked the worst time to begin beating around the bush.

"Your mother had another clutch. Four eggs, maybe a little above normal in size. It left her surprisingly weak and your Grandfather Blaka ordered a lot of bed rest. Of course, I still had to work." His father looked over the city and seemed to gather his thoughts.

"One day, I got home, and I found your mother crying in the nursery. She had to separate the two of you. You were only three and you'd tried to… beat Kudzu off the eggs. He was almost five and already a big boy. The eggs had been sliced open… and if they hadn't been fertile eggs, it would have different. But…"

This struck a cord deep within Frosty, yet he could not concentrate with the roaring in his ears to make sense of it. His father gave a little hissing hiccup and the sound produced an image from the two tone Rept's past. *Kudzu grabbing at him. A knife flashing between them.* Frosty glanced about for Dr. Ice, as a witness. Dr. Ice seemed to have wandered away.

"Kudzu denied it, of course. But he wouldn't tell us what happened. You were only three and hadn't even grown into your tail yet. So, it was either Kudzu or your mother. And if she had wanted to kill the clutch, she'd have just turned off the incubator while I was at work."

"You thought Kudzu had destroyed those eggs?" Frosty muttered, unable to fit that in with the preferential way his big brother had been treated over the years.

Daddy nodded his head in agreement while the rest of his body was as still as a charcoal etching. "I knew. Looking at him, I realized how much he looked like my mother. I blamed myself for not seeing it before. Anyway, Blaka came over as soon as I called him. He gave your mother something. Then he gave Kudzu something and talked to him, but your brother wouldn't let himself be knocked out. Blaka gave him three times the dosage for his age and weight before he keeled over."

He shuddered and took out a pack of cigarettes, inhaling them like a nosegay. "Blaka ruled your mother out, but he couldn't rule out Kudzu. Not that your grandfather was that kind of doctor, but he knew my mother, had visited her in the asylum. She'd given 'cold blooded' a bad name."

Frosty's father shook his head NO in a very universal head gesture, very warm blooded. It almost seemed exaggerated and he realized that his father was hiding his physical reaction to whatever he was recalling. The cigarettes went back into his tail pack with an obvious effort.

"Blaka said that he could tell that Kudzu was hiding something. He absolutely knew that what he'd done was wrong, yet, the same time, he'd been unable to stop… himself. Blaka said that he needed attention: monitoring and socialization. So, I concentrated on his development. I tried not to show you any favoritism… because… well, jealousy was my mother's trigger. Jealousy and attention."

Images spun in Frosty's head. Kudzu's face, spinning and spinning, lips moving. Begging. Pleading. Promising… none of it made sense. Mimic's unreadable face spun off behind him. Bling Bling speaking, slurring, and then falling back into the darkness distracted him. He clung to the railing and the building swayed in the wind, blowing all the images through his mind.

Dr. Ice was there to steady him… he saw the handle, then, of the gun that the missing Anole had gotten him, sticking out of the waistband of Dr. Ice's pants. He wanted to reach for it, throw it away, but he could not let go of the railing for fear he'd fall over.

"I didn't send Kudzu away to summer camp as some sort of reward. Sometimes, he went because his counselors said he couldn't come back to school without sessions. Sometimes, he went to camp simply so I could spend some time alone with you."

Frosty sobbed a hiss and then hiccupped fiercely. His father was about to tell him what he wanted to hear all this time, but now he was in a panic. He no longer trusted Dr. Ice. He no longer trusted himself.

Insanity runs in the family.

It made sense. Kudzu was insane. It explained all his choices. Crazy people could be so surprisingly intelligent. They had to be, in order to fool themselves. It was the only thing that made sense.

Still, Frosty found himself afraid to embrace the idea. Not here, alone on a rooftop with his father. Not with his head spinning and his tail twitching so much he was afraid of losing his balance.

Suddenly, Dr. Ice pushed him towards his father. "Boo-hoo, there's nothing wrong with Kudzu. Except that he's in the way," the singer snapped at him. "What are you supposed to do, pity him?"

Stumbling, Frosty grabbed his father by his green shirt. "What, so I'm supposed to do what? Pity him? Feel bad for him," he shouted in their father's face. "He's not suffering from insanity! He's enjoying it!" He shook his father for emphasis and their tails both slapped down, telegraphing anger and frustration.

"He's suffering, Frosty. He's suffering now." The paternal voice was firm. "Maybe it's my fault that lead to Kudzu's Takfir. Enough about him. Enough! My son, we are here for you, too. I'm sorry if you felt slighted. Know that you are surrounded by love. You've seen me nurse your mother when she was bedridden, that too is love. Letting you and Kudzu pursue this dream and take the risks you've taken, that's love too... know that no matter how many miles you may travel from us, you are still surrounded by love. Our love, the creator's love, you even have Kudzu's love... but you must also have self-love."

Frosty growled at his father, his voice carrying a high pitched edge he'd never heard in his voice before. "What are you talking about?" It almost sounded like panic.

"Son." His father grabbed his arm, almost if he could see how close Frosty was to escaping. "The drugs, that furry Fox girl, and those songs you've been singing... that all comes from self loathing."

Frosty blinked hard and tried to tell his father that he wasn't a singer. That he was confusing him with Kudzu.

Or maybe with Dr. Ice?

"The Prophet Mosaic says—," His father began, but was cut off by Dr. Ice's barking, caustic laughter.

Frosty fell back into darkness.

Anxiety fluttered through him. Self-loathing. Yes, he had some of that. He was falling off the path a bit further every day. The drinking, the sex, and allowing himself to be a part of the whole industry that discouraged modesty. How had Kudzu tricked him into following this path of destruction?

This path of self-destruction?

And how was it that he should end up—so consistently end up—with a Fox BB had brought to the party for Dr. Ice. The truth swam by in the chaotic darkness he floundered in. Frosty could not grab it.

Frosty forced himself to the surface only to find Dr. Ice screaming at his father. Dr. Ice defended the trash-talking lyrics and Rept pride that the Chromatic Pillars of Righteousness seemed to stand against. Frosty felt the singer's rage as if it was his own. It was so true that the modesty preached by Mosiac made it easy for the Warms to control them; made them Meek when most Repts were stronger than most Mammals.

"We don't need Gods," Dr. Ice screamed.

"Our ancestors were Gods!" Frosty screamed into his father's face. "We could be Dinosaurs again!"

"Son," his father said, a satisfying trace of fear on his face as Frosty's peeling snout pushed into it, much too close. "You're not making sense. Is this withdrawal? Is that what this is?"

Frosty wanted to say that he didn't do drugs. But confusing images were coming to him now. Sweet Ginger on top, her moist heat burning into his loins. The violence of their awkward sex, enhanced by little blue pills at $25 a pop. Their minds burning together on lines of quality coke at $100 a line. The feel of her sweat, painting him cool and hot in turns. They sang his songs together and when Bling Bling dragged her away, she did not look all too surprised at being manhandled.

Because she wasn't surprised, idiot. It was all a part of the plan.

Frosty faltered in his diatribe.

"Actually," Dr. Ice grumbled, "I don't love nobody but myself. Sweet Ginger loves me, not you, brother from another mother. Not you."

She does what I tell her.

His father shook him something hard and Frosty felt his body spring back, he spun and roared, tail straight out, shoulders full forward, balanced on the tipping point. Ready for some serious slash and spin, he had a curiously crystal thought.

I am a killer.

Frosty had hidden it from others for years, because he thought that he had to. He'd even hidden it from himself.

Sneaking off to speak with Bling Bling, convincing him to listen to Heartland, subtly encouraging the Anole to lift tracks, pushing, and then hinting that he—and only he—could help smooth things over with the boss man. Encouraging BB that Heartland needed to die for the record deal to go through.

The expression on Bling Bling's body when Dr. Ice shot him in the face popped into his head.

Frosty flinched at the image. That hadn't been part of the plan. It was senseless. Dr. Ice had decided to improvise.

He spun then, slapping at his own face, trying to focus. His tail scraped in a circle painfully about him. Dr. Ice slashed at his face, drawing blood. "You're not a killer, Frosty," Dr. Ice told him. "You're just a shallow facade of a Rept's calm heart. You are nothing."

Frosty batted him away. The drugs in his system… that was it, or part of it. Sweet Ginger couldn't get them from Bling Bling's trusted source. No one could find BB.

He was always going to die, anyway. Time table just moved up and Heartland was too much the asset now for Large Scale to get rid of. When it had come time to kill Kudzu, Bling Bling would have turned him in.

He spun around looking for Dr. Ice and saw no one but his father. His father who was born a Sport, an evergreen skin, normal for so many other Repts but not for a Bearded Dragon.

"Frosty," his father said, "Stay calm, it's just a reaction of some sort."

Illusions kept shattering in his head. The playing of the damaged Turtle. He'd seen it. He listened to it.

On playback.

He forced himself to recall it all. Dr. Ice strumming the strings and breathing on Mimic's neck, to stiffen him… no, to straighten him. Enjoying the discomfort of the shelled boy. His groin rubbing against the Turtle's smooth backside and feeling Mimic surrender finally to him.

Frosty stood fully upright, shocked by the erotic sensations he was feeling, by the images… none of that was right.

Insanity runs in our family…

He could feel the ancient steel strings sting his fingers as they bounced off his claws, but he forced himself not to think about it. History will right itself; it always does. It always has, before.

He found Dr. Ice standing quietly near the books. They didn't look alike now. Dr. Ice was a little skinny, freakish Fox Todd. Green and white fur, a Warm Sport who'd run away from home. Frosty had been enthralled by the idea of having a secret friend. So, he had taken him to an abandoned building.

"Do you remember the place I made for you, Dr. Ice? You wanted to be a rock star, remember? To be on Cold Train?" Dr. Ice stared back from black, empty sockets. Of course, he did, of course.

You showed me warmth and love. Frosty thought, smiling with the titling of his head. *You wanted to know what being cold blooded was like, so I showed you. It hurt, being cold, but I held you still and you got colder and colder still. You changed and you never shared that warmth with me again.*

"I showed you other things," Dr. Ice said, the fur falling from his body. Maggots crawling from his eyes. His stomach bloating. "Until the cops came and took away my body."

"You've been with me ever since." Frosty nodded. "I'm sorry…"

"It only hurt a little while," Dr. Ice said. "Never mind about that. We have to finish this while he's still worried that you're going to hurt yourself."

No, wait! This is important. Frosty lashed out again, dizzy with anger. *You are surrounded by love.*

"Where is it?" he screamed in Xeno-Vox, in Click Clack, and in the blood that raced painfully through his body. "Where is all this love?"

He closed his eyes and concentrated on his name-image. It always centered him before.

Dr. Ice shook him. "No, you'll never get this moment again. You ruined Kudzu's turn. You won't ruin this for me. For us."

His father was there when he forced his eyes open. Dr. Ice pushed him into his father and Frosty wailed, overwhelmed by fear. He clutched at his father, who slowly, tenderly put his arms around his sobbing child.

"No, I just can't stop hiccupping," Frosty explained softly. He never cried. You can't cry for losing something you never had. And Love was the only thing worth crying over.

You are surrounded by love.

He could hear the chanting, the playing, as he swaggered across the stage. There he was—a hip-hopping, cold blooded demon sucking up their love. He posed as a gangster, and they ate it up. He posed as a killer, and they ate it all up.

Dr. Ice knew love. He commanded it. Love obeyed his will. Dr. Ice, he saw now, as he had seen a hundred times before, as he had forgotten a hundred times before... Dr. Ice was Death.

Death is love.

Frosty began to suspect there was more wrong with him than he had first thought.

He felt nothing in his father's embrace. Love is warmth, but they were both so cold. He now understood why.

Frosty did not deserve love. Not when he snuck away from his drugged out Vixen alibi and waited in an alley for Saint George to come by. A publicity stunt. It was the only way to get his entourage to hang back.

Frosty knew his big brother had already trained them all. Not talking increased their street cred. Not talking meant they wouldn't have to lie. Kudzu had planned everything.

Except for a disguised lunatic that popped out a hundred yards before where the "thugs" were meant to be. Where they still stood hiding, in fact, when Dr. Ice leapt forward, aiming the handgun into the spot, just under the skull, where one bullet could be instantly fatal. Kudzu's thick tail had moved at the last second. Dr. Ice nearly emptied the clip, instead, into less vulnerable spots.

Dr. Ice fled, down a preplanned path to the hospital, hid the gun in the little used rooftop bookshelf before Frosty had to sneak back into the old school and take just enough pills to look like he'd been out cold all night. A story the local police seemed to believe.

At least until Kudzu wakes up and tells them that we shot him.

Frosty burrowed closer into his father, appalled to find no warmth, no love, just a weird reflection of his own desperation.

"Hold him still, so I can get the sweet spot. Do it all in one shot," Dr. Ice said and slipped the gun out from his waist band. Frosty squeezed his father tighter and wished he was built like his monstrous brother. Yet, his father did not resist; he pulled Frosty in closer, in fact.

Frosty remembered the first time. The eggs were leathery and hard to cut, but a sharp knife and a running start, he'd been able to ruin them all. He didn't think of it as killing. But they were a threat, that's all. They'd frightened him. He was the baby and that made him king of the family in a way. When they hatched, he'd be dethroned.

So, he ruined them. They weren't even people yet. It wasn't killing, not really, just satisfying.

Then Kudzu was there, pulling him away. He was all strength and limbs. Roaring with horror, Kudzu tried to get the knife away without hurting his little brother. He was too delicate; Frosty managed to break loose.

They ran in and around furniture. Things were knocked over. The family's tea table shattered into splinters, sending a rainbow of tiles across the living-room cushions. Frosty heard his mother yelling, but did not run to her. He knew his mother and Kudzu would just team-up against him. It wasn't fair!

Eventually, Kudzu cornered him and got the knife away from him. Frosty was spent, unable to defend himself further. A part of him was almost grateful that it was over.

Then the strangest thing happened. Kudzu began to cry.

His big brother picked him up and began chanting, "I won't tell, I won't tell." The killing stroke never came. Instead, Kudzu stroked him and swayed gently. It was the first taste he'd ever had of his brother's insanity.

Frosty pushed and screamed against his brother. Only a little older, Kudzu was almost half the size of their mother, who finally made it out of her sickbed. His mother screamed seeing Kudzu clutching the smaller child in the midst of such destruction.

He clutched at his father, ripping clothes with his claws. His father did not complain. Did not resist. Instead, their father seemed to be chanting.

A strange kind of clarity settled on his brain as Dr. Ice moved the gun to the back of their father's head. His mind was making one final connection before he stepped off into a black pit of insanity. One last chance.

He was back in Kudzu's hospital room, while their mother said she had told them so, without saying it.

Kudzu opening his eyes. Dull with pain and medication, his eyes still wet and wide with shock and fear. His lips moving, pleading... he heard the words now, he could not deny it.

"I won't tell," Kudzu had whispered again. "I won't tell."

There was fear in that voice, yes, but there was also forgiveness.

"Stop this right now!" Dr. Ice yelled at him, the gun poised to enter the green man's head and scramble his brains like it was some leathery old egg. "You'll be famous. Dr. Ice will be known as the coldest Cold Blood Rapper of them all!"

Frosty felt his claws raking his father's back. But it was only his left claw squeezing and unsqueezing. His right claw was heavy and only one finger seemed ready to squeeze. He concentrated on opening both hands wide.

Neither hand paid him any mind.

"Daddy," Frosty said. It was a hard thing to say. He felt as if he was breaking apart, nothing but a head and some twitchy arms left. His father moved his right eye to meet Frosty's left. His face was flushed by a grey concern with blotches of orange. Frosty's throat was too full of hiccupping that came wide but slow, up from hidden depths. No other words would come.

As he struggled both with his voice and with his hands, his father reached up and touched a green finger pad under his son's left eye. Moisture magically streaked across his scales. "You get your tears from your mother. She's always cried for me; it's not a weakness. It's love. It's life."

Frosty shook his head no as Dr. Ice railed at him. *We have to do this. I'm using my right hand. It's cool. He doesn't love you.*

"Daddy," he said, his throat raw and thick, "How many people are here on the roof?"

His father blinked and looked about with birdlike movements. "Just us. Me and you."

"And Dr. Ice?"

His father reached up with both hands and gently wiped tears from both of Frosty's eyes. The smears of moisture felt unreal to him. "You're Doctor Ice. But you don't have to be."

Frosty forced both his hands open as Dr. Ice wrestled for the gun. "Daddy," Frosty pleaded, "I need help." His right hand would not open. He felt nothing in it. Yet, he knew everything was in it.

"There are doctors downstairs," his father said soothingly.

"Daddy, no... I mean... he... he wants to kill you."

His father went still. "Kudzu?" he asked, only half surprised.

Dr. Ice roared with laughter and Frosty wailed. Frosty was not sure what came out of his throat, but he was finally able to get his hands open.

The gun clattered loudly to the cement pad.

"Daddy, I've been a bad boy."

The world of Aligare is steeped in legends; Linden is the keeper of one of them—Castaway village's sacred shrine tree.

Reason

A Story of Aligare

Heidi C. Vlach

L inden sat down before the shrine tree, crossed her legs, and turned her thoughts greenward in prayer. Fellow aemets broke the air behind her in the Middling circle: a neighbour family was supplying Linden's sister Chard with news of the harvest, while they picked the Middling circle's green gifts. Linden held a seed of hope that the neighbours would leave soon: prayer wouldn't calm her worries for long.

They only wanted four cupfuls of elderberries, they said, to flavour their apple mull. Those five fellowkind were standing a long stone's throw away, close enough to show clear in Linden's airsense: slim, boxy bodyshapes bent toward the sheltering bushes; antennae wagging over neat-braided hair; hook-nailed hands gentle in combing berries from the Middling circle's graced branches. Their smallest child—recently out of the broodery—clung timid to her mother's pant leg, watching and learning.

Finally, the smooth-skinned berries piled high enough in the basket. The neighbours bade farewell to Chard.

"Oh, we nearly neglected to ask! How fares our shrine tree?" one asked.

As though its browning leaves and weak new growth didn't show enough truth. Linden's heart twisted. She kept allegedly praying, while Chard shrugged and gave some neutral lack of an answer.

The neighbours' faces shifted, their smiles tight. Great Verdana would provide, they said. And after last glances aimed toward Linden, they left, vanishing into the distant air.

***

And then Linden and Chard were alone in the goddess's green presence. Chard approached, boots scuffing on the leaf-carpeted soil. She took up her trowel—from where she had left it, partway through the aerating of a pile of plant trimmings—and she came to stand at Linden's side.

"They can see the trouble as plain as we can. They're just polite enough not to pry at the matter."

Guilt cinched tighter at Linden's throat. "We've all still got hope. May I dig?"

"I can do it? If you'd prefer."

Linden shook her head. She was the Middling circle groundskeeper, by virtue of Castaway village believing it so; it was her burden to know that the shrine tree was dying.

She took the trowel and scooped a hole into existence in the leafy ground, while Chard breathed over her head. Her breath and Linden's gusted through the cool, damp air, a temperature and humidity standing bold in their airsense like a streak of ocher paint would stand before their eyes.

Dampness was their first sign that nothing had improved. Digging down an arm's length only confirmed the matter: pooled water shone ominous under a slimy tree root.

"Gods," Linden murmured. "It wasn't this high an eightday ago. No tree can live like this, Chard. The elderbushes, maybe, and the small-growth, but no deep-rooted tree."

Chard hummed, like a single note of a dirge. "I don't think there's any more we can do. No one's dug clay from this patch of lakeside for well over a month. I watched the farmers lending their hands yesterday—they spent plenty of plantcasting, grew those water reeds thicker than a nurl's pelt. They said the mat of roots underneath should be plenty thirsty. But if that doesn't hold back enough water …"

She waved an open hand at the bushes and the sparse-leafed saplings that ringed the Middling circle. Beyond them was the lake, ringed with a haze of moving reed stems. The lake was far bigger than any mortal being and the same water that nourished reeds would smother the village shrine tree. Linden, her family, and all the other aemet folk in the village would mourn the loss of a fellow, a wise and ancient sister in plantcasting's life-giving magic.

Staring down into the hole, Linden gathered her fear into a tight ball and forced it away. Fear would not help right now. Studious thought, however, might. She leaned down and took a root into her pea-green palm, probing with one of her thumbnails.

"Well," she said. She turned to look up at her sister, squinting into the tree-broken daybright. "Unless great Okeos personally takes back his waters, we'll need another plan. Are there any legends we haven't considered?"

Chard smiled, her handsome face mirthless. Her antennae bobbed with a gust of wind and she wrapped both arms around herself, as though her homespun tunic and her insectoid shell weren't enough wrapping for her taste. "I was storied with the same tales you were."

"What about your bard friend?"

"She told me korvikind stories. All about wind and fire and things glowing with ambition. They're a nice change of pace from our kind's legends, but useless for solving troubles with roots."

"Mm … The travelling merchant, perhaps? The red-feathered fellow?"

Chuckling, Chard knelt. She was taller and broader-shelled than Linden; she always had been; it was a constant and calming truth. "You think the Reyardine knows a whit about cultivation? I'd be surprised if he can guess which end of a spade to hold."

"So much for our wordsmith friends, then. Maybe groundworker korvi …?" It was easy to imagine tall, muscular dragonfolk digging up the shrine tree and hefting it out of its mire. But Linden shook her head. "No—the roots are weak, we'd savage them no matter how gently we worked. If only I had noticed this sooner!"

Quiet settled; breeze carded through the tree's boughs.

"Something will turn out," Chard murmured. "If nothing else, we could take a cutting from this tree, couldn't we? Raise it like a daughter."

That would be another, separate shrine tree. A successor to the one Linden allowed to die. What Middling circle caretaker would allow that to happen? Still, she pushed a considering hum from her cotton-dry throat: Chard was just trying to buoy her spirits, after all.

Chard set her hand on Linden's shoulder just brief enough to be felt. "I'm going to see if Mother needs help cracking those acorns. Dinner should be ready soon—make sure to come eat, won't you?"

"I will. I'd only like a moment."

On hesitating feet, Chard turned. Then she left, too.

***

Being alone made Linden nervous deep in her gut, but the tree was company. She thought in barren circles for a moment before she clenched and unclenched her hands, and looked at the divots her blunt nails made in her palms. And then she straightened her shelled back and she made an effort, genuine this time, to pray. Not just to Verdana but to any and all beings that might hear the laments of peoplekind. The gods, the Legend Creatures, the wind and the earth and, strike it, Linden prayed to anything and anyone who might hear her. Barghest strike her down if she didn't *try*.

***

Linden was uncrossing her legs to stand when an odd movement snagged her airsense. She stoppered her breath; she sat stock still until her antennae stopped swaying, and she pushed her sense outward. The movement wasn't from the underbrush, nor the lakeside reeds. It came from the lakewater. A ripple that shoved the reeds like a bodily presence.

She rose and parted the elderbushes, heading for the lake. The Great Gem's evening light dazzled on the lake and among it, the movement sharpened: it was a steady-thrashing creature. Something swimming, struggling, sucking in breath not nearly often enough, and that something had a familiar head shape—triangular, long-eared, and bristling with whiskers. Just like the ferrin neighbours in the street.

Linden was hurrying then toward the drowning person, down the sandy lakeshore. She hurried open her boot laces and yanked off her heavy footwear, and wondered if she should shed her clothing's weight, fearing for her modesty, loathing her own hesitation—before the ferrin broke surface again, their gasped air spiking through Linden's awareness. She ran again, this time splashing into the water, blurting apologies to the lakeweed plants that squelched cool underfoot.

The lake bottom dropped away after a few dozen sloshing strides. Linden hadn't practiced swimming since she was a youth but she remembered how, it seemed, because she kicked off and swam. The water's pressure echoed the pressure of Linden's pounding heart; her clothing dragging with each stroke but not enough to stop her. After an eon-long moment, Linden came to the grey haze underwater that was the ferrin and she scooped them surfaceward—but that made her sink herself and she swept both arms away, panicking as water rushed her nostrils and splashed dizzying onto her antennae. The ferrin broke surface and gasped, beside Linden's ear this time, their nailpoints sinking into her shoulder through her tunic. Linden could only swim and keep praying. But as the shallows returned, she put an arm under the ferrin's thin-boned weight and hoped she was doing enough.

***

She ran. Blindly, at first, too terrified to think, but Linden was halfway down the main village street when she found that she was running to the mage. Running with people's shapes passing her by, with the ferrin's wet gurgling and stinging nailpoints at her shoulder. She wished the ferrin would speak, would say *thank you, I'm fine now* but there was water inside their chest, blocking any air, and Linden kept on until she burst rudely through the mage's door, until the mage's skilled hands circled the ferrin's tiny body and squeezed so their eyes bulged and water burst from their retching throat to splatter on the dirt floor.

***

When Linden caught her breath, she was somewhere else again. Standing outdoors, but surrounded by walls, the thatch texture stark in her fear-sharp airsense. Fellow aemet shapes moving in her periphery. Kin were nearby. The ferrin was with the mage. No more panic. No more.

Linden measured her breathing and the fog of aemetkind instincts began to lift, her vision returning to meld with her antennae's airsight. Linden nodded to her neighbours—the many bowl-eyed faces hovering by the corner of the mage's house.

"Are you all right, dear?"

"Steady, now."

"That ferrin… What happened?"

She wasn't sure, Linden told them, with her mouth shaping the foreign things that were words. It seemed as though that ferrin could have died. But the mage was seeing to him now.

That was an unsatisfying but true answer, and with a few more well-wishes murmured, the crowd dispersed. Once she had a few more deep breaths stockpiled in her, Linden straightened, and went again to the mage's door.

***

"You've done a noble deed," the mage said, quiet as wind on leaves. "He couldn't have taken much more."

Holding her cup of tea tight, soothed by its unbroken rope of steam, Linden nodded. She couldn't pull her attention from the ferrin's breathing, from the rhythmic motion of his furred side. The weaselkind fellow laid curled on a folded blanket, his tail brush pillowing his head, his long ears as limp as rags. His pelt was dark grey, the colour of charcoal on paper, with ink-black tips on his ears and tail. Linden didn't know any ferrin who looked like him: lakeside ferrin mostly had white or dove-grey fur, and they had narrower faces besides. And they stayed well away from the lake's grasping depths.

"Will he be alright?" Linden asked small.

The mage pressed her mouth, too rigid to be a smile. "I believe so. We'll see if there's more water in his lungs once he wakes up."

"You wouldn't know this fellow, would you?"

The mage raised her hands, empty and answerless. "I've never seen him, nor has my ferrin mageling. He can tell us his name. Let's just give him time, Linden."

She nodded. And it felt as though she wasn't finished, standing there hoping in the question-thick air, noticing the way a weary otherkind stranger drew breath. She had nearly sensed two drownings today.

Linden left, and her feet took her brisk back to the shrine tree; she chose a green-glossy leaf without thinking; she was back at the mage's home, tucking the shrine leaf into the ferrin's bedding for luck, while the mage murmured something else gentle about hope.

***

In morning's light, Linden sat with the rest of the Grannell family, all gathered peaceful by the hearth fire. The breakfast corn porridge was studded with acorn meat—usually a savoury delight for Linden but today it was simply nourishment to be swallowed.

Father paused, spoon held above bowl, abruptly still. He was airsensing something: a few heartbeats later, everyone was sensing the same movement, a ferrin bounding through the street air. Linden stood as the ferrin—the mageling, distinctive with the smooth facets of a gemstone collar—rapped knuckles on the door pole.

"We thought you should know, Linden," she reported, peering up bright-eyed, "that Vrin is awake."

Linden knew no one named Vrin—and then she understood, and her heart ballooned with joy.

***

The survivor ferrin was sitting up on his haunches today, although slumped like his own weight was a burden. He was as tall as Linden's knee, large enough for his kind, although whip-boned and slender under fur gone coarse with age. But his ears stood taut with consideration and his grass-yellow eyes were bright, following the shrine leaf twirling between his sharp-nailed fingers. Today, he had enough strength to take a lolloping step toward Linden and introduce himself as Vennerick Vrin, call him Vrin.

"It's good to sense your breathing," Linden admitted.

"It's a good feeling for me, too," he said, smiling wry. His voice rasped terribly, like it had rusted overnight. "Uh, thank you. For pulling me out of there. And for this leaf, I think—is this an important leaf?"

All leaves were important: each leaf was imbued with the plant goddess Verdana's generosity. Otherkind tended to forget that. But Linden hummed agreement and said, "It's from our shrine tree. You had good fortune already, that you made it through your ordeal, but I thought a little more providence couldn't do you harm."

Vrin looked again to his shrine leaf. Like that one precious leaf would share lore with him, if he could only focus his eyes enough. "Linden, was it? Might you show me the shrine tree?"

"You shouldn't be walking," came the mage's soft-stern voice from the hearth's edge. "Rest only, until your lungs are clear."

The sudden droop of Vrin's ears yanked Linden's gutstrings. She tried, "Wouldn't a holy place do him good, though?"

The mage hesitated. "It might. Still, no walking."

"If I might offer, Vrin," Linden said, "I don't mind to carry you again."

With joy-lifting ears, Vrin smiled up at her. "I'd like that."

***

The mage lent them a carrying pouch. It was made for its users' comfort, both the ferrin in the spacious sack and the bearer with the padded strap worn crossways over the shoulder. Linden wasn't used to wearing such a device: the strap chafed hot at her neck and Vrin's slight weight felt like enough to buckle her shell. But generosity was a virtue, she reminded herself. She focused on the path through the tree-scattered grassland, her well-walked route to the Middling circle.

"So," Vrin tried, "which village is this, anypace?"

"Oh, our mage didn't tell you? We're Castaway." And with the village's name came its customary legend. It was too close for Linden's comfort, too reminiscent of the shrine tree's bloating roots, but legends existed to be shared. "Have—have you heard our tale? The legend of the cast-away seed?"

"I know that your village has a namesake legend. That's all I can say, though." Vrin wormed sideways in the pouch, resting his head in the fabric's sling, sliding his grass-yellow eyes up to Linden's face. "May I hear it? If it isn't too long."

Linden nodded. Castaway residents told the legend plenty often; if it had been long in the first speaker's mouth, it had grown shorter since.

***

"It wasn't long ago. Maybe twenty generations—of aemets," she hurriedly added. "But it's said that when the Legend Creature Seasu was swimming the rivers and ponds of this earthly plane, she found seeds in the water. Seeds from trees, flowers, grasses—all sorts. Seasu always rescued land-faring animals that stumbled into her waters, but she felt that these seeds shouldn't be left to drown and rot, either. She knew that plants had casting essence inside them: that meant that plants deserved life, too. With the seeds held tight in one of her forefins, Seasu searched up rivers and down streams, raising her long serpent's neck to see onto land's domain. But she couldn't see spark nor snout of great Verdana. She couldn't return the seeds to their mother."

Spinning a tale was more difficult while carrying someone. Linden took a full draw of air and slowed her footsteps; Vrin made no comment on it, his ears held tall and wide to hear Linden's next words.

"So," she went on, "Seasu decided to give these lost seeds a home. She chose a place here in the eastern land, where mountains and hills rest their feet, and where rivers greet each other. With her finful of seeds, she realized that she knew nothing about planting. If she chose poor locations, the seeds would die regardless.

It was then that an eightgroup of aemets came walking past. They were bent with weariness, and covered in dust from their travels.

Seasu called out to them. She had a gift of seeds, she said; would the aemets be so kind as to plant them?

They would, Great Seasu, the group's leader said. But the seeds might need to be patient. The aemets were the survivors of a lost village and they were fleeing an illness demon: they had no means of trade and no home for themselves, never mind safe garden space to share.

Seasu's heart filled with sorrow. She saved those who fell into her waters, by bearing them back to dry land; she decided she would help mortalkind in another way.

So she swam circles until she wore a bowl into the land. The mud settled into lakeshores of fine red clay, and the deep waters drew fish and lakeweed fit for a Middling feast. Lastly, Seasu brought rich mud from the riverbeds of vibrant forests, and she laid it all around the new lake to make fertile fields.

A new wind blew over this place, a wind of promise, and the aemets cried out joyful at the feeling of it. They could grow anything they desired here, they said, and the lake would give them bountiful treasure, besides.

The leader held out a cloth pouch for Seasu to pour the seeds into. And then he produced a plum from his pocket, a plum from their former village's groves. Seasu's castaway seeds would be safe, the leader said, and they would have a plum sapling for company. All of them would call this place, Castaway, their home."

***

The weight of story's end hung in the air, as Linden followed the path through elderberry thickets.

"That's a fine legend," Vrin decided, his ears swivelling, thoughtful. "It must be a comfort, having a story for why you live here instead of any other place in this land."

Linden hummed. "I never thought of it like that ... I've just got roots here. My family, my caretaking trade ... Why question roots?"

Elderberry bushes murmured in the wind, their berries bobbing among smooth leaves. Saplings wagged toward the sky and among them, a lark sang alone and bold. Linden skirted the Middling circle proper— the ring of quartz stones and Legend Creature statues that guarded

Castaway's heaps of composting plant trimmings—until she stood in the shadow of the great, troubled shrine tree.

"Anypace … Here it is."

"Your shrine tree? Is this the one from the legend?"

"The very same."

Vrin stood taller in the carrying pouch, his tail a stiff counterbalance. "An ancient tree … Does it still give you plums?"

"Ah, a few." The fruit had been pale and undersized this year, a warning call Linden should have minded.

"Linden? I'd like down, please."

She bent and set her passenger down carefully on the leaf-blanketed ground, with the mage's orders echoing back into her memory. "Just don't strain yourself, please," Linden said.

"No, nothing like that. I only want to look."

On two feet, moving in a slow shuffle that didn't suit a ferrin, Vrin approached the tree. His breathing grew ragged, catching with each breath. He laid a paw on the tree's bark, and sniffed as though he might smell the lore steeped into the wood, like the Seasu's kindness still clung. Then again, Linden wasn't furkind: maybe legends *did* leave a scent that Linden could never comprehend.

"May I ask you something, Vrin?"

Linden was already imposing a question; Vrin undulated his ears and then, simply, nodded.

"Why were you out that far in the lake?"

"Ah, well." Movement flickered over him, subtleties of ears and mouth and whiskers. "Yesterday, I was out sitting by the mine—I'm an earferrin, you see. Partner to Menille of Ojerie, the copper miner. I've been with her for seventeen years."

"Oh, an earferrin!" Linden's heart swelled at the thought. Vrin was one of the generous, diligent ferrin who accompanied a korvi person like a shadow, listening for what their partner's mine-ravaged ears could no longer hear. He must have sat on his partner's shoulder like the miner and earferrin pairs Linden saw in the village street sometimes. Linden's heart always warmed at the thought of two folk braiding their lives together so honestly. "Your partner must be searching for you; we should get word to—"

"Uh," Vrin piped. He wrapped his tail about him. "Maybe—maybe you had best wait."

Linden's eyes drew wide. In the lake-touched clearing air, Vrin stood distant and he couldn't truly *mean* that he was abandoning his partner.

"Wait?! But your miner needs you! Doesn't she?"

"She's got a new earferrin training. A young kit."

"Oh ..." Reluctantly, the thought shifted in Linden's mindsight, to a partnership that would end soon because the ferrin was growing old and he would need a successor. It was sensible but still a bitter truth to chew. She missed her former thoughts of earferrin already, the unruined thoughts.

"I'm sorry, Linden," Vrin said. He had turned to face her now, and was considering the story her expression told. "I shouldn't be burdening you with this."

"Well," Linden tried, with a flick of dry tongue over her lips, "I don't know a lot about your trade's ways, and besides that, we've only just met. But if you'd like help with your burden, then ..." She knelt, her tunic rustling too loud. And she extended a hand, palm up, for Vrin's consideration.

Head bowing, Vrin took a breath in slowly as drawn rope. He tottered two-footed back to Linden and took her offered hand between his warm little paws.

Out of all the times she had offered her hand to a new ferrin acquaintance, they had never felt a need to sniff her. Maybe she seemed trustworthy, Linden wondered. Maybe all the ferrin she met simply had plenty of trust to give. Vrin made no move to sniff her either: he only stared past the creases of Linden's palm and gathered some elusive truth from inside himself.

When he spoke, it barely touched Linden's ears: his tongue and lip movement filled in the spaces.

"I've had a long life."

"Seventeen years, you said?"

He shook his head. "Twenty-one. I've had twenty-one years."

That was a full portion of a life for someone ferrinkind. They were vibrant, clever folk but they faded away when an aemet was only middle-aged, and a korvi still newly fledged. Linden looked again at the dry grey of Vrin's fur, at the creased skin hiding in the fine fur around his eyes.

"And I'm happy that most of my years went to helping Menille," Vrin blurted, "truly, I'm thankful as anything, I wish I had a hundred more years to give her. But I'll be gone soon. I only work alternating days now, with the new kit needing space on Menille's shoulder so she can learn the trade …"

He took another deep draw of breath. He scraped up more truth.

"I was waiting outside Menille's mine, yesterday. Working a piece of horse leather against a stone, I was going to shape it into a flask. And I slipped and scraped myself on the stone. Nothing serious—I could smell the blood more than see it. But it must have been enough to draw basilisks. A pair of them—big ones, nearly half your height, Linden—and they were working in tandem. I can stand against a lone beast, but two …" Vrin shook his head. "I ran. No trees near Menille's mine, so I went into the lake. The beasts wouldn't follow me into deep water but they didn't leave. Just paced the shore."

"They must have known you can't swim forever," Linden murmured. "Awful things."

Vrin shrugged. "It's true. I *can't* swim forever. I circled there for a while. Called out for Menille, but there was no chance she'd hear me when she's three furlongs deep in the mine. What could I do? I turned toward the opposite shore and kept swimming."

"This lake is the largest in the land … Gods, Vrin, you've got a strong heart."

"Ah, well. It might sound terrible, but while I was crossing that lake, I felt sure that I wasn't going to make it. That it was my time to die."

Linden's free hand flew to her mouth.

"Well, you see, I've lived my portion," Vrin added. "My children are grown. Menille has the new kit to look after her. It was my time … or, I thought so, anypace. I never thought I'd die in water, closer to Okeos than to great Ambri, but there it was. Ah, I'm sorry—this isn't your way, is it?"

"No, no, your thoughts are yours," she stammered. "You just … sound so *calm* about it."

He smiled. She could see the weariness in it now, the way his fur made a grizzled frame. "I'm confused, that's all. Why did I make it? I just don't see what else there is for me to do with this life."

"Does there need to be a reason?"

He shrugged, but his cloudy gaze spoke truth. "Maybe. Maybe the gods have something in mind for me. Or one of the Creatures. *Someone.*"

One could only hope. They sat in contemplation for a long moment, alone with each other. Linden shifted on her folded legs; Vrin released her hand and turned a fraction away, to look at the earth between his toes and groom his ears with distracted sweeps of his forepaws.

"Well," Linden said, "we should still let Menille know that you're safe. She must be sick with worry."

"Yeah ..." Suddenly, Vrin looked to her, ears stiffening with thought, his eyes searching Linden again. "Wait a beat, what if I'm—Could I be here to help you, Linden?"

She blinked. "I suppose. What gives you that thought?"

"I was drowning, but I made it out, so Seasu must have helped me. Stirred waves that washed me closer to shore, maybe. I can't believe I swam as far as that."

"I did feel waves," Linden murmured. "When I sensed you out there."

"So maybe there *was* a reason. A reason Seasu held in her heart—or just a reason out there in the earth and sky. There's something else this old fellow needs to do, and it's *here*, where you brought me ashore—with aemet folk, with Castaway's plum tree."

Linden felt a wordless void in her own mouth. She represented a place of worship and a shrine tree but she couldn't speak for the gods, nor for legends. "There might be. What, though?"

"I don't know." Vrin turned pleading eyes up at Linden, a ragged burr building in his voice. "Is there something Castaway needs? Is there something *you* need?"

"I—I don't think it's anything you have the power to change."

"No? What is i—" His voice broke into a wet cough and he brought both hands to his mouth.

"Don't work yourself up, please! It's just ... ah, I'm worried for this shrine tree. Its essence feels weaker each time I reach out to it. But the farm folk of Castaway have tried every technique they know to arrange the land to a tree's liking—so truly, Vrin, it's nothing for you to worry about."

He considered, ears working. And another coughing fit seized him: Linden pulled the carrying pouch to her frontside and held it open, inviting.

"I've upset you enough for today. Please, you should get back to the mage house."

He gulped, and stepped back into the pouch without another word.

***

Vrin was quiet on the walk back. He merely picked up the shrine leaf from where he had left it in the carrying pouch, and twirled it as slow as thought. They were nearly among the village's thatch walls before Vrin spoke, like down feathers:

"It might just be the end of your shrine tree. It's lived for eons—the legend says so. Maybe this is its time."

Linden hated that thought and she hated the way Vrin was right. Why did a legend need to die within her mere lifetime? Why did great Okeos's waters have to shift from nourishing to smothering, and why *now*?

***

They reached the mage house, and Vrin returned to his borrowed bed.

"I'm sorry to have upset you," he told Linden.

"It's not truly your doing," she replied. Her troubles were far bigger than a newcomer ferrin deserved to bear.

Their low voices caught the mageling's ear; she deliberately chose a quartz crystal from a storage bin and sat down to charge it with casting energy, aiming her ears away.

After watching the mageling for a few heartbeats, and growing shaky faith in her discretion, Linden turned back to Vrin and added, "Are you sure? I can send word."

"Give me a night to think on it. Please. It might be easier if I simply don't return."

Against the hot refusal in her chest, Linden nodded.

***

She left the mage home, took a few steps out into the flow of aemet folk, and stopped. The skylight was turning purple with dusk, shifting from day's brightcasting to night's darkcasting: even if Vrin changed his mind, it was a poor wager that a korvi messenger could fly quick enough to outpace nightfall. The miner Menille would just have to spend another night worrying.

There was too much defiance pent in Linden's heart: her feet took her away from her own home, down the market street, toward any messenger fate might let her find. But she couldn't see or sense any korvi people. Only aemets and their ferrin friends, a curious lack of fiery feathers.

"Oh, everyone with ready wings has left," a ropemaker told Linden when she asked. "We got word that Valeover town has some problem basilisks."

Another senseless turn of fate—and Linden was immediately crushed with guilt for that thought. Strong korvi friends would make sure those fearless basilisks didn't hurt any more peoplekind. There was a reason for this; maybe Vrin was better attuned to the world than Linden was.

***

She thanked the ropemaker. She trudged home. And in the blanketing darkness of night, with the Grannell home's hearth embers fading and most of the family breathing the steady rhythm of sleep, Linden told Chard everything.

Gently, she took Linden's hands between hers. Chard spent more time in the family spinach patch than Linden did; her broad hands tingled, like the day's plantcasting had left a trace of vigor.

"Sounds like Vrin is right," Chard said. "About our tree, that is."

"I know. I simply don't like it."

Chard squeezed her hands tight. "Two simple basilisks causing such a stir, though? Might be an omen of greater trouble to come."

"We'll be keeping our acorns for later, then?"

Chard hummed. "That harvest is nearly through. Maybe we'll see about some corn, to sit on for later. Feh, this isn't my point, Linden. I think we should make sure there's a shrine tree for the generations to come. Even if it's not the same one."

Linden's head felt heavy: she stared at her own pant legs.

"Doesn't mean we can't try to help our current shrine tree. Do you figure it'd help to prune her?"

Linden couldn't speak, but she nodded.

***

That thought rang in Linden's head like an iron bell, while she laid in her bed and thought of forces like fate, of all the worldly motions greater than herself.

***

In the morning, Linden again had a visitor: Vrin came on his own four feet, breathing thicker than Linden liked the feeling of.

"Great green, the mage *let* you?" She lifted the door curtain back farther than necessary for such a small friend.

"I kept a mild pace," Vrin huffed, "but I am glad I brought this."

Linden accepted the carrying pouch from him—and couldn't ignore the weight of her family's attention any longer. "Ah, everyone? This is Vennerick Vrin, call him Vrin. The one from the lake …"

The Grannell family showered greetings on Vrin, praised his good fortune and wished him well. Linden's parents both offered him porridge and Vrin squirmed as he declined twice; the mage hadn't let him leave on an empty stomach, he explained.

"Well," Chard said, kneeling to offer Vrin her open palm. "If you'd like to get straight to work, we're tending the Middling circle today."

"Sister! He's hardly on the road to health, he's not going to work."

Vrin sniffed Chard's palm, and sat stock still with realization. "If I'm meant to help you," he said, slow but firm, "I whole-heartedly will. What are you working at?"

***

They brought tree-cutting tools, blades with merciful but terrible purpose, and a wrapping cloth not unlike a funeral shroud. Accompanied but alone, Linden stepped close to the shrine tree's trunk.

"I thought aemet folk didn't cut trees," Vrin asked, quiet as a question.

"Only when mercy demands it," Chard said.

Linden laid both hands on the ragged bark. It was plain to see which branches were lifeless, but she took a moment to be sure: she extended emerald-glowing tendrils of plantcasting from her palms, inward to touch the tree's same essence.

She knew this tree plenty well. She found her answer in the time it took to draw a breath. The tree contained life, ebbing but still vitally present and timelessly complex; the taproots keened, a heart-rending silent cry that Linden couldn't answer; some of the branches were fully dead, with no green veins flowing into them, no presence except dry stillness. Linden drew her magic back inside herself, and opened her eyes to the physical land once more.

"We can certainly take some wood. It'll feel no trauma." And then, to the tree, she murmured, "Forgive us this violence, great sister. May we remove a burden from you, and build better lives from your wood."

And then she stood back for Chard to throw the saw wire over the lowest leafless branch. And the two of them began.

Terrible though it was to drag the serrated wire through treeflesh, the dead branch came off stroke by stroke. Then a second branch, this one easier to cut where it was succumbing to rot. Sawdust fell between Linden and Chard like dry rain; Vrin shuffled closer to watch, his broad ears stirring air as he tipped his head.

He waited until the second branch struck earth, and until Linden finished wrapping it in respectful cloth, before he spoke with his held breath.

"So, then, Linden—or, Chard, if you know, I'd be pleased to hear from you, too! I wanted to ask, is there any sort of gift folk give to Seasu? I've heard of folk being saved by her, but I've never heard any tale of how to give thanks."

It put a soft smile on Linden's face, however much she wasn't in a smiling mood. "Seasu doesn't ask much. She's a wanderer, after all. But she likes it when folk set things in the water. Stones, broken pottery, branches that the Middling circle won't miss—anything a water creature might find shelter in."

"Or lay eggs in," Chard added. "Seasu has a soft heart for new life."

Humming, Vrin folded his ears back with thought. "I was just thinking about thanking her. Menille will want to, I'm sure. I'm, ah, beginning to feel badly about all this."

Linden caught eyes with Chard—for only an instant, a knowing instant—before she asked, "Should we find a messenger korvi?"

And Vrin nodded, gaze turned to his feet. "You're right: she must be so worried. And the rest of our family, too. if my time didn't come in these past days—" Wetness caught his voice, and he coughed into his paws. "If it didn't come now, then ... I don't know."

"How will we get word out, though? I didn't see a single friendly feather in the street yesterday—most of our dragonkind folk are gone, they've joined the effort to deal with those basilisks before anyone else gets hurt."

Vrin deflated, but said nothing.

"I have a favour to lend," Chard offered.

"You do? How can you ...?"

"No, I mean a favour with someone else."

"Oh." Linden lit up suddenly. "Oh! The Reyardine still owes you his wings?"

Chard nodded, her delight at Linden's understanding crinkling her eyes. "He's no fighter; he's told me so himself. I wouldn't wager a pebble on him going out hunting a basilisk."

"Does he still come here to see the mushroom farmers?"

"Sure as rain. He should be here today unless someone else buys his service."

"You'd give your favour to me?" Vrin asked, brows drawing toward his ears. "That's kind of you, Chard. Can I aid you in anything …?"

She only reached around Vrin's tiny shoulders, patting him gently but still enough to shake him. "Just be well. And if you can manage it, help my little sister be well, too." Then, waving a hand toward Castaway town. "Well, I'd best go see the farm families, make sure we catch our merchant friend before someone else does. We'll make sure your family gets word, Vrin."

She waved off Vrin's further thanks, and she left on brisk feet.

***

With a smile held warm in her mouth, Linden waited. And then she said, "She's sage. She really is."

"Seems so."

"She's always given me good advice, I'm just learning to follow it."

"Good advice about?"

"Oh, well …" Linden felt right telling Vrin, and considered it a second time just to be sure. "I had a brother at first. He never seemed at home in his own shell, and he figured out it was because he wasn't a *he*. She's my sister, Chard. She picked the name herself—it suits her, wouldn't you say?"

Vrin hummed agreement. He came steps closer, near enough for Linden to sense the body heat pockets between his every strand of fur, and that heat made her want to share the best words she had ever heard.

"After she chose it, and I said it suited her, Chard … told me something. She said words could be heavier than any mountain, but she found change only as heavy as she wished it to be."

With a dozen subtleties of his ears, Vrin considered that.

"I didn't understand it when I was young," Linden went on. "I think I'm starting to."

"It's good advice. You should share it with more folk than just me—if that's alright with Chard. I, ah, guessed her secret before you told me." He pointed a clawed finger at his nose, far more discerning than any aemet's.

"Oh, she doesn't call it a secret." Linden waved a hand. "I'm sure you can understand—" And her eyes widened. Linden spoke her thought as it formed: "You understand change. You know it doesn't need to be heavy. That's what you meant, isn't it, Vrin? That however painful it'll be for your life to end, it'll be a change bringing new and good things?"

"I don't think my end is painful," he murmured. "But, yes. You're seeing what I mean now."

He wasn't meeting Linden's gaze, so she took him in again. Dry fur, creased eyelids, sure heart.

"You need a cutting from your shrine tree, right, Linden? For a new beginning?"

Her voice sounded like a stranger's: "Yes. I do."

"Uh, and if it has to be a green cutting, you'll need to reach the slenderest part of a branch, isn't that right? I think I've figured it out. You'll need help for that ... Help from someone small?"

Someone ferrin-sized would be an excellent help: Linden smiled back at him and couldn't argue with that at all.

***

She knew every fingerwidth of that clearing, and which angles the shrine tree's life flowed at. Such knowledge didn't make it any easier to throw the wire saw over a branch, pull against green wood, and hold it bent until Vrin—perched awkward on her rounded shoulder with nails clenched into her tunic's cotton—could carefully wield a knife.

But despite Linden's fears, he didn't slip and cut her, and the sprig of plum branch was sliced off clean enough to heal. Linden put it to her palm and urged roots from it. She dipped a pocketcloth in lakewater and wrapped the roots up safe. And she walked home with the carrying pouch digging into her back and her fear of things to come finally, finally allayed.

***

When Chard arrived home for dinner, she wore a smile. "Syril of Reyardine, owner of the self-proclaimed fastest wings in the land, is on his way to Valeover right this moment. Your partner will know by nightfall."

***

Vrin stayed with the Grannell family for his last night in Castaway, accepting all the washcloths and blankets Linden's parents offered for nest material. He piled them beside Linden's bed, and circled until he laid calm.

"You told me a legend," he said, quiet enough to rasp in the house's dark. "Should I tell you one?"

"I'd like that," Linden told him.

So while she settled to sleep, her friend told a story. The legend of the electric goddess Ambri gathering stray bolts of lightning from the clouds, and making topaz stones for them to call home.

Linden had heard this legend before. But coming from Vrin, it sounded like new.

***

They planted the new shrine sapling together, a moment's walk from the Middling circle where the earth felt only moist enough. They visited the mage, who tutted over Vrin's wetly unchanging lungs and told him to eat more wholesome greens. And as Linden left the mage home, resettling the carrying pouch so Vrin's weight didn't dig so badly, a new colour in the Castaway crowd caught her eye.

It was the plumage of a wine-feathered korvi. She stood out dark against aemet skin but garnet-vivid where the skylight hit her: her reptilian snout turned as she searched the village throngs. Her mane feathers were cropped short except for one bead-studded braid tucked behind her left horn, a braid that her shoulder-perched ferrin friend held between her paws like a safety rope.

A ferrin on her shoulder. She had to be a miner, and Linden filled up with mixed emotions at the same time Vrin cried, "Menille! *Menille!*"

He leaped out of the pouch, and stumbled, and caught himself and ran four-footed to the kneeling, beaming korvi woman.

"Vrin!" She snatched him into her muscular arms. "Thank the gods and the Legends!"

They embraced under Menille's mantled wings, with the new earferrin sliding down to join in and butt fondly against Vrin. Castaway neighbours passed them by, like water around stone. They were a family—Vrin's family.

Step by unsure step, Linden approached them. Close enough to hear the mucus crackling that Vrin didn't seem to care about. And close enough that when Menille looked up and locked eyes with her, Linden could see the glimmer of happy tears.

***

Life kept onward. Vrin was gone for days Linden didn't mark, except with the fingerwidths taller the new shrine tree grew.

***

One afternoon, she came home to find Menille of Ojerie at the door, horns held high but her eyes muted as dark water. Her earferrin called a greeting; Menille waved and pulled a smile halfway up her long mouth.

"I hadn't expected to see you again this soon, friends," Linden told them. "Is everything …?"

The earferrin didn't repeat Linden's words: Linden was among the minority with high enough voices for Menille's damaged ears to manage. Instead, the earferrin watched her partner with limp, honest ears, while Menille gathered her voice and said, "He's elsewhere, now."

"Oh! My apologies …"

"It was his time. He knew that as much as we did. We'll just have to hope that his goddess is taking sure care of him. And we still can't thank you enough for *your* caretaking, Linden."

Her throat was gummed closed, but she nodded.

"We've got two requests for you. The first—"

"Might we come in?" the earferrin piped. "The street might not be the best place to discuss it."

"Yes," Menille gulped. "That."

As far as Linden was concerned, they could have whatever Vrin wanted.

***

He wished to be laid to rest at the roots of the shrine tree. Linden Grannell's shrine tree—the new one. It would need food. Even after his own life was gone, he wished to lend his aid.

***

Chard joined them for the ceremony. Menille wielded the shovel: she was roped all over with muscle and far quicker at digging than Linden could ever hope to be. She dug between the shrine sapling's roots; she dropped in the paper packet full of dryness that she said was Vrin's ashes; she filled the hole back in.

With that finished, Menille picked her young earferrin back up, and the four of them stood with heads bent around the tiny plum tree decked with a legacy. The sky stirred with wind, far above and all around.

"Vrin will do good here," Linden said. "We'll make sure of it."

"I have entire faith in that," Menille told her. Then she reached to her satchel, dug inside, and produced a tin kettle so dented that it hardly resembled itself. "Well, if you two would show me where the lake is? Something might make a home of this."

"Um, why are we throwing that in the lake, again?" the earferrin asked.

Linden and Chard caught each other's shining eyes.

"It's what great Seasu wishes folk to do," Chard replied. "You must know who the Legend Creature Seasu *is*, but there are plenty of stories about her—Linden, would you mind telling her? In Castaway fashion?"

Linden didn't mind at all.

Do you hear a rattle in the distance?

OLD-DRY-SNAKESKIN

Ross Whitlock

R attler waits in the dark with the One Actual Story on his forked
tongue.

So everyone says. These days, stories float about in the
lightning-struck sky above. There's nae counting them all. They hiss
and hum and sting the ear like ashes from the broken world. One day,
you'll hear about the bears and the cracked boulder. Next day, it'll be
the young doe who sank in the swamp and came back up with pine-tar
wings and a sheen like a hummingbird's breast. The mice say that the
foxes did everything wrong, and the foxes say that the mice gnawed one
too many roots and made it all crumble in the center. Even the birds,
who all went starkers long ago, hide a story within their ragged, jagged
bird-talk. More stories than ants on the ground and blowflies in the air.
All wending their way toward the same damned punchline:

"...and that's how the world broke."

The bears' cracked boulder kept cracking. The doe from the swamp
was nobody's messiah. The foxes fumbled; the mice gnawed. And that's
how the world broke.

Still. Ask about the One Actual Story, and you'll tease a consensus
from the muddle of crossed tales. Rattler knows. Rattler and only
Rattler. Oh, there's plenty of rattlesnakes out there, blending with the
matted carpet of rot in what used to be forests, nestled in cracks under
the too-big, too-close sun. But there's only one Rattler. And the other
snakes'll nae speak of him, but to spit and call him outcast, heretic,
starkers. His head got split, they'll say, and his brains got well and surely

pithed. Maybe you'll listen close and hear how they're all afraid, all those snakes. Afraid of Rattler and what he knows.

Three things folk agree upon: Rattler knows the One Actual Story, he'll tell it to you, and you'd best be bringing him a pretty present. That's his toll.

And, any-old-way, you have to find him first. He's down in the dark. Is he North? East? West? It'll nae matter, on account of there being nae compass any more. The world broke. Nobody (unless it's Rattler) knows how or why or even when. Every creature's inside-clock is busted, wires and cogs in a tangled bouquet, so nobody can say how old they are or what they were up to before the world broke. But it did. Bits of the world are nae up nor down any more. Some parts have crumbled while others have reached for the sky, knife-edged pinnacles every which way, as if to stroke the lightning. Half the world's covered in swamp, and there's things under the muck, long and ropey and hungry, that just keep going. The sun, when it shows its sickly face, is too big, too close. The moon's nae just one moon any more.

In a broken world, eating and mating and staying alive are all and everything. Nobody sleeps. Time is in shards. The wolf sings with the stag, a melancholy duet, as one's teeth tear out the other's greasy innards. The birds are mad, starkers without their compass bearings. They batter themselves to pulp on cracked stone cliffs, dive giggling into the swamps, swallow hot coals and ground glass. The humans are all gone, their cites reduced to gravel and burning gasoline. Nobody knows where. Underground. Or up in the sky. Nae dead, on account of there being nae bones or clothes left. Gone.

In all this, how's a creature to find Rattler? The best option is, you find where the world's broken worst, and go that way. If you see anything safe, pretty, or normal, avoid it. Turn away. Go toward the worst ruin, the deepest calamity, the deadliest obstacle. Start every morning with the urge to kill yourself. Go starkers. Stay alive. Hold tight to your pretty present for Rattler. Keep on.

When you find his hole, you'll know. It'll gape at you, all a-glimmer. Rattler's tunnel bores deep, deep into the world. A greenish, toxic stream of water, cool and burning at the same time, flows up and out against all laws of gravity. The tunnel floor is mud and the walls and ceiling are a church, a cathedral. Rattler's taken all the pretty presents given to him, all the shiny stones and colored glass, the butterfly wings and glossy feathers, the chrome from human machines, the obsidian and jade and fool's gold, the dead Christmas lights and circuit boards—all of it's gone up on those tunnel walls. Every time some pretty fragment is dug from the shit of the world, it's found its way to Rattler. Because that's how badly folk want to know the One Actual Story.

Rattler takes the green, deadly water and mixes it with earth and mud, and pastes his presents, glues them into the mosaic. Some stretches of tunnel, you can nae see the stone through the mask of mud and glimmering, twinkling trinkets. Snakeskin weaves everything together. Rattler sheds it often, far too often for a normal snake, but what's been normal since the world broke? Rattler's old skins become braided tendons that hold his whole church of mud and pretty presents together.

Keep going. Deep and deeper. You'll find Rattler in time. The tunnel nae ends; it keeps on boring into the black, airless core of the world. But Rattler's made himself a nice nest, a tangle of mud and snakeskin, stretched across the tunnel like a spider's web. In the middle of the web's a hole, and when Rattler's nae working on his mosaic, he drapes himself over the bottom edge of the hole like a tired, threadbare stocking. He's always tired.

"Welcome, friend-o-friend," Rattler will say to you. His voice is like a mouthful of sand. "Come all this way, have ya? Come to hear old Rattler flap his jaw? Gimme my pretty present."

You've got to hold it up for his inspection. If you've brought him more than one pretty present, so much the better. If the distant daylight reflects off your present just so, or if you're one of those creatures with dark vision, you'll see that Rattler's a sorry, sorry sight. His left eye is gone. So's his right fang, taking the venom sac with it. Worst of all, the other snakes got one thing right: Rattler's head's been split. Right between eye and socket. His hide flaps open and his skull pokes out. You can almost see his brains. He must be starkers. If only there were nae such terrible, furious sanity in his one leftover eye.

"Very fine, very pleasant," Rattler will rasp, after he's tilted his split head this way and that to assess your present. "Drop it on the ground, friend-o-friend. I'll find the perfect spot for it later. Now, you'll be aching to hear the One Actual Story, yes?"

Yes.

Rattler will laugh and wheeze in his voice of sand. "Of course. Everyone has to know. How the world got broke. How everything turned to baked shit. Unclog the wax from your ears, friend-o-friend, and have a seat."

You'll find a dry patch, well away from the toxic green trickle. You'll rest your tired paws, or claws, or talons. You'll scratch your fur or fluff your feathers. Maybe you've got dark vision or maybe you're blinder than a mole, but you'll fix your eyes nonetheless on Rattler where he dangles limp. You'll unclog your ears.

"Now," Rattler says.

"You may well smell a rat. How come a measly snake knows it all? When the world broke and everyone lost their way, how come I nae lost mine? Well, friend-o-friend, I could lie and call myself The Chosen One. Plenty have done so. But I'm humble. It was pure luck. I rolled snake-eyes, and that's a mighty fortunate roll for a snake, so it is.

"When the world broke, I happened to be out in the driest, parchiest, most remote little stretch of desert I could find. I was a young snakelet then, all puffed up with self-worth, taking my slinkabout. The slinkabout is something young rattlesnakes do now and then, to prove their moxie, or to find their purpose in life, who knows, but we've always done it. What you do is, you catch a mouse, but you nae eat it right away. You keep it close and you see to it that your mouse gorges itself on a very particular type of cactus with very, shall we say, esoteric properties. Once your mouse is fat to bursting and so starkers it can nae tell up from down, you take your mouse to the farthest desert, far from any other being, and you scarf your cactus-poisoned mouse right down. So I'd done. Once it takes hold, your mind goes to all manner of interesting places and you forget who and what you are, and you nae care. I could nae tell you if I saw anything during my little trip, anything useful or relevant.

"All I know is, when the world broke, my mind was in that other space. And I figure that might be what kept my mind safe. Why I nae lost my way, lost my compass, forgot what came before. So I figure.

"But, any-old-way, sooner or later I came back to myself and immediately kenned that something had gone wrong, wrong, wrong. The sky was nae any one color, and the sun was too close, too swollen. The desert was blasted and twisted and drippy like pine sap. I knew I could nae still be on my trip, 'cause I felt hungry and itchy and scared. I nae knew which way to turn; nothing looked familiar. But I saw a cluster of hills in the distance, so I figured that'd be a place to start.

"I slithered my gingerly way over what had been the desert, and I approached the hills, and they were nae hills.

"They were the gods.

"You'll know all about the gods, of course."

At this point in his story, Rattler will pause portentously, as though his tale needs real, true validation. Of course his listener will know all about the gods. That's one thing nobody's forgotten. There's the Bossman, the first god, who made all the others and then left, back to wherever that sort of being goes. The littler gods took it upon themselves to make the world, although it's a point of exceeding controversy which god actually did so. You have Big Flanks, the bear god, and Weave-the-Grass, the rabbit god. The frog god is known as Ruggalumph the Sonorous, and the mole god is Honorable Sniff and Sift, and the fox god changes his name every week to confuse people. There's one bird god who is also a million bird gods; it's tricky. Nobody can pronounce the name of the alligator god, but if you snap your jaw a few times, that's close enough. There's too many more to count. We know it. Rattler knows we know it.

Once he's got the proper affirmation, Rattler will go on.

"The gods. Each and every one, splayed and sprawled over the shattered ground. I should've been honored, but I was pissing-myself terrified. The gods were in a horrible, loathly state. Big Flanks and Weave-the-Grass, Thundering Hoof and the bird god, or bird gods, and even that clever red foxy. Nae really alive, nae exactly dead. Their bodies were torn and riven. Their fur, scales, and feathers made a gory carpet. Their eyes, those that still had eyes, were milky marbles, staring miserably at nothing. I saw things reflected in those eyes, things that have nae business existing anywhere. Worst of all, the mouths. Where each god had once had a mouth, muzzle, beak, or snout, each god had a ragged black hole with stringy edges.

"I slithered through the fallen gods, trembling and jittering, scared that they really were dead, even more scared that they were nae dead, and would move and look at me with those awful, hopeless eyes. What could've done such a thing? In my jitters, it took me a bit to realize who was missing. I clenched my nerves and made the rounds again, just to be sure. Nae mistake. One god was nae there. My own god. Old-Dry-Snakeskin.

"I left the poor, rotting gods, picked a direction, and stuck with it. It became clear to me that the whole world was broke, and when I met other creatures, I saw that they'd all lost something. Wit and memory had given way to confusion and frustration. I nae told a soul what I'd seen, what had become of the gods. Why make the broken world even more hopeless? But I held in my snake's heart a flicker of hope.

"Whatever had befallen the gods, Old-Dry-Snakeskin had escaped. I was nae surprised. Old-Dry-Snakeskin is one tough god. He's the one who really made the world, friend-o-friend. Let no one tell you different. Old-Dry-Snakeskin spit the world into being, crafted it from venom and his own shed skins. And his mighty, thunderous rattle beat the stuffing out of any god who tried to stick their paw into his work. Don't you interrupt, friend-o-friend. I'll nae have any creature butting into the One Actual Story. This is gospel. Old-Dry-Snakeskin is the reason we have a world at all.

"So if the world had gotten broke, figured me, then Old-Dry-Snakeskin could fix it.

"But where to find him?

"Well. Old-Dry-Snakeskin likes dark, dry spaces. He likes to be cool and shady. These days, most of the world's surface is swampy, knife-sharp, overly parched, or all at once. Nae good places for Old-Dry-Snakeskin. But below the surface, that's another story. When the world broke, an impressive portion of it crumbled and fell into itself. A lot of folk went with it, and plenty more have fled into the depths, away from the too-huge sun and the blowfly swarms and the terror. I figure there's at least as much world below the surface as there is above it. It's nae any less dangerous or wrong. But, figured me, it'd be the place to start questing for Old-Dry-Snakeskin.

"So down I went."

Rattler will usually pause at this moment, shift his scales and languidly crick his neck. His awful split head bobs from side to side. Behind him, the deep blackness yawns and seems to draw nearer.

"Now.

"Down below the surface is a whole 'nother set of unnatural-type tribulations that I had to learn to dodge pretty quick. Oh, I had me some close calls. Thick wormy things that wanted to suckle me down. Mushrooms walking like people and people stuck to the rock like mushrooms, that'd whisper all my dark secrets to me as I slithered by. I saw birds who lived on the ceilings of caves, upside-down forever. I fled from something that was legs, legs, nothing but legs. Had myself quite the set of adventures, but nothing we need trouble ourselves with just now, friend-o-friend.

"Nae till I came to the poison lake.

"This was long after I'd gone down. I'd learned what to eat and what to drink. And I'd found myself a compass of sorts. See, I'd nae idea where

I might find Old-Dry-Snakeskin, in all that rock and tunnel. But I soon learned that the underground was hit by mighty quakes on the regular. Deep, wrenching quakes that crumbled rock and rewrote all that cave geometry. I imagine, to most of the creatures living down there, the quakes were just another occupational hazard. But rattlesnakes can feel rhythm. We know our percussion. If I sat really still during a quake and attuned my inner hearing bits, I knew. I was certain. Each quake was a rattle. A deep, angry, sad snake-rattle from somewhere far below in the black.

"So whenever a quake hit, I'd head toward where it seemed strongest. And that's how I came out a narrow tunnel and stopped dead on the lakeshore.

"Only a fool would stick a toe in that lake. Can you picture behind your eyes a cavern so big you can nae see the far side, or even the ceiling? Now imagine the lake reaching from wall to far-far-off wall, hissing and sizzling, purplish in places, piss-yellow in others. Huge bubbles rising and exploding like ticks on a brushfire. One slip and I'd be a goner. The lake would take my body apart; I'd be a grisly scum across the surface. And no path led around the cavern's edge; the walls sloped right down to the poison froth at the edges. So what was I to do?

"I sat there for a spell, pondering. Figuring I'd need to backtrack, find a new way, waste time. But then I saw something bobbing across the lake toward me. A boat? The lake would eat any boat just as readily as flesh. But it drew closer, and I realized it was a stone boat. Yes, a stone boat, a floating basin of rock, its sides pitted from the acid, but holding firm. How can a stone boat float? How can any of this be possible, friend-o-friend? I see the doubt on your lower lip. Feel free to turn tail and leave if you've ceased to believe. It was a stone boat, I tell you, and standing at the bow, poling the vessel along with a stone rod, was the rattiest, scraggliest, sorriest-looking magpie I'd ever laid eyes on. Or so I thought, until I noticed an even rattier, scragglier, sorrier magpie huddled at the stern.

"You've got to be careful with birds. They're all starkers. But that stone boat looked mighty promising.

"'And hello to you,' said me.

"'And more the same,' said the magpie poling the boat.

"'Fancy giving a snake a lift?' asked me. 'For safe passage, I'll not bite. By my honor.'

"'Plenty of folks want to cross,' said the magpie. 'Damned if I know why. But it's good to feel useful. I'll pole you across, friend-o-friend, but not for free.'

"'I've nae much to offer,' said me. 'Perhaps my next snakeskin. Weave it into a cloak, keep off the poison splashes.'

"'Don't want to wait,' said the magpie. He cocked his head and looked at me this way and that. Magpies, they love their shiny, pretty things. After a spell, he said, 'Gimme an eye. I fancy those peepers of yours. All those little rainbows deep down. Your eye's my price.'

"'I'm greatly sore to think of losing an eye,' said me.

"'An eye or no passage. Take it or leave it.'

"I could nae see as I had much choice, so in time, I nodded assent. The magpie hopped off the boat, his beak flashed, and just like that, he'd taken my eye. All hurt and aching from my loss, I slithered into the boat. The other magpie at the stern watched me. The first magpie waved a wing toward her and said, 'My sister,' though she looked awful old to be his sister.

"He began to pole us back the way we'd come: him in the bow, his sister in the stern, me coiled up in the middle, still aching. He held my eye under his wing as he poled, held it close and covetously. His sister quickly took to staring at him, at my eye where it peeked from under his wing. I'm nae much for reading bird expressions, but the look on her beaky face disquieted me. It must've taken hours to cross that lake. In time, I could nae see any cave walls at all, just bubbling, hungry poison and acid in all directions.

"Somewhere out there in the middle of that awful stew, the sister-magpie spoke. 'Gimme the eye, brother,' said she.

"'You can see it when we're safe across,' said he.

"'Gimme it now, brother,' said she. 'All that you've taken from me. All that you've left me hurting and sore. All the tears I've shed on your behalf.'

"'It's my eye,' said he. 'I took it, nae you. Maybe I'll let you look at it now and then.'

"With that, his sister hunched herself down, a knot of ragged black and white. I thought that was the end of it. But then she flung herself at her brother, right over me and into him. I kept very still as the two magpies fought and cursed and tugged my eye back and forth, back and forth. 'All you've taken from me,' she kept saying. 'All you've taken.' Her brother gave as good as he got, and I saw that he'd lost his grip on his stone pole and it had slipped down below the surface. We were adrift.

"When it happened, it happened too fast for most to see. One minute, they were still kerfuffling over my eye, the next minute she was gone. Over the side without even a scream. Her brother and I looked over and watched as the lake took her apart, spread her out, dissipated her. Pray you never see such a thing, friend-o-friend. Her brother knocked his head against the stone boat, over and over, and made sounds like a kitten in pain.

"'Listen here,' said me. 'I'm awful sorry for your loss. But if we can't find a way to make this boat move, we'll drift until we die.'

"The magpie hauled himself up and looked at me like he was already dead. 'I said I'd get you across,' said he. 'I've nae had an unsatisfied customer yet and I nae plan to.' Then he dipped his ragged wings in the acid and pushed. Again. Again. He ferried us the rest of the way across with nothing but his wings. It must have hurt like anything, but he made nae sound. Finally, after more hours, we reached a stony bank with fresh tunnels leading away to more caves.

"'I'm greatly obliged,' said me.

"He looked at me. His wings were down to a little bone and tendon. 'Thanks for the eye,' said he. 'May I be cursed. I did it all for her. No one sees. I did it all for her.'

"He rambled like this for a bit, and I figured I'd nae get nothing more from him, so I turned to slither away. All I heard was the slight ploosh of the magpie's body slipping over the side of the boat and into the poison. I watched as the lake took him apart. He held my eye tight against his breast until there was nothing left of either one. I lay there, looking down into the burbling stew, long after there was anything to see. Then I turned away and continued on my journey with many strange new sorrows in my heart.

"But, any-old-way, that's how I lost my eye.

"Now.

"Some space of time after the poison lake, I found myself in a maze of tunnels, all twisty and turny like coral. In this maze were a great number of fuzzy little bats, all flapping this way and that, all squeak and chitter. They pretty much ignored me as I slithered through hard, caked layers of their guano. Best I could tell, those bats seemed locked in some great political and military strife, fighting battles, making and breaking alliances, backstabbing, scheming, politicking. For what? For another ten feet of tunnel? It nae made sense to me, so I kept on slithering. Let the bats have their madness.

"Then luck kicked me right in the rattle. Another one of those deep earthquakes hit the tunnels, and as always, I turned my head towards where it seemed strongest. But I nae counted on the crumble, the jagged spray of broken rock that cascaded down on me before I could dart out of the way. The rockfall pinned me tight, so only my head and a bit of my body could even be seen. And limber as I may be, those rocks held me tight and fast. Things nae looked good.

"I lay there for some time, getting hungrier, wondering if this was it. I tried hissing for help, even though only those fuzzy little bats were around to hear. Finally, one bat flew down and landed to have a look at me. A tiny little thing he was, ears as big as the whole rest of his body, eyes all popped out. He shimmied left, then right, and I gave him what I hoped was a friendly snake-grin, and that's when he squeaked in righteous excitement.

" 'By mine troth!' cried he. 'But the legends are true, for I see with mine own eyes! Thou has the twin swords of Daghm-har! Thou bears them within thine maw, waiting the grasp of a true hero! Mine time has surely come! Though I am but the runtling of the Clatterskap Clan, youngest heir, though the war goes ill for us, mine destiny is upon me and all true wingèd!'

" 'The hell you talking about?' asked me.

" 'Crimson moons and riven rock!' chittered he. 'Scrape and ruin upon mine foes! All shall tremble! Long ago and far away, the Great Cratered One hid the twin swords in a place only the most stalwart would find! I never dared to dream it would be I, Onin of Clatterskap, who would wield such glory! Noble sword-keeper, give to me the blades and let me take up mine father's father's mantle! All shall tremble! The Ancestress and her eighteen earless husbands! The red guard of the Isenken Crevice! Fat Pellik and his bullyboys! The faithless ones who scheme against us, who break our bones in battle, now shall taste the dread fears of old! All shall tremble!'

"I could see this Onin of Clatterskap was no less starkers than the rest of those bats. I let him rave and froth in his euphoria, and when he quieted down a bit, I asked him if he could shift the rock and set me loose.

" 'I will assist thee once I clasp the twin swords of Daghm-har in mine claws, noble one,' said he.

" 'But I need my fangs,' said me.

" 'But I need the twin swords,' said he.

"'Tell you what, friend-o-friend,' said me, knowing he had the upper hand. 'I'll give you one fang…that is, one sword…and once you've shifted the rocks and set me loose, you can have the other.' I figured once I was loose, I'd eat him and take my fang back. Losing an eye is bad enough, but a fang is truly tragic.

"'Thou art silver-tongued, sword-keeper,' said he. 'When the twin blades allow me to conquer mine foes and win the great war, when I sit upon the Onyx Throne and wear the Micah Sigil upon mine brow, I shall remember who bore the swords to me, by the grace of the Great Cratered One. Give me one sword, and I shall free thee forthwith.'

"So I opened my maw nice and wide, and Onin reached in with the little claws at the joints of his wings, and he tugged and twisted, and just like that, he plucked out my fang, and the venom sac too. Oh, how it ached. And how he chortled waving my fang around with the sac all a-dangle beneath.

"'Now shift these rocks,' said me.

"Onin got a very calculating look on his wrinkled little bat face. 'Now that I think on it,' said he, 'one sword should be more than enough. If I need the other one, I know where to find thee. Farewell, sword-keeper. Onin of Clatterskap is off to write a new history and turn the tide. All shall tremble!'

"And off he flew, taking my fang with him, the two-timing little bastard. I heard his all-shall-trembles fading off into the gloom and I despaired.

"Nae ask me how long I was stuck in that rockfall. All around me, the bats were warring in earnest, and it seemed Onin was using my fang to great effect. I nae ever saw him again, but from what fragments I caught, he'd murdered all his brothers and sisters and was leading the Clatterskap Clan on a campaign of bloodthirsty slaughter that'd make your hide crawl. I stayed alive by luring more bats down to where I lay trapped. After all, I still had the other sword of Daghm-har. I'd promise them power and victory, let them reach into my maw for my other fang, then snap my jaws shut and chew and gulp. Bats are stringy.

"Finally, a mighty quake occurred, and the rocks shifted, and I was able to writhe my way to freedom. Funny thing, but it seems the quake happened at the very moment Onin was leading his army in the final campaign against the Baron Starlicker, his mightiest foe. Victory was within Onin's grasp after so many campaigns, betrayals, and massacres. But just as the two armies flung themselves at one another, the quake broke loose a mighty stalactite that plummeted from above and squashed Onin and his army into raspberry jam. So that was the end of Onin, and his beloved sword, my fang, got squashed along with him. Probably his death began a new epoch of scheming and backstabbing and politicking, and probably those bats are still there, too starkers to stop their eternal war. I nae stuck around to see.

"But, any-old-way, that's how I lost my fang.

"Now.

"Deeper down, always deeper down. Figuring I'd better find Old-Dry-Snakeskin or just curl up and die, 'cause I'd nae be much of a snake with one eye and one fang. It became hotter, the air thicker. I began to hear many new sounds. Booming, clanking, clattering and crunch. Machine sounds. Human sounds. Scraps of ash flittered in the air and smears of black oil sullied the rock. I saw metal in the rock too, girders and rivets, a rusty skeletal framework. So dark and deep, yet humans had come here to take what they could. And what terrors had been birthed from steel and axle grease when the world broke?

"The ash got thicker and the oil got smearier, and everything reverberated and echoed off the metal. A mournful, orangey-red glow seeped from cracks and crannies. So much heat threw my senses out of whack. I didn't sense the first human until he came right up behind me and snatched me below the jaw. For all my thrashing and snapping, I could nae do much to free myself. This human had black oil smeared across him in purposeful markings, and ash stuck to him all over. He looked me over and I could see he was starkers like every other soul I'd met down here. He carried me off.

"Dangling and mightily uncomfortable, I was carried into a great chamber, lit by torch and the flowing of molten metal through troughs. Ash swirled like a blizzard; black oil dripped from every surface. An entire self-made tribe of humans awaited, all bowing and caterwauling before a fearsome sight indeed. The far wall of this great chamber was all rock that had melted and dripped over unknown epochs of time, a frozen stone waterfall. Fused to this was a titan of machinery, oil-dripping, great chimneys and spidery pipes, vents and shafts, billions of rivets and continents of rust. It chugged and snarled, belching smoke to stain the ceiling, flashing sparks. It was tall as the cave itself. Who knows what it was, or had been. The breaking of the world had given it new purpose.

"'I bring a sacrifice!' cried the human who held me. 'Fresh meat for the Bossman.'

" 'Come and be honored!' responded another. 'How long it's been since the Bossman tasted real meat!'

" 'What now?' asked me, trying to make myself heard over the echoes thundering about the cave. 'What's all this?'

"The second human looked vaguely chieftain-ish, with old bones haloing his shaved cranium. 'The Bossman, snake,' said he, indicating the towering machine. 'The first god, he who made the other gods and left for parts unknown. We have found him, see! He grows strong on meat and oil, and soon he will lead us back into the daylight with our newly-smelted blades. We are his chosen, his only.'

"Well, that great machine was an impressive sight, but I could tell it was no Bossman, no god. I'd seen the real gods. It was just a big machine from the old times. But I knew arguing with these crazed humans was useless. I'd have left them to their worship if they had nae been about to offer me up.

"I struggled and tried to bite, but got nowhere. They carried me all the way forward, to a little stone altar. Its top was metal mesh, all caked and crusted with the blood of the poor creatures they'd sacrificed. I could see how my blood would ooze through the mesh, trickle down a pipe and into the belly of the machine. My captor flung me down on the mesh and held me there, while the chieftan brandished a dull chrome knife and chanted a multitude of complicated obeisances.

"I could nae get free. I could nae bite. I could nae talk nor bargain nor threaten with starkers humans. Things looked bad. Only one little freedom remained to me, one little trick: I could rattle. So rattle I did. I shimmied and shook my rattle this way and that. I rattled from rage and frustration, from all the hurt I'd seen and caused. Shicka-shicka-shicka!"

As he tells this part of the tale, Rattler will rattle. He'll shake and shimmy, and the dry, eerie rasp will echo all throughout his tunnel. It's almost possible to imagine that from behind him, from deep in the dark, foul void, one echo, faint and insidious, is nae an echo at all, but an answer.

"Shicka-shicka-shicka! All around the great cavern went my rattle, stirring the ash. Bouncing here and there, its echoes finding new cracks and crannies, whispering deeper. It made the humans fretful; they stared at each other with their yellowed, red-rimmed eyes, all a-wonder. I rattled with all my might as the chieftain raised his chrome knife to slit me open, to let my blood and guts ooze into the machine they so revered. But just then, a whispery trace of my rattle found its way right down into the world's core…and was heard. And he answered, friend-o-friend. Old-Dry-Snakeskin answered.

"Up it came—his great, furious, rattle. The biggest quake of all. Divine justice for those who would carve up his kith and kin to a false Bossman. The quake hit and all went to chaos. The walls shook and haroomed and cracked, and the machines snarled and squealed. Metal warped; magma roiled; rivets gave way with a pop-pop-pop. The humans all flew into a wretched panic, running in circles, wailing, clasping their hands over their heads and begging their lousy fake Bossman to deliver them. But with the swirling ash everywhere, soon all they could do was sneeze and wipe their eyes. My captor let go of me and joined the rest in stumbling about, sneezing, wiping his eyes. Chunks of rock and pipes and metal shards came tumbling down. I bolted for the edge of the chamber, for a crack or cranny I could shelter in until the quake ended. I was feeling good, feeling fine. Old-Dry-Snakeskin had heard my distress and saved me. The end was in sight, and what a story I'd have to tell my god!

"I was nae quite that lucky, sad to say. I'd just about made it to shelter when a great fold of metal, knife-edged, plummeted from above. The great machine wanted my blood after all. The knife-edge struck me right between the nostrils, between eye and socket. The pain was worse than anything I'd felt, worse than losing my eye or my fang. It erased all my senses, sent me into oblivion.

"I have a pretty good figuring of what happened to those crazed humans, though. The rock came down on them, and the metal of their machine, and all was buried in gray ash and black oil. They nae died, nae all of them, but they were left all crushed and squeezed. So they rallied and tried to squirm their way up and out, back to the daylight. But all that writhing and squirming through tiny rock veins compressed those humans, made them small and squat. And the ash covered them and stuck to them so badly it became like fur and a tail. And they wiped their bleary eyes so much it left a permanent eyemask of black oil. So when they finally did make it back to the daylight, they looked like nae humans anyone had ever seen. And when anybody asked them what they were, all they could do was sneeze from the ash: 'Ra-ra-ra-cooooon!' So folk called them raccoons, and that's why we have those now.

"Oh, you thought raccoons were already around before the world broke? Just shows how badly everyone's forgotten about everything, friend-o-friend. Remember, you heard it from Rattler: a raccoon is just a compressed little human covered in ash and oil. Maybe that's how the real Bossman punished them for having a fake Bossman. Who can say?

"As for me, I awoke buried under the ash, in the tiniest of coffins, all surrounded by rock. My wounded head hurt like you could nae believe. I wanted to die. But I knew Old-Dry-Snakeskin had to be close, so I stirred my aching body and forced some sense into my throbbing skull and hunted for the next little crack to slither through, and the next, and the next.

"But, any-old-way, that's how my head got split."

Now Rattler will lift his poor, wounded head and tilt his chin up. His one eye gleams; you can make out an entire universe of tiny lights, all the pretty presents he's glued to the walls of his tunnel, reflected. His hiss will grow quieter as his story takes on reverence.

"Now.

"I found it very dark and quiet, down near the core of the world. Nae new quakes hit—Old-Dry-Snakeskin had ceased his rattling. But it nae mattered, 'cause I could sense him near. I just could. He's a god, my god. Ask any creature and they'd be just as sure of sensing their god nearby.

"I sought out cracks and crevices, forced myself all the way down. I left a few scraped scales behind me, nae caring. In the end, I poked my split head from a crack and all around me was space. Vast, black space. You have nae idea what real darkness is, friend-o-friend. I had nae hope of seeing a thing at first. I rested myself with my head hovering over that great void, so big as to be its own world. I let all my senses attune themselves to the dark. I waited patiently.

"In time, I figured I could ken what lay before me. More than just nothingness. A world-sized cavern, nae floor below, but a ceiling. I knew there must be a ceiling, 'cause hanging down from it were stalactites, fangs of stone wider than the thickest redwood, longer than the tallest, silveriest tower ever crafted by human hand. A fringe of stone older than creation itself, if such a thing could be.

"More time went by, and my attuned senses made out new shapes, and there came a moment when I saw the whole picture and was awed and humbled. He was there. He'd been there the whole time. I realized him all at once. Draped and coiled around the vast cones of rock, stretching from one limit of my senses to the other.

"Old-Dry-Snakeskin.

"But once I'd realized him, I almost wished I'd stayed blind. I can nae describe in how sorrowful a state Old-Dry-Snakeskin appeared. He was all bones. Dry, dusty ribs and vertebrae, a great fanged skull with nae eyes nor tongue, just a tiny bit of god-light glimmering in the sockets. Nae scales, nae skin, nae meat and guts. The skeleton of Old-Dry-Snakeskin dangled from the rock, long as a mountain range, worse than dead. Nae moving a single inch.

"One thing he'd still kept: his rattle. One small amount of his old godly glory. Such a fine, glossy rattle, longer than any mortal snake's, almost as long as the stalactite from which it hung. Old-Dry-Snakeskin had nae tongue, and so he could nae hiss. But he could rattle. I waited, 'cause it's unseemly to announce one's presence to one's god. After a long space of time, he noticed me. He nae moved, but I felt his attention shift. His glorious rattle twitched and shook, whispers running down its uncountable chambers. In that faint rasp, I heard his words.

"'You've come upon me in a sad state, snakeling,' rattled Old-Dry-Snakeskin. 'A sad, sad state.'

"'I guess we're both in a sad state, Old-Dry-Snakeskin,' said me.

"'It pains me to have one of my own see me like this,' rattled he.

"'O, Old-Dry-Snakeskin,' said me. 'My lost eye aches and my lost fang aches more and my split head aches like no one would believe, but worst of all is the ache of seeing you all stripped down to bone. Who did this to you, Old-Dry-Snakeskin? Who committed this act upon your godly self?'

"'All of them did it,' rattled he. 'All those faithless, harebrained, no-account bastards, all those gods. Took me apart, ate and drank me, wrung me dry. But at least I can say I'm nae worse off than them, eh, snakeling?'

"'Why, I saw them out in the desert,' said me. 'All the gods. Nae dead, nae alive. Their bodies in shreds and their mouths turned to stringy holes. Old-Dry-Snakeskin, the whole world's broke. I figured you'd be the one god left to fix things.'

"'Just look at me, snakeling,' rattled Old-Dry-Snakeskin mournfully. 'I'm nae fit to be seen. My fine and glossy scales, gone. My venom, gone. My eyes and my tongue. I'm just bones and a rattle. A dead god, nae equipped to fix a damn thing.'

"'How'd it happen, Old-Dry-Snakeskin?' asked me.

"'It all started with a rumor,' rattled he. 'A vile little rumor. Y'see, snakeling, I'm the one who made the world. The other gods all say they did, but it was me. I made the world out of venom and shed skin, and my rattle clobbered any god who tried to meddle. The other gods know this, so I scare the hell out of them. They'll nae admit it. They wonder how I did it. It eats at them. They wonder what's so special about my scales, my venom, my bodily matter, that it can make a world.

"'So there was this rumor. I'd nae be half-surprised if that damned Reynard-the-fox-god, or whatever name he goes by this week, started it. Or maybe some other trickster. Who's to stay where rumors start; it nae matters once they get rolling. The other gods began to whisper that whatever I had in my bodily matter was the good stuff. The powerful stuff. The One Actual Nectar, the elixir and the panacea. Every god wants to build their own world, y'see, and the rumor whispered to them that Old-Dry-Snakeskin contained all the world-building stuff they needed. The rumor grew and grew until it was all the gods could think about. So they all decided to eat and drink me.

"'They lured me into the desert, telling me there were signs of the Bossman's return to this world. I fell for it, 'cause what god would have dreamed all the other gods were planning to eat and drink him? They got me out in the middle of nowhere, and they all fell upon me, and I could nae fight off every god at once. They tore me all up, snakeling, and they ate me. Scales, skin, meat, and guts. A god can nae die entirely, but I was about as close to dead as could be. And then they did the worst thing of all. They plucked out my venom sacs and passed them around, drank and guzzled down my toxins. It got them drunk, and nothing's worse than a drunk god. They drank, and they waited for all the power to come upon them. And they drank, and they argued. And they drank, and they fought. And they drank, and they fought harder, until all the gods were tearing each other to pieces in one big ball of drunken, divine chaos. Struggling, thundering, raging, the gods pulverized one another, and kept on guzzling my venom until it ate away their mouths and their insides.

"'And that, snakeling, is how the world broke. It's because all the idiot gods got drunk and wrecked themselves beyond repair. I made the world, but the world needs all the gods to run proper. Now the gods lie piled up in the desert, wrecked. Only the Bossman could fix them, and I doubt he's gonna bother. I'm so sorry, snakeling. You came all this way, lost your eye and your fang, got your head split. Just to hear me say this. The world's broke for good.'

"'But you can still do something about it, Old-Dry-Snakeskin,' said me. I nae wanted to believe what I was hearing. 'You made the world.'

"'I already told you,' rattled he. 'I'm fit for nothing any more. I need scales and flesh. I need venom. I need a tongue. But without all that, I'm too weakened to help myself in any way. All I have left is my rattle, but I'm tired of rattling for nae purpose. I can make the underground shake and quake, but up there on the surface, they nae even feel a thing. If I go up there, I'll just be a long string of bones, baking in the sun. That's all.'

"Now, after all I'd been through, all I'd suffered, it might've been easy to give up right then and there. I thought about it. And then I said, 'Old-Dry-Snakeskin, let me help. Let me help you get back what you've lost. I figure I'm the only rattlesnake left who nae suffered the madness and forgetfulness of the world breaking. Maybe it's for a reason. So I can help you.'

"Old-Dry-Snakeskin looked at me with his empty, glimmery eye sockets. 'Well, snakeling, you're bold enough. But can you make me a new hide of fine scales? Can you conjure up new flesh for my dry bones? Fresh venom? Can you find me a new tongue? If you could do all that, why, I'd come back up. Oh, would I ever. I'd come barreling back to the surface, and the whole broken world would tremble. If only.'

" 'Let me try, Old-Dry-Snakeskin,' said me. "I nae care how long it takes. Let me try to make you everything you need, scales and flesh and venom and a tongue. So you can come back. Come back to the world. You're all the world has left now.'

"Old-Dry-Snakeskin's rattle was quiet for some time. I stayed still, my head hanging over that huge, vast blackness, waiting to see if my god had given up the ghost.

"Finally, his great skull moved a little; his rattle twitched. 'Try, then,' whispered Old-Dry-Snakeskin to me.

"He rattled no more. I turned myself right around and began the long, tired slither back the way I'd come. I had a long way to crawl before I'd see the lightning-struck sky again. I might die a thousand times over. But now I had a reason to live. A purpose. A duty. I was the one chance Old-Dry-Snakeskin had of returning from his tomb in the world's core. He'd given me permission to try.

"I had plenty more adventures on my way back up, but I'll nae waste your time with talk of those. I lived. I came back up, felt the bloated sunlight, the bite of the blowflies. The world on the surface was nae less broken than before, but still I saw beauty in it. The beauty of purpose.

"Old-Dry-Snakeskin told me I could try. So ever since then, I've been trying."

Now Rattler will fall silent. It's nae the poised silence of a pause between chapter and chapter. It's final. Even though he has more to say, it's final. He's waiting for the argument.

It always comes. You'll be rolling your rebuttal around in the back of your throat right now. Because Rattler's story nae sits well with anyone. Some fragment or detail always sticks. And within a moment or two, you're going to spit it out, just as everyone does.

The brown bear will grumble and growl, "But that's nae how the world broke at all. See, there was this boulder that cracked..."

Or the crazed, giggling bird will gasp out, "Nae magpie ever lived underground. That's starkers even for us!"

Or the salamander will roll his eyes and declare, "Old-Dry-Snakeskin nae made the world. It was Rollumbol the salamander god, who took the leftover slime from his tongue and—"

Or the raccoon, all bristled and puffed out, fit to bursting with outrage, will blurt, "Now, just one gods-damned, piss-drinking minute!"

And that's when Rattler's sandy hiss will cut back in, cut off the argument. "So. Do you want the One Actual Story, or do you nae want the One Actual Story? Eh? Eh, friend-o-friend?"

He'll wait for the sullen silence, and smirk. "You came all this way. You brought me a pretty present that'll look fine here in my church." He'll bob his head, encompassing the tunnel of awful prettiness, a thousand thousand glittering remnants of beauty, stuck to the walls in the mass of clay and snakeskin. The green, toxic stream, flowing uphill. The nest of tendons running in from the walls, to the webby hole where Rattler dangles. The terrible black, choked, dusty void behind him. Now you'll see: it's a shrine to Old-Dry-Snakeskin.

"You're correct, though," Rattler says. "There's no right or wrong. That's what's so interesting about gods. Somewhere out there, a fox is building a church to his god-of-many-names, and a salamander is constructing a chapel to drowned Rollumbol, one bubble at a time. A bird is making an eyrie for his many gods, who're also one god. Nae one of them is wrong. Even those humans with their big machine, thinking it's Bossman returned. Nae wrong. Everyone's right. Right about which god made the world, about how the world broke, about how to fix it.

"They're all right. But me, my story, is the only one that's real."

Rattler's grin is terrible. Terrible.

"So now you know, friend-o-friend. You know what's waiting down there in the world's core. And you can see. My church to

Old-Dry-Snakeskin is also his skin and his meat. When it's done, when I judge it ready, I will rattle a message down into the depths. He'll hear. And Old-Dry-Snakeskin will come barreling up. All dry bones, he'll come. His skull will hit this nest of clay and skin, and it'll stick to him. As he passes through this tunnel, he'll strip the walls inside-out, slide the clay onto his bones like a pretty lady sliding on a stocking. All these pretty presents will be his new scales. The clay will be his meat. He'll drink down this toxic stream as he goes, and that'll be his venom. By the time Old-Dry-Snakeskin reaches the daylight, he'll look better than ever. He'll be ready. A brand-new light will blaze from his empty eye sockets, and the broken world will tremble."

Rattler's voice is worse than his grin. And the sanity that still blazes in his one eye is worst of all.

And then? you'll ask, afraid to know. He'll fix the world?

Rattler will laugh, low and vicious in his throat.

"Fix it? Fix it, friend-o-friend? Nae. Old-Dry-Snakeskin has enough rage in his bones to write new gospels of ruin. This world's too broke. I nae saw that when I was young, but I see it now. I love him for it. He's got big, big plans for the wreckage of this world. But he is nae planning to fix it."

You don't want to stay. You want to turn tail and run. But you have one more question. What does Rattler think will happen to him when Old-Dry-Snakeskin comes up?

Rattler will tilt his split head back and sigh. "Ahhhh. Well. I'm nae fit to be a snake any more. But Old-Dry-Snakeskin has more in store for Rattler. When he comes up, I'll stay right here until his jaw closes around me, and I'll root myself right down in his mouth. With my split head, I'm perfect for it. I will be the instrument by which he rains his gospel down upon the doomed world. I will be his tongue."

His one eye will finally close. "I'm tired. Go. Thank you for the pretty present, friend-o-friend. Go."

You'll go. You'll shuffle out of that glimmery tunnel, back out into the light of the too-big, too-close sun. You'll leave that dark void behind and return, or nae return, to the places you know. You'll hope they haven't crumbled or shifted or gone away. As if it mattered. You can nae outrun Rattler's words.

There's one thing that holds true about each and every creature who goes to hear the One Actual Story from Rattler. Each of you, with nae an exception, regrets it.

But it's just a story. A confuddled tale from a starkers snake. Let him build his church, you'll tell yourself. Let him stick his pretty presents to the walls. It nae means a thing. Some other god will fix the world. Some other story is the one which matters.

So you'll tell yourself.

And then you'll begin to run, sprinting and stumbling over the blasted remains of the world, cutting yourself on rock shards, bit by blowflies. Always glancing behind you. Over and over. As if you could hear a deep, cruel, enraged rattle from somewhere far below. You'll run. You'll shut your tired, teary eyes tight.

You'll pray that when Old-Dry-Snakeskin surges into the light, all coated and bejeweled in a brand-new skin, with his living tongue hissing and slavering and raving below his great, dripping fangs, you'll nae be alive to witness it.

Even though Rue is a legendary creature, her kitsune magic is limited. She doesn't know if she'll ever reach her full potential and unlock the secrets of foxfire and human transformation.

KITSUNE TEA

E.A. Lawrence

Rue hated the cruel truth that she was not even one year old and she would probably die before her first birthday, but she didn't plan to go quietly. As Rue hunted using the spells her father had taught her, like how to fly sparrow-shaped all the way to nests to get the really fresh eggs—she thought of how he died empty stomached and alone under the tires of a convertible before his fourth birthday. Rue trembled at the thought every time. Her stomach grumbled in harmony. What was the point of being kitsune if you could die on a human's tarmac or between incisors like a rabbit? Shaking her shoulders, Rue tried to gauge if she had enough in reserve to shift form.

Shifting wasn't easy to learn. As a kit, Rue learned basic spells to hide and to hunt. It was easy to surprise a mouse if you floated down next to it as a leaf. But that took practice, energy, and talent; Rue was only ten months old. Master level kitsune mages could achieve human form, but kitsune mages weren't plentiful, especially in Manitou State Forest. Dinner was rarely plentiful in her patch of the forest but she persevered. Rue bent and twitched her nose over the path, inhaling and processing the smells. Rabbit was especially strong today. Her tongue darted over her chops as Rue set off after her dinner, keeping her kitsune form this time.

Evening sun streamed into a small clearing in the wood, a small oasis of rich gold tinged with woodland green in an otherwise shady forest. Rue liked this particular clearing. Yes, it was a trifle exposed, but the open canopy let a thin turf of grass, ferns, and seedlings grow, which attracted rabbits. Even if rabbits weren't available, this time of year Rue could find some berries growing along the edges and on the old oak stump. It wasn't meat, but berries would keep her alive.

Rue crept forward on her belly, nose twitching. Human scent filled Rue's nose instead of rabbit-tinged earth. Rue froze in place, heart beating as fast as a mouse's. Rue was too hungry. Nothing short of divine grace would let her turn invisible or sparrow-shaped now. Odd though—Rue couldn't hear the human. Humans usually made noise no matter what they did. Rue sniffed more deeply. Yes, that was human scent but it was stale. Gathering courage, or perhaps bowing to curiosity, Rue lifted her head above the cover of a fern to take a look. Balanced on the old oak stump stood an enormous wooden dollhouse. Rue couldn't have been more surprised if the nine-tailed Goddess herself appeared to say hello.

The dollhouse reeked of human but the smell was old; the humans who brought the dollhouse hadn't been back in days. Rue regarded it with great interest, ears pricked and whiskers on end. The thing that struck her most beyond its very presence in the wood was its size. The dollhouse was palatial, four stories, with fancy gables, cedar shingles, huge windows which glinted like eyes in the evening light, and a big bay window which gaped in a faux smile. Rue paced around the edifice, giving it a lot of space, distrust from the human musk making her keep her distance. She found the dollhouse curiously appealing, especially the gabled porch that ran the full length of the house on its front. If she stretched out there she could nap safely, and dream, really dream, wondrous things. The back was partially open, showing every floor of the house equipped with tiny engravings on the walls, minutely patterned rugs painted on the floors, and even tiny little cherry patterned curtains fluttering in the kitchen windows. A rumble in Rue's stomach reminded her that she could not afford to tarry. Nothing edible resided within and the scent of human, stale though it was, was still potent enough to make Rue's fur stand on end, an instinctual attempt to increase her paltry size and a futile one. Rue went back to the trees to look for her dinner, but she cast many a backward glance to the dollhouse waiting alone in sunny finery, marooned in the wood.

***

Curiosity made up a large percentage of Rue's nature. As she sat back on her haunches, enjoying the rich smells of the dollhouse, rain, wood, paint, plastic, and glue, Rue began to ponder tactics for how best to explore all of its crannies. A rich meal of momma mouse complete with mouse pups filled Rue's stomach comfortably. She could do magic if she chose and have energy to spare. The question was, what spell would be best? The house was large enough for Rue to explore the lower stories as herself, but things would be knocked over in the process, and some sort of small creature was necessary for the upper floors.

Rue concentrated on the sparrow spell, calling on the power of the Goddess and her ancestors. The familiar tingle swept over her pelt; simultaneously, she was fledged and shrunk until finally with a sort of pop! she felt more than heard, Rue found herself flapping in the air, a song sparrow, peeping into a living area that suddenly seemed quite large. Landing inside, Rue decided to explore the marvels of the main floor and then move up, exploring along the way, for as long as the spell endured.

The blue chairs were actually padded and upholstered in old velvet. Rue pressed her right foot upon the cushion, reveling in its softness. An oak stained wooden hutch gleamed beside the beautiful bay window. It was filled with shiny little things. A real flower patterned china set glinted softly at Rue from the wooden shelves. When she pecked the biggest piece, it made a distinctive tinkle. Rue didn't know all the uses of these wonders, but she vowed that someday soon she would, these things and everything else in this strange human house. Of course, she would need to see the whole house first. Flapping mightily Rue flew up to the second story. Hopping quickly through a bathroom, she came to a detailed miniature gallery of framed portraits and hunt paintings done on paper in petite frames. The next room proved even curiouser to Rue.

A toy baby grand piano, just a little too big to be to scale and shining invitingly, occupied the corner of the room. Rue hopped forward and boldly tapped at the keys with her beak. She was rewarded with tinny notes registering high on the scale. A thought, vague though it was, began to form in Rue's mind amidst the thrills of sound; *so this is what humans feel like, this power of making something new happen.* Rue's feathers began to tingle; she knew her magic would slip soon.

Tearing herself away from the mini music room, Rue fluttered up, skipping the third floor and going straight for the fourth floor at the top, knowing she was missing rooms. She found herself in a room filled with even tinier tiny things. Little wooden trains, colorful blocks, a wooden crib, an assortment of minute bears, bunnies, and a rocking horse that even had a string mane and tail. It was hard for Rue to hop without disturbing anything.

With a lurch in her tummy and a bit of giddiness, Rue knew her time was up. She had strength enough to topple over the floor's edge before pop! Rue was kitsune once more in midair between the barely explored fourth and the unexplored third floors. She fell fast. Rue landed with a painful thump on the ground at the base of the stump. Rue's stomach began to grumble just a little. The magic had been costly. Part of Rue, perhaps the rational part, knew that she should regret the frivolity that wasted a meal that could have sustained her through tomorrow night. She couldn't care less. Rue felt light-headed, like a kit who opened her eyes and found there was a world beyond the dark warmth of the den. It was vast, wonderful, and she burned to explore it, to know the secret meaning behind every strange little object contained in the miniature mansion. Lying in the dirt, staring up at the dollhouse that eclipsed the afternoon sun, Rue began to hope that perhaps this strange edifice would be her ticket to kitsune magehood. This was a hope worth hunting for.

***

Rue trotted along the old sidewalk. She hadn't been to this part of town in a few days. Too many rival kitsune and unfriendly foxes lived in the human communities, where the hunting was good, and a puny vixen like her was not welcome. The sidewalk ended in a ragged chain link fence hung with a red diamond sign. Half-finished housing frames, draped with flapping sheets, lined the grassy sidewalk. Rue knew mice and rats frequented the frames, but she was too polite, or too fearful, to contemplate poaching. The territory of the old vixen was rich in prey and a good trot from Rue's range. Earlier she got lucky on her lands and caught a robin, her grandmamma's favorite prey. Rue took this as a sign from the Goddess that it was time to go ask her grandmamma for some advice. Finally, Rue arrived at a raggedy gravel strewn clearing. Rue sat down to wait. If her grandmamma was alive, Rue would find out soon enough. A human bag lady appeared in front of Rue.

"What a pretty little vixen you've grown up to be!"

Rue felt her eyes widen; her fur went up; and she made ready to run. Then Rue was helpless, clutched by the scruff of the neck, dangling from the bag lady's hand.

"Your name is Rue, isn't it? My Lulu's child."

Rue realized with a shock that the bag lady was speaking kitsune, not human, and that this old human was her grandmamma. Rue's heartbeat quickened.

"Yes, Grandmamma, I'm Rue."

"What brings you here? Not poaching, I trust." A shake underscored the point.

"No, Grandmamma, I brought a gift actually."

"A gift, eh? Well, Lulu raised you right then after all. I take it that you've come to talk then."

"Yes, Grandmamma."

The woman looked hard at Rue. Rue noticed the pale eyes that could barely be called brown, the vivid red hair that anyone would think was fake, and the pointed teeth glinting through her smile. The lady set Rue down and sat facing her, legs crossed, arms resting on her thighs. Rue had no doubt that one or the other of those arms would grab her if she misspoke at any point.

"You may speak, child. I'll let you know when we're through."

"Well, Grandmamma—" Rue began.

"Wait. You said you had a gift. Let's have that first." Without a word, Rue regurgitated the robin only somewhat worse for wear. "Oh! Robin meat is my favorite. Go on then, child."

Rue kept it simple, asking how Grandmamma became a mage and what Rue would have to do to make the same progress. The bag lady gnawed at the partially digested robin, thinking a moment, before speaking.

"Well, I've been a mage these two winters now. Right about when this project site got abandoned and I moved in, I figured out the spell."

"And?"

"And what?"

"The spell. What is the human spell?"

"I can't tell you." Grandmamma crunched a robin wing as she said it. Rue was angry now.

"Can't or won't?"

"Can't, child. See, here's the dirty little secret about magic, Rue. It's not one size fits all. The spell I use to take this form might do nothing at best if you said it; at worst it would do something you didn't want to happen to you."

"But spells can be taught. Spells like invisibility, being a leaf, or being a sparrow. My parents taught me those easy enough."

"Sure'n they did. But let me ask you this, child. When you do those spells, is it like pushing water uphill or following a river down?"

Rue was puzzled, cocking her ears at the imagery. "It's easy once you get the knack."

"Exactly. You're going from kitsune to something simpler than kitsune. That's a uniform transition, easy to teach. It's hard to teach someone how to know themselves."

"What?"

"Look, since you've been polite enough to give me a robin, I'll tell you what you need to ask yourself. Then you're on your own. Wait. Here, have a chunk." The bag lady gnawed off part of the other wing and threw it to Rue.

"Ask?" Rue swallowed the offering in one gulp.

"Don't interrupt. Now the questions you need to figure out: Who are you now? Who do you want to be? Why be a human? That is what you need to know. Answer that list, child, and I'm positive you'll figure out the spell to tell the Goddess."

"But how do I figure all that out?" Rue wanted to howl.

"I don't know. But I figure you wouldn't have come here if you weren't working on the problem." Both kitsune sat in silence a moment. Finally, the elder stood, robin finished. Rue took the hint promptly, taking to her heels and shouting, "Thank you, Grandmamma," over her shoulder as she fled the old vixen's territory.

***

Rue had another good hunt. She'd gotten lucky and found a litter of baby rabbits hidden in one of the few grassy spots in the wood. Rue liked rabbit meat the best and the babies were just so tender. This, of course, meant that Rue practically skipped all the way to the dollhouse in the wood. Despite inhabiting the wood and all the elements, the dollhouse was holding its own upon the oaken stump, still a beautiful shining structure in the afternoon sun. Rue paused to sniff the dollhouse. It smelled entirely of the wood now, not a trace of the human world lingered on its surfaces. The grasses were beginning to grow up around it. Pollen, leaves, and twigs littered the wooden floors. A feeling stirred in Rue, a feeling of perhaps rebellion or perhaps grief. The dollhouse no longer seemed an interloper in the forest. Rue couldn't let this happen; she just couldn't stand by and watch the dollhouse get destroyed, not before learning its secrets. The words came from her lips, words she just felt, somehow, would work, and Rue found herself to be small, impossibly small, but still herself rather than any sparrow or leaf, standing inside the living room of the dollhouse.

"Thank you, Goddess, thank you," Rue spoke aloud to She who might have been listening. Rue set to work, a kind of work that it wouldn't otherwise have occurred to her to do. Methodically, she began to clean the dollhouse. Using her tail as well as her paws, her tongue a little on the upholstery, she swept out all the debris a forest produces. Rue clambered up the floors, banishing cobwebs, spiders, beetles, and twigs from all the nooks and crannies of the dollhouse. With delight, Rue realized that she was finally on the third floor.

The first room she entered had a giant four-poster bed complete with pillows and a multi-colored fabric cover of little squares. Rue reached out, tracing the stitches with her paw. She didn't know what it was, she hadn't seen this through the human windows in the town, but she admired its energy. Some sort of weapon with a weighty globed knob and pointed metal tines sprouting from a metal bole stood sentinel in the corner of the room, with a red cloak hanging on one of the tines. Tentatively, Rue touched the fabric. It had been crafted with tiny little stitches in thick wool; it felt soft and looked like it was waiting. Rue looked at it in its mystery and suppleness one last time before she clambered round the wall to the next chamber.

This room held wooden bunkbeds complete with more colored tops and pillows. A large wooden box was against the wall partitioning this chamber from the next. Fumbling with the clasp, Rue managed to lift the lid. Small flowered dresses, denim trousers, shirts, handkerchiefs, and white cotton underthings were tightly folded within the box. Rue cocked her head and scratched her chin. What possible purpose could there be to crafting tiny little clothes no human would ever wear and putting them in a small, hinged box? But as she closed the lid she couldn't help but be impressed in spite of herself. As carefully as she could, Rue repacked the little garments into the trunk and even managed to close the box.

Scrambling around the wall, Rue had to catch herself to keep from falling off the edge. She found herself standing inside a well-appointed library. Shelves filled the walls of the room, a room as large as the two chambers she had just visited put together. The shelves were filled with beautifully crafted miniature rectangles of what smelled like paper. An expert hand had lettered the spines in minute gold letters of human script. Rue navigated around the leather wingback chairs, the tiny little side-tables, and a round table complete with functioning drawers, as well as a giant blue greenish orb that seemed to be importantly placed on a central table. Rue gently prodded it with a toe, almost jumping into the shelving when the orb began to spin gently on its base. Rue spun the orb several more times after the initial surprise wore off; she marveled at the blur of colors as it spun and the slight breeze it produced whirring on its axis. It reminded her how once, just a little while after she first opened her eyes, she saw her grandmamma and parents produce foxfire together. Rue didn't know why they did this or why she was never taught how to produce the fire herself, but she did remember how it looked: blue, green, and alive, hanging against the night colors of the copse in which they lived.

Rue suddenly heard a nightmare sound. The eerie halloo of a pair of feral dogs echoed through the wood. It wasn't hard to know where the dogs were. Kitsune ears are keen and hungry dogs pelting for a meal can be loud. Rue didn't want the dogs to corner her here; they might damage the dollhouse, or she might, in a premature transformation. Rue would have to run and run fast if she wanted to lead the dogs away from the clearing. Rue leapt from the third floor, leaving behind the wonders of tiny clothes and spinning orbs, and landed on her feet in her full-size. It was time then to do something Rue never thought she'd ever even think of: run towards a pair of hungry mouths determined to kill her, run for everything she was worth.

Rue ran until she saw the white markings on their faces, startling them on a deer path in the wood. The dogs were large and lean with hunter eyes; these dogs had known no human comforts, only the hunt. Rue knew the hunter look, she knew it in herself and she knew how feeble her own eyes must look to them in her small face. Rue bared her teeth and cocked her head. Yes, she may be the prey. But she was kitsune, the most cunning prey of all. Rue lolled her tongue and grinned at the dogs, turning forty degrees to the side. She leaped off tree trunks and stumps as she ran past their dumbfounded faces. Rue could hear them turn around, away from the dollhouse and its wonders, to chase her red brush through the wood on the path they had just run.

The chase seemed interminable. Rue knew the ground, knew the feeling of her claws raking across its surface, felt the rhythm of her pursuers' paws through her own footpads. Rue stuck close to the trees. Every chance she could she zigged and zagged or leapt up or across any stump or rock that might slow the dogs' pursuit, occasionally kicking any sticks or rocks she could to inconvenience them.

As Rue ran, part of her, a part she never knew she had, began to notice something. She noticed the blur of the trees, the colors of green and brown melding together into an impression of shadowed light that struck her, illogically and perhaps foolishly, as beautiful. The word beautiful was basically alien to Rue, hardly something in her everyday lexicon, yet it floated to her mind like a gift from the Goddess as she looked at the trees at speed in the afternoon sun.

Gradually, the trees began to thin. Rue heard the approaching hum of a road. Blurs of color and engine noise and the scent of exhaust attacked Rue's senses. She knew enough to pause a moment for the cars to pass, but Rue knew it couldn't be more than a moment. The dogs weren't deer to freeze at the roadside; they would use it to press their advantage. If only she had some sort of spell to cover her escape once she reached the other side, something to dazzle the dogs so they wouldn't follow her across the road into the human neighborhood. Foxfire. Rue could have howled. If only she knew that spell.

Foxfire is part of kitsune nature. Why didn't she know it? She ought to know it. Foxfire should be easy, like following a river downhill, as her grandmamma said. The dogs' footfalls approached; one of them hallooed. Rue didn't have a lot of time. Taking a deep breath, Rue filled her mind with fire, focusing and amplifying the memory of her parents' shining blue fire filling an evening sky so that it filled her mind. Suffused with the warmth and color of remembered fire, Rue threw herself into the road with a running leap, caught the pavement with her paws a quarter of the way across, and ran for all she was worth. Rue felt the invulnerability of the truly desperate with nothing left to lose as she flung her life across the roadway.

The gambit worked. Rue found herself alive and alone across the road from where she had started when she finally stopped for breath behind a potting shed in a bed of hydrangeas. For a while, Rue couldn't guess how long, she simply lay among the hydrangeas in the flowerbed catching gulps of air back into her lungs. It was a marvel to her that she managed to find her fire within such a desperate circumstance. To conjure the flames, Rue just had to think them. By the time she was breathing at a normal rate, Rue found herself juggling seven little globes of foxfire between her front paws. She felt like a kit again playing with her new toy.

The sun was beginning to set. It occurred to Rue that perhaps she ought to investigate the neighborhood, since she was there anyway, and give the dogs time to find other prey. Rue couldn't support a transformation spell; she was surprised enough that the foxfire hadn't cost her more energy. She'd just have to rely on plain sneakiness for the moment. Carefully, Rue snuck up to the house next to the potting shed to explore. The lights were on in most of the windows. The house was small, not as palatial as the dollhouse in the wood, and only had one apparent level with a deck. Rue stood on her back legs to look through the big window. Humans, adults and juveniles, were gathered around a table. Rue recognized the shape of the big china thing being used as identical to the delicate pieces on the shelves in the dollhouse. The adult human held the handle and the lid while pouring an amber colored steaming liquid into little cups. Young human females grasped the cups with exaggerated care, small fingers extended for balance, as they brought the steaming beverage to their lips. Rue watched as cups were refilled, sugar passed round with delicate metal tongs, and the cream liberally added from a small matching jug. The band of human females seemed both grave and happy as they used each piece of the mysterious set of vessels in turn. Rue had no idea what the ritual meant, but she found herself curious to someday sip from the dollhouse's version herself.

A smell of angry male fox assaulted her nose. Rue was on her paws and at bay to a male twice her size.

"Poacher!"

"Easy now, I'm just passing through."

"Not even in heat?" The male sniffed. "Why would a foreigner be passing through if not to poach then?"

"I'm not poaching anything." Rue tried to sidle to the left out of his snap range.

"You're not here to screw, so you must be here to poach, foreigner. You're going to have to fight me first if you want to hunt here." The male's chin jutted out. His lips exposed his canines for her inspection. Rue could feel that she had edged away from the wall and round the corner. She could bolt for it, but a rumble in her gut told her the effort would cost her dear.

"I'm not fighting anyone. I'm leaving."

The male made a snap at her just as Rue leapt backwards and away. The moon was up but low, since the last rays of sun were just caressing the western sky. The neighborhood was at rest in the human homes, but the animals were awake. Some were just getting the day's foraging started while others were calling it quits. Rue could hear the low hum of the locals as she fled for her life yet again.

***

Rue collapsed in a heap of leaves piled against the roots of a big red oak just inside the borders of her territory. For now she was safe from the ire of other kitsune and local foxes. Her paws were sore and Rue could feel the hollows of her stomach. Even within her own lands, she felt unprotected and vulnerable. With effort, she tucked her sore paws up under her fur and curled her proud brush around her like a mantle. The kitsune in the human lands were older than Rue, stronger, and meaner. No quarter was granted; Rue had not run two seconds from one territory to the next before the resident kitsune or fox took up her chase where its neighbor left off. Rue was small, young, and weaker than all of them, but she was fast. Not for the first time, Rue thanked the Goddess for her paws even as she licked their sores.

At least there was the dollhouse. Rue lifted her nose out from behind her brush and pointed it in the direction of the dollhouse and its clearing, inhaling deeply. A scent touched her nose. So close, the sweet smell of vole; the scent wafted on a breeze toward Rue where she lay in the leaf litter. She needed this kill. She hadn't eaten in almost two days and nothing would replenish her like meat. Rue hauled herself up and began to stalk toward the scent.

It was a slow stalk. Every paw placement mattered with something like live meat. With a delicate twitch of her whiskers, Rue could sense the vole moving through the top layer of detritus. Rue knew her best chance would be to stun it with a high pounce from above and that she would have one chance at that. The muscles in Rue's legs trembled a little with weakness and the effort of not making noise. Rue could just barely see the vole now; the ovoid outline of that plump little morsel shuffled underneath some lacy oak leaves. The moment was now. Clenching up her hocks, Rue got ready to spring. Faster than a blink Rue pounced, paws punching the leaves with enough force to stun the vole and enough muscle to hold it in place for her jaws.

As soon as Rue's paws hit the leaves, she knew she had failed. She'd been fast, but the vole was faster, darting out from under her paws at the last millisecond. With a scramble, Rue went after it, but quit quickly; her nose told her the vole was out of range and she couldn't sense anything else in the area as a second choice. This was the hunt: usually it was a failure and that was part of why the successes tasted so sweet. Grass could keep her alive, as could acorns and berries, but it would be meager and she wouldn't be able to refill her reservoir of magic, much less cast any spells, eating only plants. With trembling limbs, Rue set off at a trot towards the dollhouse. If she was going to feel sick and eat grass, she might as well do it within sight of the dollhouse, all the better to ponder her grandmamma's questions.

***

Perhaps because it was such an essential part of the kitsune character, a part of the soul, foxfire didn't cost Rue a thing to use, but rather helped comfort her on her herbivorous diet. So night after night, Rue sat in the grass in front of the dollhouse, casting balls of foxfire up around its walls. The dollhouse looked so beautiful on the oak stump lighted by the blue green orbs of foxfire floating in and around it, illuminating the interior and casting the illusion of living shadows on its walls. Rue found herself, as the days passed, doing more than just having balls of foxfire brighten the dollhouse. With practice, Rue could make smaller and smaller balls of foxfire and have them dance around in the rooms. Foxfire flitted through the library while a different orb bobbed around the kitchen and another danced in front of the little porcelain set.

***

Kitsune don't sing much. Or at least they don't generally sing a song just for the thrill of using their voice. When kitsune sing, it is usually for an occasion like a large birth or at a remembrance service like the one for Rue's father when they sang his spirit to the realm of the Goddess. Yet Rue found herself, on these nights with her foxfire and the dollhouse, singing. Sometimes the rhythm was upbeat, especially if her orbs were moving quickly around the rooms of the dollhouse, sometimes together, sometimes apart while other times the rhythm was slow, thoughtful, almost wistful, but always a dance of light illuminating the dollhouse set to a music of Rue's own.

This was how she wanted to live her last moments. After all this time, Rue felt so ill and weak that she knew her day to meet the Goddess was nigh. Curiously, Rue felt calm about this. No longer did the prospect fill her with the rebellion it once did. It felt like Rue had failed at being a kitsune. What kind of hunter can't hunt properly? What kind of kitsune lets herself get so weak and frail using magic on something that doesn't net her any food? Whatever that kind was, and it was probably not a very good kind, Rue accepted that she was it. She had tried, really tried, to live. She had tried to hunt. Rue even kept eating grass and weeds; it just felt like that wasn't going to be enough anymore. If it wasn't going to be enough then so be it; at least Rue could choose to spend her last days the way she wanted: in front of the dollhouse, working with her foxfire. Foxfire would probably not help Rue get food; at least Rue couldn't see how it would catch food since it didn't burn or injure, but Rue knew she didn't want to meet the Goddess without at least getting really good at using foxfire. As impractical as it was, it was part of her, so she would practice it as much as she could while she had the chance.

Night after night, Rue's foxfire became more intricate. Not only could she manipulate multiple orbs at once, soon she managed to make not just orbs, but also little shapes. First they were crude ovals and lines, columnar shapes of blue green light floating up the stairways and moving through the chambers. One particular night at long last, small human figures made of foxfire and one small kitsune-looking bit of foxfire took shape. The figures were gathered round the little table in the dollhouse, little arms gripping little pieces of porcelain and seeming to be holding a merry sort of conversation. Rue alternately sang and hummed as she manipulated her imaginary figures of foxfire and the not-imaginary bits of porcelain.

As Rue sang and spoke and hummed, telling the story of her light doppelganger and friends as she acted out their kitsune party, she finally knew what that strange feeling was she'd been feeling more and more even as she grew thin with hunger. It was joy. Rue reveled in pointless impractical imagination in front of the dollhouse in the wood. She forgot her own hunger as she practiced her craft. If this was the mercy of the Goddess, the mercy that comes as the last boon before death, then the Goddess was truly merciful indeed.

In this way, in this joy of song and story and imagination, Rue made a miracle. The magic reservoir, the place inside herself from which the power of spellcraft came, that place that had felt so hollowed out, felt suddenly not only full, but overflowing with energy and that energy could only flow in one direction: downhill into a waterfall ending in a rainbow.

It took Rue a minute to realize that she was standing on two feet, toes curling into the soft dirt and stubbly grass she had gnawed to the root. Rue was really convinced of her magehood when she began to topple backward and saw what were normally her paws stretch out in front of her face for balance and turn out to be two human hands, four fingers and one opposable thumb apiece. For the longest time, Rue marveled at the spaces between those digits and the way the stars above looked between them as she began to teeter backward. The stars looked so beautiful within Rue's hands; she smiled at them as she fell.

Rue landed on a few leaves covering the stubby grass. She felt weak, but as she marveled at the way her hands could move, she knew that this wasn't going to be the end. Carefully, Rue managed to stand, though she had to lean on the dollhouse a little for balance. But then, Rue smiled. The dollhouse had been letting her lean on it for a while. She looked at the wondrous plaything in the starlight. Even with human eyes, it still looked grand and beautiful on its stump.

Rue sniffed the night air. Her nice kitsune nose seemed to work even in this tiny human face. Step by step, Rue set off towards her grandmamma's territory. Even if nothing she found was strictly practical, Rue felt her grandmamma would want to be the first to know Rue had found the answers to her questions. Humming a song of gratitude to the Goddess, Rue, clad in the finest foxfire, walked into the morning light.

Sometimes the most powerful legends are our own personal ones—for George Brewster that means a Teddy bear he hasn't seen in thirty years.

A TOUCH OF MAGIC

John B. Rosenman

George Brewster hadn't seen his Teddy bear in thirty-four years, so he was a bit surprised when he opened his office door and found it sitting on his desk. Or *her*, rather. As the door clicked shut, he remembered he had called her Susy Burkabine. He also recalled that his parents had disposed of her in the incinerator one day when he was six.

What was she doing here? He took a couple of steps forward before the oddness of the situation fully registered. What was left of Susy was long dead ashes, yet she sat with her knees crossed on the edge of his desk as jaunty as ever, just as he remembered her.

"Hello, Georgie."

"Susy—is that *you?*" The words seemed to pop out by themselves, and then he had to sit down. He fell into the chair before his desk, staring at her.

"Course it is. Who did you think I was, Winnie the Pooh?" Her brown glass eyes regarded him with pride and delight. "My little boy has grown up into such a strapping big man, a regular grizzly." She laughed fondly. "And I see you've put on a bit of weight too, Georgie."

"I know." He poked his stomach. "Karen's a darn good cook and she always gives me second help… Now, wait a minute!" He was on his feet, the unbelievable fact that Susy had returned after all this time suddenly crashing down on him. "How can you be here? My parents burned you to a crisp when I was six."

"No, they didn't," she said soothingly. "I knew they wanted to get rid of me because they felt you were too old to be so attached to a Teddy bear. So I had to split."

225

His eyes bulged. "But where—where did you go?"

She waved a furry paw. "It's hard to explain, really. Call it a kind of Teddy bear limbo where we go until we're needed again."

"I see." A sweet sense of awe swept over him. So Susy *had* spoken to him as a child and been able to move! All his life he had told himself that his memory of their relationship was a persistent delusion. Still, confronted with her at forty in his office, it was a bit hard to believe. He was a responsible Insurance Sales Manager, concerned with profits and premiums, not fluffy balls of fur who called him "Georgie."

"Oh, dear." Susy's round felt nose wrinkled in distress. "You're starting to doubt."

"Pardon me? I don't—"

"Don't you *dare* pardon anything, Georgie. That's adult language. You'll chew me up in that paper shredder of a mind if you're not careful." She held her breath and then slowly released it. "Whew! That's better. I thought I was a goner for sure."

"Would you mind telling me—"

"It's very simple." He watched her rise and stretch her two foot length. "Most of us teddies are just toys—balls of fur and glass eyes. But occasionally, once in a great while, we're lucky enough to find a child who loves and believes in us so much, we actually become alive." She stopped and her eyes softened. "One like *you*, Georgie."

"Susy—"

"But if you start to doubt, even for a moment, then it's like dying. That's the way it is with us, Georgie. We can't stand Doubting Thomases, not even for a moment. We're meant to be held and loved, not questioned."

He rose, his eyes brimming with tears. Tenderly he picked her up. Her soft, wooly arms. Her fuzzy ears. Yes. As a child, he had dragged her by them all over the house until his mother had to sew her back up to keep her from falling apart. Trembling, he pressed her to him.

"Susy," he whispered, "it *is* you! How could I have ever doubted?"

"Hummmphf! You've gotten stronger, Georgie. Don't squeeze me so tight!"

"Oh, sorry!" Carefully he moved her away and looked at her. "Are you all right?"

"I seem to be."

He watched her inspect herself and adjust the bow around her neck.

"I'm a little lumpy, though. You practically squeezed the stuffings right out of me."

"I'm sorry."

"It's O.K. Only no more bear hugs, huh?"

"I promise."

They gazed at each other.

"Hey, Susy," he said, her presence in his arms sparking his memory. "Do you remember the times my dad looked for us and we hid under the porch?"

"Sure! And we'd see his legs winking beyond the wooden lattice. You'd be giggling so hard I thought for sure he'd find us. But he never did." She poked him. "Or how about the times we slept together and you'd hold me tight and tell me about all the wonderful places we were going to go some day and all the wonderful things we were going to do?" Her eyes glistened. "Good times, huh, Georgie? *Good* times!"

"You bet. The best!"

She pulled a little away to look at him. "And how are you doing now, Georgie? You making it O.K.?"

He shrugged, rocking her a little. "Well, I'm a District Sales Manager for an insurance company, and I've got a nice house, a fine wife, and two great kids." He faded off, feeling inane.

"Well, that's not so bad!"

"Yeah, well. It's just..." He looked at her. "Remember all those wonderful fairy tales I made up, Susy?" He glanced about the office. "It's just that I expected something more than this."

He felt her paw stroke his cheek. "Everybody has to grow up, Georgie."

"I...guess."

"Only they have to grow up in the right way. Remain a kid in some part of their heart." She glanced around the office at some drawings of his older daughter Tammy which he had displayed on the walls, and a Cutty Sark he had built as part of his ship collection. "And from where I sit, you're doing just fine."

"You sure?"

"Yup. Only it's your other kid I'm worried about. To be frank, she's the reason I'm here."

"You mean you didn't come to see *me*?"

She leaned forward and touched her nose to his, just as she'd done when he'd been a child. "No, Georgie," she said gently. "I wish I had, but there are only so many of us to go around. And our main concern is *children*. That's why I'm so worried about Sylvia. Do you know she's eight years old and never laughs? And she does things, Georgie, bad things which hurt others."

He nodded. He had worried much about his younger daughter. Unlike twelve-year-old Tammy, who was so popular, Sylvia was distant and mischievous in a way that seemed slyly calculated to hurt others. Just last week she had damaged a model schooner he had built and cut up her sister's drawings. And while she was a pretty little girl, usually she seemed more serious and reserved than most adults. Susy was right. She never laughed, and he and his wife had wondered constantly if her being four years younger than Tammy had something to do with it. Perhaps she felt alone, and her destructive behavior was her way of reaching out. Still...

"So you came to help Sylvia?" he asked.

"If I can. But frankly, Georgie, she looks like a tough nut to crack. Have you tried—"

The door opened and Ed Turner barged in, not even bothering to knock. George looked at him, forgetting about Susy.

"Ed, don't you ever bother to knock?"

"Can't. Got a hot customer on the line and I need those new annuity rates. Pronto!"

He watched Ed go to the filing cabinet and start searching through it. Ed was his number one salesman, a brash kid just out of college who would one day climb to the top of the company ranks. Still, he wished Ed wouldn't storm into his office like he owned it and would treat him with a little respect. He swallowed and rubbed his mustache. Although he was a big, powerful man well over six feet, he felt a little intimidated by Ed Turner, partly because he knew Ed's eye was on *his* job.

"Got it!" Ed slammed the drawer in and started out with a file in his hand, not even asking permission. Then he stopped.

"What's that you're holding?"

He looked at Susy, feeling foolish. "A Teddy bear."

"A *what?*" Ed moved closer and poked Susy. "I'll be damned! I didn't think they made those things anymore. Where'd you get it?"

"A toy store," he extemporized. "Bought it for one of my kids."

"For one of your *kids?*" Ed looked at him like he was nuts. "George, why'd you want to do that for? Those things belong in the nineteenth century."

"Are you kidding? I see them in toy stores all the time."

"Makes no difference." Ed transferred the file to his left hand so he could gesture with his right. "Look, I don't want a toy around which doesn't *do* anything. When I get my kid a toy, it's something educational which will prepare him for the future. Like the latest Max-Box 900 where you can stream a thousand different games and fight wars amid the stars."

He looked at the smaller man. "Ed, this is for my eight-year-old. I want her to have something soft she can—"

"George, look, this is the age of interactive games. Teddy bears which just lie there belong with the dodo." He waved the folder. "And paper records are out, man. That filing cabinet you insist on keeping is obsolete." He patted George's shoulder. "Take my advice and get your girl a smartphone. Kids are crazy about them."

They watched him leave. George wished he had said something, done something for once to put him in his place. If Ed had wanted the file so much, why hadn't he downloaded a copy in *his* office? But of course he knew the reason. Ed wanted to intimidate him, and he had. What must Susy think of his cowardice?

Susy glared at the door, looking as if she were about to roar. "Damn, I wish I could have given him a piece of my mind. Would his ears burn! Toys which don't do anything and belong with the dodo. Huuumphf!" Angrily, she twitched the small ball of her tail. "Don't get me wrong, Georgie. I don't have anything against Mr. Hot Shot there. It's just that he represents all those who think computers, tablets, and mobile phones are everything."

"But..." He fumbled for words. "All these things aren't bad, are they? I mean, you need them."

"Sure. But when you make a religion out of it, you're going too far. Keep it up, and kids will be extensions of machines and won't recognize a book unless it's on a screen." She nudged him. "C'mon, let's split."

***

On the way home, Susy insisted on using a safety belt. She looked a little odd with her brown fur bunched over the buckle and her head not even reaching the window, but he didn't say anything. Her only response to his stares was a slight smile and a wry comment, "Guess I'm getting a mite cautious in my old age."

"Are you, Susy? Getting older, I mean."

"You better believe it." She pointed at her head. "See these white hairs? I'm not exactly a spring chicken anymore, if you'll pardon the expression. Course, most of them are due to you."

"Me?"

"Sure. From up there I see a lot of things, like the time two years ago when you almost totaled your car."

He shivered at the memory. "It was the other guy's fault."

"I didn't care about the other guy, Georgie. *You* almost checked out. Anyway, I've watched you grow up, get married, have kids. The whole ball of wax."

He glanced at her, suddenly embarrassed. "Then you've seen all the stupid things I've done."

"Aw, Georgie, I just cover my eyes. And if I'm not fast enough..." She shrugged. "I didn't even mind the time you drank too much and spilled your Singapore Sling down the front of Patty Lawson's dress. You wouldn't be my Georgie if you didn't do such things. Besides, I'm proud of you. You've turned out just fine. You're a good husband, father..."

A pickup truck pulled even with them at a stoplight and a man with a cigar glanced over at them. George saw him notice Susy strapped against the seat and give a snort.

"Hey, buddy, who's your girlfriend?"

Embarrassed and hating himself for it, he turned and gazed into the rearview mirror at his rugged face with its thick brown mustache. Six feet five and two seventy, he told himself, yet he couldn't even answer. His huge hands, immensely powerful, gripped the wheel. How he longed to face the man, stare him down and say something bright like, "What are *you* gawking at, Turkey? Ain't you ever seen a Teddy bear before?" But he couldn't do it.

After a moment he sneaked a look at the man, hoping he had lost interest. But he still sat watching him, his eyes amused and contemptuous above his cigar. George looked away.

When they reached home, Karen met them at the door. "George, a Teddy bear! Where did you get it?"

He shrugged. "Some toy store." He kissed her affectionately, relieved by her enthusiasm. "Like it?"

"Oh, it's beautiful!" Her brown eyes danced as she touched it. "And so soft! I didn't think they made those anymore."

"Hmm." He held her slender form, aware that Susy was silent. What would happen if she spoke up, broke her code of silence concerning other people? Somehow, he thought Karen would be able to handle it.

With a playful pat, he released her. "Is Sylvia home?"

Her eyes darkened. "She's upstairs."

"Good. I want to show her this."

He passed her and went inside. At the foot of the stairs, Buford, a shaggy, seventy pound dog (Heinz 200, Tammy called him) perked up his head and thumped his tail like a trip hammer on the tile. Grinning, he set Susy down and buried his hands in Buford's fur while he squirmed to lick him.

"Hey, Buford, how ya doing? Yeah, that's my boy!"

Then, remembering that Susy wanted to see Sylvia at once, he picked her up and started up the stairs. Behind, Buford laid his head down on his paws again and went back to sleep.

Halfway up, he heard Karen's voice and turned.

"Yes?"

"It won't do any good, George," she said. "She won't even want to look at it."

He paused and then more heavily, continued up the stairs. On the landing, he saw that the bathroom door was ajar and went to it.

Inside, his twelve-year-old daughter Tammy stood in a half-filled bathtub in her swimming suit. She had a multicolored scarf in her hand and the other end was tied to a small, yellow, plastic tugboat which she pulled gently back and forth the length of the tub. In the boat was a tiny turtle, barely two inches across.

His face split into a grin.

Back and forth, back and forth the turtle sailed the seas in its own private yacht. George felt his heart thump as he gazed at Tammy. Almost a woman, and yet her face wore such a look of concern for the turtle's welfare. He recalled how proud she was that she had decimated most of the house's fly population and fed them to the turtle, who regarded them as a delicacy.

Then Tammy looked up and saw him. "Daddy!"

Instinctively, he thrust Susy behind him, ignoring her protest. Tammy stooped, lifted the tugboat, and stepped out of the tub. She held the tugboat before his eyes so he and the turtle could look at each other.

"Doesn't he look great in it, Daddy? I call him Camouflage."

"Oh, you've found a name?"

"Yeah." She stood stroking its mottled shell, then peered around him. "What have you got behind your back?"

"Nothing."

"Yes, you do!" She tried to outmaneuver him and peek behind his back while he dodged, amazed again by what he called her "invisible antennae." Tammy. Just bring a box of candy or something new into the house and somehow she knew about it. Sometimes she was even into it before your back was turned.

At last, giving up, he brought Susy out in plain view.

"Whooooo!"

He watched her get excited the way she usually did, with her whole body. Legs, arms, eyes, mouth, even the dusting of freckles on her nose got into the act. Clearly, he thought, Ed Turner was wrong about Susy being a relic of the nineteenth century. For Tammy, she was right at home in the present.

"Boy, it's hu-mung-y! Where did ya get it, Daddy?" She grabbed one of Susy's ears and tried to pull her out of his hands. He held tight, sensing if he let go he wouldn't get her back.

"Toy store," he answered. Susy was emitting a low tone which sounded suspiciously like pain, and he raised his voice to cover it. "And you'd never guess what I decided to call it!"

"What, Camouflage?"

"No. Susy Burkabine."

Tammy laughed, released Susy who sprang back with a grunt.

"Susy Burkabine? Oh, Dad, what a flip! Why do ya call her that?"

He started to tell her that he had originally named her after a playmate in nursery school thirty-five years ago, but checked himself. "Hey, Tam," he said, "is Sylvia around?"

Instantly he saw the same look he had seen on her mother's face. "Aw, why do you want her?"

He gave Susy a little bounce. "I thought she might like *this*."

Her face told him otherwise. "She ain't going to—"

"Isn't."

"She isn't going to like it, Daddy. She doesn't like anything nice. All she likes to do is cut up my drawings." She lowered her voice. "Did you know I caught her trying to kill Camouflage this morning?"

"*Kill* him?"

"Yeah, with a hammer. And Marion Webster told me Sylvia took her little sister's brand new school books which she liked so much and threw them in the drainage ditch. Laughed at her too when she did it."

He felt stunned. Usually Sylvia's pranks (if that was the word) were comparatively mild and restricted to home. But killing a pet? Maliciously destroying a student's books? If she kept it up...

"If you ask me," Tammy said, "Sylvia's weird and gives me the creeps. She needs help, Daddy! She's sneaky, but one of these days she's going to go too far. And when she does..."

Silently she drew a finger across her throat and rolled her eyes, then placed a covetous hand on Susy's chest. "Please, Daddy," she said, the subject miraculously dropped, "can I keep her? Just for a little while?"

He sighed. "We'll talk about it later. Where's Sylvia?"

Tammy looked down at her feet. "In her room," she mumbled.

"Thanks." He kissed the top of her bent head then started out, pausing at the door. "Hey, Tam, I know your sister's difficult, but please make an effort, huh? And you might play with her now and then, O.K.?"

Still sulking, she didn't look up. He frowned and walked toward Sylvia's door, passing Tammy's. On it were two pictures she had drawn of Justin Bieber. One of them was in color, the other in pencil. Both were quite good. Just beneath them was a hand-lettered sign he had considered talking to her about but hadn't.

If
You Don't
Like
Justin Bieber
Get
The Hell
Out!

Sighing, he moved to Sylvia's door which was bare and without personality. He gripped the doorknob, considered knocking, then rejected the idea. For a moment his face twisted. Two girls. One twelve, the other eight. Yet it was the former who seemed a little girl at times. As for the other...

He took a deep breath and entered.

***

She sat at her desk, gazing out the window. Quietly, he closed the door behind him.

"Hi, Sylvia."

She turned her head, her dark hair swirling about her shoulders. "Hi," she said, then looked out the window again.

He went over to her bed and sat down next to a picture of Mr. Babadook, a monster from a movie Sylvia had watched on TV when he hadn't been around. Glancing at the creepy, cartoonish figure, George remembered Sylvia's disturbing interest in the character.

Perched on his knee, Susy almost tumbled to the floor. He caught her just in time and studied his daughter. As he did, the words of an old song drifted through his mind.

Who is Sylvia? What is she...

"So how was school today?" he asked.

"Fine."

"Any school work?"

"Yes."

"Well, may I see it?"

Dutifully she went to the bureau and returned with some papers, which she gave to him. She sat down.

He went through them, making sure Susy could see. English 98. Spelling 95. Math 100. *Excellent!!!* her teacher had written. No, whatever was wrong with her couldn't be found in her grades. She was a bright, efficient student, but she seemed to take no real pleasure in anything and had no friends. In her closet, long neglected, were the toy cars and trucks she had once loved. He could still hear her laugh and shout "Beep! Beep! Zoom! Zoom!" as she rolled them across the floor.

Worst of all was the matter of her behavior. Cutting up Tammy's drawings had been bad enough, but attacking her pet was far worse. It was vicious, it was... He shied away from other words, fearing where they would take him. Of course he'd have to call the girl's parents and apologize for the school books, pay for them if necessary. But he knew it didn't solve the problem. Maybe Tammy was right, he thought, and Sylvia *did* need help.

"These are great, honey," he said, handing them back. "You must feel pretty good."

Her mouth curled. Slightly. "They're the highest in the class," she said. If she saw Susy (and how could she not?), she didn't seem to think it worth mentioning. Even her high grades didn't seem to matter. She took no joy in them.

234

He cleared his throat. "Sylvia, why did you try to hurt Tammy's turtle?"

"Tammy's turtle?"

"Yes. And Tammy said you took a student's books and threw them in the ditch."

"Tammy told you that? *Tammy?*" Sylvia glanced in the direction of the bathroom where they could hear Tammy splashing. Her eyes hardened, and what he saw in them made his stomach cold.

"Now, look, honey," he said quickly, "it doesn't matter who told me. What matters..."

He stopped. Sylvia's eyes were narrowed to slits, and he had a crazy notion she could see *through* the walls to Tammy. Impulsively, he leaned forward and took her shoulders.

"Why, Sylvia?" he said. "Why do you do these things?"

"Things?"

He shook her. "Yes, why do you do them? *Tell* me!"

For a moment her eyes flickered. "I...I don't want to do them, Daddy." A tear formed in the corner of one of her eyes. "I keep trying to stop, but it..."

Then it was as if what he'd glimpsed had never been there. He watched her return to her chair and gaze out the window.

Stunned by the suffering he'd seen in his daughter's eyes, he let her go. What was wrong with her? Why had she almost cried? He found himself remembering how lovely, bouncy, and full of spirit she had been as a baby and how proud he and Karen had been when they'd brought her home from the hospital. But somehow, he couldn't say when exactly, she had begun to change. What had happened? They had consulted doctors and he had turned the mystery over and over in his mind, but it was a blind labyrinth leading nowhere. Except for one thing: a feeling. A feeling that in some way his beautiful, bright-eyed baby had been taken from him, leaving a shell in which something was pervasively missing.

He felt Susy nudge him.

"Oh, yes," he said, remembering. He wet his lips. "Sylvia, do you notice anything different?"

She turned. Her large dark eyes gazed at him.

"About what?"

"Anything."

"I don't think so."

Just that. *I don't think so.* No excitement. No giving back. No *What is it, Daddy, did you buy something for me?* No jumping excitedly out of her chair and throwing herself all over him like Tammy would, trying to find it. No nothing.

"Are you sure?" He held Susy upright, then made her bow.

"Yes."

"Well, what about this?" He made her do a cartwheel in the air.

"Oh, you mean the Teddy bear. Is that what you're talking about?"

He started to answer, then stopped. Slowly, Susy was leaning forward in his hands, one of her brown paws extended toward Sylvia's knee. George felt his throat tighten. Sylvia watched her expressionlessly. Then, as Susy's paw made contact, something happened. His daughter's face contorted and she lurched up, knocking the chair over. She screamed.

He was on his feet too, dumbfounded. "Honey, what's wrong?"

Susy nudged him, harder than before. "Outside!" she hissed.

"What?"

"Outside. *Now.*"

He gave Sylvia another glance, seeing that she had backed all the way into a corner. Reluctantly, he opened the door and went out.

"Why did you do that to her?" he demanded. "You scared her out of her wits!"

"Shhh!"

He looked up. Tammy was standing in the door of the bathroom and Karen was just reaching the top of the stairs.

"George, what is it?" she said, coming toward them. "I heard a scream."

"Did you? I didn't hear anything." He bolted past them, ignoring their stares, and almost ran down the stairs. At the bottom, he nearly tripped over Buford, who growled and lumbered off where it was safer.

"All right," he said, "tell me. Why did you—"

"Not here, Georgie. The *bathroom.*"

He turned and went to the downstairs bathroom. Closed the door and turned on the light. "All right, now tell me. Why did you do it? I can't believe you'd hurt my little—"

"*Listen* to me." Something in her face stopped him. "At first," Susy said, "I hoped Sylvia was just a shy girl who resented her big sister and was trying to get attention. But I'm afraid it's something worse. Far worse."

"What..."

"One of the Others has her, Georgie. And it won't let her go."

"The Others?" His breath locked inside him and he glanced confusedly around, seeing white tiles everywhere. "What are…"

"The Others, Georgie? They're our opposites, the enemies of Teddy bears everywhere. And as you just saw, they can't even bear our touch." She crossed her arms, which he noticed were a little frayed. "Ever wonder why some children turn bad, Georgie, why they start off so well and then seem to wither, grow mean and empty? *Have* you?"

He thought of Sylvia, who had been such a warm, loving baby, one who had smiled in her crib and made soft cooing sounds whenever they had touched her. He nodded.

"Yes, I know you have," Susy said. She hesitated. "You see, Georgie, the Others hate us. They hate life. And especially, they hate little babies who are brand new and just starting out, with their whole lives before them. So they wait for just the right moment, and if it comes, they *take* them."

"Take them?"

"Take them *over*, feed on the lives they destroy. Oh, sure, the children still live, but all that's beautiful and good and funny in their lives is gone. Life's like a flat canvas, cold and barren, and as they get older, the evil inside them starts to reach out and destroy. The Others are very good at hurting, Georgie. They can detect desires and weaknesses in others and manipulate them for their own pleasure, tell just where someone is vulnerable so they can inject their poison. Without love and compassion themselves, they know precisely how to twist and pervert people to serve their own ends."

He thought of Tammy's turtle, of the new school books which had meant so much to a little girl. "But where do they come from?"

"No one really knows, Georgie. All we know is that they hate life and their only pleasure is to hurt and consume it. They see little babies in their cribs, and if they spot an opening, they *pounce!*"

"But not all babies…"

She smiled. "No, not all. We don't know that either. We don't know what makes one child vulnerable and another not. Maybe it takes a special openness and ability to love to open the door for them, while others who are harder…" She raised a paw and blotted away one of his tears. "You see, it's a battle, Georgie. A worldwide battle between two forces. Between the Others who want to destroy little children and…"

"And *you*, who want to save them."

Susy nodded. "Fortunately, we're not alone, Georgie. We have a lot of help. Anything which makes a child happy is an enemy of the Others. The natural beauty of the world. Other toys. And especially, parents."

He opened his mouth to protest, to scream down the horrible insanity he was hearing. But he couldn't. He knew she was right.

"What are we going to do?" he asked. "We can't leave her like this!" He thought of what her life would be like, what she would be doomed to suffer, and gripped Susy even harder than he had in his office. She didn't complain.

"You want to help her?" she said.

"Yes!"

"Then you must help me."

"How?"

"You must hold her while I cast it out, make it leave her."

"What?" He looked at her, trying to understand. "Is there any danger?"

"Yes."

"What could happen?"

Her expression changed, and his fingers froze on her warm fur. Impossible. Impossible to believe that brown glass eyes could look so sad.

"We...could lose her?"

Slowly, Susy nodded.

"But what should I do?"

"I can't tell you, Georgie, even though I know what *I* would do. It's *your* decision."

And now he *did* doubt her. Angrily he dropped her in the sink, not caring that it was cold and uncomfortable.

"Let me get this straight," he said. "You want me to help you perform an *exorcism* on my daughter?"

"You could call it that."

"But if it doesn't work, she could die."

"Would you rather have her condemned to remain what she is now? Flat and lifeless? Fated to hurt others because she can't help herself and perhaps one day even attack her own sister?"

"Her own sister? You don't mean—"

"Georgie," she said quietly, "you don't really think Tammy's turtle is the end of it, do you? Believe me, it's just the beginning. You saw how she looked when you told her Tammy said she tried to kill her turtle. The Others thrive on hate and devour life. They try to conceal and protect themselves, but once they get a taste of another's pain, their presence becomes more and more obvious."

He gazed blindly at her, a nerve leaping in his temple. No! She was saying Tammy was in danger, that her own sister... He took a step backward. Finding Susy again after thirty-four years had been wonderful. Now he wished he had never seen her. Or if he had, that she'd remained as simple as before, a wisecracking companion who was fun to be with and the best friend he had ever had. Anything. Anything but what she was now.

Suddenly he saw dismay on her face. "Georgie, don't!"

"What?"

"You're beginning to *doubt* me again, and I told you before what happens if you do. "I'll *vanish*, Georgie. I'll become just another Teddy bear."

He started to deny it. "No, I..."

"Yes, you *do*. You don't think I can even do it. And if you keep it up, in another minute you won't even believe in *me*. You'll be just like the man in your office and that truck driver who saw a lump of fur and nothing else. And worst of all, you'll be just like your parents thirty-four years ago who wanted to burn me because they felt a six-year-old boy was too old even to have a Teddy bear. *Stop it.*"

He swallowed and closed his eyes, then opened them. Miraculously, it was Susy again.

"All right," he said softly, picking her out of the sink. "Tell me what I have to do."

***

It was 8:30 Sunday morning, and neither Karen nor Tammy wanted to go to church without him. He stood at the door, his mouth twisted in a smile.

"But George, I don't understand," his wife said from the front steps. "Why don't you want to come with us?"

"Like I told you, honey, I just want to spend a little time alone with Sylvia. Thought we might get to know each other better."

Karen and Tammy exchanged looks. His reason had sounded unconvincing the first time he had given it, and it didn't improve on retelling.

"Reverend Whitcomb will ask about you."

"So he'll ask."

"But—"

"Daddy, *please* come! I don't want to listen to his moldy old sermon without you."

If it were another occasion, he thought, he would laugh. Tammy's restlessness during sermons was a family joke.

"You go on, now. Sylvia and I will be just fine."

"Well…all right." Karen leaned forward to kiss him, and he held her a little longer than he should have. When she drew back, he saw her frown.

"George, is everything all right? You look—"

"Sure, I'm fine. You hurry along, now." Gently he closed the door.

He heard the click of heels on the sidewalk, moving toward the car. Tammy, he recalled, was proudly wearing hers too, and he felt a twinge. It seemed only yesterday that she was his little girl. Soon she'd be dating, bringing boys home to meet him who would probably regard him as a superannuated old fogy. Soon…

"Are they gone yet?" a voice called from the living room behind him.

"Not quite."

Through the white linen drapes he could see them at the car. Karen had the keys in her hand. For a moment she hesitated and cast an anxious look in his direction. A chill ripped through him. What if she could see him through the drapes and came back? But then she turned and opened the car door. He watched her let Tammy in on the other side and back out of the driveway. A few seconds later she was accelerating up the street.

He turned around and entered the living room, passing Buford who thumped his tail and opened a hopeful eye.

Susy was waiting there for him, her feet planted firmly on the carpet. Reluctantly, he faced her, wishing he could go fishing or smoke one of the evil-smelling panatelas Karen complained about but which he relished.

"Well, Susy, I guess this is it."

Numbly he went over to her and picked her up, thinking of the past three days during which they had gone over and over what he must do. He knew there was nothing else to say.

But Susy stopped him at the foot of the stairs. "Wait a minute, Georgie, I have a couple things to say."

He swallowed. "What is it?"

She looked up at the stairs, then at him. "I know how you feel about going up there," she said. "Only half of you really believes what I told you, but the half that does is scared. Scared silly. Am I right?"

He didn't answer.

"Well, get me straight, Georgie. There's nothing wrong with being scared. It would be dumb *not* to be. We could all get hurt, or *worse*, in Sylvia's room." She leaned her cheek against his. "Only you've got to handle your fear, Georgie, make it work for you. You can't let it walk all over you like you did that salesman in your office or the truck driver. This time, *you've* got to be the boss because Sylvia needs everything we have if we're going to set her free."

He blushed and started to deny what she'd said about Ed Turner and the truck driver. Only he couldn't.

"Sounds like you want me to grow up," he said.

"Oh, you'll do just fine. You're almost there already." She paused and then looked away. "And Georgie, there's just one more thing I have to tell you."

He waited.

"Georgie," she said, her voice breaking, "I can't be...your Teddy bear anymore."

He blinked. "What?"

She turned back. "Don't you see? If we can save Sylvia, she's going to need all the help she can get, and especially, the kind of help that only I can give her."

"But she has a family," he blurted. "After we free her from this demon or whatever it is—"

"It won't be *enough*, Georgie. She needs a touch of magic in her life, the kind of magic all little children need if they're going to grow up to be strong and good. Without it, she'll never be much more than what she is now. Oh, you and Karen and Tammy will be important to her, but..." She gazed at him. "You *do* understand, don't you?"

He closed his eyes, feeling just the way he had as a child when he had thought she'd left him, only to find her later under the bed.

"Sounds like you want to leave me," he said, his voice almost a whisper.

"Oh, George, I could never want that. I'll *always* be your friend. Your very best. It's just that I'll have to give all my love to Sylvia from now on."

A thought struck him. "You mean...you won't even be able to *talk* to me?"

She dropped her eyes. "A Teddy bear can belong to only one person, Georgie," she said quietly. "You ought to know that."

And somehow, despite his pain, he did know. The knowledge hurt him, but he knew there was no other way. Sylvia was the one who was important, not him.

"All right," he said huskily, raising his eyes to the top of the stairs. "Let's go."

He mounted the stairs, Susy cradled in his arm. Outside Sylvia's door they paused and exchanged a last glance. Then he opened it and went in.

***

Sylvia sat at her desk just as she had before, gazing out the window at…what? Nothing, perhaps, if what Susy said about her was true. For an instant the name of Tammy's Turtle leaped into his head. Camouflage. That was what the parasite was doing to his little girl, using her as camouflage while it fed invisibly upon her mind and spirit.

But was Susy right? Was there actually an "Other" inside her? He grit his teeth and lowered Susy to the floor.

"Hi."

Sylvia turned. "Hello."

He took a step and concentrated on what he must do. "Honey," he said, "would you stand up for a moment?"

"Stand up?"

"Please."

Her eyes blinked, large brown ones like Karen's but curiously lifeless. He remembered how she used to shout "Beep! Beep! Zoom! Zoom!" while playing with her toy cars and trucks.

Sylvia rose and looked obediently up at him.

Quickly he picked her up and sat down in the chair with her on his lap. He held her tightly so she couldn't move.

"Hello," Susy said.

She stood on the floor just three feet away, her eyes riveted to Sylvia's chest. As he watched, she inched forward.

"I speak not to Sylvia but to the coward inside her, the sneak thief who picks on defenseless babies and doesn't even have the guts to show itself."

Under his arms, Sylvia sat motionless, quietly watching her.

"Come, you *worm*," Susy said, spitting out the words less than two feet away, her face looking different than he'd ever seen it. "Come to *me*.

Or are you such a sniveling, contemptible craven that you're afraid even to face a toy, a ball of synthetic fur and stuffing?"

Closer. Closer and closer, and still nothing. Sylvia did not jerk, did not recoil, did not do any of the things Susy had told him she would. He felt doubt steal through his mind like a burglar. Surely she should have moved by—

"Come, you cesspool, you vermin, you disgusting bag of filth, have the courage to show your miserable face. Stand up to me. Stand up to me—now!"

She touched Sylvia.

And then something happened. Beneath his arms he felt her start to writhe. Sylvia's head shot back and her mouth opened in agony. She strained upward.

"Sylvia!"

But she was beyond him now. He felt her buck and lunge in his lap and held her with all his strength. Held her as Susy had told him he must to keep her from exploding.

Something rose from Sylvia's mouth, eddied and materialized above her head as a green cloud. Horrified, he watched it expand and crystallize, assume a shape.

He tried to scream but couldn't. Susy was backing away now, her mouth opened in fear. In his lap Sylvia screamed, sounding human for the first time in years. "Daddy! Daddy! Help me, Daddy, don't let it get me!"

The thing turned, searching.

He fought down his panic and the urge to run, his mind struggling to classify and cope with the abomination before him. A gargoyle, yes, one of those grotesque ornaments projecting from medieval churches. But taller, taloned, unspeakably vile. He saw it turn, its green scales glittering, its furnace eyes blinking as it adjusted to its new environment.

Then it saw Susy.

It roared, a sound torn from the depths of hell, and lashed out with one of its talons. Susy staggered back and fell, her insides spraying from a gash across her chest as the thing's tail swung and caught his chair, throwing him from it. He landed against the wall and scrambled to rise, seeing his daughter's terrified face as she fell against the bed and the Other turned and found her again.

"Daddy! Daddy, help me!"

He moved quickly and stepped between them, braced his two hundred and seventy pounds. "Try me for size," he said.

Its smoldering eyes widened. *Not a gun or a knife, Georgie,* Susy had told him. *You alone can save Sylvia. It must be good against evil, love against hate. Only you can give her a chance to live.*

The Other darted, moved to get around him.

Just as quickly, he blocked it. *Yes, it is true,* he thought, *they are cowards. They prey on vulnerability and avoid strength.* He saw it dart again to outflank him and watched its movement. Tammy had tried to get Susy from him and he had partly surrendered her, but he must not, *must not* surrender this time.

"You scum," he heard himself say, "you took my little girl."

As if saying the words opened the floodgates of hate, he felt his whole being focus on a single purpose. He leaped forward.

As he did, he knew he had only one chance. He must not miss. He saw the thing's arms enclose him in a monstrous embrace and then he had it by the throat, his fingers sinking into the loathsome flesh. It roared and seized him up, whirling him about the room. He held on, tightening his fingers with all his might, his eyes fixed on the hated face.

"You took my little girl!"

Claws raked the skin from his back now, and its wings opened till they almost spanned the room. He felt his feet leave the floor as he was borne upward, the wings buffeting the air as if to escape. Screeching, it drove him against a wall but he held on, fixed and determined as his fingers whitened.

At last, he felt the tide turn, felt himself drive *it* back, force it over and down upon Sylvia's bed. Slowly, its head descended to the picture of Mr. Babadook on her bedspread and the glowing eyes dimmed.

Then its mouth opened and it spewed a sickening jet of green slime all over him, a noxious ointment which coated his face and chest. He barely noticed. Relentlessly he gripped its throat, feeling the talons drop from his back as the thing shuddered and lay still.

Then it was gone.

He knelt over air, his hands fastened on nothing.

Gone.

He forced himself upright and peered about the room. "Where... where did it go?"

"Probably back to hell," Susy said. "Or to torment some other poor child." She was kneeling in the corner, ministering to Sylvia's still form.

He staggered over and knelt down. "Is...is she all right?"

Susy had her head to Sylvia's chest, listening. He saw her smile.

"She'll be fine. The poor thing just fainted."

"Thank God." He felt tears spring to his eyes. "But what about you?" Trembling, he pointed to the ragged gash across her chest. Bits of cotton protruded from it.

"This?" Susy examined it. "Pooh, I'll be fine. A little needle and thread and I'll be good as new." She glanced at him. "Hey, what about you? Your back looks a fright."

He smiled. "Iodine."

Susy nodded grudgingly. "Well, anyway, let me wipe some of that pea soup off you." She unbuttoned his shirt and started blotting his face with it.

"Here, I can do it." He took the shirt and looked at his daughter. "You sure she'll be O.K.?"

"You bet." Susy gazed fondly down at her. "You've got yourself a beautiful little girl there, Georgie, and she's going to have a crackerjack life. Boyfriends by the bushel-full. Parties and good books. Plus a family and all the love she can get."

He nodded and wiped his face. "Thanks to you, Susy."

"Naw, Georgie, *you* did it. I just got the thing's attention."

Without thinking, he reached out and took her in his arms, held her for a long time. At last, reluctantly, he let her go and gazed at the miracle of his daughter's sleeping face. Somehow, it looked different, as if the healing had already begun.

He bent and kissed her on the cheek, knowing he himself had already healed. No matter what happened, he'd never be frightened of anyone or anything again.

"Well." He straightened and stood up. "Guess I better go now. You'll want to be alone with her when she wakes up."

"Yes," Susy said. "I think it would be best."

He hesitated, for the first time feeling awkward with her. Then he went to the door.

"Georgie."

He turned around, and it was the same old Susy again. She stood gazing at him, grinning painfully but with fierce pride.

"I just want you to know, Georgie," she said, "that in my book you're tops. Strictly Triple A!"

He smiled, fighting down the ache. "Goodbye, Susy," he said.

"Goodbye, Georgie."

He opened the door and went out.

On the other side he closed his eyes, the ache rising in his throat. But it was a good ache, the kind of pain which could make him whole, and he knew that never, *never* had he felt as good as this. Not on his wedding day, not on the days his children had been born. Not even on the day two years before when he had opened his eyes after a car accident and found himself still alive.

There was a murmur in the room behind him, and he pressed his ear to the door.

"Hello, Syl," he heard her say. "My name's Susy, and we're going to be great friends."

*We aren't always aware of the spirits that travel beside us,
but our legends become their lives.*

LONG TIME I HUNT

Erin Lale

The sky is the peculiar blue color of ice from a deep, old lake. It burns over my spirit-eyes, bright and clear. Such terms as solid, liquid, or gaseous mean nothing to me before I first become embodied. I know nothing of touch, or taste, but the waves of light and sound I understand, vibrating through my insubstantial self. The concept of "first" is likewise lost on me until "first" happens.

Humans delight me. I love your cleverness: the way you bring forth new things out of nothing but your mind and what you find around you. In the early days these new things were simple, but wondrous. Pottery, made from earth and fire, still seems more amazing to me than the earth-metal and fire of your rockets blazing pillars through the sky. Oh yes, that sky: I know now that sky and earth are not equally passable to the embodied kind.

How can I describe my very first breath? I have lungs to fill and twin scent organs in my skull. One tells me the ground is wet from recent rain and the smoke coming from the burning wad of whole-leaf tobacco in the human's hand speaks to me in a way that nothing else ever can; and the other organ that tells me the body I inhabit has a sister of its kind nearby, strong pheromones in her urine-marking on a nearby tree calling me away to find a mate.

I delay, listening to the medicine man, sniffing his offering of tobacco, for it is a human who calls me here to this earthly plane, far from the spirit world where my prey passed through me and rose again. Favors the human asked of me; favors I bestowed.

I go to hunt, in my new form. Muscles contract under my skin, burning chemical energy that must be replaced. Long time I hunt the spirit world, but not like this. Now the hunt is not a reflection of my nature but a necessity, and the prey I grasp in my jaws does not rise again, save by a miracle the spirit world has not and envies: birth.

I scent a deer, and chase him with jaws of bone, amazing constructions of calcium and pattern. His hooves crash through the undergrowth like cymbals; my heart is a drum. My teeth puncture his flesh. I taste iron, that ancient killer of stars, in the liquid made of solids and spaces and tiny galaxies of energy and motion that was blood. How amazing is the world of matter, for on its most basic level, it is the same as the world of spirit.

The sky now is not ice but ether; I feel it on my fur when the wind evaporates liquid from me, cooling my long, graceful body. My fur is the color of the sun. I lick the blood of the deer from my fur, and the slight chill moves through nerves of flesh to a brain of solid mass and weight. I move through green hills that recede in the distance into grey mist.

Many times I come to the medicine man, when he calls me, until the life of my body draws to a close. Then I come unbidden, and lay down by the circle of his fire. I fold my paws and rest my head upon them, blinking at him slowly in the way my body's kin express friendship. He comes to me then with tobacco and flowers and the fresh blood of a rabbit in a pale clay bowl. I lap it, and give up my last freedom to him and his descendents. When my eyes close for the last time in that body, he carefully removes my skin, and all my flesh, cleans my bones and paints them with sanctifying blue paint. He paints symbols known only to him and to his sons; it is long, long before his people would write in the syllabary known as the Tsalagi letters. The symbols inscribed on my bones are not representative of sounds, but of holy concepts tying my spirit to the bones and to the place where they were buried. So my spirit form could ever find a new body near the children of my human friend.

Many times they call me, over the years, until the secret of my bones is forgotten. It does not matter at first, for the children of my friend still live on the land above my burial place, and I come to them easily in form after form of sunshine and sinew, the Mountain Lion Spirit.

One day I see them making symbols, new symbols, the syllabary and other symbols unknown to me. They make a building to house the symbols, which are cast in metal and fitted onto a machine like a cider press that makes words. How clever my humans are still.

Then one night I hear the old words spoken at the place with the metal. I am being summoned. I come. There are two groups of the children of my friend, one dressed in the familiar skins of deer and the other in a mix of traditional garb and unfamiliar things, things that remind me of the webs of spiders, spun and woven. How clever, my delightful humans. But no: this is not a hunting ceremony. This is no night of delight and honoring, for the fire is in torches carried in the hands of the spider people, and no tobacco is offered to me.

I do not understand what the two factions war about, so I will it that I know the speech of humans, and I hear the spider people say the deer people tell lies with their metal words and the spider people want to put their own ideas into the metal so that more people would agree with the spider people. The deer people say the metal words are truth and the spider people are wrong and they will not give up the metal words to them.

There is one among the deer people who is pale as a dead man. But he bears the Lion Tooth in a small pouch bound at his neck, and I respond to him.

There is fire and blood between the children of my friend, and my heart grieves. But I must respond to the power of my bones, and out from the dark of the trees I leap, my green eyes flashing in the firelight. The spider people pull back from my snarls, and the deer people go into the building and take the metal words, and go off with them. Then the spider people come forward, daring my jaws, to burn down the temple of the metal words. One points an object at me. I have not seen its like before, but I recognize the threat carried in his scent and stance, and I retreat. Loping along in the woods just out of sight, I follow the deer people.

In disarray they come to a settlement, set a watch, sweating fear stink into the air as early dawn comes pale and rainy. Soon they have their fantastic machine set up again, carefully arranging each piece of metal. In goes the spew of octopi from far away oceans. In go the flat leaves that are not leaves. Down come the metal words, and the ink dries on the paper. Folded, bundled, carried by runners and men on horses, the news of the spider peoples' attack on this thing the deer people call 'newspaper' goes far and wide.

The man with the lion tooth smokes at last, sighing in contentment. I creep closer and inhale the scent. This is a different sort of tobacco, less hallucinatory, sweeter. I wait for him to say the words as he puffs, to fan me with the smoke, but he does not. Eventually he comes up with his own words to thank me, and I turn and go into the trees, now green with the touch of the sun.

Long time I hunt. Uncounted days in the green hills flow down the little streams to the lake as I pad softly on the deer trails. I lose track of time, existing in the great Now of cats and spirits. That is the long time, the time out of time.

Then the Lion Tooth goes beyond the river. I am pulled in two now. My anchoring spot on the ancient land of the Ani Yunwiya is far from the Lion Tooth. I must divide my power to remain with the shaman who calls me. I become smaller. I am a lynx, now.

I hunt with the Full Bloods in their new home—I understand they call themselves this because they wish no part of the invaders' life and want to hunt and trap and not farm, but in my mind I call them the deer people, for this is a matter of what humans call 'politics' and not parentage—and we take many skins.

The Lion Tooth is passed to a wife. I follow the widow of the shaman back closer to my place of power, as she returns to the family which gave her birth before her marriage, and I hope for my old form, larger, stronger, gold as the sun. It is not to be.

She tends a small garden, full of tomatoes purple as hearts.

She is still young, with much promise in her limbs and soul, but among the spider people she is not safe from the outsiders. They come to her garden. The Lion Tooth is going far from the rest of my bones once again.

I see the widow in the soldier place, many people about, illness and thirst and death. It is some soldier illness, strange to me, but it strikes the children of my friend as they swelter in the hot sun, waiting for boats to take them where the soldiers wish them to go. Some of the children of my friend pass the time by gambling while their brothers die around them. Brown rivers of disease run into the dust.

I see the widow go into the bushes with a soldier. In my lynx form, I can hide near the soldier place and watch over her, but she does not call to me for protection, nor would I know what to do if she did. I am a hunter. Never have I seen an avenging angel come down from the sky with a sword and a merciless arm, but if such a spirit came from the world of bodiless entities that was my ancient home, surely it would come for the soldier's silver metal that he wears around his neck, not for the Lion Tooth around hers. It is the thoughts, the words, the expectations of the humans that give shape to those of us who leave that realm for this one when the humans call.

All I can do for her is be here, ready if she calls. The tufts on the tips of my lynx ears sway in a slight breeze as I swivel them, listening for a call that does not come.

She argues afterwards with an old man of the People. She says, "You tell me to think of my future now, when we are torn from our land and given money in exchange, sent over the hills? What future do I have, grandfather? Our seeds will not fit the land and our healers will not know the plants, that is what the cousins have said of the lands of the Fullbloods, and we are going farther than they. To a land filled with enemy tribes. If we do not die of this bad water first. What future should I save myself for?"

He says nothing. He squints into the sunlight and sees no answer.

The future finds her nonetheless. I skip ahead, falling into the future, falling asleep. It is a trick I have learned from you, clever humans. Each night you go into your beds, your time travel devices; you close your eyes, and you skip ahead to morning. Such a wondrous ship of time is your bed; full sleep ahead.

Now I see her old and surrounded by her children, and I understand how her firstborn came to have the eyes of the sky. It is to her firstborn that the Lion Tooth comes next. This son will not stay in the exile place the enemies call Oklahoma. He has heard the stories all his life of those who escaped along the trail, and those who went before, long before, on their own and willingly, to hold to the ancient ways of trapping and hunting and not be bothered by the white men and the Half Bloods anymore.

The stories said that even the Full Bloods were not left in the peace they had been promised, and the land they had been given on which to hunt, in exchange for the land taken from the People, had in time become interesting to the white men as well. So the Full Bloods had scattered on the wind, some coming on to Oklahoma and the Western Band, and some returning to South Carolina and the Eastern Band, and others disappeared into the wilds and became indistinguishable from the Mountain Men, still trapping as before. There was a rumor that somewhere there was a settlement of the Full Bloods, where the old ways were still kept. This blue-eyed son is a Full Blood in his heart.

He dreams of me, and feels the power of the Lion Tooth around his neck. Each night he awakens from the hunt in the spirit realm where his dream self and mine stalk spirit deer beneath the icy sky. Each morning he looked out on parched farmland and the soldier-road.

So this son goes out from the western lands and fares south. Once out of sight of other humans, he stops in a little clearing off the road, with the green herbs bathed in sunlight in the midst of the shadow of a stand of trees. He does not know the old words, but he calls to me with his heart. "Lion, come to me. Let us hunt."

I am being summoned. I come.

I bound joyously out of the trees to him, and reach his side with one great leap. He laughs. I blink at him in the way of my kind, and he blinks back. We set off, hunting and walking.

He sings as we travel, for with every step he thinks he will come upon Full Bloods living the old ways and he will join with them and be as one with the ancient traditions. We tramp through many woods and meadows, and across many rocky ridges. We hunt, and we share our hunt and our prey and our lives. After years, he concludes there are no Full Bloods left, and that they faded into the hills like the whites said the fairies did long ago.

My lynx body does not live as long as a human's. Eventually I have to give it up. But this son of the line of the medicine man still wears the Lion Tooth, so I come with him in spirit.

He walks in the damp and sweltering wilds, teeming with life, and he sees the juicy ducks and the water snakes, and at night the fireflies dance with the sparks of his small fire as he roasts what he caught, and the sparks fly up into the stars, and he decides he would stay there, wherever there was. He traps and he skins and he goes into town to sell his skins and buy iron tools and he sees others like him, selling skins, wearing skins, kissed by the sun, and he knows he has finally found his people. But no one would speak Tsalagi or praise the old ones, wearing crosses every one, and boots with lug soles. They all have log cabins and property despite the law that forbids Indians from owning land in the state. This son of the children of my old friend understands. He has to make him a cabin too, and then he would put on lug sole boots and a coat with brass buttons and he would go down to register his property and he would not say he was of the People at all.

I watch him hunt and trap, but my lynx form would not stretch so far. The Lion Tooth calls me, but my bones were far away, and I have to divide my power again. I hunt with him then in bobcat form, always running in parallel with him as he sets his lines and walks his route. He does not see me, except the one time.

I am deep in the swamp, but I am being summoned, so I come. He is there, with the Lion Tooth around his neck, though perhaps he does not know it, for it is an old amulet, and the small leather pouch in which the Tooth rides has not been opened in his lifetime.

"May the spirits watch over you, and keep you safe in the far lands," says this son who is now an old man. He puts the Lion Tooth amulet around his grandson's neck. The grandson stands tall in white, with a white hat and crisp white uniform and black markings, reflecting in the water around the porch like the wings of an egret. "See," says the old man, "the spirits have heard us and they are here to see you off."

"That's a bobcat, grampa," says the young sailor. But he wears the Lion Tooth.

The Lion Tooth goes where I can not follow: far, far across the vast ocean, to a land where even the cats are strange to me. Visions I catch of him, far away, where the ground suddenly erupts like a geyser where no geyser is, and no water, and strange metal birds fly overhead and men run from them like ducklings from the eagle. What birds were these that could kill men? He fights, but I cannot go to him, cannot protect him in those alien lands.

At last I feel the touch of the Lion Tooth upon the shores of this land again, far away where the ocean of the West beats watery fists against black rock until shaped into the spires desired by the sea, leaving sand as a sculptor's sawdust lined for miles along the shore.

I would come to him then, sloughing off my bobcat form for another, smaller form again, but he does not call me. He puts the Lion Tooth medicine bag in a glass jar along with some metal disks and a few raw crystal points and these odd bars with cloth on one side and a small piece of driftwood. There it sits, and I wait, wait.

I hunt by the old cabin, and take my share of rodents, but no one calls me for help in hunting. No one calls me to watch over them, no one calls even "the spirits," let alone me myself by name. The other powers of the world must have been called, though, because they do not come by to visit, not even to tease me about my smaller form or how sometimes in the old days they would send me to a call for "the spirits" because no one else wanted to go.

I feel the keeper of the Lion Tooth move closer to me, some years later. In the mountains, he is, up a broad black highway and over a mountaintop to a gravel road and down to a stream. Many animals drink from the stream and lick from the salt lick on the hillside and roam in the deep shade of straight, tall trees whose leaves never fall, not even in deep snow, but he does not hunt. He fishes. I like fish. I cannot catch them myself, but if he offered one to me I would come to him and we would hunt together all the days of his life. But he does not call.

So I hunt. I hunt in the spring and the summer, when the light falls on the feathery blossoms, and I hunt in the autumn in the tall grass, and in the winter I rustle through the leaves and skid across the ice. I never smell wood smoke here anymore. No one lives in the log cabins, though some still have the smell of humans on their doors and there are things inside. No one poles through the swamp on a flat boat, no one sets a trap line under the falling leaves, and no one calls me.

I feel his death, many turnings of the seasons later. To what end humans go when they pass from this earth, I do not know, for I am bound to the world by my bones and the Tooth. But I hear the coins rattle against the glass as the jar containing the Lion Tooth in its little pouch of leather on an old rawhide cord is taken from a drawer. Far it goes, perhaps a little closer to me, away from the foggy coastline and the endless voice of the sea, but the Tooth goes to a place strange to me. No trees grow but what were planted, and the tall straight things that dominate this forest are made of steel and concrete and plastic.

In this place of buildings full of corners, there are also gardens. In this place where little flowers are grown in sterile plastic pots and fed with blue stuff that came from a factory, there is also a garden of the old ways. It is a grandmother's garden, where the corn, beans, and squash grow together, and the purple tomatoes of the old line are watered with carefully collected rainwater, even if it first touched the roof of a house of squares.

It reminds me of the deer people wife who had gone back to her spider people family, before the Removal. These ways are old, but not as old as I. Yet they were old enough to recall the days when I was Mountain Lion, hunter of the hills.

A woman stands in this garden, and she wears the Lion Tooth. She wears a wide brimmed straw hat and her hair is uncut and she stands barefoot on the earth among her tomatoes, and she calls. She does not know my name, but I hear her call me nonetheless.

"Kitty, kitty," she calls.

I am being summoned.

One last transference, across many hundreds of miles, into my smallest possible form. There is no smaller cat that I could become, now; this is my permanent form, and my permanent place, unless the Lion Tooth be reunited with my bones in the misty hills of far away. My eyes glitter green now. Gray is my body, with the stripes and eye markings of lynx and bobcat made into this monochrome like the wide grey streets on which these humans park their it-stares.

"Kitty, kitty." She holds out her arms to me, and I run to her, and for the first time a human touches my form. She grooms me as a mother grooms her kitten, her hand petting my fur like a mother's tongue. "Hello, my sweet kitty, my dream cat." Then she turns and walks to the house of corners and opens the door. The house? Perhaps there are mice to hunt in the house? "Kitty, kitty. Come on in, kitty."

I am being summoned. I come.

Long time I hunted. Now I sit in a patch of sunlight, a square patch, the shape of the window that admits it. My green eyes glitter as I watch over the clever humans. I am watching you right now.

The costs of war are high; legends are made, but lives are broken.

THE BUTTERFLY EFFECT

Jay "Shirou" Coughlan

We stood in the tent alone with two humans of the city's army; it smelled of dirt, sweat, and, best of all, ginger. The ginger was sourced to a table with a steaming cup of what I assumed was tea and the scent drowned out all others. It was a familiar smell, a delicious smell. It reminded me of my time as a young pup with my mother and father. I straightened.

Me and Rahni stood side-by-side. Before us was an opportunity no one of our kind could have dreamed. But the tension was thick in the air, and not just from the war outside. The humans before us bickered between themselves about this. The tall, dark skinned one was against our presence entirely. He was an officer of some high ranking. I hadn't yet learned what ranks matched with what armor, but his was opulent silver plate-mail with golden embroidery and several commemorative medals on his chest. The other man was old, short, had milky skin that matched his white lab coat, and only a few wiry hairs on his head. He ignored the officer's words with an exhausted expression, like he'd heard this a million times before.

All four of us wore masks made of silver and stuffed with incense and herbs over our faces. Ours were made specifically to fit over our muzzles but they weren't comfortable, especially for as long as we had been wearing them. No doubt the humans were feeling the same, despite their better fit. They were a constant reminder of what kind of war this was.

"They're a couple of pelts!" the officer scoffed, voice barely muffled. His bulky armor clanked with every minute movement and made my ears ring. They flicked in annoyance, but I held otherwise still.

"They're two able-bodied young men. Whether they have tails and fur is irrelevant," the Spell-master spat back. They referred to our species. Not human like them, but wolves that stood like men. I was more surprised by the light-skinned one's apathy than the officer's disgust. Most humans thought us lesser than themselves. Perhaps they were just too used to the obedient feral dogs and wolves that walk among their mother country. Perhaps they just thought us weird.

My fur prickled in excitement. This war could change that. To be called into service for the war as a spell-weaver was more honor than anyone of our kind could expect, but to be asked for aid by the Spell-master himself was beyond anyone's expectations. I didn't risk a glance to Rahni, but I knew he was just as excited as I. Things would be different after this war.

Between the officer and the Spell-master was a short pedestal holding two odd looking eggs. At first I thought they were dragon eggs, for their size was too big to be anything else and their colors were odd; one was blue as the ocean and the other was a brilliant lavender. But when I looked closer I noticed they weren't made of shell and scales at all. Instead they were made of intricate intertwining metals woven into impossible patterns. The eggs outer casings were silver with a design of swirls, alchemic symbols, and almost illegible lines of ritual casting carved into the surface. You could look through deliberate gaps in the casing and see thousands of tiny interlocking pieces, gears, cogs, and screws all lying dormant within. The eggs, I realized, weren't actually colored but were lit with an inner glow that pulsed with pure magic. The color reflected against every piece of metal within, and reached the outer world with an amazing brilliance. As I realized the complexity of whatever spell these eggs held, my eyes widened.

"It's good to see you two realize the power in these." The old man chuckled. The officer seemed to have given up his tirade and settled for glaring at us instead. I looked over to Rahni who had an expression similar to how I was feeling, excitement, intrigue, and awe, only he was far less contained. "I knew you'd be able to appreciate it, unlike some of the mundanes around here," the Spell-master said, shooting a glare at the officer. "Before any of us continue with anything, I must warn you. These are very strong magical devices. They can work separately, but are at their strongest when connected with you. But if you're connected to them for too long… well, just don't wear them for too long if you can help it."

I nodded, and glanced at Rahni who hesitated and then did the same. I felt Rahni's tail press against my leg, and I knew he was nervous about these strange devices too. The risks sounded high, if nebulous, but we couldn't deny the opportunity given to us here. I pressed my tail back against his for reassurance.

"We're ready," I said.

"Yeah, we'll do it," Rahni followed with a goofy grin.

"Excellent." The old man smiled. He beckoned us forward with a hand. "I would explain these in more detail for you, but it's better if I just show you." The Spell-master smiled, taking a hand from each of us and leading them to the eggs. The glow within them began to crackle and brighten. Power coursed through my fingertips as I got close to touching their silver surface. Once my hand was on it, I came to a brilliant and terrifying conclusion.

These eggs were alive.

***

Roi's eyes blinked open. He lay on his back, half covered in sheets, and turned to look at his clock, a round crystal orb with illusory blue numbers suspended within. It was exactly six fifty-nine, sixty seconds before the alarm would sound. He lifted his arm and waved at the device, silencing it early.

Sun streamed through his drapes and filled the room with a warm glow. His house was small, it had a kitchen, a bedroom with a closet, and a connected bathroom. Wood floors covered the entire area; they always looked filthy in the summer when his fur shed, and his claws often scratched the surface. Carpet would have been nicer, but it was harder to maintain and harder to get these days.

Roi sat up, removed the sheets, and sat on the edge of his bed. He looked over himself, gray and white fur with patches of brown that grew smaller with every summer shed. A careful hand traced over the large bald patch on the left side of his stomach. It was rough, wrinkly, and about the size of a small plate. He felt a few brave, new hairs trying to reclaim the pink and brown splotched skin but he held no hope. It had been over twenty years since the injury; the fur would never grow back.

His hand continued to wander over his body. The fur he did have had clumped and matted in his sleep, and he tried to rake it smooth. His dull claws clicked against metal bands made of tiny intricate scales wrapped around his limbs and upper body, all of them connected with even thinner strips of the same silvery material. They shifted and adjusted as he moved with clinks as quiet as whispers. Every piece was eventually connected to a single point at his back, surrounding and protecting a large sapphire gem. He had long since gotten used to the silver that was pressed against his body and idly wondered if he still had fur underneath it.

Roi stood and walked into the attached bathroom. He stopped at the sink and stared into the mirror. Tired, yellow eyes stared back. As he rinsed his face, he felt the metal hub on his back begin to shift and wake.

"Good morning Roi!" chittered a metallic voice as thousands of scales and gears shifted into the form of a small silver gryphon. The tiny metal beast, about the size of a crow, sat neatly on the wolf's shoulder, his tail dangling down, still connected to the metal that spider-webbed from Roi's back. The gryphon flexed its wings, showing off the glowing stone that now sat in his chest, and made a show of preening his always perfect, silver feathers.

"Good morning," Roi said.

"Oh dear! There seem to be a few more gray hairs on your muzzle today! You must be getting old!" the gryphon joked, playfully pressing his beak to Roi's cheek. Roi grunted in response, brushing his teeth. "Heh, I remember when you were just a young pup, you were so worried about this very thing. Look at you now! I think you look quite distinguished with it."

Roi spat out his toothpaste and rinsed, ignoring the comments. "You've only known me since my mid-twenties, Archimedes," he reminded the bird.

"Oh, right." Archimedes' tiny metal ears swiveled back in embarrassment. "I must have been reading your memories by mistake again."

Roi's ear twitched back as he rinsed his face. Memories. Those were his dreams last night. Those had been his dreams every night. Old, touchy, sensitive memories. Sometimes they were good memories, sometimes they were terrible ones. More often they were just normal, mundane events. It was odd to know your dreams had actually happened. To know that every action in them was something you knew, something you could think of just as clearly during the day. Dreams were supposed to be something more. Fears, desires, a breakdown of how you're feeling, visions of the future, or even visions of another world. Roi hadn't had a proper dream in years. But he had memories.

"Oh! Don't forget your breakfast with Erin today," Archie said, adjusting his weight as Roi walked to his wardrobe and swung the doors wide open. "You should wear your red robe. She likes that one!" he suggested. Roi pulled out a pair of thin, silver-silk pants and began to put them on.

"I have work today." He grunted as he felt the fabric catch on his fur. He would have to get the pants re-spelled or buy a new pair. He grabbed his usual robes, blue with silver and gold trimmings, and slid them on. They too were getting old; some of the trim was fraying, and there were a couple small holes that threatened to turn into larger problems. He would have to have those repaired as well. Archimedes looked disappointed, but remained silent.

They walked to the restaurant in silence. The summer sun shone down from beyond the clouds, and several kids of varying species ran up and down the cobblestone streets. Roi saw Erin sitting at one of the patio tables of *La Crepe*, watching the kids play. Some were fooling around with what magic they had learned at school and others were smacking each other with sticks in mock swordfights.

"My apologies if I kept you waiting," Roi said as he pulled in across from her. Erin turned and smiled at him. Age had hit her harder than it had hit Roi: her eyes were tired and weary; her muzzle had gone from rich reds and browns to stark white; and her skin seemed to cling to her skeleton. She had lost a lot of weight.

"I wasn't here long," Erin said. Even her voice sounded slower, more deliberate, as if she'd lose it if she weren't careful. Her ears perked forward as she looked over Roi. "You're always exactly on time. I could set my schedule to you. Have you been sleeping well?"

"Yes, fine," Roi said. Erin nodded, but didn't seem to believe that answer.

"Have you seen your therapist lately?"

"I have not. There hasn't been any need," Roi said. Erin didn't believe that either.

They ordered their breakfasts as usual, scrambled eggs and toast for Roi, a lemon crepe and sausage for Erin. Erin took charge of their conversation, telling him about her job at the academy, about rumors of the staff and students, and about one of her students who had made a great jump in learning since he started. Roi nodded and made affirmative grunts where appropriate, and every so often Archimedes would pipe in with a comment or quip, which would make Erin laugh.

Erin was about halfway through another story when she trailed off with a sigh. Roi perked his ears forward. He considered asking what was wrong, but he knew she'd say anyway. Instead he waited. Erin looked at him, expecting something, but when he offered no words she began to speak.

"What is wrong with you, Roi?" she said.

"I don't understand."

Erin dropped her fork with a clatter and stared at him. "We come here week after week because we promised not to lose touch, and every week it feels like you want to be here less and less."

"I simply don't have much to say," Roi responded. A flicker of motion next to Erin caught his eye, but was gone too fast to see.

"That's the thing! Do you even do anything beyond this and work? Do you even do anything at work?"

Roi shrugged, his eyes searching for the movement.

"He's been reading, although it's mostly for research on the shield," Archimedes piped in from Roi's shoulder.

"Archie." Erin let out an exasperated sigh, pushing her half eaten food away. She shook her head and returned her focus to Roi. "Have you even spoken to our daughter recently?"

"She made it clear she wasn't interested in talking, so I've left her alone," Roi said. Erin rolled her eyes and ran a hand over her ears. The movement appeared again, and Roi's eyes snapped to where it had been, but it was gone. He eyed the flower box hung on the fence behind her.

"Roi." Erin put her hand on his half of the table, reaching forward to him. He looked down at it, confused. "Roi, do you ever regret our divorce?" she asked, her eyes staring into his. He looked back into hers with an unwavering non-expression on his face.

"No."

The flicker returned and, before Roi's eyes even locked on to what it was, his hand was out. In one swift motion his palm was beside Erin's cheek. He had grasped the movement and immediately seared it with flame. Erin recoiled as the heat licked her face and stumbled out of her chair.

"By the gods!" Erin shouted. Roi stared at his closed fist, head tilted curiously.

"Apologies. I didn't mean to scare you," he said as Erin stood up.

"You nearly gave me a heart attack!" Erin snapped, picking up her purse and coat. "You can pay for breakfast today. I'm done." She kicked her chair and, with an angry swish of her tail, left.

Archie watched her leave before butting his head against Roi's cheek. "What were you thinking! What was that!" He clicked. "Am I bound to a madman now?" He hopped on Roi's shoulder to get his attention.

"I thought this was you," Roi said. He stared at his fist. "I never meant to do this."

"It certainly was not me!" Archimedes huffed, annoyed. "What did you scorch anyway?"

Slowly Roi opened his clenched fist. Ash fell from his hand onto Erin's discarded breakfast, as well as one half of what used to be a butterfly. Archimedes gasped, although it sounded mechanical and false due to his lack of lungs.

"Is it one of them?" Archimedes asked, peering at it.

"You wouldn't need to ask if it was." Roi leaned back, and brushed the rest of the ash off into his own breakfast. He threw some money on the table, more than enough to cover the breakfasts, and left for work in silence.

Work did not go well.

"That was a disaster," grumbled Fehri. He was a short, brown-backed, white-bellied stoat the size of a small man, and was the current head of the Amalian cultural office of Toriel. Despite being much younger than Roi, the stoat was technically his boss, but he rarely felt like it. Roi had just told Fehri about the events of the council meeting, and the stoat was furious. "What were you thinking!"

"I was thinking of the future of our city and way of life." Roi knew the question was rhetorical, but he felt his reasons were obvious.

"You told the council the entire topic was pointless!" Fehri's fists slammed against the paper strewn desk in front of him, sending several wayward sheets flying. He would regret that later.

"We're trapped behind a shield; we're terrorized by butterflies and their possessed souls; our land becomes more crowded every day; and the council wants to talk about weather magic. It was pointless," Roi said.

"For the love of—the King was there, Roi! You couldn't have pretended for her sake?"

"I was hired for my knowledge and expertise, not to pretend there is nothing wrong with our strategy," Roi said. He idly petted Archimedes as the gryphon sat on his shoulder. Archimedes wasn't certain now was the time for it, but accepted the strokes anyway. "Besides, she seemed amused."

"Life doesn't stop just because there's a threat on our doorstep, Roi!" Fehri shouted. "Not everyone is able to fight, not everyone is able to research. What would you have us do? Put them in a cave while everyone else tries to fight bloody little butterflies!" He grumbled nonsense in frustration.

"I don't think you comprehend the severity of our situation," Roi said.

Fehri rolled his eyes.

"I know the 'severity of the situation.'" He raised his hands and mimicked air-quotes around the phrase. "But those who can't help still need to live! You're supposed to represent a large number of them! Do you know how many Amalian would be pissed off if their ability to cast spells like this was taken? *It's a slippery slope!* they'll say, *How long before we can't cast spells at all!* they'll cry," Fehri said, mocking the people as his voice became squeaky in agitation.

"I'm not saying these aren't subjects to consider," Roi said, straightening his robe. "But until we can prove we have a future beyond these few years, our time is better spent elsewhere."

Fehri took a deep breath.

"Is this a post-traumatic stress thing? I talked to Erin this morning; she told me about your 'breakfast.'" He air-quoted again. "Do you need a week off? Your benefits include therapy; should I give you the details?"

"No," Roi said.

Fehri stood up and paced the tiny office and his thin, wisp of a tail flicked. He couldn't stand still when agitated. Archimedes watched him pace from Roi's shoulder.

"I think a week off would be a wonderful idea!" the gryphon chimed. Roi shook his head immediately.

"I don't need time off."

"Too bad, you're taking it," Fehri decided, sitting back at his desk and shuffling about the mess of papers on it. "I know you like to work and everything, but you clearly need some time to put your head on straight."

Roi put a heavy paw on Fehri's desk with a thump and stared him square in the eyes. "There is nothing wrong with my head. I have done nothing but try to help this city."

Fehri matched the wolf's gaze. Roi was smarter and stronger than him, and often Fehri let him do what he wanted because of it, but this was an exception. "You're supposed to be our liaison, our representative in the King's council. You're so obsessed with this war you haven't even been doing that." He tugged a sheet of paper from under Roi's massive hand and began scribbling on it.

"I'm not taking any time off," Roi said.

"You're not. This is a suspension." Fehri handed Roi the slip of paper and sighed. "You're a brilliant guy, Roi. But you just..." Fehri shrugged. "I don't know how to say it, something's been off. You need a break."

Fehri leaned back in his chair. Roi stood with a cursory but snappy thank you and left.

***

"Can I come in?" I asked. I stood outside a small personal tent, listening to the murmurings inside. I couldn't make them out, and I didn't try. This was Erin's tent, and despite my own curiosity, I didn't want to eavesdrop. There was a shuffling within before I heard a muffled "come in" in response. I opened the flap and ducked inside.

Erin sat on a bulky sleeping bag, legs crossed and tail trailing behind her. Rahni was slumped against her with his head resting on her shoulder. I felt a pang of jealousy ripple through my chest but ignored it. I knew there was nothing between Rahni and Erin; Rahni just wasn't that way.

"How are you holding up, Ra? Ready to go back out there?" I asked with a smile. I stuck my thumb out behind me. Rahni groaned. Archimedes walked into the tent and over to Hermes, Rahni's wolf-shaped spell-forme. The two exchanged a glance and then settled next to each other, watching us.

"Really? Already? I hate it out there," Rahni grumbled. He sat up, but didn't look ready to actually move. His eyes were locked on the floor and his ears drooped back.

"I hear you, Ra," I said, sitting down across from them both. "But one of us needs to be out there. I can't support everyone by myself for long."

Rahni didn't move.

"Go on." Erin nudged him with a smile. "With Hermes at your side, you two are unbeatable!"

Rahni didn't say anything. He was slow to stand, and made an exaggerated show of stretching. He lowered an arm towards Hermes. The metallic dog jumped on his hand and seemed to melt into the wolf's armor, unfolding and covering every inch of Rahni in full plate.

Perhaps it was my own exhaustion, or just the lighting in the tent, but the armor had lost some of its sheen. I shook the idea out of my head and gave Rahni a pat on the shoulder as he passed.

"Don't worry. We're close to a solution, right Erin?" I said.

Erin tensed. "We were just discussing that. Erm, no, no we're not."

I let out a sigh. Of course they had been discussing that. Just my luck.

"It's fine, Roi," Rahni said, brushing my hand off his shoulder. His voice did not sound fine. He turned to me, his eyes looked as dark and tired as I felt. This war was taking so much from him. I gave him a reassuring smile but he simply turned and left.

"Those masks the spell-weaver's keep handing out are failing. Rahni's own squad turned right on him," Erin said. I sat next to her, replacing Rahni's head on her shoulder with my own. "Poor guy is losing it."

"I didn't know," I whispered, letting the comfort of her closeness wash over me. I wasn't sure what to say. The idea of those you trusted in one instant becoming enemies in another was terrifying, more so when the reality of it was right outside this tent. I breathed in Erin's scent, letting it clear away the thought. She kissed me between my ears.

"You okay there, bird-boy?" Erin whispered into my ear. The nickname had become her favorite since she discovered Archimedes was my spell-forme.

I chuckled a little. "Not as bad as Rahni," I finally said. "Just tired." I leaned in closer and pressed our bodies together. "What's going on with the butterflies?"

"Not a lot." Erin sighed, idly stroking my side. "The butterflies are too dangerous to get close enough to research them, and anyone who is possessed by them is out of our control. All we know is it has something to do with the air, and that they are more than normal butterflies."

My ear perked. "There's a difference?" I asked.

"Yeah, these butterflies have a distinct magical signature. It's how the shields can keep them out of our tents. We're trying to make a smaller scale version for the masks, but it's not as easy as you'd think. Especially since we're running out of time."

"Well wait, what if…" I paused to let my brain catch up. Thoughts were beginning to connect and an idea was forming. "What if we made that shield surround the city? It would be temporary, but it would buy us more time."

Erin thought it over for a moment. "We considered that. But it was agreed the power required to keep it up would be way too much."

"Not if the shield was blood-bonded, kind of like our spell-formes."

"Not bad, but who would take on that responsibility?"

I shrugged. "The king?"

"Roi, you're a genius."

Erin grabbed my cheeks and kissed me so hard I nearly blacked out.

***

Roi blinked awake. The sound of fist pounding on wood echoed through his home. His head rested on the table, books spread out in front of him. He didn't remember deciding to take a nap; age must have been catching up on him. He shook his head to forget the dream. There was another knock, and Roi stood, giving his wayward fur a quick brush so it stood somewhat straight, and answered.

"Hey, Dad," said Rin. She did not sound happy.

"Come in," Roi said. Rin pushed past him into the house.

"Hello, Rin." Archimedes greeted, forming himself on Roi's shoulder.

"Hello Archie," she said in a much nicer tone.

Rin was Roi's daughter. She stood a head shorter than him with rusty red fur and a sour expression like a grumpier, younger version of her mother. Her arms were crossed as she stalked in silence to his kitchen.

"Apologies for the mess; I wasn't expecting company. Can I get you a drink?" Roi offered, clearing books and notes from the table. He knew Rin would refuse, but it was polite to offer.

"How have you been, Rin?" asked Archimedes.

"I'm not really in the mood Archie. I'm here about him." She spat that last word with venom and pointed. "You told mom you have no regrets about the divorce?"

Roi started preparing himself some tea anyway. "Yes I did.".

"Why in the world would you do that?" she snapped.

Roi snapped his fingers and a small flame appeared in the boiler. "I saw no point in lying."

"I'm not surprised you don't care. Prick." Rin growled. She sat in a chair with a heavy thump. "But you had to just tell her? Do you have any idea how people work anymore? Are you just a golem now? Input orders please," Rin said, mimicking the emotionless, stilted tones of primitive golems.

"Technically I'm a golem," Archie piped up with a forced smile.

Rin rolled her eyes, but her expression softened. "Good point, Archie. You have more damned sense than he does." She crossed her arms and leaned back in her chair, looking like the annoyed teenager

Roi remembered. "I'm here because Mom's hysterical about what you said. She hasn't stopped crying all day. She even called in sick to work. Do you know how rare that is?"

"She is a dedicated woman; it's one of her best qualities."

Rin slammed her fist on the table. "Damn it!" Archie tensed. "I knew you wouldn't bloody understand. It's like I'm arguing with a wall!"

The water boiled, and Roi put the teabag into his mug, carrying it with care to the table. "Please do not hit my table," Roi said, sitting down across from her. Rin stared daggers at him and began rhythmically slamming her fist on the table, shaking it with every thump. "Now you're just being petulant."

"You're being heartless!" She stopped banging her fist on the oak table, likely due more to pain than any satisfaction.

Roi placed his tea on the table, confident Rin wasn't going to slam her fist into it again. "I didn't mean to hurt her, but I make a point of not lying, and I don't intend to break that."

"Really? You couldn't pull out one little lie. All you needed to do was say, 'Of course.' And move on."

"I'm not going to lie just to save her heart. She's a tough woman, she'll understand."

Rin shook her head and placed it in her hands. She couldn't find the words. Frustration welled inside her, and she resisted the urge to scream. "Am I making any sense to you here? Archie, tell me I'm not the crazy one," she said, golden eyes pleading with Archie's own blue orbs.

"She has a point," Archimedes said before shifting uncomfortably on Roi's shoulder. "You were a bit cold this morning. It wouldn't have hurt to lie a little."

"Thank you!" Rin said. Archimedes bowed his head with a quirky smile. She turned her attention back to Roi, who sipped his tea. "Look, I don't give a dyce's ass what you do, but if you're going to be this heartless then stay away from Mom!" she spat.

Roi sipped his tea and Rin refused to make eye contact. Silence sat between them, thick and heavy.

"It's a pleasure to see you again," Archimedes said, trying to break the silence.

"It's nice to see you as well, despite present company." She flicked her eyes to Roi, who seemed disappointingly unfazed at her comment. "You ever want to get away from him, Arch? Just detach yourself and wander around alone."

"I can't say I do. Your father would be crippled without me," Archimedes admitted.

"Pretending he wasn't blasted in the war. Would you?" Rin pushed.

"Well…"

"I hear Rahni's spell-forme did all the time."

Roi put his cup down, hot tea spilling over the side. "The point is I was shot, and Archimedes cannot detach," he said.

"It was just a question," Rin spat back.

"A pointless one."

"God, you're worse off than Rahni." She stood up, chair scraping behind her.

"How do you figure?"

"Because no one's expecting him to be normal like everyone else! No one's being disappointed when it's easier relating to a damned thesaurus!" Rin slammed the table again, the tea spilling everywhere and splashing on Roi. "Stay away from Mom!" she shouted before storming out and slamming the door.

Roi stood and cleared most of the books off the table to prevent them from being damaged. He padded across the kitchen, claws clicking against the hardwood, grabbed a cloth, and dried off the hot water from his robe, grunting in discomfort.

"Are you okay?" Archimedes asked.

"The burns are minor at worst. I'll be fine," Roi said.

"I'm glad, but that's not what I meant."

"Then I miss your meaning." Roi said. He walked back to the table and began drying it. He finished cleaning up, putting his notes and books back onto the table and resumed his research without another word. Archimedes returned to his hub on Roi's back. They both remained silent until, eventually, Roi finished his research for the night and went to bed.

***

The battlefield was nearly devoid of bodies. The sun was setting on the horizon before us, illuminating the oncoming army in a fiery glow. It was terrifying. Our men were all retreating, grabbing whatever wounded had not been compromised. We were only able to retreat because our enemy's new recruits took some time to get properly coordinated.

"We have to go, Rahni!" I shouted. In an instant the blue light of magic lit up my shoulder, and traveled down my armor through my hand. I threw up my arm at my oncoming opponents and in moments they were all frozen.

"Stay away!" I heard Rahni scream. I turned to him, three of our allies who were set to keep him safe had turned on him, swinging their weapons in savage arcs. His spell-forme armor had crafted small shields to deflect the attacks but he couldn't focus enough to get a clear shot with any of his spells.

I whispered a silent apology, brought what dredges of energy I could muster, and shot damaging spells at the three, knocking them to the ground, likely maiming them for the rest of their lives. It was too late for them anyway.

"Come on, Rahni!" I shouted, waving towards our retreating army. "We have a plan; we need to go!"

He stood stock still and silent. I ran up closer and I finally got a good look at him. Madness had twisted everything about him, his spell-forme armor, once silver and gleaming, was turning black and rusting; his magic aura, once clear and violet, was foggy and infected with brown tendrils; and his eyes, once young and excited, were bloodshot and dominated with fear. "Rahni?" I whispered.

"Go away!" Rahni screamed, he waved his hand and a pulse of magic shook the earth around him, nearly knocking me off my feet.

"Rahni come on!"

"What's happening?" shouted a voice behind me. It was Erin, running out from the now-abandoned research tent.

"Rahni's gone crazy!" I shouted back to her. I reached a hand out to him, hoping he'd come back to his senses. Instead the mad wolf shot a spell at Erin, who thankfully had her defense spell active. The violet pulse of Rahni's spell smashed against her prismatic bubble, but she remained unharmed. "Stay back!" I snapped. We locked eyes for a moment and shared the same thought. I had to try and reach Rahni; we couldn't leave him behind.

Rahni's eyes shifted between me and Erin, not daring to let us out of his sight. Paranoia racked his brain, and all reason had been thrown aside. I was afraid his mind was lost and he'd be nothing more than a two-legged feral like the wild wolves we descended from. I stood up straight and raised my hands in a sign of peace. My movement alerted Rahni and he shifted focus to me, his own hand was up and ready to fire whatever mad spell he had prepared.

"It's me, Rahni. We're going to take you home," I said, forcing myself to be calm. I saw his hand begin to glow as he prepared a spell. I didn't move. He didn't fire. Time was running short.

"Archie, disengage armor," I said. A mental command would have worked too, but I wanted to prove to Rahni that we were still his friends. I wanted him to hear the words.

"Sir, that is not advised."

"*I don't care. Disengage armor.*"

With reluctance, Archimedes obeyed, and my armor began to fold back upon itself, getting smaller and smaller until it had detached and returned to the form of a small gryphon by my feet.

"*Don't come any closer!*" *Rahni begged, the energy in his hand crackling its threat. I had to try. I took a step forward. He screamed and shot the spell, hitting me in the stomach. The world lurched, I couldn't feel anything. I clutched my hand to where I was hit, and felt blood. Archie was already on me, calmly telling me to count to ten as he began to wrap me in his armor once more.*

One, two, three.
Erin was screaming and firing spells faster than Rahni could react.
Four, five, six.
I hit the ground. Others were joining in to detain him.
Seven, eight, nine.
Rahni, why?
Ten.
Everything went dark.

***

A heavy weight on Roi's chest woke him from his memories. His eyes flicked open and adjusted to the dawn sun peeking over his windowsill. Even though his eyes were having trouble focusing, he knew what was on him. A perk to having a soul-bond.

"Might I ask why you are formed on my chest?" Roi said over the rough carpet of his tongue.

Archimedes clicked his metal beak but wouldn't meet his eye. "I've been worried about you," he finally said. "You've been acting… well." Archimedes bounced on his front paws, nervous. "You simply haven't been acting."

"I don't understand."

"I went through your memories, from since before we connected and—"

A knock on the door caught Roi's attention. Archimedes looked at his host, eyes pleading for him to ignore it, but Roi was already standing. Defeated, the silver gryphon disassembled into his host's exoskeleton as the wolf made himself decent.

"One minute!" he called.

The door knocked twice more before Roi answered it. On the other side was a woman dressed in simple silver armor with a gold crown emblem on the chest. One of the king's royal guard. In her hand was a letter, sealed and facing Roi to show off the royal crest—a hand seizing a four pointed gem—stamped in the wax.

"You have been summoned for an audience with the king," she said in a booming voice, as if she was speaking to him from across the street. Roi took the envelope, opened it, and quickly scanned the contents. "What is your answer?"

Roi's response was simple. The king was an important figure, her attention was valuable and a request should be responded to with haste. He could feel Archimedes' desire to reject the offer; something important was on his mind. But they were soul-bound, even if they could separate they would always have each other. Their conversation could wait.

"I accept. When shall we depart?"

The king waited for them in one of the side halls off of the main chambers. The hall was made of light gray stone with blue carpet that led the way from one end to another. Large windows overlooked what was once a beautiful garden, but since the war, had been re-built as small homes to house the serving staff and guards. The king stood facing one window and looking pensive over the new walls. The guard announced Roi, much quieter than when she gave his summons, and the king dismissed her with a wave of her hand. King Julia then turned to Roi, her lips quirking into a small smile as her hand rested naturally on the pommel of her sword.

"Roi, thank you for coming to see me," she said with a nod.

"A pleasure as always," Roi responded with a light bow. Julia began to walk and Roi quickly joined step as they wandered the halls.

"You worked with my father, correct?" Her armored shoes clanked with every step.

"For a brief time, as we set up the city's shield, and some work in the council before his passing."

Julia nodded solemnly, the memory of her father must have still been fresh in her mind. "It was the shield that eventually did him in, correct?"

"You know this answer as well as I do, your highness. Yes, it did. Why?" He had expected this conversation to be about his poor performance at the council, but the way the conversation was turning confused him. He hadn't been confused like this in a long time, the sensation was foreign to him. Like a book read once as a kid being re-read as an adult for the first time. Julia stopped walking and turned to him.

"Did you already forget?" she said, harsher than her diplomatic persona usually allowed. Roi looked into her eyes; they were sunken in, red. Dark circles ghosted around them from exhaustion. It was easy to miss the circles at first, but a closer inspection made them impossible to avoid. Roi could never forget. They were the same eyes as her father's, and it was because of Roi and Erin that they were there.

"Of course not." He dipped his muzzle in respect. "I was only meaning, why are you asking now?"

"Because I feel it happening. It's draining me. Every day it's harder to wake up, to move, to think. Even if I conceived an heir now, they would have this curse from me as a child. Father only lasted fifteen or so years, and I know I won't do much better."

Roi nodded and understood. The reality of her situation had dawned on her and she was panicking. The shield was supposed to be a temporary measure, only meant to last a short while until a solution came. Or worse.

"It would be possible to create a second shield and pass the responsibility to someone else." Roi offered, but Julia shook her head.

"The king's responsibility is to protect their people. It wouldn't be right." She smiled a mischievous grin, and looked Roi in the eyes. "But I have another idea, and I need your opinion on it. Your honest opinion." She put emphasis on 'honest', like she expected Roi to sugar coat his answer, or beat around it, or straight up lie. Clearly she hasn't been talking to his ex-wife. His only wonder was what her solution was. Then it clicked.

"You want a spell-forme," Roi said.

"You're the only sane person left who's been connected to one of them. My advisors are split on the idea, and I need you to either make it or break it," Julia said.

The "sane" comment made something stir within Roi, but he ignored it. "Have you spoken to Mr. Gerald about it?"

"No." Julia shook her head. "He won't be making the spell-forme anyway; we got his research notes when he retired. Perhaps you'd run it by him?"

"We'd love to, your highness," Archimedes spoke up, forming himself on Roi's shoulder. Julia's face brightened. The gryphon made a show of bowing, spreading his wings as he did so. "I do not believe we have properly met. I am Archimedes, Roi's spell-forme."

"Charming," Julia said with an amused smile. "Are all spell-formes gryphons?"

"Not at all! Rahni's was a small wolf, for instance. We choose forms based on our hosts. We are meant to work alongside our partners as well as a part of them, although I'm constantly connected to Roi for health reasons."

Julia asked them both questions, although they were targeted more to Archimedes than Roi. He let his gryphon answer them as Roi couldn't focus on the task before him. No matter how hard he tried, he couldn't stop his mind from wandering.

"You're the only sane person left who's connected." The words echoed in his ears. Rahni's haunted eyes flooded his vision. They nearly looked like the king's own, but while Julia's eyes were exhausted, his were terrified. The war had broken him. The war had broken many people, but Rahni suffered the most.

Or had his spell-forme broken him? This wasn't the first time he had humored the question. The spell-forme came out just as bad, if not worse than Rahni had. Did it accelerate his condition? Did it cause it? Or was it the other way? Did Rahni corrupt his spell-forme with paranoia? He didn't know.

With this question in his head, he couldn't endorse the King's proposal. If she were to gain a spell-forme, and it affected her like it might have Rahni, or if her panic about the shield corrupted her spell-forme, it could be a disaster.

But Roi stood here as a bastion of success for this magical tech. He was proof the spell-forme would work, right? And the benefits for this were grand; a stronger shield, a long-living king, and another force to be reckoned with on the battlefield.

Assuming he was a bastion of success. Roi recalled Archimedes this morning, worried and invasive. His spell-forme had never scanned over his memories before. Why now? Was he malfunctioning? Was Roi malfunctioning?

When Julia's assistant came to remind her of her next appointment, the king requested Roi's answer, but he still couldn't decide.

"I need to think it over," Roi said. "Let me talk to Mr. Gerald, and I will be back to you as soon as possible."

Julia looked surprised, but seemed understanding. "Please be fast. We don't know how long it will take to make one."

Roi bowed deep in respect; Julia nodded her head; and they both went their separate ways.

Archimedes stayed quiet the entire way to Mr. Gerald's home, only forming himself as they came up to his door. Roi knocked three times and waited.

"I'm comin', give me a minute," came a voice from inside. It was slower than they remembered, but not any less energetic. Eventually Roi heard footsteps on the other side, a click of the bolt un-doing, and the door opened.

"Hello Mr. Gerald, we're—"

"Well now!" Mr. Gerald cut him off, happily surprised. "It's been so long since I've seen you, come in, come in." He shuffled back and waved the wolf in. Thomas Gerald was a short man with pale skin and only wisps of white hair touching his head. Besides some balding and changing his lab-coat for a house coat, he hadn't changed much since Roi first met him on the battlefield.

"Sir, we are here on royal business," Roi said as the door closed behind him.

"Oh hush, we have time. Sit down, have some tea. It's been years!" Mr. Gerald rushed behind him as best as the old man could, and prepared a kettle for some tea. "How have you two been getting along? I haven't been able to see my creation in such a long time."

"I'm doing quite well, Thomas," Archimedes said with a short dip of his beak. "I think."

"You think?" Thomas said with a raised, oversized eyebrow as he dropped tea bags into mugs. "Not the confidence I want from one of my creations. What's been botherin' ya?"

Roi shifted and Archimedes jumped onto the back of the overstuffed armchair they sat in, his tail still connected to the wolf's exoskeleton.

"Honestly nothing, sir. We are here on official business."

"Roi, you have to admit something's off."

"Nothing is off, Archimedes." Roi shook his head. "You're simply overreacting to an issue that isn't there."

Thomas tsk'd. "You should listen to him, Roi," he said with a smile. The water began to bubble as it heated. "My spell-formes are smart devices. They don't get up in arms over nothing."

"Regardless, we are here on royal business, not a checkup."

"Oh, I'm sorry, Roi. Did you have something better to do?" Thomas's words dripped with sarcasm as he stared down the larger wolf.

Roi didn't respond at first; he had no job to report to, and his own research hadn't been heading him anywhere. "We shouldn't keep the king waiting," he said.

Thomas chuckled. "So the rumors were true. You have been suspended." Roi and Archimedes looked at each other, caught off guard. "Oh come on." Thomas smiled. "You're not the only friends I have in the castle." He began pouring water into the mugs, the steam rising high like misty spirits. "Are the rumors about you and your ex true too? I heard you said some very insensitive things."

Thomas walked over to sit in the chair opposite, offering Roi his tea as he passed.

Roi took the mug with a small "thanks" and stared at the rising steam. "I suppose they are true," he admitted. Despite his ambivalence, Roi couldn't keep his ears up; they kept sweeping back like weights were put in the tips. He took a sip of tea, and Thomas joined him. "I didn't say anything that wasn't truthful."

"That is a shame," Thomas said in a voice that betrayed his age. The usual twinkle in his eye faded for a moment. "You two were a great couple. So cute together. Like puppies."

"Please, sir," Archimedes said, jumping onto Roi's shoulder. "Roi used to be so excitable, empathetic. I ran through his memories last night, and ever since the war… His emotions have just ebbed away."

"Meanwhile, you have more emotion than I could ever have dreamed!" Thomas gave Archimedes a wide smile, proud of his creation. Then the smile faded, and he set his cup down on a side table. "I did warn you."

Roi's ears perked. "I'm sorry, sir. Warn me about what?"

"About this," Thomas said, waving his hand at the wolf in general. "About being connected all the time. Spell-formes were never meant to be permanent life-support."

"I don't understand," Roi said. His ears fell back down.

"I remember both you young pups when you walked into that tent. I knew giving anyone spell-formes was dangerous, but it was a dangerous time, and we were out of good ideas. You two were the best part of that terrible plan. You were capable of magic so you could properly use the 'formes, and smart enough to not let the power drive you mad." He paused. "Bad choice of words. I mean greedy and stuff. Like the tales you hear of ancient spell-weavers determined to find 'ultimate power', as if it ever existed. Have you visited Rahni since then?"

Archimedes fluttered his wings. Roi remained silent. "He hasn't been able. Rahni's at Gimaldi Asylum and I deactivate when I get too close to the azuchite. It's not pleasant for Roi," Archimedes said.

"Ahh, drain stone would do it," Thomas said, grabbing his tea and sipping from it. "But I told you, your body is not meant to be a continuous vessel for this." He waved, again, at Roi in general. "You should have disconnected as soon as you were hospitalized. They could have stabilized you and you would have only needed an extra week or two to recover. three weeks during the war was bad enough, but two more afterwards? That was too much." Thomas took in a ragged sigh and sipped the tea. "You should have at least disconnected as soon as you healed."

"I tried," Roi said, setting down his own cup. "But I collapsed as soon as we did. I couldn't even lift my arm. Erin and I feared it was too late." Roi's hand rubbed his bald patch. "But if it was such a problem, why didn't you mention it the many other times I visited?"

Mr. Gerald looked away, holding his cup in his lap as his eyes seemed to wander to another time. "A little bit of hope. A little fear. I didn't see you again for a month after you recovered, by that time I, too, thought it must be too late. After seeing the chaos that was Rahni's mind, and seeing you acting as what I thought was normal, I thought you could handle it. You were much more…" He mulled for a moment, looking for the right word. "Straightforward than usual, but I thought it was just the war that had changed you. Maybe it still is but…" Thomas sighed and brought his tea to his lips. "You're not the same wolf who touched that egg."

They sat in silence, sipping tea and not looking at anything in particular. Roi couldn't grasp Mr. Gerald's words. He understood their meaning, their definition, but their intent was muted and empty. They both sipped their mugs.

"You haven't noticed the tea," Thomas said.

"Excuse me?" Roi asked.

Thomas nodded his head towards Roi's mug and lifted his own for emphasis. "It's ginger. I remember it was your favorite because you loved how the aroma cleared your nose of all other scents. You told me once that one cup of it had you smelling ginger for days. If that's not proof something's wrong then…" Thomas shrugged, and let his sentence trail.

Roi looked at his mug. He hadn't noticed the yellow tint of the water, or the taste, or, of course, the smell. Now that he knew it was there, he could get the faintest whiff of the flavor he once loved, but only for a moment. He set the mug down and stood up.

"Thank you, Mr. Gerald."

Thomas shook his head. "I don't deserve it. Thank you."

Roi walked to the door and had his hand on the handle before Thomas spoke up again.

"What answer did you give the king?"

Roi could only guess how he knew. "I told her I didn't know."

Thomas shook his head. "Me neither, Roi. Me neither. What answer you do give her, I support. You would know better than me at this point."

Roi gave a silent nod and left.

Gimaldi Asylum was a tall, three story mansion that stood looming over the street. It had a red brick exterior, large windows, and a triangular roof. It would look like quite a comfortable place to live if it didn't have the eight-foot-tall fence made of spear-like protrusions and the patrol of armored guards at the perimeter.

Arcadus Gimaldi sponsored this building nearly three decades ago to house the "incurables"; people whose minds had been impossibly addled by magic. His daughter's mental state had been all but destroyed by one of Gimaldi's own experiments, and he took the guilt to his death. But before he died, Gimaldi donated his estate to the asylum, making sure residents were given the proper care and treatment they deserved: a full rotating staff of nurses, proper food for those still capable of chewing, plenty of room to move about, and (ignoring the steel doors, triple locks, and barred windows) all the comforts of home. This made the idea of leaving Rahni here for nearly twenty years more palatable.

Roi sat on a public bench across the street, staring up at the building. All was silent except for the occasional breeze through the trees and whispered conversations between the guards. Roi took in a deep breath, the faint scent of grass filling his lungs. He let it out, and for the first time since he left Mr. Gerald's, started talking.

"Archimedes. I want you to disconnect."

The metallic gryphon, already formed on Roi's shoulder, huffed and made a show of preening his silvery feathers. "Not on your life." To emphasize his point Roi felt Archimedes tighten the bands around his arms and legs, as if he was worried the wolf would try to tear him off.

"Archimedes," Roi repeated, slower. "I need you to disconnect."

Archimedes tightened his claws on Roi's shoulder, nearly piercing the wolf's robe. "Roi, if I disconnect, you'll die," he said. His voice shook with worry. Roi reached a hand up to gently pet the gryphon. At first,

Archimedes tensed, fearing a more aggressive action, but soon let himself relax against the wolf's rough palm.

"I'm not certain I'm living now, Archie," he said in a voice barely above a whisper. Archimedes stayed quiet, not knowing what to say. "The king wants to know if she should put effort into getting a spell-forme. I haven't been able to answer her, and Mr. Gerald hasn't either. There's only one person left who might have the answer I want, and I've been long overdue to visit."

"That can't possibly be the reason why you want to disconnect!" Archimedes said, blue eyes growing wide.

Roi shook his head. "A convenient excuse. Now please, before I convince myself otherwise, disconnect."

Archimedes tensed, mulling over his host's request in his mind. He couldn't just let Roi go, but this was the closest Roi had ever come to pleading with him. Archimedes' solution had been to go get a therapist, not to risk death to see a long lost friend.

The memories Archimedes had watched mulled about in his mind: a young pup excluded by his peers, reading book after book to escape the taunting; a teen daring Rahni to jump in the lake during winter, caring for Rahni when he had inevitably caught hypothermia; meeting Erin in the middle of the library and laughing about a story they both had read; the terror and excitement he felt when he had been chosen to go to war.

These emotions were completely cut off to Roi. He hadn't laughed in ten years, hadn't smiled in seven. Archimedes had no memory of his own of Roi being sad or angry. He himself was a magical-mechanical being, and he had gone through the gambit of emotions. He simply assumed Roi had always been like this, but looking back proved him to be very wrong.

"Archimedes," Roi said, a fuzzy finger stroking the gryphon's metal neck.

"I don't want you to die, Roi," Archimedes whispered, a low metallic groan.

"I don't plan to."

He couldn't stop himself. With a great heave of his chest and a thousand clicks of metal pieces overlapping and rearranging, Archimedes quickly detached from Roi. The circlets around his wrists, biceps, chest, waist, thighs, calves, and ankles all clicked open, dragged away by the thin strands of silver metal connecting them all. Air suddenly breathed on parts of Roi that hadn't been free in years; they were so sensitive that it felt like shards of ice were prickling his skin. Finally, when every piece had returned to the central hub on Roi's back, the whole thing fell off, and Archimedes stood fully formed, fully separate, on the back of the bench.

Immediately Roi felt like all his blood had turned into thousands of sharp knives, their blades white hot. The searing pain coursed through his veins and spread through his entire body. He immediately grabbed his stomach, curled over onto the ground, and opened his mouth to retch. What came out wasn't food but a blood curdling scream as his body tried to process the pain. Then his body stopped moving and he collapsed on the ground, conscious, but only barely.

Roi could feel Archimedes hop down from the bench and climb over him in panic. His metallic stomach had opened up like a terrifying creature come to devour him, but those worried, glowing blue eyes made him look vulnerable rather than fearsome. He could hear Archimedes talking in panicked tones, but already Roi could hear so much more: the rustle of grass against his fur; the chittering of birds several trees away; the crunch of gravel underneath a guard's boot as they crossed the street. The words Archimedes used were lost in the cacophony of sound, but he could guess their meaning. As fast as he could, Roi shook his head and Archimedes climbed off of him with some reluctance.

"Sir! Sir! Are you alright, sir?" a guard cried as he approached.

Roi strained to filter out the sound as a thousand more smells filled his nostrils. "Y—yes," Roi grunted. His lungs felt frail and getting air in them was laborious. Every breath was full of the stench of dust, grass, and sweat.

One of the guards, clad in a mix of steel and leather armor, rolled Roi onto his back and checked his vitals. Archimedes jumped back when their night-sticks got too close, likely they had azuchite at their core.

"Can you hear me, sir?" the guard asked, keeping very deliberate eye contact. "What's your name?"

Roi thought it was unlikely they didn't know who he was, few people didn't. This was likely a tactic to see how mentally aware he was, and to keep him conscious. Good thing too; his mind began to fog. "Roi Henkha Longfang." Roi took in a deep, shuddering breath. "I need to see Rahni."

The guard was confused by the request and made that clear with an unnecessarily long "Uuuuuh." The smell of his breath made Roi cringe, but he couldn't muster the energy to get his head to move. He was lucky he could speak at all.

"Sir, we have to take you to hospital."

"No, I need to see Rahni." Roi tried to shake his head, but it did little more than vibrate slightly. "Archie!" he called. His voice was raspy with exhaustion and he couldn't waste more energy arguing. Archimedes was quick to aid, talking rapidly to the guard about the situation. Roi couldn't pay attention to his words, he was just trying to keep himself awake long enough to make this worth it. Just like last time, he couldn't move his arms, legs, head, or tail, and was at the mercy of these guards. Or Archimedes if he decided enough was enough.

And then it hit him. Like he stepped out of time for a moment and relived his whole life for the past twenty years. Flashes of memory came back: his wedding, his daughter's birth, getting hired at the council, his divorce, meeting the king, scaring Erin, hours upon hours of research, all of them at once, with every emotion he should have felt. It was a good thing he couldn't move, or he'd be bawling his eyes out in front of all these guards. As it was, he clamped his mouth shut and let the tears burn at the corner of his eyes.

Whatever Archimedes told these guards must have been good, because when they put him in a wheelchair, they didn't immediately start pushing it to the nearest hospital. Instead they brought him through the front gates of the Asylum, earning him many strange looks by other guards and nurses when they processed him as a guest.

The asylum was well spaced out to make it feel like both a home and a care facility. To Roi's surprise, inside the building was almost brighter than it was outside. Large lanterns hung from the ceilings, filled with little flitting orbs of bright white light. Lightning bugs were often the choice of lighting for institutions with lots of azuchite; they didn't suffer magic drain like most practical lighting did, and were perfectly safe in case a patient got violent.

The azuchite wasn't hidden either. Tall pillars of the stone went from floor to ceiling, and likely made up most of the building's skeleton. The stone looked like lava rock the color of storm clouds with tiny shards of luminous blue crystal speckled throughout its mass. Azuchite was infamous for it's strange properties; it was extremely light, stronger than diamond, and absorbed all magic that came near it. As a result, most prisons and mental asylums used it as the core material for their buildings, or in this case, decorative pillars.

Moving his head was a draining task, and keeping it upright and forward even more so, so Roi let his head dangle limply on his neck, bouncing as the wheelchair hit uneven surfaces. He didn't see most of the decor in the place or the mental patients in their augmented cell-bedrooms. The drain rock sapped at his now pitiful magic reserves, and his whole mind was focused on staying awake and lucid. His lips curled into a faint smile; maybe they were just wheeling him to his own room in this place. He'd fit right in.

Eventually they came to an almost empty room. It held a table, chair, and a nurse. The room itself looked like a tasteful light blue, but it was entirely white; the blue came from the soft glow of the azuchite pillars in each corner. Arcadus spared no expense making sure the building was completely magic-free. The only meaningful detail in this room was a window on the left side. Behind it, Roi could see a single guard sitting down and watching.

"Are meetings always this homey?" Roi mumbled.

The guard pushing him gave the nurse some papers, and the nurse smiled at Roi. "Not always, Mr. Longfang. This room is for our more violent tenants. I'm afraid the person you wish to see is quite unstable," the nurse, a human with olive skin, said with a soft smile.

"Ms. Patty here is going to take care of you while we sit and watch behind the window there. Usually you'd be left alone, but I don't trust your health right now," the guard said.

"I understand," Roi said.

The guard gave his shoulder what tried to be a comforting squeeze and left. Immediately Ms. Patty began fussing with him. Lifting his arm, taking his pulse, and generally checking him over.

"Rahni will be brought in soon. Is there anything you need? A glass of water? A pillow?"

Roi scrunched his nose. "No, thanks. I don't think I'll be here long."

Ms. Patty nodded her head as the door across from them opened.

Roi made an effort and lifted his head. A short, pudgy otter in a lavender nurse's scrum walked in the room, holding the hand of a much taller wolf in sky-blue, oversized pajamas. The wolf's head hung limp and his feet dragged across the marble floor. Roi could hear the *scratch-click* of the newcomer's nails as he labored to lift his feet and mumbled something to himself. That was definitely Rahni.

"You're in luck," Ms Patty said, failing to be assuring. "He's in one of his mellow moods."

"They fill your mind with countless lies," Roi could hear Rahni mumbling as he approached. "Prepare to lose familial ties, beware the devil's butterflies."

"Here we go, Rahni," the otter nurse said as she lead him to his seat. "Mr. Longfang is here to visit you." The words seemed more tradition than effective, as Rahni didn't react whatsoever, allowing himself to be lead into his seat.

"Beware the ones with glassy eyes, as you fall their armies rise, slaved to devil's butterflies." Rahni's ears were flat against his head, like he couldn't be bothered to lift them. Roi could see patches of his friend's greying fur were completely missing, and he became keenly aware of a cold spot on his stomach.

"Rahni?" Roi said, mustering up as much energy as he could to speak clearly. "It's me, Roi."

The nurses shared a look with each other. They didn't expect this meeting to go for very long. Roi couldn't blame them, he was lame and Rahni was mad. More productive conversations could be had with particularly lazy snails.

Then Rahni's eyes blinked, and he stopped his muttering. He lifted his head, eyes wide and his ears were perked and swiveling. Rahni looked between Roi, the two nurses, and then back to Roi. His hands went to his muzzle in shock, although his ears never stopped moving.

"I killed you," Rahni hissed, terrified.

"You tried." Roi gave a light chuckle. "But I'm fine Rahni, Archie made sure of it. I'm sorry it's been so long."

"Archie?" Rahni's head tilted in confusion.

Roi nodded. "Yeah, Archimedes. He's my spell-forme. Do you remember?"

Rahni's began frantically turning in his seat, as if looking for something.

"Are you okay—"

"Where's Hermes!" he snapped, now half standing on his chair as he looked at the ground. The otter nurse tried to get him to sit down, but he smacked her hands away as she tried to calm him. Clearly this sort of thing happened often.

White began to creep in at the edges of Roi's vision as his energy wavered. He didn't have long. He blinked his eyes to clear it away and re-focused. "Hermes has been put away so he can't hurt you," Roi answered calmly.

"I need him!" Rahni screamed, then he leaned over the table and began whispering. "He's the only one I can trust. Everyone else lies. He told me secrets." Rahni's eyes locked on Roi's and Roi could see that all his years away from the war, away from the spell-forme had done nothing to improve his friend's mind. His eyes were still twitchy, red, paranoid, and lost. Ms. Patty coughed and without moving his head Rahni stared at her, eyes as big as saucers. She returned the stare with a smile and after a minute he turned back to Roi.

"I need him, Roi. I need Hermes. Everyone wants to kill me, or hurt me, or give me to them." He spat the last word out as if giving the butterflies a name would summon them.

"No one wants to hurt you, Rahni," Roi said. His chest tightened. Even though Rahni was right here in front of him, breathing his breath right into Roi's nose, it became clear his friend had died long ago.

"They all turned on me!" Rahni shouted, leaning back. "Fred! James! Eric! Ben! Nihk! Rahk! They all turned on me! They tried to kill me! The butterflies got them all! They're coming for me, Roi! They're coming for me!" Rahni raved and raved, but Roi heard none of it. As Rahni listed off names, Roi's vision swam, tears rolled uncontrollably down his cheeks, and his determination fell apart. Darkness filled Roi's vision as he slumped forward and smashed into the table.

Rahni screamed.

***

Roi took a shuddering breath as his eyes blinked open. He was in a strange bed. The sterilized scent of cleaner filled his nose, and he could hear the soft hum of magic powering some sort of device. He tried to sit up, but found his body didn't want to cooperate. He turned his head instead. At least that was willing to work.

Something metal beside him began to shift and move, eliciting a soft "Hmm?" from someone else to his side. Roi could see Archimedes, now the size of a small feral dog, resting on Erin's lap. Next to her was a large crystal orb, decorated with spell-weaving runes hovering in the air to monitor his vitals. He was in a hospital.

"You're awake," she said with a playful smirk. She was absently petting Archimedes, who enjoyed the attention. "Would you like to try that stunt again? Or do you realize how stupid that was?"

"He's had a rough day. Leave him alone," the gryphon grumbled, sitting up to look at his host.

Erin's expression softened.

"She's right," Roi said. His tongue felt dry and his throat was like sandpaper. He found enough strength to raise his hand and lay it gently on Erin's knee. She knelt forward and grasped his frail bones in her firm grip, and rubbed his hand with her thumb. "I'm sorry."

"Well don't do it again. Gods know you nearly died today."

"No." Roi shook his head. "I meant for yesterday at breakfast. For what I said."

"Don't do that again, either."

"Being connected to Archie just—"

Erin put a finger on his nose and shushed him. "Are you feeling better? Is your mind clear?" she asked.

"I'm not sure." Roi shrugged. "To be honest, I can barely think as it is. My mind is clearer but there's still a fog in there." Roi exhaled and gave Erin's hand a squeeze. "I'll have to return to being connected soon."

"Maybe this time you'll go see a therapist again?" she said with a chuckle.

Roi smiled. "Erin, I know I'm asking a lot, but..." He swallowed, attempting to clear his dry throat. "Will you stay with me? I'm not asking for marriage again." He looked into her eyes, his tired yellow locking with her old gold. "But I do miss you."

Erin's muzzle spread into a huge smile, and she leaned over and kissed him on an ear. "You sound like a pup again." She chuckled, pulling away. "I will, but tell me you don't care about our divorce again, and I'll punch you in the balls."

Roi chuckled and nodded. "I can accept that." He turned his head. "Archie? I think it's now or never."

"Of course, Roi," Archimedes said, climbing over the bed and onto Roi, careful to avoid stepping on anything sensitive. Erin stood up and helped Roi sit up as Archimedes began disassembling himself into a swarm of thin silver chains. They slowly snaked beneath Roi's fur and wrapped themselves around their familiar positions. As the cool metal settled in place, Roi could feel his strength returning, and his mind becoming cold and distant. He fought against returning to what he was, but couldn't hold it off completely. He was still exhausted. What part of Archimedes didn't disassemble into silver serpents climbed onto Roi's back and solidified itself as the central node, tiny pinpricks sticking in to finalize the connection. Gingerly, Erin let go, and Roi remained sitting up.

"Thank you, Erin," Roi said with a solemn nod. Archimedes appeared on his shoulder, once again connected by the tail, once again the size of a small owl.

"You going to say more insensitive things?" Erin asked, crossing her arms and looking dubious. Roi chuckled, and she relaxed.

"I can feel it creeping on me, but I think if we're wary, we'll manage," Roi said. The wolf laid back down with a deep, satisfied sigh. "I think I know what to tell the king."

Erin's ears perked in surprise. "Was Rahni actually helpful?" she asked.

"Rahni's lost," Roi breathed. His eyes flicked down. Archimedes ruffled his feathers. "But Hermes didn't drive him mad; the war did that to both of them. They just made it worse for each other." Roi yawned, exhaustion beginning to take hold of him. "But I think, if she avoids making one vital mistake, a spell-forme is a good idea."

Roi yawned and closed his eyes while Erin held his hand. She couldn't be sure what affected Roi's mind; maybe it was Archimedes' fault, maybe it was the war, maybe it was regret for Rahni. But as she looked on his resting face, Erin knew she would stay next to him as long as she could. Someone had to watch over him.

***

"Hermes has been stored away," Erin said as she walked into our living room. Our house was small, but we knew it was for the best. If a solution to the war couldn't be found, we'd run out of space within our shield. There's only so much the king could protect.

Erin sat next to me on the couch. I didn't speak. She grabbed my hand and stroked my fur flat with her gentle thumb. "You should probably disconnect from Archimedes," she said. Her hand traced a silver strand between his wrist and elbow.

I shook my head.

"Didn't Mr. Gerald say—"

"My stomach still hurts," I interrupted her, rubbing the sore spot where my fur had yet to grow back. "Just a little longer."

Erin sighed, but didn't argue. I pulled my hand out from her grip and wrapped it around her shoulder, pulling her closer. I buried my nose in her fur and was comforted by the smell.

"Did they dismantle him?" I asked.

"No. Something about studying him and finding a cure. Honestly, I think he was just too expensive to dismantle. Or too volatile." She waved her hand to indicate that she didn't much care for their decision and hadn't listened beyond that.

We were silent for minutes, enjoying each other's presence, but something gnawed at my mind.

"Rahni has been put in the Gimaldi Asylum."

I could feel Erin tense. "For the best, probably. At least I hear it's a nice place."

"He will likely never leave. Even if he does, he might be sent to prison."

She doesn't say anything. I don't say anything.

And that was okay.

Even in its own time, the mighty Tyrannosaurus rex was a legendary monster.

Note on pronunciation: the characters are more closely related to birds than mammals, and their names are meant to be read as approximations similar to transcriptions of bird song, where a sound from nature is filtered through a human brain and crudely recreated. "Aaw" is the croaking vowel sound in a raven's call; a capitol "C" is a click, and, for example, "Ikherrja" could just as faithfully be spelled "I-heard-ya!"

THE ROAR

John Giezentanner

The flowers are past their peak, white petals blowing off the trees, but their carrion scent is still strong. We should not be here. There are scent lines we shouldn't cross; it's palpable; it resists me more than the thick understory of ferns. But we're starving, and there is that other scent, flesh-smoke, so new and enticing to the boys. With the wind, Djuxhaawtig smelled it all the way up on our mountain soon after we saw the bolt.

I pause at the edge of a clearing—acrid, burnt feather stink. Djuxhaawtig strides forward and the boys follow. The clouds keep flashing and roaring, but it has not rained and the ferns are brown. Near the middle of the clearing they are stomped down from grazing, and there lies two dead animals.

Fresh enough.

I join the others, noticing scattered shards of horn. The animals are bigger than me, and one is nearly as large as Djuxhaawtig. At first glance their profile is similar to ours—long tail, two-legged, small arms, but their bodies are cloaked in long, drooping plumage—heavy looking, silly. Their small hands have more than two fingers (jealous) and their heads are all covered in spikes and knobs surrounding a single, massive horn that recurves from the top of their head, reaching past their shoulders. The larger one is missing his; there's only a big bloody dome where it attached.

"This is why we hide from lightning."

"Except for right now." Thrutsee-e, one of my little brothers, nods flippantly.

My feathers bristle… but I did consent to this. Djuxhaawtig is already tearing at the larger horned one's belly and I join him, thrusting my face beside his into the rip.

He growls, and I only get my nose wet before he slaps me away with his head. I stagger, surprised by the force of the blow; he's already back to gulping still-warm entrails. The boys notice and get to work on the smaller one instead.

My belly tightens and I growl too.

"Share, brother."

I work my snout into the wound again but keep an eye open this time. Djuxhaawtig rumbles, but leaves me alone. So lustful pulling and gulping until Ikherrja, the other little one, startles me with his high pitch.

"TraawkCnara! I think there's some lightning left over here!"

I throw back some gore and look over to see him peering at a mass of trampled litter. Thrutsee-e can't be distracted from fresh meat, but Ikherrja might starve himself if he notices the beetles crawling in the tree flowers.

"That's not how lightning works. Eat," but then I see the little flame being stirred by the wind. I head him off quickly. "Don't touch it. That's fire. It'll lick your skin off fast as you can lick the horned one's blood."

"I know." He doesn't know, and is already stretching a toe towards the warm, rippling color. Thrutsee-e turns with guts in his mouth, still attached to the horned one, to watch it play out; a low, gravelly moan rolls overhead, and it isn't thunder.

Ikherrja jumps and runs before realizing the sound didn't come from the fire. Thrutsee-e loses his mouthful, swishing his tail with laughter.

"We have to go. Now."

They both look at me, then at our banquet, wondering if there's time for another gulp.

"Run!" For once they don't argue.

Djuxhaawtig's still up to his cheeks in the other animal. I nudge him, then nip at his tail. He turns to me, red faced and bristling. Another roar issues through the clearing. Djuxhaawtig draws breath, lifts his head and bellows defiantly.

Fear spikes in my belly. "No! We have to go!"

"Ours!" he growls.

"No, Djuxhaawtig. You're not that big. We run from monsters."

He looks down at me, eyes yellow as the fire, longing to fight. I plead with them.

"*That* will kill us if it doesn't."

He sniffs, noticing the quickly spreading flames and his tail finally curls with alarm.

"Go!" He takes longer to get up to speed than the boys but we soon overtake them—I assume that's them, rustling the fronds they pass beneath. The plants are only up to my elder brother's knees; my head is above them, but they brush my chest and tickle down my belly while the fire tracks us home. It files along the base of the cliff, eating the big ginkgoes by the river before jumping it and starting uphill, roaring into the cycads and tall pines, finally dropping into the fern meadow beneath us. Up at the cave I watch pensively. The boys are enthralled, sniffing and sneezing, asking questions I remember asking about the nature of lightning and fire.

"Some things aren't for us, little sister," Djuxhaawtig used to say. That still annoys me, though it rings truer than it used to.

"I don't know," I tell them. The rain finally comes with curling smoke and steam.

***

Ikherrja's hiss outside the cave wakes me when he charges Thrutsee-e. It's not yet morning, but they've already found something to tussle about. They grunt as their chests connect and necks slap together; two-fingered foreclaws hook onto shoulders, and their feet scrape the gravel. Thrutsee-e still finds breath to goad his brother. Despite being nestmates, Thrutsee-e is a little bulkier than Ikherrja and always has the advantage at wrestling. But the uneven ground puts Ikherrja a little higher, and I wonder if it will go his way this time. My tail's twitching; I've a mind to challenge the winner, but it wouldn't be sporting, even against both of them. I miss having an even match. They are getting bigger, though. We all are.

Djuxhaawtig rouses suddenly and shuffles out of the cave, forcing me out before him. His back scrapes the ceiling, and I lament his formerly sleek brown coat, which remains thick and ruddy only about his neck. He no longer preens. Gray skin shows in patches, and the flags of white feathers on his arms and tail tip are nearly gone, making him harder to understand when he talks, if he talks. We stretch our legs and tail.

"Hungry." He marches downslope on one of our trails, not waiting.

I head-butt the boys apart—their game will have to wait. "We're hunting."

***

Our home is steep and rocky, mostly unforested, and there is little game. That's why it's ours—it isn't worth claiming by the monsters and forms a buffer between their expansive territories. Now it's also charred. The ferns were consumed, leaving the ground bare, black and with the rain, muddy. Beyond the heavy burnt-mud smells there is a large animal odor redolent of the river. But that is not what Djuxhaawtig stops to scent. Filtering through the skeletal pines, rippling in the breeze, now softer, now harder, a beast at a far edge of our turf calls out in death. I do not acknowledge it.

"Smells big," says Thrutsee-e.

"No."

Ikherrja's nose is pointed in the same direction. "Can't we just go get a good sniff? It might still be good."

If it's been dead long enough for the aroma to permeate this far, "It isn't." I leave it at that, continuing our patrol.

"Hmm…"

The boys press on either side of Djuxhaawtig. "Can't we at least try?"

Djuxhaawtig pauses, sniffing. He begins to turn toward it.

"Jux!" I resort to the abbreviation he prefers these days as I shoulder Thrutsee-e aside and lean into him, trying to turn him back. "We can't! Remember?"

He rumbles, seems unconvinced.

"You're starving us with your stupid rule, TraawkCnara," says Thrutsee-e.

"It's NOT stupid!" I clap my teeth at him. It's always been *our* rule. I am hungry too, tempted too. But we do not eat carrion.

"Let's try the other thing." I nose toward the river, though it sounds foolish and even Djuxhaawtig seems surprised at me. I pull in more air, sifting for something useful.

"I think it's alone."

"Probably still has a tail, though."

"So do I!" I slap Thrutsee-e, knocking him over. I did not mean to hit him hard. He glares at me; I look to Djuxhaawtig. I think the boys are wondering if I'll contradict him. I wonder, too.

"Yes…" He has that knowing look as he starts toward the river, still sniffing. I sigh, relieved, though I'm not sure what we'll do when we get there.

I hear the river filtered through crispy cycads, their waxy fronds blackened but intact, before seeing it and the cliffs beyond. It's strange in here now, black coating my feet, quieter than usual. Some of the wrecked ginkgoes still smolder. We follow the scent downstream, and I finally catch what Djuxhaawtig has smelled all along: the tang of distress. The armored one is squalling, water rushing up and over the domed shield of its back, splashing across its horned face as it struggles out of the main channel and into a calmer pool.

Armored ones are big. We could maybe take a young one if we found it alone and managed to flip it over, but their skin is stone and their broad bodies and stubby legs keep it all low to the ground and they know it. They don't run when threatened—they attack with their club tail. We avoid them.

This one is grown enough to be alone, big enough for that tail to hurt, but—but!—something's gone wrong for it. Looks like it was trying to cross the river and was overcome by the current, still high from the rain. Now it's just trying to get out, but it chose a poor spot, right through the deep water and deeper mud of the pool. Mired but too stubborn to change course, it's plunging its tree-trunk legs into the mud and muscling forward, little by little. It won't drown on its own, and when it hauls ashore the game will be over for us. Ikherrja and Thrutsee-e are pacing uncertainly, looking at it from a little upstream, a little downstream, but I rub against Djuxhaawtig.

"Lovely big nose! This might work!"

I splash into the river, immediately losing my toes in the ashy mud. The bank drops off fast; I'm up to my hips, and I gasp, unprepared for the cold which sinks in, becomes pain, and I'm thinking this might be a mistake. But I take a few awkward steps to the right, letting the eddy current help me, and though I have to work against the muck, at least I have proper broad, three-toed feet and can get a little traction. I turn to face its shoulder, and it isn't bothered by me yet. I'm taller, but it's bulkier than me, and I know better than to mistake its lack of fear for stupidity. I glance back to Djuxhaawtig, who is watching, looking a little confused.

Well, get its attention then. I scream and charge, counting on the water to slow me down while I make a lot of noise and splash. The armored one tosses its head up, putting one brown eye on me, and struggles to turn, bringing its tail to bear. I dig my toes in the mud and jump back, the current still on my side, and the club wags by, slinging cold water. There is one part of this beast that can move fast. Still, my plan is working so far—it isn't moving toward shore anymore. It's wriggling backward toward me instead. I can keep a safe distance, though this way will eventually lead to dry ground as well.

"Jux—Other side!" He grunts and splashes in, sinking farther into the mud than me, but he's still only up to his knees and he moves through the water with ease, slogging around to the armored head. The boys wisely stay ashore. They would be swimming—too slow against the tail.

I hope Djuxhawwtig has the idea, but he goes full in for the beast's neck. It won't work—between the armored shoulders and short but broad horns, sweeping down from its cheeks and back behind its eyes, it only has to toss its head up, and I bet he just lost a few teeth. Now it wants to turn its weapon on him, but he follows the head, both of them turning toward me.

"Stay there!" We only have to keep it switching between the two of us, use the beast's stubbornness against it until it's too exhausted to keep its head above water. But Djuxhaawtig takes a big step forward—the armored one still turning—lifts his foot out of the water and... he's stepping on it! He plants his foot on the beast's back—the knobs of armor only give his claws grip—and puts his weight on it. The armored one is strong enough to support him, but the mud is not, and it gives a last, surprised cry as its snout goes down. It thrashes wildly, tail still slapping and churning the water. Jux hops on his other foot to keep balanced and wastes no time getting his teeth down to the knobby back, looking for something to tear.

I watch, heart pounding; the cold no longer stings. Brilliant! Djuxhaawtig is so big now he can just step on an armored one and hold it underwater until it stops moving. Much faster than my plan. Brilliant. And I get a little scared. He only needs to wait, but he rips off a scute and goes again, aiming for the bloody mark.

But the beast isn't dead yet, and the foot Jux has in the water hops too close to its head; he cries out in pain, trying to pull away from the sharp beak. I rush in to help—the head is curved toward Jux, neck exposed to me; I bite hard with the satisfaction of flesh on my teeth. It jerks its head around and those horns hurt as I pull away. I back off from its gaping beak, and Jux is off of it too, backing up, too close to the hind quarters—a wide arc of water—he screams, falls sideways and I startle as the splash rains.

The armored one makes a few quick jumping motions, gets its head back above water, and comes at me, swinging its head side to side like a smaller version of its tail.

I let it push me back.

Djuxhaawtig's claws slash the water as he tries to right himself, his snout reaching for air. We're nearing the shore, and I try to work my way around the beast. Finally finding itself on better footing, the rotten one lets me escape, and I tromp through the clouded water to Djuxhaawtig while it hurries ashore and away.

He's managed to roll onto his stomach, but is not rising. "It hurrrrts."

"Come on." I plunge my head underwater, under his chin, and lift hard, afraid in my stomach. If one of his knees or ankles is twisted or broken... but slowly, with protest, he rises, and I gasp, muddy water flooding my mouth as I come up. With a few staggers he gets his balance and struggles out of this mud pit. Thrutsee-e and Ikherrja are stretching tall, watching from shore, and I'm ashamed. Djuxhaawtig limps, bleeding from his right ankle and his left shin already showing a lump. He settles down on shore grumbling, muddy feathers looking more ragged than ever. I notice those he's left floating in the water.

I bathe the mud off in a clear running part of the river and preen until I start pulling feathers out. Djuxhaawtig only licks his wound. He is in no mood to travel, and it becomes clear that we are here for the hot part of the day. I hunker down by him and try to clean him off, but he rumbles at me.

Fine. Thrutsee-e licks the cut on my nose, but Ikherrja tarries by the water, looking past it, up at the cliff.

***

My stomach wakes me. Alone, I groggily preen and then sniff after the others, tonguing the throbbing spot where I lost a tooth. Must get food soon, soon.

I should not have overslept. The carrion we smelled is this way. I trot, and run when there is a clearing, more afraid, angrier. I find them in a clearing at the base of a gentle slope near the water, crouched over an already scavenged carcass. Heavy death smell, flies. I hiss and chase off the boys. Thrutsee-e tries to take a bone with him, but I grab the end of it, lifting him off the ground before he lets go. I yell and gnash until I'm sure they're done with it, then turn to Jux, who hasn't budged.

"Stop It!" I charge, but he growls and guards his prize. I stop short. "You promised! What about NgCerif?"

He snaps a bone and keeps gnawing. How can he forget my nestmate sister? We used to eat carrion in the old days before we found Ikherrja and Thrutsee-e—until she got sick, got those rings around her mouth. She hurt too much to eat or drink, then she screamed until she couldn't anymore, until she couldn't breathe. How dare he forget?

I try to grab the bone from him, and he lunges to his feet with a growl, swinging his tail, and I'm on the ground, stunned. I roll to my stomach; my tail curls, and I lift my head and gape, crying like a nestling.

The boys come to see if I'm all right, but Djuxhaawtig surprises me, nuzzling my shoulder and neck.

"Hey. You're all right. What's wrong? Hey." It is the gentlest he's sounded, the most like himself, in a long time. It only stirs more memory.

"So stupid," he mutters. "I should go."

"No!" I jump up and press myself full against him, hook on with my fingers.

"Not you too. I won't let you."

"TraawkCnara?" Thrutsee-e nips me for attention. The boys are watching this curiously, cautiously. "If we can't eat this, then *what*?"

My head's swimming. I have no answer.

"We could try the cliff," Ikherrja offers.

Thrutsee-e sighs as though we've been over this. "No, *thin tail...*"

My head's cocked. "What about the cliff?"

***

We stay alive a few more days, catching some fish. The boys chase bugs and furry things; Ikherrja even manages to snag a bird. But we need bigger prey, especially Djuxhaawtig, who is more irritable than ever, and thin. So we keep our noses to the wind and wait. When the moment comes, we ford the river at a better place than the armored one knew of. The boys and I swim; my claws occasionally scrape cobble; Djuxhaawtig slowly walks across.

We shake off on the far side and walk along the cliff, where the flaking rocks have spirals on them I've always wondered about. The ground has dried here, and the ash coating my feet starts to work its way up, getting in my feathers, annoying. But when Ikherrja realizes he can change his color to all black he rolls in it and has a way to threaten Thrutsee-e, who does not wish to be all black.

The cliff falls in elevation, finally disappearing into a hill we can climb. Into monster territory. Which is so big, I tell myself, that it's very unlikely the resident will be anywhere nearby. We were able to smell the herd moving through and are thus downwind, scent concealed. The trees and big, bushy cycads hide us (and them) from view.

I hate splitting up, but when we are close enough to hear snapping branches, we leave Ikherrja behind and begin to circle around. Already I can tell by scent, and by a lesser extent sound, that there's more than I can easily count—some young, some mature, females and at least one male. I stop a good distance from Ikherrja, and Djuxhaawtig and Thrutsee-e continue on. There is nothing to do but wait, shifting from foot to foot, tail twitching, muscles tightening.

Finally Jux roars, a deep, resonant, proper roar, and I answer with my own, as loud as I can, and charge the herd. Tails come into view. They are... other ones. We never see them unless they happen to move through down by the river. They run on all fours, though I have seen them stand on two to reach higher; their oddly featherless green skin is pebbly, with white stripes on their long tails. I know the males by their bright blue heads—there's one out front bigger than Djuxhaawtig, and females bigger than me, along with young.

Djuxhaawtig and I push from the back while the boys steer from the sides and it's working, but I hope we haven't bitten off more than we can swallow. Jux is already falling behind on his sore legs. If we are exhausted—or they are—too soon, it all fails. They start to slow, but a roar, close and strong—Jux?—puts fresh fear in them.

Through the foliage ahead I see a clearing and horizon—our mountain, the sky beyond. Suddenly the lead male drops out of sight along with a big female, then another, pushed by those behind, before any of them can cry out. A small one follows its mother as the remnant skids to a halt and turns as we close in. Mothers circle up around their young, ready to fight, but it doesn't matter.

Ikherrja and Thrutsee-e look over the edge and report back with joyful yips. The top of the cliff may be monster territory, but the bottom is ours.

A feast!

I start to back off the remaining other ones, but Djuxhaawtig will have to be persuaded. He hasn't spoken since the other day. I flinch at a roar, near and loud. Not Jux. I have time to turn around before it trails off. The boys abandon the other ones and draw in to us. With our tails turned, the other ones quietly flee. Jux is drawing himself up, facing the roar. He huffs and a low, hard growl wells up from him. He does not look at me, and I know he will not run. My heart sinks.

This is happening now. Have to make it work. "Herrja! Thrut! Away from the edge! Nip its tail if you can, but stay AWAY from the mouth, understand?"

They look at me, feathers fluffed in shock, but then bolt off together toward the trees. And it's crashing through the forest, nearest to me. I back up. What else can I do? It's bigger than the four of us combined, all naked gray skin except for a bushy, blood-red mane.

Jux brushes up beside me, answers the beast with his roar, and its charge stutters to a halt, stones sliding on the bare rock near the edge. At least he's big enough to give it pause. We show it our teeth, and it gapes back at us. Thrutsee-e or Ikherrja could curl up whole inside that mouth.

It steps, and we have to step back; I can see the precipice on my left, and we don't have much ground left to lose. I cannot see making the first move against those massive, many-spiked jaws, but neither do I intend to go over like those other ones, not while my brothers remain up here.

Thrutsee-e is running up behind it; it sees our anticipation and lunges in, snapping at Jux. I go for the ankle, and it keeps me off with a stomp. Thrutsee-e bites its tail, which whips back, and he flies, lands hard. I look for another opening, glimpse the monster's head swinging away from Jux's counterattack and—

—lightning fire in the black—

My head. I need to get up. I see it… then I *see* it, right beside me— *the monster!*—backing Jux along the cliff, jaw to jaw. Ikherrja, still black with soot, screeches as he leaps, impacts the base of the monster's tail and clings there with tooth and claw. I'm left behind. What am I doing? I plant my four little fingers on the rock, shove up to my feet, and stagger away from the battering tail.

Jux is outmatched, his front half all bloody, but he can't turn away. I'm no help here, and there's no approach from behind, with the tail still trying to get rid of Ikherrja, who is dug in for his life. So I pace out to the side, giving myself space to run, and before I can think better of it I charge, aiming for the legs taller than me.

It knows. It's turning, chancing a bad bite from Jux to finish me off. It arches its back to turn faster, but it's so big it takes a precious moment too long and I know—triumph!—I will close the distance before I'm caught in the maw.

"Hang on, Ikherr—!" The foot on my side is in mid stride; I open wide and feel the shin slam into my mouth. Jux gets his bite, full on the opposite shoulder, and throws his weight in, twisting, and I'm crushed. But it's only the leg fallen on me so I'm still alive. I scramble out beneath the kicking upper leg and turn to avoid the edge—a claw catches my side and rips me thigh to tail, but I'm out. Jux is still locked on, moving around to get a better angle. With a wild kick and roll, the beast rights itself, but its other foot is sticking out, crossed awkwardly beneath it.

No longer pressed to the ground, Ikherrja climbs onto the beast's hips and springs off—it snaps, but he dashes away, losing only tail feathers as far as I can see.

Jux comes in from the other side, and it turns to fend him off, the back half of its bloodied tail now sticking out over the cliff, and it roars defiantly—*My cliff, my ground! Mine!*—and it pushes itself up—on one leg. The one it landed on is not right, and the moment it feels weight, the beast screams, staggers a half step back and collapses on it with another piercing scream. It tries to turn on this new enemy, and moves its full tail and good leg out over the abyss in the process. It faces us abruptly, feeling its weight shift, and rights itself again. The claws of its four little fingers score the stone as it tries to get a hold. I gulp air. I feel my pulse in my chest, my neck, my tail.

I am looking at prey.

Jux growls, blood dripping from head and neck and shoulders, and eyes the beast as I do. We roar at it, as if the combined strength of our voices will finally push it off. But the betrayal is complete—its own body drags it, slowly, slowly, then all at once it tips away, roaring, and disappears. That roar shivers me, but vanishes just as fast.

Ikherrja is over with Thrutsee-e, who is back on his feet. My mouth isn't closing right. Annoyed, I shake my head, keep trying—a pop, pain, and it works again. I look myself over and give my tail an exploratory lick—it stings, but isn't deep.

Jux took the worst of it. Bites all over his face and neck and shoulders, but I'll clean him up whether he likes it or not. He looks too much like the one we just fought, with all that red, and his body feathers so few and scraggly now, thick only about his neck. A mane. And he's still growling.

The boys are coming over to greet us, and when we get back down I intend to give them both a good bath as well. Thrutsee-e is still a little shaky and falls behind Ikherrja, happily trotting up. Why is Jux still growling? No—

"Did you see that? Ha! That was great that—"

The growl becomes a snarl as Jux reaches down, jaws agape, and snaps up Ikherrja. I scream; Thrutsee-e doesn't know what's happening. Ikherrja is impaled, lifted up and shaken, his little tail and head whip violently and he's flung away, crashing somewhere in the trees.

The monster roars—*My cliff! My ground!*—then notices me crying out. He turns to me, deep, bloody maw, long teeth and small eyes, and I don't know if I will fight, but I haven't the strength to run. He swishes his tail in confusion, dips his head submissively, and moves as if to comfort me.

I roar in his face and snap at him.

He backs off, grumbling, and stomps away into the forest.

I sink. I won't move, won't think, won't feel. But I hear Thrutsee-e chirping like a chick and I have to go to him. He is with Ikherrja's body, crumpled and bloody beneath a ginkgo.

He looks at me frantically, his nose ashy from nuzzling his brother. "He can't die! He can't!" That isn't like him.

My throbbing jaw slurs my speech, but I give the truth. "Of course he can."

He shakes all over, suddenly enraged, "*Why?*"

After my oldest brothers left him and NgCerif and me, I still hoped it would be different with Djuxhaawtig. I tried. "The monsters are us, if you haven't noticed."

Thrutsee-e's plumage is all slicked back, his trembling violent. "You too?"

I huff. This is my nightmare: "When I've forgotten he was ever my brother, I might let Jux mount me and leave eggs where they drop for some other little ones to find and raise."

I want to say I'm sorry, but I'm so angry I rake the dirt with my claws instead.

Thrutsee-e stands, looks away from me, toward the precipice. "Not me."

I know what he's thinking, because I'm thinking it too.

He gets two steps before I've straddled him, caught him with my foreclaws and forced him to the ground. He panics, thinking I've already turned on him.

"Not today," I promise. I cannot protect him from time, from what I will become, from what he will become when he is big enough to have no need of family or memory, when he loses himself in the roar. But I am no sister if I can't keep him away from the edge of a cliff.

He relaxes, and his warmth is the only thing. I want to stay here, with both of them, but it might return.

"Up!" I goad him onto his feet with annoying wrong-way licks and prod him until he attains a steady march.

There is a feast to be claimed beneath the cliff. We will not have to hunt for a good while, and when we do it will be easier without having to fill Jux's big mouth as well. I will be sick—no. Tonight, in the cave, when our bellies are too full to do anything else, Thrutsee-e and I will bathe each other. So we go on.

Allen and Will are a fox and a coyote in love, but Will has a secret.

TRUST

TJ

The coyote stretched and laid his arm around the gray fox beside him as the credits started to roll. "That wasn't as bad as I was expecting."

The fox slid up against him on the couch, cuddling. "Why did you think it would be bad?"

"Because it's a foreign film about a guy who deals with dead people in a non-supernatural way and plays a cello. Death like that is dark, and classical music is boring." He pulled Allen closer.

He nuzzled into the hug, then slid his head onto his lap. "You just like movies with explosions," he replied, accenting the last word with a poke to his chin.

The coyote yipped. "Hey, that felt weird; don't do that." He playfully glared down at the fox below him.

"It's my birthday and I can do what I want," he giggled, then closed his eyes and swayed to the music coming from the TV. "You hear much about the Supreme Court ruling on gay marriage?"

Will shook his head. "Just that it's coming soon."

"I hope so. It would be nice to be recognized in the rest of the U.S."

"You thinking about asking me to marry you?" the coyote scratched at Allen's belly.

He smiled. "Maybe. I don't see why not."

"Yes, everyone should be allowed to experience the hell that is marriage," Will joked. Again, the fox poked his chin. Again, Will twitched. A quick, short laugh turned into a cough. He pulled his arm back and used it to cover his muzzle as the cough became deeper.

"You okay, Will?" He placed a paw on the coyote's chest. "Can I get you some water?"

One last deep cough and Will cleared his throat, shaking his head. "It's okay. I'm fine, Little One." He scratched the fox's belly again. "Why don't you stay here and enjoy your boring cello-music while I clean up the dishes?" As he finished his question, he stood up, gently setting Allen's head on the couch.

"Okay," the fox replied. "I'm just a little worried for you, hon."

"I'm fine, Allen," he said from the kitchen. "Trust me."

The fox sighed and rested his arm over his eyes. "But you've had that cough for a while," he muttered to himself, sighing. "You never talk to me about your health." Taking another breath, he listened to the piece. As it ended, he scooted back on the couch, lying flat. "So," he said to the coyote, "a well prepared steak and a movie with cuddles. Anything else planned?"

"The night is young, Little One," he whispered as he picked the fox up.

Allen smiled and wrapped his arms around the taller male's neck. "Last time I checked, thirty-five isn't little. Especially to your thirty-eight."

"I'm not talking about age, silly." He nuzzled the fox's neck and took in his scent. He then kissed him as he carried him into their bedroom.

As Allen broke the kiss and opened his eyes, he gasped. "Oh, Will."

Along the sides of the room, both dressers were covered with red and white candles of many shades and sizes. Each gave off a luminous glow, gently lighting the room. On the bedside tables were vases, each filled with a dozen roses. As Will gently laid him on the bed, he noticed it was also covered in rose petals.

"When did you have the time?" the fox asked, eyes wide.

"I have my secrets," he answered with a smile. "As I said, the night is young, Little One." And Will closed the door.

***

"He did not!" the ferret said, looking over her cubicle.

"He did," Allen repeated. "Roses everywhere." He spread his arms around him. "Lit by candles. It was beautiful. You should have seen it, Candice."

"Sounds like you had a good birthday," she said with a smile.

"We did." He smiled back. "We even talked a little about the big M."

Candice gasped. "Really now? After five years he finally said something."

Allen shook his head. "I brought up the Supreme Court hearing. I'm just testing the waters. I think I may ask if it's a ruling in our favor."

Candice sighed. "You two are so cute. I wish Joe was as romantic as you two are." She sighed and rested her head on her hands.

The fox chuckled. "Some guys have that romantic touch. Lord knows I've dated enough who didn't."

"When they're hot, they're *hot*," Candice said, snapping her fingers.

"And when they're not..." Allen shrugged with a smile.

"They're Joe." The ferret broke into laughter and Allen joined in.

As his chuckle died down, he shook his head and sighed. "I'm just worried for him, you know? Like, he's had this cough that won't go away, and it's been there for at least a month. And I think it's getting worse. I can't tell." He hugged his arms.

"I don't know a single man that *likes* to go to the doctor," the ferret said. "Try talking to him about it. If it gets bad enough and he still doesn't do anything, schedule the appointment for him and drag him there." She winked at him.

Allen smiled. "I thought I was the sly one here."

"Oh, time," she said as her phone alarm chimed. "Break's over. Gotta get back to the calls."

"Yay calls," Allen responded sarcastically. "Just think of our special men at home waiting to help us unwind tonight. Or over the long weekend."

"You can still unwind more after last night?" She winked again.

"You know what you—"

She raised a paw. "Hi, my name is Candice, how can I help you today?"

Allen glared at her. "Lucky you got a call," he said as he flopped back into his chair. He adjusted his headset, just before he heard the beep. "Hi, my name is Allen..."

***

"I'm home, hon," Allen called, hanging his jacket by the door. "It is so comfortable outside."

"I know what you mean," Will called over the sound of sizzling on the stove. "But it's a bit toasty in here."

"That's going to happen when you are in front of a hot stove." Allen stepped into the kitchen and hugged the coyote, pressing his nose to the tawny, strong back, and taking in his scent. "You smell good."

"Just cologne from this morning and natural me. Maybe a hint of spices here, too," Will said with a raspy tone, lifting the pan and stirring.

"Mostly you and cologne." Allen frowned a little. "Are you losing your voice?"

The coyote shrugged. "Maybe I'm coming down with a cold. It will probably go away here soon. I'll be better in the morning, I bet."

Allen nodded, pressing against Will. "Food smells good. What's being served with the veggies?"

"Chicken Cordon Bleu. Keeping it warm in the oven while the rice and veggies finish."

"Sounds good." Allen let Will go and grabbed silverware and napkins. "Wine with dinner?"

"Riesling is already chilling in the fridge," Will answered.

"You know me so well." After setting the table, Allen opened the bottle and poured two glasses. As he finished, he heard Will turn off the stove, then open the oven and grab plates. Moments later, he arrived with two fully dressed plates.

Once seated, Allen looked the coyote over. His fur, usually a sharp and glossy black, brown, and cream looked dull and listless. Keeping his concerns to himself, they ate.

As the meal carried on, they talked about their respective days; Allen about the people he talked with, and Will about the groups he guided through the downtown history museum.

"And this cub was just so appalled that to bathe, a cowboy would jump in the river and scrub down, depending on the time of day and where they were." Will chuckled and sipped his wine, sliding his mostly full plate away. "I almost wanted to tell him how sometimes, more than just water flowed downstream from the cattle." He waved his hand. "But of course, that would have started a riot with this group." He started to laugh in earnest which, again, turned into another cough—a cough that started in his diaphragm and moved through his lungs, forcing his shoulders to quake.

"Are you okay, hon?" Allen asked, worried again.

Will nodded between jarring coughs. When the cough subsided, he answered. "Yeah, why?"

"You just…" Allen paused. "I'm just worried. You didn't eat much and your coat has lost its luster. And you still have that really bad cough." He reached a gray paw across the table to Will's.

The coyote smiled, holding Allen's paw and rubbing it with his thumb. "You don't need to worry about me, Little One. Trust in that."

"Well, you aren't worrying about you, so someone has to." The fox sighed.

"How about this," Will started with a grin. "Let's go to bed early, sleep in a little, then go see a movie or two?" He leaned in. "You can pick both," he sung.

"Hmm." Allen put his other paw to his chin. "Any movie?"

Will nodded. "Any movie."

The fox smiled. "The independent theater downtown has two I want to see, actually." His tail wagged behind the chair.

"Sounds like you already know what we're seeing." Will continued to smile as he stroked the fox's paw. "Since you're picking the movies, can I pick food between viewings?"

Allen nodded. "Sounds like a date."

***

The fox took a deep breath as he started to wake. Feeling Will wrapped around him every morning made him feel safe and secure, and today was no different.

Allen gently wiggled his way from under the coyote and made his way into the kitchen. "Early to bed, early to rise," he muttered to himself as he set up the coffee pot. He looked up at the clock briefly and saw it was 7:30am. "Very early." He chuckled.

As he waited for Will to wake up, Allen puttered around the kitchen. He filled a pan with water and gently heated it as he cleaned. With every creak of their bed, Allen's ears would perk and his hopes rise that his lover was waking, but no coyote joined him in the kitchen.

"I'll just help him along a bit," he muttered to himself. He poured two fresh, strong cups of coffee and put a splash of milk in one and carried them into the bedroom. Setting the black cup on Will's bedside table, he stood by the door and waited.

Moments later, Allen saw the coyote's nose twitch as he sniffed the air. He then took a deep breath. "Coffee…" Will said, still in a raspy voice. He sat up with his eyes closed and reached for the mug. He sipped from the mug and moved his head towards the fox. "What's for breakfast?" he asked with a smile. His voice was still horse.

"I was planning on poaching some eggs, if you were interested."

Will sipped at his mug more. "That's sounds nice. But, now that I think about it, I'm not really hungry."

Allen tilted his head. "Really? You used to eat like a pro swimmer. Barely any food last night and no food this morning." He walked up to the coyote and felt his nose. "You feeling okay, hon?"

"Don't worry, Allen," he said, gently pushing his paw away. "I'll be okay."

The fox sighed, pressing his head to the coyote's black and brown one. "How long have you been hoarse for?"

"For the past few mornings and last night. It usually goes away pretty quick. Coffee will probably clear it up," Will said as he scratched the back of Allen's head. He kissed his nose, then sipped his coffee again.

Allen sighed and stood up, watching the coyote. Then Will started coughing again. He held the mug up to the fox. Allen grabbed it and set both cups on the end table and rubbed the coyote's back.

As the hacking coughs got worse, Will pressed his arm to his muzzle. When he finally stopped, there was blood on his sleeve.

At that sight, Allen became serious. Setting his jaw, he stood and moved to the dresser. "That's it. Put some clothes on; I'm taking you to the ER."

"Allen, I'll be fine," Will said. He didn't move from the bed.

The fox glared. "If you don't let me take you to the ER, I'm calling an ambulance and I'll have them strap you down."

Will sighed. "I don't think it's that easy."

"Well, watch me try." He glared over his shoulder to Will.

"Okay," Will sighed. "You win." He crawled out of bed and started to dress.

***

Allen sat beside the hospital bed where Will lay and continued to hold his paw.

"The X-ray is not conclusive so I'd like to order a few more tests." The otter turned a computer around to face the two. "These are two pictures of lungs. The one on the right is what a healthy lung looks like."

"And the left one?" Allen asked.

"Is Will's." The otter pulled out a pen. "See this darker spot right here?" He circled around Will's left lung. "I don't want to worry you, but I'd like to look further into this."

Will sighed. "What do you want to do first?"

The doctor put his pen in his pocket. "I'd like to start with a CT scan. Can you two come in on Monday?" He looked from Will to Allen.

"Shouldn't be too much of a problem," Will said.

Allen nodded. "I'll call off if I have to; I'll make sure he's here."

The otter nodded. "I'll let the nurse know and we'll schedule you in. After that, we'll get you on your way for now. Just try to take it easy. And we can get you a prescription for the cough if you'd like."

Will shook his head. "I think I will be okay until Monday."

"Okay," the doctor said. "Just don't push yourself."

The coyote nodded. "Yes, sir."

"Do either of you have any questions?" Again, he looked from Will to Allen.

"What do you think it is?" Allen asked.

The doctor sighed. "It can be a few different things. But I don't want to make any assumptions until we have a better understanding. Let's just try to not worry too much yet."

Allen nodded. "Sounds like a plan.

***

The two sat in silence as Allen drove them home.

"Still want to catch the movies?" Will asked with a smile.

Allen shook his head. "I don't think I would be able to focus on them. My mind is all over the place right now." He sighed. "Waiting is awful."

The coyote nodded. "I know." He rested a paw on Allen's leg. "Then want to go rent something? Maybe with an explosion or two?" He squeezed the fox's leg with a smile.

"You are supposed to be taking it easy," Allen replied. "*Explosions* indeed."

Will sighed. "Are you going to be able to enjoy any of the long weekend now?"

Allen took a deep breath, running his fingers through his head fur. "I'm sorry... I'm just distracted." Now he sighed. "Not knowing upsets me. I mean, how much should I be worried? A little? A lot?" He took another deep breath. "I can't help but worry, hon." Blinking back tears, Allen pawed for a tissue. Will pulled one from the center console and handed it to the fox. "Thanks," he said, dabbing his eyes. "I just don't want to lose you."

"I'm not going anywhere, Little One." Will squeezed Allen's leg again, trying to comfort the fox.

"Not now, that's for sure." Allen chuckled. "Let's see if NPR has anything interesting to distract me." Without looking, he reached down and turned on the radio.

"—and with today's historic ruling from the Supreme Court, same-sex couples should be able to marry within the week around the nation." The reporter continued to remark on the ruling, but Allen didn't hear anything past that.

"Well, that's some good news at least." Allen chuckled. Then laughed a little. He laughed more and more and Will noticed, slowly, he started to cry.

"You can't drive and cry, Little One," Will said with a hint of both seriousness and playfulness.

Allen pulled over. "I'm just... happy and scared all at once, and I can't tell which feeling is stronger." He took a few deep breath. He met Will's eyes and saw a somber look, then really started to cry in earnest.

"Hey, I'm here, Allen. You don't need to cry," he said, petting the fox's leg.

"The doctor thinks you have cancer. He didn't want to say it, but I will. And you don't look like you care."

Will sighed. "Trust me, Little One, I care." He rested his head against the fox's shoulder as he turned the car off.

Allen laid his gray head against the coyote's and wrapped his arms around him. He bawled, shoulders rising and falling along with the tears. The two sat there while Allen cried out the stress and fear that had been building.

After a while, he finally calmed down again. Wrapping his arms tighter around Will, he sighed and sat up. While his ears were low, his shoulders looked less wound up. The fox looked to Will. "Look at you: you're the one going through this and *I'm* a blubbering mess." He laughed at himself as he wiped his face with another tissue. "How do you keep it all together?"

Will chuckled and stared in front of himself. "Practice," he said, setting his left paw on the fox's shoulder"

Allen saw he had a faraway look on his face. "What do you mean?" He put a paw on the coyote's thigh at the same time.

Will was quiet for a moment before responding. "Do you trust me?" He looked deep into Allen's eyes with a seriousness that the fox had never seen before.

"Of course," Allen responded immediately. "Why would—"

"No," Will cut the fox off with a curt wave of his other paw. "Not like that. Do. You," he tapped his right paw to the fox's thigh, "Trust me?" He moved his paw to Allen's chest. "I don't want an automatic response." He held both of Allen's paws in his own. "I want you to *honestly* think about your answer."

Allen held his gaze as he thought. How much did he trust the coyote? His past was unknown to him—and every time Allen would try to talk about his family, they quickly moved on to a different subject. But he was honest and straightforward in every other way. Hobbies, interest, politics. Morals.

"With my life," Allen answered.

"Even though you may not—"

"I don't care about where you came from. I know you now. And I trust you with. My. Life." Allen shook Will's paws with each word.

Will nodded. "Good. Let's go home. We can get some clothes and my truck."

"Your truck?" Allen started the car again and merged back into traffic.

"Yeah," Will said, nodding. He took a breath to answer, then had another coughing fit. "Sorry," he coughed. "This part will only..." He cleared his throat "...get worse for a while." He grabbed a tissue and wiped away some red from his muzzle.

"Really?"

Will nodded.

"And you're sure?"

Will coughed again. "You trust me, right?" He smiled.

The fox sighed and nodded. "I trust you."

***

"Can you go pack us a bag, please? Probably three days' worth of clothes should be enough." Will pulled himself out of the car and walked towards the garage. "Can you push the button, too?"

Allen quickly hit the electronic opener for their garage and chased after the coyote. "Three days? Where are we going, hon?"

TRUST

"I'm never really sure until I'm there. Now please, I'd like to get as much driving done today as possible, and that is probably going to be a lot." He walked in and moved right for his camping gear and started tossing pieces here and there into his truck bed.

"Do you really think we should be camping now? In your condition?"

"I'd rather have the gear and not need it," Will said. "Now please, can you go pack us some clothes?"

"Can I help you with anything, hon?" The fox had his arm against his stomach while his other paw was balled near his heart.

"I'll be okay if I take my time," Will said, focused on the task in front of him.

"Will," Allen started, "you're starting to scare me a little."

Will stopped, and looked up at the fox, seeing his gaze was glued to the floor, ears were down, and his tail wrapped around his leg.

"Oh, Little One." He walked to the fox and hugged him. "You don't need to be scared."

"Things are just moving so fast and I have no idea what is going on," Allen said, hugging the coyote fiercely. "I mean, I'm worried about you being sick and here you are packing to go camping." Tears stung his eyes.

"Hey," Will said, rubbing the fox's back. "Think of it this way: you and I are going on a little adventure." He pressed his head to Allen's. "I'm still here and everything will be alright."

Taking a few deep breaths, catching the coyote's natural scent, Allen started to calm down and feel safe. "Okay," he said. He took another breath. "I think I'm under control. Still scared, but at least I can think straight."

Will continued to hug him. "You don't need to be scared," he said again.

Allen chuckled. "You can keep saying that, but until I know what is going on, I'm going to be."

The coyote sighed. "Fair enough." He paused. "How about this, I'll explain everything when we get there." Allen nodded. "Okay, now could you please go pack some clothes for us?" Again, Allen nodded, then went inside.

About twenty minutes later Allen returned with two small suitcases. As he put them in the cabin of the truck, he called to Will. "Can I help you load anything?"

"No," the coyote answered as he loaded one travel pack into the truck bed. He lifted the second pack, loaded with a tent, into the bed and slid

314

it back. He took a deep breath and started coughing again. He pulled out a rag from his pocket and covered his muzzle.

Allen ran back inside. Moments later, he returned carrying two sports bottles and handed one to Will. He took a small drink from the bottle and the coughing subsided. He took another sip to rinse his mouth and spat red into the lawn. "Sorry," he said with another small cough. "Thanks. Water helps get the taste of iron out of my mouth."

The fox nodded. "You're welcome. Not what I expected, but happy to help." He closed the truck bed and opened the passenger side for the coyote. "I'll drive, just to be safe. Where are we going?"

With Allen's help, Will climbed into the passenger side. "I usually start in Dodge City and work my way south."

"Wait, Kansas?"

Will nodded.

"And we *start* there?"

He nodded again.

The fox sighed. "Really glad we just got paid. This sounds like an expensive weekend."

"At least gas prices are down," Will said.

The fox sighed again and got in the driver's seat. "Well then, to Dodge City," Allen said as he started the truck. He shifted into reverse, and they were off.

***

Later that day, Allen stopped for lunch, then that evening for dinner. He was the only one to eat lunch, but he made Will eat something that evening to keep his strength up. Late that night, they got into Dodge City.

"Okay, hon, where to from here?"

Will smiled. "South."

The fox nodded. "So I'll head for 283, then."

Will shook his head. "We'll never find it that way."

"What do you mean?"

"Do you know much about cattle drives?"

"Only that they are much easier now." Allen sighed. "I need some coffee; you want some?"

"Sure. It gives us an excuse to get off the highway." Will continued to smile.

As Allen flipped on his turn signal, he asked, "What should I know about cattle driving?"

"Nothing in particular. We're just following the Great Western Trail. Time willing, we may make a detour to visit my home town."

"In Kansas?"

Will shook his head. "Texas."

"Texas?" Allen sighed. "You weren't kidding when you said south."

The coyote chuckled. "You may learn some stuff about me." He smiled at the fox. "Let's get to Oklahoma, then find a place to camp."

The fox sighed. "Are we allowed to just camp on the side of the road?"

"Not sure," he replied with an upbeat tone. "Probably not. That's why we aren't going just off the road."

Allen sighed again. "I think something stiffer than coffee is starting to sound better."

***

The next morning, after coffee by a campfire and a breakfast of eggs and toast, they drove through Oklahoma and into Texas.

"Where did you learn to cook like that?" Allen asked, patting his belly happily. "That was really good, for something so simple."

"Lots of practice. I did a good deal of camping when I was younger." Will's rasp wasn't getting any better. "The pan you use can make all the difference, too."

"Well, at least one of us was active when we were younger." Allen sat in silence for a few moments, thinking. He looked over at the coyote; his coat looked duller than it had the day before. He started to feel worried again.

"You got quiet, quick," Will commented.

"You still haven't told me where we're going," Allen said.

"I guess I can tell you now; we're going to cure cancer."

"We're *what*?!" Allen spun his head towards the coyote. He spun his head so sharply, he tugged the wheel, causing the car to swerve.

Will was thrown to the left, locking the seatbelt across his chest. He started coughing again.

Allen cursed. "Sorry, hon," he said as he corrected the vehicle. "But what the hell did you just say?"

"Hey, be careful. I'm sick you know." Will smiled at the fox. Allen reached over and smacked his arm, and Will chuckled. "We're going to cure cancer," he said again, pulling out the now red-stained rag. "My cancer, at least. Lung cancer." He coughed a little more before reaching for the bottle of water. "Hopefully that takes some worry off your chest."

"How the *hell* does that 'take some worry off my chest?'" Allen said, getting louder, as he smacked the coyote again. Will tried to scoot away and chuckled. "And how can you say that so calmly?" Will let out a raspy giggle. "Because I've come to terms with it. It just another fact. The sky is blue; the sun is hot; this coyote has cancer." He put a paw on Allen's leg. "And you are the only other person that knows."

"And *now* is the best time for a road trip?" Allen was shouting now. "Trust me, Little One," Will croaked. "It is."

Allen growled as he drove on. "I am more than half tempted to turn us around and take us right to the doctor." Will squeezed his leg. "And where the hell are we going?"

The coyote shrugged. "This way," he said pointing down the road. Allen glared at his answer. "I'm not sure yet. And why are you so upset?"

"I feel lied to," Allen shouted again, striking the wheel.

"I never lied," Will replied

"You just never told me everything." Allen huffed, losing a lot of steam. "I feel like I've been stressing over your health while you sit back and laugh."

"I've never laughed at you. You think I like watching you worry?" Will cracked his window. As air swirled around them from outside, the coyote closed his eyes and took in the air. "In any case, you'll get your answers soon. Could you pull over for a moment?" Will smiled at the fox. "*Gently?*"

Allen looked from the road to Will and back. He huffed again. "Damn that cute face," he said as he pulled over.

Once the truck stopped, Will opened the door and moved to jump out. As his feet hit the ground, he fell to his knees.

"Will!" The fox jumped out of the truck, leaving the engine on, and ran to the coyote. "Hon, are you okay?"

"Yeah. Just wasn't expecting weakness in the legs yet."

"Yet?" Allen asked while helping him up.

"Yeah. Don't worry, we're only a few hours away now." Will's tail wagged slightly. He closed his eyes again and took a few steps from the truck, sniffing the air.

Allen mimicked the coyote. "What are you smelling?"

"Grit and dirt; steer on the trail." Will spoke as if he were far away. "I think we can get there by about late afternoon if we're lucky. Maybe early evening." He walked back to the truck. He sighed as he reached the door. "Here's a part I don't like," he said, turning to the fox. "Can you help me in?"

After helping Will in, getting back in the driver seat, and maneuvering them back on the road, Allen asked, "How could you smell that? I mean grit? Steer?"

"Longhorns specifically."

"And how can you identify the species by the scent?"

Will smiled. "You know how a smell can take you back in time? These are the scents of my younger days." He lowered his window further, letting the Texas air swirl around the cabin.

"It just smells like the outside to me."

Will chuckled. "We all know the scent that shapes us."

Over the next few hours, Will directed Allen south along the trail with periodic stops to take in the air. They drove along dirt roads and paths for mile after mile. About two hours south of Fort Griffin, in the heart of Texas, Will had Allen stop before a river crossing. The fox helped him out of the truck and he took a few steps.

"We're getting closer," he said to Allen. "Can you drive along the river there?" He pointed upstream.

"I don't see why not," Allen answered.

After helping the coyote back into the truck, he drove along the river. About twenty miles later, a dense grove of trees cut into their path. Allen helped the coyote get out again. Will walked towards the trees and sampled the air. "Cactus flower; now we go on foot."

With his tail wagging, Will climbed up to the truck bed and grabbed the packs. He unloaded the tent from one and dug through it. After pulling out a compass, he sat on the gate and slid off.

"Grab a pack and let's go!" he called to the fox. Without another word, or time for Allen to process what he was told, Will started walking through the trees.

"Will, wait up!" Grabbing a bag, he ran after the coyote. "What do you mean, 'cactus flower'?"

"Smell the air," Will said, glancing towards the fox, but not stopping.

"This doesn't seem safe, hon. Besides all I smell is what's around us. Trees, water, dirt."

Will kept smiling and his tail kept wagging. "The sweet scent is faint. Hard to catch unless you're looking for it." As he walked into the woods, the coyote stumbled on a tree root and Allen barely caught him.

"See, dangerous. And you are sick." Allen helped Will up. "Remember, the doctor told you not to push yourself."

"Sorry," Will panted. "I'm just getting excited. I've never done this with another person before." He smiled at the fox.

"What? Go hiking in the woods? I think we could do this at home." Will closed his eyes and took a deep breath. "You'll see," he said.

Allen shook his head. At a much slower pace, he helped the coyote navigate through the trees. He tried to smell the air. "I still don't notice anything new in the air."

"Trust me, Little One, we're almost there." The two continued to walk upstream, following the creek's twists and turns. After about a mile or so, Will pointed. "See that, Allen?"

The fox looked further upstream and saw two channels feed into the river, one that went further upstream, and a cave. "Yeah," he said. "That's where we're going?"

Will nodded.

As they walked up to the mouth of the case, a scent crossed the fox's nose. Under the smell of damp dirt there was a slightly… different scent that was hard to place. It was almost flowery, yet old and musty.

"What is this place? A cure for cancer's here?"

"Aren't you just full of questions?" Will teased. "Just wait and see, Little One."

As they walked inside, a gust of wind pushed against them. Allen closed his eyes and raised his arms as the wind blew. For a moment, he stood there in darkness and he noticed it did not have a musty smell anymore and smelled more of flowers.

"Come, everything's okay." Will took Allen's paw with a soft touch and the fox opened his eyes. Together, they followed the smaller creek inside as it curved.

As they rounded the bend, Allen gasped. He saw a pond lit from above by a natural skylight. Along the edges, the pond was covered by flowering cacti of all shapes, types and sizes. Short and tall, bright colored and dark, fleshy and full of spines.

"Welcome, Little One." Will smiled to the fox as he started to remove his clothes.

"What are you doing?" Allen hissed. "Is this really the time for a swim?"

"No better time than the present," Will answered. Folding his clothes and setting them on top of his pack, he took a few slow steps into the pool. Once he was about mid-calf in, he turned to the fox with arms outstretched, beckoning him to join.

"We'd better not get caught," Allen said with a huff as he set his pack down.

The coyote continued to smile. "We wouldn't be here if there was any chance of that."

Allen braced himself for the cool water, and he gasped when he stepped in. He looked from the water to the coyote. "It's warm."

Will nodded. "Always has been." He moved deeper into the pool.

As Allen caught up, Will took his paw, and they walked hand in hand to the center of the pond. Once they were knee deep, Will scooped a paw full of water and sipped. Allen watched as water ran down his cheeks and splashed back into the pool.

After a few paws full, Will turned to Allen, offering him a drink. The fox gave a nervous look.

"Trust me," Will said, still smiling. Allen nodded and lapped at the water from his paw. His eyes went wide again; he had never tasted water so clean and crisp. He dipped his paws into the pool himself and drank in earnest.

As the water entered him, Allen started to feel warm from the inside out and he closed his eyes and rested his arms at his sides. His heart started to race, spreading the warmth further. He grew warmer from his ears to his tail and he started panting. He gasped out loud as the temperature peaked and, just as quickly as it started, it stopped.

"What was..." Allen stopped as he saw Will. The coyote's eyes were closed and his fur was standing on end. Allen watched as his coat regained its color from root to tip and became bright and full of youth again. When he opened his eyes, Will let out a deep breath, letting out a light cloud with it.

"What *was* that?" Allen's eyes were wide.

"I'm fairly sure that was cancer." Will's voice was clear and youthful again.

Allen gasped. "Your voice!"

Will smiled. "Symptom of the cancer. With it gone, I'm back to normal."

"Normal? You look ten years younger. What did we drink?" Allen asked softly.

"I've been calling it the Fountain of Youth."

Allen blinked. "The... fountain of youth?"

The coyote nodded. "I stumbled on it in about 1887 and I've been—"
With a splash and a yip of surprise, the fox's leg gave out.
Will sat beside the fox, helping him stay up. "Deep breaths, Little
One. Everything's all right."
Allen sat there, staring at the wall and blinked. "So you are almost
130 years old?"
Will coughed. "Closer to 160."
"Can we, uh, move over there?" Allen pointed to the edge near their
bags. "I think I need to lie down."
Will helped the fox to the water's edge where he sat down. Sitting
quickly turned into lying down as Allen curled his legs under himself
and his tail wrapped around himself. He continued to lay there, staring
at the far wall. Allen didn't realize he had fallen asleep until he woke up
with a blanket over him. He looked around and saw he was still in the
cave, still by the pool, and still surrounded by flowering cacti. But now
the place felt... different.
"Will?" he called out.
"I'm right here, Little One."
Allen spun around and saw the coyote sitting by a small fire pit.
"Oh. Where'd that come from?" Allen nodded to the fire.
"I found out that if you dig around here, there are roots that work
well for a fire. I wanted you to stay warm."
Allen noticed that Will looked tired. "Thanks," he said as he scooted
closer to the fire. "So, you've been doing this for a while?"
The coyote nodded. "But I've never trusted anyone enough to bring
them here. You're the first I've shared my secret with."
Allen nodded. "And your cancer is gone?"
This time, Will shrugged. "For now. Over the years, I've come to find
that drinking from the pool doesn't so much heal, as it returns us to our
prime. Probably about early to late-twenties. I think I have anywhere
from ten to twenty-five years before I need to come back again.
"But when I've come to find this place in the past, I wasn't in a
serious relationship." Will looked into the fire. "I'd just disappear and not
worry about going back. I'd create a new life for myself." He looked back
to Allen with worry and concern in his eyes. "I had friends and lovers,
but no one I was *that* close to. But you were different. I didn't want to
just leave you. I want to be with you for the rest of time—if you still
want to be with me."
Allen was quiet for a moment. "I get to meet you all over again."

"But you already know me. You know who I am. Whether I go by Will, Bill, or William, my personality doesn't change."

"Do you have any family?" Allen asked.

Will shrugged. "Probably. Cousins, or nieces or nephews, but I don't know them. My family was told I died in 1896."

Allen scooted closer to the coyote and put a paw on his leg. "How is that not lonely?"

"It can be, at times." Will shrugged. "I had people around me, had companionship, but no one that I trusted. But, well, I was hoping I wouldn't have to be alone anymore," he said as he looked hopefully to the fox.

Allen met his gaze, then looked into the fire. "I don't know." He was silent for a moment before looking back at the coyote. "I love you. I really do. And I want to spend the rest of my life with you—I have no doubt about that. I have questions for days, and I want to *really* get to know you." He looked around for his pants and reached into a pocket, then moved closer to the coyote. "But I still trust you, and I want to grow old with you. Instead of asking me to stay with you," he started, holding out a box, "will you stay with me?"

The coyote reached out. Inside were two rings made of dark wood, one lined with silver and one lined with gold.

"I was thinking of asking *the* question, since it seemed like you never would," Allen said. "Now though, I need to rethink all of this. But I still want to be with you and be there for you."

"But I still have cancer."

"You think I care?" Allen chuckled. "Cancer isn't a death sentence." Allen put a paw on his leg. "You said the symptoms don't start for a number of years; if it is detected early, it is easier to fight."

"But it can be expensive."

Allen smiled. "Again, you think I care? I said I want to grow old with you and that is what I plan to do. I want to be with you, get to know you." He smiled at the coyote. "Trust me, Will."

Will smiled and a tear rolled down his cheek.

"I do."

Sushil has withdrawn from a world that covets his horn.
Hidden away in an ashram in the mountains, he has
become a legend, when he was once a friend.

THE GOLDEN FLOWERS

Priya Sridhar

The little black martin landed on the sage's ear and chirped. His eyes shot open as he registered the message.

"A visitor, you say?" he murmured. "How long has it been, little one? Days? Months? *Years?*"

The bird flew away; its wingtips grazed his face. Dewdrops scattered from its flapping gusts.

Sushil meditated in the great field in front of his ashram. He would let his four stubby legs splay out in front of him, on a patch of often-flattened grass. Only a shaved-off stump remained for a horn, and he wore a loincloth that wrapped around his leathery, grey skin and covered his tail. His eyes blurred the horizon, so he kept them shut as he breathed in and out deeply. Silence coated him, like a thin veil, and it tore easily when someone broke the silence.

He heard the sound of hooves, thin clopping. Sushil's eyes popped open, and he straightened up. He blinked several times, but his vision remained blurry.

"Sundar?" he gasped. "Is that you?"

The figure stopped walking. It was white and had black horns on top of its head. Sushil lumbered to get up, and charged towards the figure. He smelled wet fur, grass, and engine oil. Nevertheless, the rhino pressed against him, as a form of an embrace. The figure bleated, and went limp. Sushil caught him with his flank. He heard a stick press into the ground. Metal clinked against grass.

"Sundar was my grandfather," the figure gasped. "I'm Emery. Emery Brittle." Sushil backed away, and the figure used the stick to gain better footing. Now that he was closer, he could see that the figure had bright black eyes, curled horns at the top of his head, and wore bright white clothes that had neat stitches.

"Emery," he said. "Sundar has grandchildren?"

"Yes. You must be the Guardian of the Flowers," Emery said, clutching his chest. "My grandfather told me about you."

Sushil cast a backward glance; the ashram blocked the garden, but the golden flowers gave off a scent much like marigold and jasmine blended into one.

"How… how is he?" he ventured to ask.

"All right," Emery said. His legs stopped buckling. "A little grumpy, and sickly, but still the same goat I remember from when I was a kid. He told me to come find you. He said you could help."

Hope perked within Sushil's chest. He locked eyes with the small goat, and adopted a regal stare.

"What did he say?"

"He said I had to give something to you, as an apology," Emery said, waving his cane. Sushil now noticed the rucksack he was carrying, which Emery struggled to take off. He rummaged into the bag before coming out with a wrapped bundle.

Sushil took the bundle; its weight felt familiar, as was the smell of chalk. The hope crushed his insides, like a fist.

"He says he's sorry, and that he hopes you can help me with my condition. Our condition, I guess."

A shard of rhino horn nestled in his palms. He weighed it; sharp memories came back to him. A saw cutting through the horn, as if it were a twisted tree limb; the final glare in Sundar's arms as he had left.

"He said the flowers can help with my condition," Emery said, face turning red under the white fur. "But also that I have to ask your permission first, before I can acquire a few. He said to be mindful."

Sushil pondered the horn. He touched the stump on his head, fingering the eroded surface, the nicks and furrows that had emerged over time. Old pains emerged.

"I need to think about this," he said. "Hasty thinking only leads to wasteful actions."

***

They ate a meager meal when the evening came. The martins had returned with berries for Sushil and blades of grass. He sucked the dewdrops from the berries and blades. Emery pulled out a small brown log and nibbled on a few pieces. They knelt under the covered part of the ashram and ate as the sun dipped behind the mountain and the air grew colder.

"Fruit cake," he explained to Sushil. "Keeps your energy up and is filled with healthy nutrients."

Sushil nodded; he chewed at his grass slowly. The martins climbed all over him and pecked insects and ticks off him. Emery's cheeks tinted green, but he stuffed his mouth with fruitcake instead.

"I haven't seen this horn in fifty years," he said. "You don't see many of my kind with horns in this day and age. The martins tell me that the few surviving rhinos cut them off and sell them, to pay for grain and for their houses."

"Grandfather told me that he stole it from you," Emery said, with some shame. "He said that you were best friends, but he wanted to see the world. And he took your horn, which you had hoarded away."

Sushil turned over a berry in his hands. He blinked rapidly, for Emery seemed to turn into Sundar the longer the shadows grew in the ashram.

"That's not exactly what happened," he said. "Did he tell you the full story?"

"Not very well." Emery looked down at his fruitcake. "Grandfather isn't well, sir. He can only talk for maybe half an hour at a time, and then his limbs act up and he needs his medication."

"Call me Sushil," the rhino said. "None of this 'sir' business. I'm not a wise rhino. I just happened to survive. My story with Sundar started a long time ago. A *lifetime* ago."

Once upon a time, he said, *there were dozens of rhinos like me. Rhinos do not like cities. We do not even like towns. We like our solitude. Rhinos have heavy thoughts, and heavy thoughts ask for heavy thinking. It is hard to think together. We did not seek out friends. We did not seek out each other even.*

When other creatures learned that rhino horns could become magnificent jewelry, crowns for kings, musical instruments that curled in the air, no one spoke for the rhinos. The vicious monkeys hunted us down one by one—shot in the gut and our horns lopped off. I was only a juvenile then, but I knew how to hide. I knew how to run, and how to charge. Yet I wished only for solitude, to be alone with my thoughts again.

One night, scavenging in these mountains, I came across a strange herd of goats. They had thick wool and hearts as soft as feathers. They allowed me to trade labor for food, and asked me to give rides to their kids. I did so, and earned a peaceful existence.

One of the goats was your grandfather: Sundar. He was more bowlegged, more prone to falling than the others. Yet he kept getting up, and he conversed with me. He could not believe that I had chosen to run rather than fight. He said my horn could be used against the hunters.

"I do not fight," I said with dignity. "It is not the way."

"What is this way you speak of, Sushil? Are you an agent of the spirits? The ones that say our material lives are immaterial."

"No. I am no one's agent. But I know the way."

You could say it was arguing, except we enjoyed it, and arguing is not supposed to be fun. My thoughts felt lighter around him, for he did not accept things. He changed them when he could. He designed new ploughs for farming and drew quicker routes to grazing grounds.

The hunters came. They always came when a rhino horn dangled in the distance. The martins that roosted on my flanks flew south of the mountains for winter, caught wind of their plans, and they warned me. With a heavy heart, I prepared to leave in the dead of night, long before the hunters came and razed the goats' meager village to the ground.

Sundar approached. He asked where I was going; I told him I had no idea, I did not know where I would live. He told me of a sacred grove where the peaceful could stay. He gave me directions, and the martins listened.

"Nothing is peaceful," I said, "so long as I have my horn."

"Let me cut it off for you then," he said, a strange glint in his eyes. "We can give it to the hunters while you make your head start. It will make everyone happy."

He had a saw in his hooves; I knelt and let him cut. It did not hurt. He sawed neatly, so that there were no nicks. When I stood, I realized how light my head felt. The horn had been heavy.

"I like it this way," I said. "Thank you, Sundar. You're a good friend."

He looked uncomfortable as he brushed away the horn powder.

"When it's safe, come looking for me, Sundar. Let me know that the village is alive."

"I will," he promised.

So I left the village, entered the dark of the mountains. When I found this grove, I found the empty ashram. I donned the cloth that the last person had left, and started to meditate. My thoughts had never felt so light.

In time, they grew heavier. Day after day, I waited for Sundar, strained my ears for the heaviest footstep. He did not come. The martins flew to the village and back, telling me that the monkeys came and left with a quarter of a horn.

That seems odd, I thought. Sundar cut off more than that.

I realize now what must have happened. Sundar took the horn for himself, trudged down the mountain, and sailed abroad to make his fortune. I do not blame him for that; better that my horn was in the gentle hooves of a friend than in the bloodied grip of a hunter. And now he has asked you to find me, after I have renounced the world. How blessed I am.

Emery put away his fruitcake. Tears ran down his face; he wiped at them.

"That's such a sad story," he said. "After all that you did, Grandfather left you and took what made you valuable. No wonder he feels awful."

"A horn is a horn," Sushil said. "I'd rather have Sundar back than my horn, if I had a choice."

Emery nodded. Guilt clouded his face, and he brought his knees up to his chest. In that moment, the comparison to Sundar faded; Sundar had never looked that guilty, or so fragile.

***

Days passed. Emery meditated with Sushil and chewed on the golden flowers. He imitated the rhino's poses and told him about his life across the ocean, going to school with a cane and using his cane to knock away bullies. He walked more steadily, but the slightest surprise could cause him to faint. He would bleat, collapse to the ground, and then lift himself up again. The grass stained his clothes, so that he was green and white all over. Occasionally pollen coated his nose.

"It helps," he said when Sushil helped him up. "Grandfather's in a wheelchair now, a kind of seat that moves, and he can't get out of it without help."

The martins brought more news: Emery's parents and older siblings were roaming the mountains, searching for their son. They asked all the birds that traveled, but the martins went unnoticed amidst the flocks of foreign pigeons and crows. They came up to the goat village.

Emery on hearing this took out a small piece of paper and gave it to the martins. He had scrawled a quick note on it and rolled it into a tight ball. It was high noon, so the sun shone brightly.

"Make sure it gets to them, but don't get caught," he said. "My parents are probably frantic. The note just says I'm safe; don't come looking for me, nothing to worry about."

He took out a larger piece of paper then, and started writing. Sushil occasionally looked over his shoulder but could not make out the scripture.

"I have an idea," Emery explained. "But it's going to need a messenger. The martins, have they ever flown across the ocean?"

Sushil asked the birds, who clicked and chittered. They said no, they hadn't. Such work was for foreign pigeons.

"I need you to get this message to my grandfather," Emery said. "Or at least passed onto him. He needs to make the journey to the ashram."

"Is that even possible?" Sushil asked. "If he is as old as you say he is, and unable to walk, it will be difficult to get him up the mountain. Unless…"

He stood up and paced around the ashram. Heavy thoughts banged against his mind.

"I could come with you, to return you to your parents. They must be frantic, and they could get a message to your grandfather."

"No!" Emery exclaimed. "Bad idea!"

Sushil stared. Emery before this had never raised his voice, even when startled into fainting. The goat kid took a deep breath.

"My parents, they are clingy. And think they know everything. I had to run away to come see you because they laughed when grandfather told me to seek you on the mountain. They think he's a crazy old goat that's becoming senile."

"That can't be true," Sushil said. "Surely they must love him."

"Love and respect are two different things," Emery said. "Yes, they do love me, and they love my grandfather, but all their love comes out as worrying, and they stopped respecting my grandfather when he suffered a major fit and had to cede control of his company to my father. They don't notice when I can do things, or when he actually makes good points."

Angry tears sparked in his eyes. He turned his head away to wipe them.

"It's not right to make them worry," Sushil said. "Why didn't you tell me before?"

Emery didn't answer. He walked around, thinking.

"You need to go back, Emery."

"I can't," Emery whispered. "I need the flowers."

"You could have just taken the flowers, and left," Sushil pointed out. "Why did you stay?"

"Because leaving you wouldn't have been right," he said. "You'd be alone again, and I would have given you nothing for the flowers."

Sushil started pacing with him. His feet thumped against the ashram floor.

"Let me talk to the martins," he said. "Perhaps they can deliver a message from *me* to Sundar."

He talked to his youngest martin, a fledgling named Ravi who had traveled as far as the end of the mountain. Ravi's eyes widened, and he chittered that of *course* he would go and find the strange goat man. He only needed a map, and villages had *many* maps.

"I can't write," Sushil said, "But you can, Emery. I want you to write down a letter to Sundar, from me."

Emery nodded with understanding. He took out two larger pieces of paper. They were thicker and cream-colored. Sushil thought, and spoke slowly. Emery copied the loving, laborious words on both sheets. He laid the sheets in the sun so that the ink could dry, getting black smudges on his hooves. He gave one dry sheet to the martin Ravi, which expertly tied the note to his leg as a tiny scroll. Emery tucked the other letter into his shirt.

"I'll keep one copy with me," he explained. "For when I go back to my family. Maybe one message will get through."

In the evening, they picked the oldest flowers, enough to fill two woven baskets, and Sushil showed the dense seedpods.

"I sometimes dry out the seeds for long winters, and there are bushels of them," he said. "I keep the bushels in a cave."

He showed the cave to Emery, who could only accept one bushel, since that was all he could carry. There were enough seeds in there to grow a hundred fields of golden flowers, enough to last him a lifetime. The more Emery took in these baskets and dried seeds, the more resigned he became to returning.

"I guess going down to the village where they pointed me here is better than coming up," he said. "I was scared I would never make it up here with just my cane. It was amazing I didn't have fits on the way up."

Sushil stared at him. He felt heavier, older, *blinder*.

"Emery, you are not going down there alone," he said. "Strap the baskets to my back. I can carry them easily."

"It's not safe for you," Emery insisted.

"Then it isn't safe for you either. At least let me carry these down to the goat village."

They left in the dead of night. No moon shone, but the stars did, and Sushil smelled out the path. His bones rattled inside his grey skin, but Emery must have been feeling worse, walking like a calf facing unjust execution. He stumbled more despite having stuffed himself with flowers, and Sushil caught him twice.

"On my back," he ordered.

"Sir, no—"

"Get on my back," Sushil said. "You won't be any good to your family with a broken leg."

Emery relented and climbed onto the rhino's back. His hooves scraped against the grey skin and knocked against the baskets. Sushil despite the heavier load found himself moving faster. Emery leaned against him.

"It makes a difference when one has a goal," Sushil said aloud.

"Yes. Provided that goal is positive," Emery said bitterly.

The village lights greeted them first. Sushil saw kerosene lamps and carts with larger wheels. Figures started approaching them.

"There you are!" A female goat came, hooves fisted against her knees.

Emery gave out a bleat and sank on Sushil's back. The rhino quickly lowered him to the ground and nudged him upright. The goat recovered himself but gazed sourly at the figure.

"Hey, sis," he said without amusement. He yelped as she grabbed his shoulder and slapped him.

"Just a minute!" Sushil exclaimed.

"You are in *big* trouble, mister!" Emery's sister said. "Do you know how long we've been looking for you? Do you know how many goats Mum and Dad have hired?"

"I left a note!" Emery retorted.

"Yes; to chase after one of grandfather's fantasy creatures. Like there would be a rhino in this mountain!"

I'm standing right here! Sushil wanted to shout, but his voice seemed to have died. The approaching goats from the village came forward and stared.

"There is a rhino, and he didn't do anything!" Emery shouted. "I went to him, for the flowers! They actually helped! If you would just see!"

"How can you trust a word Grandfather says?" the girl goat demanded. "He'd say the sky were purple if the nurses would let him! Just wait till Mum and Dad get here!"

Emery twisted his head and shot a dark look at Sushil, not one of anger, but of warning: *Go. This isn't your problem.*

Sushil thought slowly, which was hard with the female goat yelling, and the pricking around his neck that meant danger. Then he made his decision, to become angry.

"Stop that nonsense! That is not how one treats a brother!" he snapped. "Do you not realize he is ill?"

The female goat stopped shaking Emery and turned to him. She paled.

"Yes, I am the rhino that your grandfather befriended. I am the rhino whose horn he took." Sushil took a deep breath. "Your brother was kind enough to return the horn to me, and in return I gave him these baskets of flowers. They have helped him. Maybe one day, they will help your grandfather become well enough so he can come visit. I miss him."

He grabbed for the tethers that bound the baskets to his back, and untied them. The baskets sailed to the ground with grace.

"I said this world wasn't safe," Emery said, a red mark blooming on his cheek. "It isn't a kind world. It's one where no one listens to you even if you're right."

"I understand," Sushil said, turning. "I am going to return to my ashram. You and your grandfather are always welcome."

"You can't just leave—" Emery's sister said, but Emery collapsed in her grasp, and she had to catch him. Emery dropped his cane, and it rolled.

Sushil tore up the mountain, not in fear, but with understanding. He had witnessed an ugly part of the world, something more intimate than a heart, and something far more damaged. Small wonder Emery had tried to escape it.

***

Although only a few months, it felt like another lifetime. Ravi the martin returned, his feathers tinged with frost, returned with a note that Sushil couldn't read and a song he had learned from Western martins.

Sushil meditated. He ate grass and berries. He sent the martins to the goat village. Emery's father, a large goat with thin hands, came up the mountain path, but Sushil met him a short distance away from the village, and the goat's eyes remained on the remaining horn stump on Sushil's head and lectured about how terrible it was for Emery to visit him. There was no warmth in that goat's face, not like Emery's.

The martins led other visitors astray, for many creatures coveted Sushil's horn or his privacy. The one visitor he wanted, as new flowers sprouted and bloomed in the field, never came.

Until one day. He awoke to hearing the sound of wheels squeaking and a familiar voice.

"Keep moving, you laggard! We're almost there!"

Sushil sat up from his meditation. He blinked, and sniffed the air. Two figures stood in the distance, one being wheeled in a strange cart.

"Sundar?" Sushil asked with hesitation.

"Hey, old friend," Sundar responded, with a long beard and grey in his fur. "I got your message."

The goat that had come with Sundar yelped as the rhino charged at them, but Sundar laughed as Sushil nuzzled him and capered around in joy. Then Sushil had to ask.

"Emery?"

"Says thank you," Sundar smirked. "He always smells of pollen and nectar."

To the stars…

A Thousand Dreams

Amy Fontaine

Tarascus was a wolf made of stars. He used to be a wolf made of blood and muscle and fur. An Earth-wolf, coarse and untroubled by philosophy. A meaty thing that killed and ate.

But Tarascus was a wolf with a destiny. There was a prophecy among the wolves concerning the year Tarascus was born. It said that the first wolf born under the Northern Lights in that year would grow to be a great leader. He would live a passionate, fulfilling life. Rather than going into the Earth when he died, he would take his place among the stars. Tarascus turned out to be this wolf. Born under the Northern Lights, he quickly became a well-respected alpha with a mate and six hearty pups. His family grew and prospered every year of his life. When he died, his spirit climbed a tall, snowy mountain and ascended into the heavens.

Tarascus lived in the heavens after that, and he was quite a sight to behold. His coat was woven from white stars. His eyes burned like two fierce yellow suns, staring down at the world below.

In the daytime, the sun's brilliance kept Tarascus from seeing the world, but the night—the star-time—was the perfect time for him to observe Earth. He saw wolf packs running across the snow. He saw blood spilt, red on white, the victory of a fresh kill. Mothers storing food in their bellies to take home to their pups.

Tarascus burned with longing. He yearned to race across the frozen ground, to feel the cold snow on his paws and the icy wind in his lungs. He longed to taste fresh blood again. He wanted to romp with the pack, to nuzzle his mate.

But Tarascus could not do these things. He was a star-wolf: distant, silent. Alone. He could not taste or feel or play. He could not love. He watched helplessly as his mate died, returning to the Earth. His pups, too, were claimed by the Earth, one by one. Now his pack consisted of only his great-great-great-grandchildren. They would never know him, except as a few specks in the sky. He was only a vague story, passed from one wolf to another.

Tarascus's once-brilliant star-coat faded to a dull moonbeam gray. He watched generations pass. His descendants slowly forgot him. He grew frustrated with his life as an elevated being.

"What does being a legend get you," Tarascus cried, "if there is no one to share it with?"

Tarascus's sunspot eyes widened. He had spoken! He wasn't sure how, but he had broken the silence of a thousand years. It did not matter, though, for the wolves of Earth could not hear him. They frolicked happily amidst the snowflakes falling from the sky, unaware that these flakes were the star-wolf's frozen tears.

"What is there to live for?" sobbed Tarascus.

"Plenty," said a voice.

Tarascus turned toward the voice. Instantly, his fur lit up again.

In the sky before him was an owl, perched upon a star. She was poised as a statue, old as a redwood tree, and twice as beautiful as either one. Her feathers, white down laced with gold, sparkled against the blackness of space. A warmth filled Tarascus as he looked at her—like the feeling of nuzzling his mate, like the taste of fresh blood. Yet something... truer, something more.

"Who are you?" breathed Tarascus.

The owl chuckled. Her laugh was like the sea, lapping at a thirsty shore.

"I am many things," she said. "I am the pains and joys of your heart. I am the goal you never accomplished. I am the God you never believed in."

"God?" asked Tarascus. "Who is God?"

The owl laughed. With a windy rustle of wings, she flapped away into the far reaches of space, disappearing from sight. With a strangled cry, Tarascus gave chase. Soon he had left Earth far behind him.

Tarascus followed the owl for a thousand years, tracing her path through the universe. The centuries were a blink of an eye to a star-wolf, but the time still felt unbearable to Tarascus. He had found a companion at last, only to have her vanish again. He almost gave up the search several times, but then he would spy a little white feather that revived his hope. So he kept running, flying through the stars.

He grew so tired from traveling that he almost collapsed. Then he spied a whirling vortex in the center of space. For the first time in a thousand years, he stopped running. He stared, transfixed, at the vortex. His heart was moved; it stirred like a half-frozen animal recovering beside the hearth. The vortex was endless; it seemed to contain all of space and time. Purple, blue, black, and green, it spiraled down into a strange, wondrous funnel. The brilliance of a thousand stars shone at its core.

"There is much to live for," said a voice. "The universe is full of beauty."

Tarascus whipped around. There was the owl, perched on a star at the corner of his vision.

"You!" he gasped. "You, at last!"

The owl's luminous eyes seemed to smile.

"I have been with you all the time."

The wolf stared at the calm bird. He sank to the velvet floor of space, relieved and exhausted. He gazed up at the owl, who still floated upon her star.

"You are a marvel," said Tarascus. "What shall I call you?"

The owl preened herself, dipping her beak into her luscious feathers. The wolf's mouth watered as he watched her head's delicate movements. He had not felt hunger in a long time, but this was no flesh-hunger. This was some kind of spirit-hunger, a feeling that was powerful and odd. He got to his feet, staring at the owl with keen eyes.

The owl stared back at him. She spoke without vocalizing, as did he. Space-speech is all thought-projection and ether: no physicality required.

In this projected voice, which seemed to come from all the stars, the owl said, "I have been called many names. Peace, Faith, Prosperity. None of them suit me."

"Well then, what shall I call you?"

The owl gazed into the vortex. Then her eyes met the wolf's sunspots.

"You may call me Ranslei," she said.

***

During the next thousand years, Tarascus followed Ranslei deeper into the universe. She showed him things he had missed before: little brown comets, full of holes; suns like flaming rose petals; moons like frozen tears. He felt a delight the likes of which he had never experienced. He was learning things, blazing a path through new territory. And all around him was beauty, every step of the way.

Ranslei showed him a cathedral suspended in the air. Its stained-glass windows glimmered in ultraviolet hues. Ranslei sat upon a star, gazing at the building.

"There are a thousand colors in space that creatures on Earth don't see," said Ranslei.

Tarascus gaped at the building.

"These colors don't reach Earth?" he asked.

From her glowing perch, Ranslei flexed her wings, like a white-and-gold butterfly on a bright star-flower.

"They reach Earth," Ranslei said. "The creatures there just don't see them."

Tarascus stared, mesmerized.

"I don't think I appreciated my eyes when I was young," he said.

Ranslei fluttered into the air. "It is hard to appreciate a gift when one is in a hurry. On Earth, every living being hurries. That is why they have no time to see the thousand hidden colors." The owl soared to the top of the cathedral, alighting upon the pinnacle of the structure.

"This is space," she said. "Here we can stop and stare for a thousand years, if we wish."

The star-wolf stood on his hind legs, hoping for a better look. He cared not for the cathedral any longer—he had eyes only for Ranslei. She looked like an angel: standing at the tip of the steeple, her white wings spread wide. He wanted to stare at her for eternity.

A thousand years passed in reverent silence. At last, Ranslei flew off the steeple.

"There is always time," she said, "but there is always more to learn and see."

Ranslei soared deeper into space. Like an ocean pulled by the moon, Tarascus followed. She had become the blood of his being; a form through which only stardust once flowed had taken on new life. He was no longer a ghost-wolf, doomed to watch other wolves live their lives while doing nothing himself. He was an active participant in this universe, engaged in his own personal journey. He knew not what lay at the end of it, but his heart leapt with joy. He pranced across the stars, eager to learn whatever new secrets Ranslei could share.

For another thousand years, the owl and the wolf traveled together. They saw stars being born. They danced across asteroid belts. They met many constellations: Delphinus the dolphin, Cygnus the swan, Vulpes the fox. Tarascus had never felt so free. But throughout his quest, he never saw a thing more beautiful than Ranslei. He felt a deep connection to the bird. She carried him onward with a force stronger than gravity, yet kinder than love. But she always waited just at the edge of his vision. When he moved toward her, she would glide away towards their next destination. There was always more to do, more to see.

Ranslei brought him to a blue-and-white planet, frozen and cold and lovely. At the top of this planet was a tall, white mountain, similar to the mountain the spirit of Tarascus had ascended to join the stars. From the atmosphere, Tarascus and Ranslei savored the view. Blue and white plains stretched for endless miles. Flocks of four-winged gulls skirted over the land, mewling mournfully. Spiral-shaped clouds drifted lazily over the ice. On the ground grazed glowing green does. Pawing the snow, they lapped it up with their long tongues.

"Life is beautiful," said Tarascus.

Ranslei turned her head to look at him. "Yes, it is."

Grazing over the deer, the eyes of Tarascus fell at last upon the desolate mountain peak. A thousand unspeakable longings swelled inside him. He turned his head, gazing at Ranslei. As always, she perched at the corner of his vision. He longed suddenly to touch her, to unite with her, to take her inside of himself and make her his own. Overwhelmed with the vastness of space, he yearned to latch onto the one certainty in this inconstant universe.

"You are beautiful, too, Ranslei," murmured Tarascus.

His voice was smaller than the tiniest snowflake. After he spoke the words, his star-mouth went dry.

Ranslei turned away. "Please do not say that."

Tarascus's astral body burned with a fleshy heat. Rage flowed through him.

"Why shall I not say it?" he snarled. "I love you!"

The universe gaped, staring in shock at a starry wolf and a white-and-gold owl.

Tarascus felt horrid for confessing his love in such a rash, inappropriate fashion—and with such anger in his voice. But he was consumed by desire, so he stood his ground, refusing to amend his bold statement.

"It is impossible," said Ranslei.

"Impossible?" shrieked Tarascus. "Impossible! Are you so cold?"

Ranslei's unblinking eye shed a single tear. The wolf's throat rumbled like thunder.

"You always position yourself just out of my reach, even though you've known all along how I feel for you, how I long for your soul to meet mine. Why? Why can I not touch you?"

Growling, Tarascus leapt at Ranslei.

"I shall touch you now!"

His claws met Ranslei's form and—passed right through her.

Tarascus blinked. He stood upon a single star, overlooking the planet below him. It was blue-white, frozen, with not a trace of life upon it. He stood upon a single star, a star on which an owl had once perched.

"Ranslei?" Tarascus called. "Ranslei."

The universe was as speechless as his heart. The birds were all gone.

A wind moaned against the blue-white planet, brushing away the spiral-shaped clouds. The barrenness of the surface became even clearer. A chill crept into the star-wolf's heart.

"Ranslei? Ranslei!"

There was no answer.

***

Tarascus now roams a lifeless, empty universe, searching for the one who showed him a thousand hidden colors. His once-brilliant coat is now a midnight-black. His search is mostly fruitless, though every now and then he spies a single white feather that spurs him on.

The wolves of Earth can now hear their unfortunate comrade. The sounds of his sorrow upon losing his beloved penetrated the barrier between his world and ours. Humans cannot hear the star-wolf's cries, but the wolves always can. They send him their sympathies in the form of a song to the sky, a song for all the things in life that are just out of reach.

We end our journey with the story of Stargrave, forsaken but not forgotten, a truly legendary hero.

PUPPETS

Ellis Aen

// LOADING ACADEMY EMI SIMLOG PRIMER;
// AUTHORITY OF: WAR PROFICIENT FIRST CLASS
COMMANDER LADELY;
// SESSION 012114 ...

***

==NEURAL SENSORY FEEDBACK LIMITER SET:
PHYSICAL / EMOTIONAL==
==AUTHORITY: COMMANDER LADELY==

***

// EMI IMPRESSION d15.11.2072.AF;
// STARGRAVE (ROOT $SOOK);
// DOCUMENTATION PROVIDED BY: SIMSTIM
TACTICAL DIV.

***

@003.
    "We've got company: hillside, eight o'clock. Skiff coming in low."
    Stargrave pivoted in place and cycled his visor. The display zoomed and isolated multiple targets on his heads-up display. Three of them. All in armor, too. "Probably scavengers," he said. "As if we don't have enough problems with the war by itself. Hey, I've got a great idea: let's add infighting, too."

The lioness beside him was already loading a charge cylinder into her firearm. The brilliant afternoon sun glinted off of the sharp edges and ebony polymers of her power suit. Stargrave could see his reflection cast back on them, his lupine visage accented in the black and neon-orange of his own suit. His hellfist power gauntlets made his already-large-enough wolf paws look even larger still—ridiculous, even. Not that the horns jutting up, out from under his angular helmet, looked any less ridiculous. "It's bad luck, what with no survivors," Rey said, pointing out the star-ship's wreckage, "but we're beyond our responsibilities, now."

Stargrave groaned. Time was money. Especially in a personal-augmentation suit. "We're bleeding beats like pumping blood from a gaping wound. A hundred and thirty of 'em already. Even if we head back now, it's already a bust. EDD only fronted us for a hundred."

The mission had been an urgent (but mercenary-accessible) assign-ment from the ISF's Emergency Deployment Division. A search-and-rescue job on a fallen starship from a battle up in the heavens. It was a small frigate; the survey told them that most of it had been wasted in landfall.

The Ikaile-Artyom spinner, however, was still intact.

Rey thumbed off the safety on her rifle. "So what's the deal, boss? Running or gunning?"

"One of the FTL drives is still in one piece," he said, with a slow lilt. "Our visitors must've picked it up on LRS." Long range scanners would mean that the incoming flight-craft knew they were going to have company. Stargrave bunched up his fists and bounced them in place. His gauntlets were heavy, yet satisfying with their weight. "What's one of those things go for these days, anyway?"

Rey grinned under her helmet; Stargrave saw the expression in the display on his HUD. The lioness had a pretty muzzle for missing two teeth and a quarter of her nose. "Enough to warrant taking a risk on the IBM."

Stargrave whistled. "The Interstellar Black Market, huh? Guess the question answers itself then, dun-it?"

"Was hoping you was gonna say that."

"Eh," Stargrave said as his combat overlay kicked in, "I haven't punched anything today, anyway. And I'm feeling grumpy." He held his massive palms skyward in a throwaway gesture of disbelief. The energy-projection circles on them glowed an eerie blue. "Someone forgot to refill the merc-hall coffee machine this morning. Can you believe that?"

"Not for a second, boss. Godsdamned travesty."

"Worthy of a tail-hanging," he confirmed. His armor was already conveying commands through his neural interface. Navigation points appeared on Rey's HUD. The lioness's suit-camouflage kicked in, light bending around the multi-faceted surface of her armor. The only way Stargrave would be able to track her would be through infrared thermal imaging or her suit's broadcasted notifications on his comm-band. "We split up. Flank 'em. They'll hit the anti-mag-field any second."

The skiff in the distance dropped thirty feet straight down, as if on cue. Stargrave immediately flipped the field-bubble around the crash site from the anti-magnetic to a thermal-overload containment barrier. Visors could mute out the flash of heat and light, but with a periodic pulse, infrared was now effectively useless.

Rey shot up the hillside to the left; Stargrave rounded the hind-end of the busted starship. The skiff collided with the ground. Dust and chunks of turf plastered in overgrown dry grasses flung outward in long, forward arcs.

It was a terrible layout. A flat grassland with half a mile of rounded hill ridge the only other feature. A faded gold-green croissant baking in the hemispherical oven of the containment field. Their only option was the element of surprise. Thanks to a little bit of planning ahead, they had it.

The crack of gunfire exploded at the top of the ridge as Rey opened up in randomized bursts into the billow of dust. Stargrave, meanwhile, made a beeline straight for the cloud. He opened his gauntlets up and thrust the palms backward. Then he leaned forward and discharged them. The burst from the palm elements threw him skyward and blew a crater in the earth behind him.

They had the drop. Home-team advantage.

This'll be easy, Stargrave thought.

Stargrave had second thoughts when he met a brawny little female vibrodancer, midair, just below the apex of his jump. The vibroblade axe she leveraged against him was nearly as big as she was. He barely managed to shift his posture in time for the block.

She swatted him out of the sky like an insect.

He spun wildly for a second, contorted himself, and discharged his left palm for stabilization. It was an awkward recovery. He would've used both palms, except he was gambling on there being a follow-up strike—and he was right. He met it on the ground with a right hook that broke the sound barrier.

The dust cloud vaporized from the impact wake.

"Shit, boss! She's fast!"

Stargrave's ears were still ringing from the collision. There wasn't time to linger, either. His hearing gradually came back amid the auditory clapping, explosive chaos of battle. He deflected blows from his assailant's axe with the edges of his paws like the hard edges of a blade; his gauntlets matched the axe's frequency, nullifying the enhanced cutting power, but not the force behind the swings. Behind the vibrodancer, Stargrave could see the telltale flashes of blaster fire zapping off in Rey's direction. Hot bolts of blue plasma splashed and ignited the hillside with pink flame. They came from only one firearm. The third combatant was missing.

"Watch your tail!" Stargrave shouted. "The third's a lightbender, like you!"

"Working on it," Rey grunted. She was trading fire with the gunner, in and out of camouflage. "Kill the thermal interference! I need a bead; this blind to pot-shots crap is bullshit!"

Stargrave disabled the bubble's heat flash instantly. Instantly just wasn't fast enough.

The lioness took a stream of laser to the chest. The polymers there morphed into the silver of reflective defense, but the line cut across her breasts ran like mercury. Stargrave could hear her coughing over the comm-band from the smell of liquefied metal. The lioness's power suit notified his tactical display that its temperature regulators had been fried.

Stargrave caught the vibrodancer's axe between his power gauntlets in the middle of an overhead swing. He discharged both palms, shattering the blade. He kicked the assailant back fifteen feet into the dirt and turned for Rey. She was on her knees, pawing at her chest and the release mechanisms on her armor. Her face was writhing in agony on his HUD.

"Right in the godsdamned tits, boss!" she was screaming. "Right in the godsdamned tits!" Her voice was wet sounding, as if she were a chain-smoker drowning in a sea of mucus. In the back of his mind he knew she was already dead, but he couldn't help himself. The reaction was automatic. He ran for her.

Stargrave slid across the earth and slammed a wall-shield from his hip into the ground. It deployed in front of the lioness, phasing into its solid energy shape. Plasma hit it not but a second later. He embraced her, twisted, reached around her to scoop up her rifle, and fired blindly around the shield's barrier. Infrared was still recovering from being flashed out, but he caught enough of a blur to hit his mark. The gunner went down.

That left the vibrodancer and the other lightbender.

Two bolts of plasma hit him in the back. He discharged his left palm against the ground, launched upward and into a twisting backflip, and thrust the firearm forward while accelerating his right gauntlet—and drove it clear through the lightbender's throat and out the back of his neck. Splinters of armor and spinal column came away as he jerked it back out. The muzzle was a smashed mess from the violence of the blow.

Warning alarms notified him of plasma clinging to the back of his suit. While his temperature regulators held out, the fur on his back was singeing inside his armor and his flesh was cooking into blisters. He ignored it the best he could. He had to focus. There was still the vibrodancer to contend wi—

The shoulder of the vibrodancer's fractured blade impacted the side of his helmet mid-turn and cracked the right side of the face clean open. Light spilled in from the outside world and half his HUD died out while the other half became a mess of indecipherable, spiderwebbed red and blue. Then the sharp point on the end of the broken blade went right through his stomach. It caught in his armor, and he was lifted and driven downward into the earth.

Over it all, he heard the flatline of Rey's life monitor.

"So you're Stargrave, huh?" The vibrodancer laughed. She flipped up her visor. "Nice horns." Her voice was a deep basso oddly at-and-not-in conflict with her visage. She was a jaguar with facial piercings and an attitude that showed in the curl of her lips. She twisted the blade in his guts, and he barked out in pain. "Must have one *hell* of a record to get a custom head-job like that."

Stargrave tried to bring his left gauntlet around, but she fired a slug from her sidearm into the palm when it appeared. He felt three of his fingers break from the concussive blast. "Ballsy, too," she said, and pointed the sidearm at his head. "Neon-orange armor accents? How gauche. Could see you from two klicks out, even without LRS."

Stargrave brought Rey's rifle to bear. The cooldown charger on the laser-fire had a quarter-beat to go. Rey must've fired it before catching a beam herself. His eyes flicked up from the readout to the jaguar.

Keep talking, bitch, he thought.

The jaguar pulled her head back slightly, glanced at the rifle, and dismissed it with a smirk. "The muzzle's busted," she said. "What good is that gonna do yo—"

Stargrave pulled the trigger. He thought of Rey: *Here's to you, girl.*

The weapon expanded like a molten balloon. Rays of wild, hot light exited in every direction at once. First in microscopic needles, and then in wide beams.

And then the world froze and became gray and flat. Like a blanket laid across the face and pinched at its center, the world pulled back and away, puckering in on itself. Reality collapsed, and Stargrave became someone else.

***

// EMI IMPRESSION d15.11.2072.AF;
// ROOT $SOOK;
// DOCUMENTATION PROVIDED BY: ADEX MINING INC.

***

@010.

SIMULATION RELAY ERROR; the message blinked in place inside the gray cube of Sook Callowain's environment interface, SERVER DISCONNECTED.

"What the hell?" the wolf heard himself say. He could feel his body responding to his brain outside of the environment. He reached behind his head and depressed the latches of his neural shunt and disengaged the connection cable. He dropped it onto the floor and leaned forward in his flow-foam recliner. He cupped both eyes in his palms, adjusting to the light. He blinked several times, shaking off wake-disorientation.

Server disconnected? Since the WarSim's inception, there had never been a service interruption. Not once in eight years of runtime had the system gone down; it was designed to be as foolproof as possible. Lives depended on it.

Sook pinched his nose-bridge. He flipped his recliner upright and blindly reached across the black desk in front of him. He found his portable work-slate and held it up. The holoplastic slate recognized the prints on his finger-pads and came to life. He checked the time.

d15.11.2072@011.AF.

ETA to destination: 95 years, 2 months, 14 days.

It was eleven beats into the fifteenth. He had been in the WarSim since three hundred on the fourteenth—the morning of the previous day. That explained why he was so damned fatigued and hungry. He had been ignoring the limiter warning notifications, again.

***

@019, Sook was in the middle of stuffing tasteless glop into his face, imagining it as a breakfast cereal from when he was a pup (yesterday, it was imaginary bacon and eggs), when his slate notified him of a relay message on his personal band. He pushed fur aside and pulled the personal micro shunt out of the back of his neck. He inserted it into the slate.

[What the hell happened?] $Chey telepathed. He heard it in his mind as if she were speaking to him directly. [Are you seeing this? The news is freaking out. MWN says the whole relay went down. The whole godsdamned thing. Wild.]

Sook brought up the Many Worlds News feed on his slate; he only had to think about it for it to appear. With a gesture he flicked it off of the slate and onto the interactive surface of the table. The window expanded under his bowl.

"—brief, simultaneous network-wide relay interruption of an unknown origin," the newscaster was saying. Which was about the only thing of substance before the babble started. Wild speculations droned on in the background while the wolf ate. What could it be? A prank, harmless, but on a grand, interplanetary scale? A system-wide government wire-tap? What about the religious angle? Could it be the gods, striking out in warning at the hubris of daekind? Who knew?

Sook made a face and killed the feed. He keyed to reply.

[Oh, *surprise*,] the wolf thought, [religious fear-mongering, as usual.]

[$Chey: Yeah, but still. A system-wide interruption? That's big news. We're talking, like, a hundred and fifty worlds—lights-out, poof. Just like that. Kinda scary. Wonder what it was?]

[$Sook: Whatever it was, it managed to take the WarSim down with it. This close to the ARP's integration, too. Wondering how the NAI is going to handle that one.]

The WarSim's Narrative AI could analyze behavioral patterns and come up with an assumptive list of activities that a character might have been doing in a player's absence, effectively filling in the gaps and making for a seamless, uninterrupted stream of in-sim memories—but how would it handle generating a list of assumptions with a data gap?

[$Chey: SimStim's CEO put out an apology for the service interruption a few minutes ago. You probably just missed it. Said they're working on a fix and writing in some new variables for the NAI. The server's back up, but everyone that had been actively engaged—combat or political—is stuck in OOC or flashback until the patch. The ARP will have to wait.]

[$Sook: Great.] The wolf dropped his spoon into the bowl. [How long is that gonna take?]

[$Chey: Couple of days, supposedly.]

A couple of days stuck in death-and-not-death limbo. Sook sighed.

[$Sook: What about you? I mean, shit. *Rey.* Gone. Three years of investment right down the shitter.]

[$Chey: Hurts. Correction, *did* hurt—damn pain-emulators get better with every iteration. But I'm doing okay. You don't play the WarSim if you aren't willing to let it, well, simulate. Shit happens. Sometimes you take a laser to the tits and that's life.]

Sook seized on that last line as a quote; it appeared on his slate as text. He pinched it over to his social media portal. He cycled through his Extra-Memories Implant and recalled the moment where Rey had gotten blasted across the chest—a moment that was now framed with the context of reality, rather than being isolated from it by the alternate reality of the WarSim.

The memory became a repeating loop. Rey flailing and pawing at her chestplate's release mechanism while her breasts and armor liquefied. He attached the quote to it and flicked it off through the portal.

The post accrued a good seven hundred and fifteen thousand likes in less than a minute. Sook didn't even blink. Melancholy had long since stripped him of the cheer of being a "celebrity". Petition to have your time-limiters disabled inside the WarSim and suddenly the entire relay knew you existed ... and wouldn't leave you alone. Until he got the bright idea to start controlling his own media presence, anyway. Things calmed down after that.

[Nice,] $Chey telepathed. Then, after a brief delay, she added: [Ass.]

Sook grinned to himself. [Thought you'd like that. Anyway, I'm gonna hit the hydrosonic and wash up. Take care of a few chores after that. Promised my mom I'd give her a call to help her out with one of her wearables. Tech support, yay.]

[$Chey: Guess I'll grab Savede in the meantime. Haven't logged any time on her in a month or two. Skunkie's gonna get a whole lot more lovings now that Rey's gone. Message me when you get back?]

[$Sook: Sure thing.]

***

@044, Sook stepped out of the shower and headed down the long hallway back to the command deck, naked. He hadn't bothered dressing immediately. There was no need to. He left wet paw prints on the floor that dried in the quiet, pressurized halls of his metal home. He was alone, and had been for a long time.

He sighed, unable to parse his mother's attempt to explain the problem with her glasses. He was listening to her via his neural interfacing; she was using an old verbal calling device. "You know, this would be a lot easier if you'd just get an EMI, Mom. Wearables were on the way out before I even *left*."

"Daniel," she said, using his middle name, "we've been through this. I don't need an EMI, or a neuro-whatsit or … whatever it is. I just need a pair of glasses and a call screen. Tap a name, make a call. Simple."

"Yeah, that's not working so well right now, is it?" He grabbed a shirt out of the pile of laundry stuffed into the corner of his makeshift bedroom and pulled it on. Underwear was next.

"And that's why I called you. I can't get the video feed to pipe through."

"And I've told you, I can't do anything without being there, or getting you to run me a diagnostic. You know I can't do the first. Which is why it would be easier if you just had an EMI." He tried to explain how to get her to send him a readout, earlier, but it was futile. She sidetracked the conversation and started talking about some medical procedure she was supposed to undergo soon. She had a habit of doing this often. "Hell, Mom, we could *visit*. You know, I could see you for once. Like, *really* see you. A call screen doesn't even come close to what you can do in a sim." He stuck a foot through a pant leg and hopped across the floor while working on the second. He leaned against a wall with one shoulder for balance.

"Those things *change* people, Daniel. They're not the same afterward. They spend all of their time on the relay, hardly even notice the world around them! For what? Some adventure in an digital world? Fancy games? We have our imagination for that. We're not expanding the mind, we're just finding excuses to distract it."

Sook pulled on a pair of socks and headed for the hydroponic vegetable farm. "The WarSim isn't some 'fancy game', Mom. It's saving lives. We're responding to data passed back from the battlefront—*real* situations—running hundreds upon thousands of tactical simulations in seconds. We're helping people fight for their lives." He stepped into the slippers by the entrance, and padded across the room to the suspended rows of plants. "And, anyway, I don't see how having instant access to information *isn't* expanding the mind."

"You're not *learning* anything if it's just *there*, Daniel. Take it away, and what do you have? No practical solutions. You become reliant. Just magically getting answers to questions isn't a way to expand your mind. It's a way to let it rot."

"It's not *magic*," he said, ducking under one of the low-hanging water piping units. He palmed one of the tomatoes and gave it a gentle squeeze. Not ripe yet. He wandered toward another row of vegetables, stepping over a few wires and bits of tubing. He didn't much like vegetables, but they were better than the glop that made up his other option. "It's science. There's nothing magic about it. This kind of stuff could *save your life*, Mom. Like, with the ARP, we could get you in *another body*. You wouldn't have to be sick anymore."

"Ah yes, the 'Avatar Redundancy Program'. Let's just make it so people can change their physical selves, too, why don't we? Even the name is an affront. Our bodies are not *avatars*, Daniel."

"Ugh. You don't have to change, Mom. It can be the same as you are now."

"Except it won't be, will it? It'll be another me. Without the cancer. A vessel that isn't even *mine*. Grown in a vat."

"They'd be genetically identical, Mom."

She ignored him. He could hear the growl in her voice. "And let's just use some procedure to move the soul over. Like that's okay! What *gall*. To play around with someone's *soul*. To say that we understand it, and can measure it. And just move it around from body to body like we have any right to? My body isn't just *property*, Daniel. It's *me*."

Sook flinched. Property. His tail tucked between his legs. Like he needed a reminder. "We don't even know if what they've quantified *is* the soul. We just know it's something we missed. Something necessary for making the transfer."

"Playing around with things we don't understand, then? What does it matter. We are not gods, Daniel, and we should not pretend to be."

He pulled a few tomatoes and a cucumber off of their vines and dropped them into a plastic tub. He sighed and pinched his nose-bridge. "Dammit, Mom, you've got more than enough money to take care of yourself. The mining company's made sure of that. I've made sure of that. You need to use it. Don't just let it go to waste."

"I've told you. I'm not. Why do you think I keep going back to the doctor? The radiation treatments?"

"But it's not *working*. You won't even take an organ transplant! Look, I know I can't see you in person, but, gods, that doesn't mean I don't worry about you. You're suffering, Mom, and you don't have to be."

"Sook Daniel Callowain. That's enough. If you're not going to help me, I'll just have to find someone else to do it."

"I'm *trying* to help you, but you're just not listening."

"No, you are not listening. I do not need this right now. I have a med-scan, tomorrow, and I do not need my stress levels up any higher than they already are. Especially at my age. Why won't you just let it go?"

Because I'm never coming home and I want to see you again, dammit! He wanted to shout it. Scream it at the top of his lungs. But he took a deep breath instead. He willed his hackles back down. "Mom." He set the plastic tub down on a table and leaned over it, paws on the surface. "I haven't changed. I'm still *me*. I'm as stubborn as Dad was, and you know that. That's how I've *always* been."

"Yes, well, there are some things that I do wish would change. Your father didn't see it my way, either. And look who's still around."

"What is that even supposed to mean? Dad wasn't being *punished* with the accident, Mom. It was an *accident*." Another flycar had caught his in the side. The other driver was joyriding, running manual controls illegally in the city. "What the hell."

"I'm going now, Daniel. We'll talk about this later."

It took a moment for Sook to realize his mother had disconnected the line on him. When he did, he slammed his fists against the table and screamed.

***

@048, Sook dropped into the seat of his recliner. It hissed and adjusted itself with air, conforming to his shape with its glossy-black rolls of flex-padding. He picked up the neural shunt cable and reached around behind his head, inserting it into the base of his neck. He leaned back into the recliner, settled in, and closed his eyes. He thought of the WarSim, and then he was in it.

***

// EMI IMPRESSION d15.11.2072.AF;
// ALEKSANDER (ROOT $[REDACTED; PRIVATE SESSION]);
// DOCUMENTATION PROVIDED BY: SIMSTIM TACTICAL DIV.

***

@055, Aleksander Wright stared up into the sky with tired, tired gray eyes. The coyote wouldn't bother looking down; he didn't need to. Why bother himself with the world when it would greet him soon enough? He would instead enjoy the brilliant blue and the little silly puffs of white scattered across the horizon.

The wind whipped at his fur and clothing. It rattled noisily as he lay on nothing, paws fanned out as he considered the clouds. They were majestic peaks, billowing as mountains in the heavens. Soft, fluffy, carelessly drifting. Like him.

The world below was alive, he knew, moving about with the bustle of day-to-day business. A symphony of people of all kinds traversed the innards of a city he knew would rise up into his peripheral vision any moment now. Even the sky was alive, filled with mechanical creatures dancing among the clouds, aircraft moving with their traffic patterns. It was all so busy and common that one would, more often than not, simply tune it out. With places to go, and people to see, nobody stopped to consider the clouds. Nobody bothered to look up. Nobody would see him falling.

He didn't flinch when the tops of the buildings punched into view, stabbing upward all around him like a thorny ring. He welcomed their embrace with open arms.

The pavement greeted him back.

***

Aleksander stayed for a while and watched the body cleanup. He was an apparition to his own corpse. The world went on without Aleksander just fine.

***

// EMI IMPRESSION d15.11.2072.AF;
// STARGRAVE (ROOT $SOOK);
// DOCUMENTATION PROVIDED BY: SIMSTIM TACTICAL DIV.

***

@226, Rey responded to Stargrave's invitation by popping in like a ghost—both mechanically, and physically.

"Not on Savede?" Stargrave asked while scratching at the root of one of his horns. He was sitting on a bench in civilian clothes, also ghosted. A few flycars zoomed by in the distance just off the edge of the high-rise park's precipice. He was in the upper quarter of one of Zoan's tier-cities. He could still see the street three tiers below if he leaned back and looked down.

Rey strolled across the park with her thumbs in the pockets of her slacks. She stopped in front of the bench and squinted into the sun even as the light passed through her. "Nah. Just wanted to get her caught up with the NAI, that's all. Thought I'd come hang out with you for a while. Figure I can't give a proper send-off to Rey until we know what happened to you. Would suck if you were alive and missed the funeral." She pushed her elbows outward, arms akimbo. "Flashback?"

Stargrave dismissed the floating UI in front of him. It was over-loaded with messages he didn't want to deal with right now. He took a breath and stood up just as someone else sat in his place. Neither was aware of the other. Ghosts were non-interactive and invisible to characters who were not out-of-character. The effect was momentarily disorienting. "Yeah, sorry. Media spam. Probably want my feelings on the relay collapse or something similarly asinine. Oh and I guess word is getting around that I might've maybe got my ass kicked. Hooray." He nodded at the park behind the lioness. "Here good?"

"Why not? Let's make it a lazy one—throw some pigskin."

Stargrave shifted into flashback-mode, pulling Rey in with him. Things went fuzzy for a moment as the muted colors of the out-of-character world faded back into the clarity of being in the in-character world. He thought about the narrative and it began constructing itself. It was a simple phased instance. The NAI filled in all the gaps of his proposal and populated the world with player-absent characters. The football appeared in his paw—and in the extra-memory the scenario would create, it would already have been there. He tossed it to himself a couple of times before winging it across the park like a missile.

Rey caught it with a slap of her paws. She fired it back. "It's just thug bullshit," she started—which would later be only a part of a much longer conversation about her military aspirations—military aspirations that her player now knew would never come to fruition. "Mercs do the dirty work; they aren't out on the front lines pushing back the mages. I want some real action. Not this small-scale pushover nonsense."

"Mercs get paid; front-liners die," Stargrave said, catching the ball in the chest.

[Oh, hey, by the way,] $Chey cut in with a telepath, [that vibro-dancer has been messaging the hell out of me. Picked up my ID tags after her party got the kill. Says she wants to meet you.]

"Yeah, but front-liners get *glory*. Imagine being a part of the battalion that actually pushes the mages *back*." She snagged the ball with extended claws as it went a bit wide. "We'd be godsdamned legends."

[$Sook: Probably to talk about what kinda NAI decisions we'll be looking at, I guess.]

"As if we aren't now?" His tail wagged.

[$Chey: Want me to give her your alias?]

"You're a special case and you know it."

[$Sook: Yeah, go ahead. I'd rather work something out in advance, just in case the NAI allows for any personal input.]

Stargrave whipped the ball harder this time. The lioness still caught it. "Luck's just been on my side. I don't expect it to last forever."

$Chey telepathed a confirmation. He replied with his thanks.

"Nothing lasts forever," Rey said. "You just gotta make the best of it while you can." The lioness held up the ball, as if to make her point. It was slightly deflated. That time her claws had gone too deep. "Wanna do lunch?"

***

@234, they were sitting ghosted outside of the noodle place they agreed upon for "lunch" when Stargrave received a message from the vibrodancer's player, $Anneda. Her homeworld ident was the same as his: Havari.

[$Anneda: Hey, horns! You busy?]

[$Sook: Not particularly. Just idling with a friend at the moment.]

The distraction must have shown on Stargrave's face. Rey was looking at him funny. "The vibrodancer," he explained. "Mind if I invite her to the party?"

***

// EMI IMPRESSION d15.11.2072.AF;
// REY (ROOT $CHEY);
// DOCUMENTATION DONATED BY: CHEY JAINA
BECKAM ($CHEY)

***

@240, the argument broke out while Rey's player was away to use the bathroom. She popped back in right in the middle of it.

"You don't know that," Stargrave said. "It was a gamble—and a stupid one on my part, sure—but we never got a chance to see it through."

"But I had a personal energy-barrier deflector on me," the jaguar—Turmoil—argued back, "in addition to reflective plating!" She was practically shouting. Her tail, all puffed up, lashed irritatedly.

"And how do you know you would've been fast enough to initiate the former? Let alone position it in a way to stave off most of the blast radius? And reflective plating is about useless against a laser of that intensity, anyway. Ask Rey how well it did for her."

Rey crossed her arms. Her pom-pom capped tail twitched up to one side as she cocked a hip. "I was breathing molten metal up until I stopped breathing."

"That's with a *focused* beam," Turmoil shot back.

Stargrave sighed and dropped his head into his paws, holding it up with his horns.

"Look," Rey said, waving a paw in a loop, "no offense, but we get this kind of thing a lot. You think you're some kind of hot shot and that you actually had a chance. Against Stargrave. *The* Stargrave. You're wrong. You lost. Just admit it."

Stargrave grunted. This was going downhill fast. "C'mon Rey, that's not fair. We don't know."

"That's right—you don't." Turmoil was growling now. "So knock off the mightier-than-thou bullshit." She turned her attention to Rey. "And 'we'? As far as I can tell, he's been pulling all the weight and you've just been along for the ride. One that's over now, by the way. No need to consult the NAI for that."

Stargrave stood up. "I just wanted to talk about this," he said. "Not fight about it. It's just a sim. There's no need to get angry."

"One that you must've been spending an *inordinate* amount of time in, what with a service record like yours. How is it 'just a sim' when you clearly don't have a life outside of it?"

Stargrave frowned. He made as if to speak, and then stopped himself. Abruptly, he vanished. His alias signed off of the relay shortly thereafter.

Turmoil's tail froze in the shape of a question-mark. She hadn't been expecting that.

"What the hell?" Rey said. "How was that called for?"

The jaguar could sense a shift in intensity beyond her ability to grasp. She laughed awkwardly, trying to play it off. "What, you guys can talk shit and act all big and bad, but can't take it when it's given back?"

"Holy hell. You *don't* know, do you?"

"Know *what?*"

"The 'Havari Starcutter'. Look it up. Get back to us when *you* have a godsdamned excuse."

Rey cut her connection.

***

// EMI IMPRESSION d29.10.2060.AF;
// ROOT $SOOK;
// DOCUMENTATION PROVIDED BY: ADEX MINING INC.

***

##INCIDENT REPORT##

@115, Sook was interfacing with the ship via shunt-socket, running diagnostics on one of the magnetic rakes being loaded back into the dock, when he suddenly felt cold. His ears popped, his interface dropped, and he came to, drifting in engineering—held in place only by the cable in the back of his neck—with a vague sense that his name had been called. He had been dislodged from his chair. His head hurt and his ears were bleeding. Warning klaxons buzzed through his skull like an angry nest of chainsaw-wielding hornets. He scrambled for the cable, detached it before it could twist in his brain-stem, and flailed uselessly for a moment, trying to orient himself in zero-gravity. Even after righting himself, he still felt disoriented. Something was wrong, but he couldn't quite place it.

He pulled himself along the cable and kicked at the air, pedaling for the nearby railing. He shimmied along the railing over to a flat-panel holoplastic monitor by the window. He felt immediately ill. The ship was spinning violently. The ore asteroid came in from the left side of the window, dashed off to the right, and repeated the motion only a few seconds later. He pulled up a report and identified hull damage near the tail end of the vessel.

"Callowain!" the ship-board speakers crackled, the voice loud enough to be that of a god. "Callowain, where the hell are you?" It was Denton.

Sook mashed the comm key on the panel next to him. "Engineering. What the hell's going on?"

"Shut up and listen to me. Close the aft airlocks. Blow the tail. The laser-pneumatic bounced in cargo when the coupler went." Sook could hear noise in the background. Shouting. Denton was straining. "Fire. It's feeding off of the oxygen. You've got to separate the rig."

Sook was sorting through readouts on the ship on the flat-panel. His fingers burned as he cycled through sections of the ship. His eyes were on fire; his nose was bleeding. He couldn't see straight.

"Sir, the Cutter's in a mean tailspin and I can't make heads or tails of—"

"Stop screwing around with the terminal and blow the godsdamned tail, Callowain! That's a direct order!"

And so he did.

The hissing stopped immediately. Sook realized he must have been shouting over it. Why hadn't he noticed the hissing before? It must've been the sound of air vacuuming in toward the tail section ... because of the fire? ... no. It shouldn't have been able to draw that fast. The fire should have been moving forward, through the ship, not oxygen toward the fire. Unless ...

There was no fire. The section of the ship he was in had been *depressurizing*.

The damn ship had been bleeding oxygen.

361

The next time the view outside of the window spun around, Sook saw the back half of the Havari Starcutter wheeling in the distance toward the asteroid. The mining unit, the cargo bay, the cryo couches, the main fusion drive, all of it. On the third spin, he could see debris flying away in pieces.

Sook had been dying, and he hadn't even been bright enough to realize it was happening. Denton had just saved his life.

Fifteen minutes later, Sook had a completed diagnostic of the ship.

All seven other members of the mining mission had been in the other half.

##END REPORT##

***

// EMI IMPRESSION d15.11.2072.AF;
// STARGRAVE (ROOT $SOOK);
// DOCUMENTATION PROVIDED BY: SIMSTIM TACTICAL DIV.

***

@715, Turmoil found him sitting ghosted on the hillside under the moonlight. Moonlight washed out with the flashes of battle in cislunar space.

She sat down next to him and wrapped her arms around her knees. Her tail looped around her ankles and she stared down at the grass, watching her shadow shift with the sources of light.

"Denton," he began reciting, "Jameson, Ripley, Anneth; Kirsten, Rashide, Morris—all unto death. There were eight miners one moment, and the next, all gone but one; in a metal tomb he travels, Stargrave, until his time too does come." He broke the cadence. "It's practically a nursery rhyme."

"I'm sorry," she said. "I didn't know."

He was quiet for a long moment. Long enough that she had started to drift off to sleep. She was tired, and it had been a long day. When he finally spoke, his voice was soft. "Why do you play?"

When the jaguar didn't respond, he went on. "I've seen your logs. You're here a lot, too; your service record isn't half bad. Why do you play? Why choose this over reality?"

"I don't understand," she said. She crossed her arms and held herself tighter. "Why is that important?"

"Nobody stays here unless they have to. This is war. A simulation of it, sure. We treat it like a game, but it's still war, all the same. People die in here every day so they don't have to on the other side, so their families don't have to. Why? Because there's hope in it. Hope that, somewhere in here, is a solution to stop the *real* war. All of us are doing our part, fighting to make a difference, whether we realize it or not."

He picked up a rock and examined it idly. "I've watched technology develop in real time through seeing it incorporated here, in the WarSim. We've invented faster than light travel. We've made new advances in medical technology. We can save lives, clone bodies for tissue and organ transplants. We've made so many leaps forward, and yet our entire species—every last race—we're all in denial. Still playing politics. Still worrying about the corporations' bottom line and not our own damn survival."

He rolled the rock over between his fingertips. "I'm here because I *have* to be," he said. "I'm not going to throw away Denton's sacrifice. I'm not going to make that a waste. I'm fighting to *survive*. Not just for me, but for everyone that died that day. To make a difference. No matter how shitty it gets—and trust me, finding out it's cheaper to let you ride out your contract and die than send out one of those fancy new faster-than-light ships to save your ass is *real* godsdamned shitty."

He sighed heavily. "Or, at least, that's my excuse, anyway." He chucked the rock down the hill. It bounced once or twice, illuminated by the flickering colors of the false-war in the sky. He turned to face her, elbows propped up on his knees. "So, why do you play?"

It took her a moment to work up the courage to tell him, but she did. She felt he deserved that much.

She started with, "I'm not a girl."

***

==INTERJECTION: COMMANDER LADELY==

Turmoil was female. $Anneda was also female. Only, no one could see it outside of the WarSim. Inside the WarSim, it was obvious.

$Anneda hated the world for not being able to see her for who she was. She felt as if she were a shell carrying around a soul that would never find peace. Her body was a puppet, and she the puppeteer.

She could get surgery, but she couldn't afford it. She had been abandoned by her family, and was out on her own working whatever job she could to get by—and only barely. She believed the surgery would only mutilate the shell, anyway. She did not want to alter something she inhabited, she simply wanted to be herself.

The WarSim was the closest thing she had to a real life. She believed that, in there, she was more than she was on the other side. That's why she played.

He said he understood, and that he could sympathize. Maybe for different reasons, but he understood all the same.

==END INTERJECTION==

***

// EMI IMPRESSION d18.11.2072.AF;
// STARGRAVE (ROOT $SOOK);
// DOCUMENTATION PROVIDED BY: SIMSTIM TACTICAL DIV.

***

@185.

"Based on all available data," the NAI said, "the results of the battle interaction between one Turmoil and one Stargrave are deemed inconclusive. There are too many variables to confirm a kill on the behalf of either participant."

The patch had come. Turmoil stood across from Stargrave in an ethereal courtroom. The NAI—the judge—floated behind the podium up front. It was a featureless eight-sided blue diamond that pulsed and stretched in time with its speaking.

"The severity of the interaction, however, cannot be ignored. It is for this reason both one Turmoil and one Stargrave will each receive an Alteration—each in the form of a battle scar. One Turmoil will receive the Alteration below the midpoint of the rifle explosion in question; one Stargrave will receive the Alteration above. You may choose how best to incorporate these Alterations into your personal narratives."

***

==INTERJECTION: COMMANDER LADELY==

When Stargrave recovered, he put out a merc-net bulletin for the vibro-dancer he had been in battle with. She responded, and the two met. There were no hard feelings. They both understood: it was just business. That's how mercenaries work.

He lost his right lung, and the top half of his right horn. She was missing her left leg from the knee down. He had the lung replaced, and she was fitted with a biomechanical leg. He kept the damage to the horn to honor Rey's sacrifice.

They buried Rey, the gunner, and the other lightbender together.

At the funeral, she asked him why he fought so hard. "I've never seen anyone fight like that," she told him.

"Because I have to," was his reply.

"We should be fighting for the same reasons," she suggested. He agreed. He said he wanted to join the warfront in earnest. To be done with the mercenary business. It's what Rey would have wanted. She asked if she could come with him. He told her yes.

For eight years, they fought together.

Until they were separated by a surprise attack. The mages had pushed into the inner colonies, hitting them where they least expected it—outside of the WarSim.

The war had come to Havari.

==END INTERJECTION==

***

// EMI IMPRESSION d08.05.2083.AF;
// SAVEDE (ROOT $CHEY);
// DOCUMENTATION DONATED BY: CHEY JAINA
BECKAM ($CHEY)

***

@344, Savede dropped herself into the barstool next to Stargrave. She was on shore leave, dressed in military casual. They hadn't seen each other in over six months.

Stargrave had his chin on the counter, an arm folded over his eyes. She could see his tongue sticking out at the end of his muzzle. He looked a little ill. He had probably been drinking for a while.

[$Chey: Hey boss. How you doing?]

Stargrave sniffed her out and preemptively explained, "Rough Day. Movement in the third quadrant, out near the Yata system. Lost two battalions. Jamesy was on the surface when they razed it."

[$Chey: I don't mean in the WarSim, boss.]

Savede ordered herself a drink, and Stargrave another round. She put her elbows on the countertop.

[$Chey: You stopped jumping.]

[$Sook: Mm?]

[$Chey: Off of things. Alt-suicide. Jumping.]

Stargrave sat up and took his glass. He idly thumbed the side of it. Then he palmed his nose.

[$Sook: How'd you know?]

She punched him on the shoulder. "Yeah, yeah, ass. Deal with it. I'm a skunk. I stink. Suck it. Drink your damn alcohol."

[$Chey: Wasn't hard to figure out. A little boredom coupled with concern for a friend, and I started doing some investigating. Wondered what you were up to with those private WarSim sessions. At first I figured you were probably perving it up or something. Stuff you wouldn't want coming back to haunt you. But after that day on Zoan—you know, where you and Rey were throwing the football in flashback?—I caught something in the newsfeed about a suicide only a couple of hours before we met up. I started looking at the public incident reports after that. Synced up pretty well with your private sessions.]

Stargrave rolled his eyes, but he did knock his drink back. When he lowered it, he looked askance at the mephit. "I don't recall giving you permission to be at ease, corporal."

[$Chey: Honestly, I don't know how you didn't do it on the other side, already.]

"Screw you. You ain't in your bars, commander."

[$Sook: Tried once. After my mom died. Hated myself. The last conversation we had, I had been waxing theological technobabble instead of paying attention to her. Doped myself up on cryo-prep. About six times the dosage. At some point, I must've priv-lined Anneda. She talked me into making myself vomit a good half-dozen times. Saved me. We spent the whole night together. I was barely lucid. Told me I couldn't back down on my responsibilities. Not after the speech I gave her the first night we met. She made me promise not to give up. Ever.]

"Heh. Still not used to that. *Commander.*"

"You'll grow into it."

"How're things back home?"

"The defensive net managed to stop a couple of the mages' Spire ships about a month back. They're starting to get the idea. You did good work. You deserved the promotion, boss. Rey would've been proud of you."

[$Chey: Still no word from Havari.]

[$Sook: Didn't expect there would be. But thanks.]

He slipped back into quiet again.

[$Chey: You're spending a lot of time in here. Like, more than usual.]

[$Sook: What else is there for me to do?]

[$Chey: Just worried about you, boss. You gotta eat and sleep too, you know.]

Savede nudged him with an elbow when the silence dragged on. "You still think about her, don't you? It's been what, three years?"

Stargrave finished off his drink and licked his muzzle. Then he wiped it with the back of his paw. He held the empty glass up in front of his face, propped up by an elbow, as if studying it. But his eyes weren't focused. "Can't stop thinking about her," he said. "She knows I won't. I promised her I wouldn't. Wherever she is, she's probably putting up the good fight. Interplanetary, groundwork, heaven, hell—doesn't matter. She's still fighting. I've got to believe it. It's the only thing that keeps me going."

***

==INTERJECTION: COMMANDER LADELY==

@145, *day twenty-nine of the thirty-day-standard month of January, 2167, the Havari Starcutter auto-parked in the orbit of a world dead in all but spirit, the debris ring of a thousand mage vessels drifting like a belt about her middle. A convoy of Havari's last bastion, the last colony of survivors, was sent to retrieve it.*

At the end of a long, dusty, metal hall, they found him. A husk, sunken into the flow-foam of a neural interface recliner. His eyes were closed. The shunt-socket was still plugged in.

He died in the field of battle, inside of the WarSim. Not from a war injury, but from old age. His last neural data request was to pull up a private-session EMI impression, set to loop.

==END INTERJECTION==

***

==ENABLING FULL NEURAL SENSORY FEEDBACK==

367

==AUTHORITY: COMMANDER LADELY==

***

// EXITING ACADEMY EMI SIMLOG SESSION //

***

d22.06.2199@300.

I exit the session early. I don't need to see the last impression. I know it by heart.

Tomorrow the cadets of the Havari War Academy will participate in a simlog session covering over forty years of tactical knowhow and battle strategies provided by War Proficient First Class Commander Stargrave—the very same strategies that helped change the course of the war. Each of them will then be fitted with a redundancy-plug and shipped off to the front lines. This session is only a primer.

A hundred and thirty years ago, the Redundancy was just a theory project. We had only just broken the FTL barrier. Now, every ship in the Interstellar Security Federation's fleet is equipped with an IA drive by standard, and we have redundant soldiers by the hundreds of thousands. They die, their consciousness dumps back into the network through the relay, and we drop them into new bodies and ship them right back out to war. We're outmaneuvering and outsmarting the mages where we were losing before, even in the face of increasingly vigorous assaults. We're pushing them back. There've even been rumors of a treaty. That the war could be over within the century.

And it's all because of him.

I pull out my neural shunt and stretch my legs. I take a stroll through the rows upon rows of cadets in their flow-foam recliners, watching their expressions change. They are experiencing Stargrave's final moments of life. In every detail imaginable. There are no neural sensory limiters in place for the final impression. They will experience his feelings, his thoughts, the sensations of his body failing him, the approach of death, slow and inescapable. The incompleteness of his heart. The will to continue where one cannot. Never to give up. To keep to his promise, and that heart-breaking moment when he realizes he cannot keep it any longer. They will know him, in that moment, as well as he knew himself.

He died in an imaginary field on his back, staring up at imaginary stars, reliving an imaginary moment. An imaginary moment more real than life itself.

I was with the away team when we discovered the Starcutter. I was the first to jack into Sook's feed, the first to see that imaginary moment.

I remember it like it were yesterday.

***

"Shh. Don't say anything," the voice says from the dark, quiet and soft. I recognize it immediately, but it's strange, hearing it from this angle. "Just let me do this."

The low thrum of a rising pad buzzes into the deep kick of a baseline. The lights come up in a neon glow. He's standing there, anxiety coursing through his veins, telling himself he can do this.

His right foot taps into the beat, the pulse of it, and then he's moving. Tail lashing, hips swinging, body dancing. He is alive with the music. A symphony, electronic; he is the conductor.

And I feel it. I feel it.

I feel it when Stargrave's heart rate quickens.

I feel it when Stargrave recoils from a twirl stopped inches in front of him, like it were a physical blow.

I feel it when the other male's paw slips behind Stargrave's back, when he walks him backward and forward in the embrace of a brief tango.

I feel their togetherness.

I feel the acceptance.

I feel Stargrave's love. From his heart, in the most intimate way imaginable. I feel it as if I were him.

The music dies down, and they stand there, together, panting, chest to chest, in the soft glow of the dance floor. Their whiskers are practically tangled with one another. He is a jaguar. A projection of the real Anneda, outside of the sim.

Me.

I see myself through his eyes, and I am perfect. I am beautiful.

I am his everything.

"If you are the puppet," Stargrave says, after he catches his breath, "then I am caught up in your strings."

***

I am War Proficient First Class Commander Anneda Marcum Ladely, and I was one of the first volunteers for the Avatar Redundancy Program. I survived the Havari invasion, because I fought for Stargrave. This is why we all fight. We fight for Stargrave. Because he couldn't fight for us.

When the cadets rise from the simlog session, one by one, they touch their pointer fingers to their foreheads with their pinkies bent at half mark—the one-horn salute.

They salute the same jaguar as in the final impression.

I salute them back.

There is nothing more that needs to be said.

War is sacrifice. Whether we pay it up front, or we spend our lives being devoured by it, it takes its toll on all of us. You can explain it in a thousand different ways, give a thousand different examples. But show it, give the experience of it, tangible and real, and it changes a person.

And sometimes it shows a person who they really were, all along.

ABOUT THE AUTHORS

Ellis Aen is the nom de plume of a genderqueer author who pretends to be a cross-dressing skunk-fox on the internet.

Back before he had any of that figured out, he was just a guy growing up with his nose lost in the pages of science fiction (*Hyperion*, Dan Simmons) and amazing animal stories (*Tailchaser's Song*, Tad Williams). Despite a passion for reading, it wasn't until stumbling upon the online furry community (FuzzyLogic, FurryMUCK) that he discovered a passion for writing.

After years of struggling with his own sense of identity, the expressive, welcoming (and sometimes a little weird) people there offered him an environment in which to explore himself and his boundaries. In creating worlds, characters, and ideas of his own, he would ultimately find the confidence to become the person he is today (who is, consequently, also a little weird).

With interests that include the strange, the furry, the occult, the future, and the complexities of the self, Ellis enjoys bucking tradition and subverting expectations, and he is a strong opponent of the demonization of sex, sexuality, and fetishism.

He can be found on Twitter as @skonqfocks

Kyla Chapek is a twenty seven year old woman living in Eugene, Oregon. Her two greatest passions are writing and martial arts. To pay the bills she currently bartends and doubles as her own bouncer. Kyla has trained in a variety of martial arts over the years, including Wing Chun Kung Fu at Leung Martial Arts in Eugene. She is also a big fan of old Shaw Brothers Kung Fu movies which greatly inspired "Crouching Tiger, Standing Crane." Someday Kyla hopes to earn enough money through her writing so she can simply write, travel and train different martial arts for the rest of her life. To view more samples of Kyla's work visit her blog at *kylachapek.com*.

Jay "Shirou" Coughlan has been a hobby fantasy author since early high school and has been a part of the furry fandom for as many years. The fandom's creative community has always inspired Jay's worlds, characters, and stories.

In his spare time, he enjoys drinking tea, hanging with friends, and watching English TV shows from which he derives his sense of humor. Jay often is found in the wilds of Vancouver curled up with a good book and a nice cup of tea.

Jay was first published in the Vancoufur Conbook (Vancoufur 2015) with the story "It Must have Been Suicide," which was later featured on an episode of *KnotCast* (episode 291). He looks forward to continuing his work in writing with many more stories to come.

John Giezentanner lives in Lafayette, Colorado, works with plants in Boulder and writes sci-fi and fantasy stories that tend to betray a deep and inexplicable longing to be an Allosaurus or something similar, like, right now. Grr.

Although, if he were honest, he probably has more in common with a Therizinosaurus, being a vegetarian descended from meat eaters who feels pretty awkward at Theropod family dinners. And what are the giant claws for, anyway? He doesn't know. Should he put them in his pockets? He doesn't have pockets because he's a dinosaur. So embarrassing. Please help.

John's fiction has appeared online in *Fantasy Scroll Magazine* and you can find him on Twitter @joginearthenzen, on FA and various sites under the alias Latro, or lurking at a local con.

Amy Fontaine is a wildlife biologist who appreciates the legendary qualities of animals. She graduated from Humboldt State University in May 2015 with a Bachelor's Degree, majoring in Wildlife with a minor in English Writing. Amy recently led a field crew studying wolves in Yellowstone National Park. She has also worked with fishers in the northern Sierras, honey bees in Michigan, and marine mammals in the Pacific Northwest. Currently, Amy is researching wild hyenas in Kenya.

Amy's writings have appeared in *ROAR Volume 6*, *A Menagerie of Heroes* (FurPlanet Productions), *Civilized Beasts* (Weasel Press), *Bewildering Stories*, and the *North Coast Journal of Humboldt County, California*. As a lover of animals and speculative fiction, she has found a place in the Furry Writers' Guild, but she plans to break into mainstream fantasy and science fiction publishing as well. She writes short stories and poetry and has a novel or two in the works.

In addition to writing and observing nature, Amy enjoys drawing, playing guitar, and traveling. She wants to be the very best, like no one ever was.

Renee Carter Hall works as a medical transcriptionist by day and as a writer, poet, and artist all the time. Her short fiction has appeared in a variety of publications inside and outside the furry fandom, including Strange Horizons, Daily Science Fiction, PodCastle, and the anthologies *Bewere the Night, PULP!*, and *An Anthropomorphic Century*. She is also the author of two books, the novel *By Sword and Star* (Anthro Dreams, 2012) and the novella *Huntress* (FurPlanet, 2015), both of which have won Cóyotl Awards. Renee lives in West Virginia with her husband, their cat, and a ridiculous number of creative works-in-progress, and readers can find her online at www.reneecarterhall.com and on Twitter as @RCarterHall.

Bill Kieffer was born in Jersey City, NJ.
He never fully recovered.
A brain injury at an early age left him with some mild issues and just enough aphasia to be amusing at parties. He tries to be very open about these. He doesn't drink, having the bare minimum of inhibitions to begin with. He also tends to describe himself in negatives.

He's happily married to a woman who encouraged him to discover and explore his sexuality. She also encourages him to keep on his meds. They both dabble in writing erotica. He is bisexual, but does not stray. She is straight and the relationship is only open in the sense that he tells her everything (they blame rumors to the contrary on his aphasia).

When he is not looking in the mirror, Bill Kieffer is actually a 6 foot tall gray anthropomorphic draft horse that types as Greyflank. He is a member of the Furry Writers' Guild and has recently published short stories in several Furry anthologies put out by FurPlanet.

His novella, *THE GOAT: Building the Perfect Victim*, is now available from Red Ferret Press.

Erin Lale is the author of upcoming sf *Planet of the Magi*, nonfiction *American Celebration, Asatru For Beginners*, poetry book *Renaissance Woman*, academic paper "Bersarkrgangr: The Viking Martial Art," contributing editor of anthologies *No Horns On These Helmets, Cat's Cradle Time Yarns*, etc., and acquisitions editor at Caliburn Press.

E.A. Lawrence is a writer, photographer, and biologist who orbits the Great Lakes doing science and telling stories while living with multiple sclerosis. You can read both her fiction and nonfiction in Playtime: An Arts and Culture Magazine and Breath and Shadow magazine. She chronicles her thoughts and adventures in life on her blog, Technicolorlilypond: https://technicolorlilypond.wordpress.com/

Your fearless editor, **Mary E. Lowd**, is a science-fiction and furry author in Oregon. She's had more than sixty short stories published, as well as several novels through FurPlanet. She also edited *ROAR Volume 6*.

John B. Rosenman is a retired English professor from Norfolk State University in Norfolk, VA. He has published three hundred stories in *The Speed of Dark, Weird Tales, Whitley Strieber's Aliens, Galaxy, The Age of Wonders*, and elsewhere. In addition, he has published twenty books, including SF novels such as *Speaker of the Shakk* and *Beyond Those Distant Stars*, winner of AllBooks Review Editor's Choice Award (Mundania Press), and *Alien Dreams, A Senseless Act of Beauty*, and (YA) *The Merry-Go-Round Man* (Crossroad Press). MuseItUp Publishing has published five SF novels. They are *Dark Wizard; Dax Rigby, War Correspondent*, and three in the Inspector of the Cross series: *Inspector of the Cross, Kingdom of the Jax*, and *Defender of the Flame*. MuseItUp has also published *The Blue of Her Hair, the Gold of Her Eyes* (winner of Preditor's and Editor's 2011 Annual Readers Poll), *More Stately Mansions*, and the dark erotic thrillers *Steam Heat* and *Wet Dreams*. Musa Publishing gave his time travel story "Killers" their 2013 Editor's Top Pick award. Some of John's books are available as audio books from Audible.com.

Two of John's major themes are the endless, mind-stretching wonders of the universe and the limitless possibilities of transformation—sexual, cosmic, and otherwise. He is the former Chairman of the Board of the Horror Writers Association and the previous editor of Horror Magazine.

Skunkbomb currently resides in McLean, Virginia, and hopes to find a job in the field of book publishing. He would like to thank his friends from the first year of the Regional Anthropomorphic Writers' Retreat for their feedback and encouragement. More of his writing can be found on www.furaffinity.net/user/skunkbomb123/. His story,

"The Pendant of Westbriar Swamp," can be found in *A Menagerie of Heroes*. He does not have a fursona, but has many characters, the most prominent being Chester, a 1920s salesweasel.

Priya Sridhar has been writing since fifth grade, a year after her mother forbade her from watching television all day. This led to several published short stories, one of which made the Top Ten Amazon Kindle Download list, and Alban Lake publishing her novella *Carousel*. She invites readers to read her blog a Faceless Author at http://pseudonymousfictionwriter.blogspot.com.

TJ is a military brat who jumped around between Northern California and Southern California before moving to Ohio, where he currently lives. He has been in the furry fandom for five years and has been writing off and on for about as long. He is incredible grateful for the community of artists, writers and fans, as they helped him find something that he cares about—the written word. TJ has grown to become more passionate about the craft of writing and enjoys creating new worlds and aiding his friends with projects of their own.

Heidi C. Vlach is a chef training graduate, a professional cook, and sometimes an overqualified waitress. She got her first Nintendo console at age 6, and video games were her introduction to magical fantasy and anthropomorphic characters. To this day, Heidi enjoys a story-rich video game as much as a good book. She lives in northern Ontario, Canada with her best friend and two cats.

Corgi W. is a fluffy writer and student, with big ears and a stumpy tail. She writes for fun, and will continue to do so, as long as she has amazing people to beta-read her stories.

Ross Whitlock has been writing fiction for about as long as he's been in the furry fandom. He loves both! Recently, his short stories have appeared in *Dungeon Grind* and *Will of the Alpha 2*, both published by FurPlanet. He's been working on a series of furry fantasy novels, and drinks lots of tea to fuel his creative juices. He lives in Colorado.

Chris "Sparf" Williams is a writer of anthropomorphic fiction currently residing in the Washington, D.C. area. His work has previously been featured in several anthologies from FurPlanet, as well as in *Trick or Treat Vol. 2: Historical Halloween* from Rabbit Valley. In addition to his writing, he is also a stage, film, and voice actor who received his MFA in Acting from The Catholic University of America. His thesis production, "What the Fur?!", can be found on his YouTube channel (Sparf1) and on Vimeo. He can be found on SoFurry, Furry Network, and Weasyl as Sparf. This story is dedicated to the attendees and instructors of the inaugural RAWR (Regional Anthropomorphic Writers' Retreat), without whose critique and support the story would not have taken the shape that it did.